FEARFUL
SYMMETRY

THE SECRET OF
the Journal

FEARFUL SYMMETRY

C. F. Dunn

LION FICTION

Published by Lion Fiction
an imprint of
Lion Hudson plc
Wilkinson House, Jordan Hill Road
Oxford OX2 8DR, England
www.lionhudson.com/fiction

ISBN 978 1 78264 198 8
e-ISBN 978 1 78264 199 5

First edition 2016

A catalogue record for this book is available from the British Library

Printed and bound in the UK, August 2016, LH26

Contents

To the Author of all things.

Acknowledgments

This is the last Acknowledgment I will write for *The Secret of the Journal* series. Although I have thanked the many people who have contributed over the years, there are many more – some whose names I never knew – who helped me with tit-bits of information, a historical reference, or words of encouragement. Then there are those on writing forums and book groups, and readers who have contacted me from the other side of the world, who have made writing this series a complete joy.

I owe much to the cheerful professionalism of the Lion Fiction team, who made editing and production (from an author's point of view) a doddle: editor Jessica Tinker; Jess Scott, who saw it through to production; Jonathan Roberts (design), and Kylie Ord (production). A special thank you to copy editor Sheila Jacobs (I hope the new orchard bears much fruit) and to Sarah Krueger of Kregel Publishing in the USA.

As always, I wish to thank Tony Collins, former publisher and editor of Lion Hudson, for taking me on in the first place and for his subsequent support throughout the series, and author Pen Wilcock for her insight and intuition.

I am indebted to the endorsement of this rookie's work by author Colin Dexter, whose encouragement and validation made the world of difference when it was needed.

To the many people who, over the years in their professional capacity, have generously given their time and advice, especially: for her insight into psychological conditions, Consultant Psychiatrist Dr Kiki O'Neil-Byrne, MB BCH. BAO Dip. Clin. Psych. MRCPsych, and R. F. D. – Director of the Royal

Engineers' Museum, Library and Archive – for invaluable access to original documents at the RE Library.

Thanks, also, to friends and colleagues, author Sue Russell (S.L. Russell), Dee Prewer and Lisa Lewin for their selfless support from the beginning, and the staff at Cobham Hall School for providing an appropriately historic setting in which to hold my launch events. Michelle Jimerson Morris, of Seamlyne Reproductions, and Norm Forgey of Maine Day Trip, who once again supplied regional information in the USA.

Special mention goes to C.P. – it is for people like you that makes writing worth while.

Nearly the last (but never the least) my chief marketing and promotion agent – my father – whom I could have hired out countless times to other authors because of his persistent and fearless approach to promoting his daughter's books to anyone and everyone, with a cheerful, "Do you enjoy a good read?" followed by proffering a card with the current book's details. How could anyone refuse an offer like that? And my dearest mother – our family's glue – holding us all together with her love, patience, wisdom and compassion.

Finally, the last word must go to my husband and daughters, whose unconditional love and tireless encouragement have kept me going from the beginning to the end.

Thank you, all, for the opportunity to bring this story alive.

Characters

ACADEMIC & RESEARCH STAFF AT HOWARD'S LAKE COLLEGE, MAINE

Emma D'Eresby, Department of History (Medieval & Early Modern)

Elena Smalova, Department of History (Post-Revolutionary Soviet Society)

Matias Lidström, Faculty of Bio-medicine (Genetics)

Matthew Lynes, surgeon, Faculty of Bio-medicine (Mutagenesis)

Sam Wiesner, Department of Mathematics (Metamathematics)

Madge Makepeace, Faculty of Social Sciences (Anthropology)

Siggie Gerhard, Faculty of Social Sciences (Psychology)

Saul Abrahms, Faculty of Social Sciences (Psychology of Functional Governance)

Colin Eckhart, Department of History (Renaissance & Reformation Art)

Kort Staahl, Department of English (Early Modern Literature)

Megan, research assistant, Bio-medicine

Sung, research assistant, Bio-medicine

The Dean, Stephen Shotter

MA STUDENTS

Holly Stanhope; Josh Feitel; Hannah Graham; Aydin Yilmaz

IN CAMBRIDGE

Guy Hilliard, Emma's former tutor
Tom Falconer, Emma's friend
Judy Falconer, archivist

EMMA'S FAMILY

Hugh D'Eresby, her father
Penny D'Eresby, her mother
Beth Marshall, her sister
Rob Marshall, her brother-in-law
Alex & Flora, her twin nephew and niece
Archie, their younger brother
Nanna, her grandmother
Douglas, her grandpa

Joan Seaton, friend of the family
Roger Seaton, Joan's son

MATTHEW'S FAMILY

Henry Lynes, his son
Patricia Lynes (Pat), Henry's wife
Margaret Lynes (Maggie), his granddaughter
Daniel Lynes (Dan), his grandson
Jeanette (Jeannie) Rathbone, Dan's wife, and their children:
Ellie Lynes
Joel Lynes
Harry Lynes
Charlie, Ellie's son

THE LYNES FAMILY TREE

Henry b. 1539
d. 1603
m
Emma D'Eresby b. 1568 -
d. 1657

Eliz'beth b. 1575   Henry b. 1577   William
m   m   m
M'tthw Monfort   Marg'ret Fielding   Susan Digby

infant d. 1611

Ellen Moore   m [1]   Matthew   m [2]   Emma D'Eresby - - - -
b. 1914   b. 1609   b.1980

Monica   m [1]   Henry   m [2]   Patricia
Davies   b. 1936   Karlesson

                                                    Rose   Theo

Ellen   Margaret   Daniel
(Little Ellen)   (Maggie)   m
                                  Jeanette Rathbone

                   Ellie   Joel   Harry

                   Charles
                   (Charlie)

THE D'ERESBY FAMILY TREE

Robert D'Eresby b. 1532
d. 1584
m
Mary Chapman

Robert   Elizabeth   Richard
m
Marjory
Monfort

Hugh Robert
m
Anne Drummond

Hugh
m
Penelope Chapman

Elizabeth b. 1972
m
Robert Marshall

Alexander   Flora   Archie
(Alex)

THE LYNES COAT OF ARMS

Dei sum leonis

THE D'ERESBY COAT OF ARMS

Fide fortuna forti

The Story So Far

Independent and self-contained British historian Emma D'Eresby has taken up a year-long research post in an exclusive American university in Maine, fulfilling her ambition (and that of her grandfather) to study the Richardson Journal – the diary of a seventeenth-century Englishman – housed in the library there.

Single-minded and determined, Emma is wary of relationships, but she quickly attracts the unwelcome attention of seductive colleague Sam Weisner, and the disturbing Professor of English, Kort Staahl. Despite her best intentions to remain focused on her work, and encouraged by her vivacious Russian friend, Elena Smalova, Emma becomes increasingly attracted to medical research scientist and surgeon Matthew Lynes, whose old fashioned courtesy she finds both disarming and curious.

Widowed and living quietly with his family, Matthew is reluctant to let her into his life, despite his clear interest in her, and Emma suspects there is more to his past than the little he tells her. His English-sounding name and the distinctive colour of his hair intrigues her, and Emma believes there is a link between Matthew and the very journal she came to the United States to study. Against her nature, she smuggles the historic document from the library to investigate further.

Events take a sinister turn as a series of savage assaults on women sends ripples of fear through the campus. Emma is convinced she is being followed and during the prestigious All Saints' dinner at Halloween is viciously attacked by psychotic Professor Staahl, leaving her on the edge of death. Only Matthew's timely intervention saves her and, as he cares for her in his college rooms, their relationship deepens and Emma finds herself battling between her growing love and her need to learn more about him.

A near-fatal encounter with a bear raises questions about Matthew she can no longer ignore.

Frustrated by the mystery surrounding his past and his refusal to tell her who he really is, Emma reluctantly flees Maine to her claustrophobic family home in England. Hidden from sight, but not her conscience, she has also taken the journal.

Years of acrimony with her family and a bruising affair a decade before with her tutor, Guy Hilliard – a married man – have left their scars. Now broken both physically and emotionally, and facing an emotional crisis, Emma drifts, until a chance meeting refocuses her attention on the unanswered questions she had left behind. Using her historical training to trace Matthew's family to an almost extinct hamlet in the tiny county of Rutland, she makes a startling discovery. Her instinct had been right: Matthew is a relic of the past.

Born in the early years of the seventeenth-century, Matthew had been betrayed during the English Civil War when a clash with his uncle left him fighting for his life. He not only lived, but persisted, growing steadily in strength and surviving events that would have killed any other man. Diary entries by the family steward in the same journal now in Emma's possession reveal that in the overheated atmosphere of seventeenth-century England – where rumours were rife and accusations of witchcraft frequent – Matthew faced persecution because of his differences, and he fled to the American colonies.

Coming to terms with Matthew's past, Emma is all-too aware that she possesses knowledge that could destroy his future and, when she learns he has disappeared from the college, sinks further into desolation. But as winter descends on the old stone walls of her family home, unable to remain separated from her,

Matthew comes to find Emma and takes her back to America.

Looking forwards to the future, Emma believes she has all the answers, but Matthew has one more revelation that could end their relationship once and for all. In a fraught confrontation in a remote snowbound cabin high in the mountains, Matthew tells her that he is still married. Over a harrowing few days with their relationship hanging in the balance, Matthew recounts his story, and Emma learns that his wife, Ellen, is a ninety-six-year-old paraplegic, and the man she thought was his father is in fact his son. Emma is faced with a stark choice: cut all ties with Matthew as she once did with Guy, or face an uncertain future with the only man she has ever really loved. Emma believes that her life is inextricably linked with Matthew's, and makes the decision to stay with him with all the complications it will entail.

As she prepares to meet Matthew's family at Christmas, the last thing on Emma's mind is college professor Sam Weisner, but it becomes apparent that she has been very much on his. After a brief, but unpleasant, encounter in which Sam acquires a broken jaw, Emma is forced to warn Sam off. But, despite her best efforts to protect Matthew's identity, wheels have been set in motion that one day could expose him to the world.

In the third book of *The Secret of the Journal* series – *Rope of Sand* – Emma meets Matthew's family for the first time when she goes to stay with him for Christmas. Here she is introduced to his son, Henry, and learns how unique the family really is. As Christmas approaches, it is clear that Emma is not welcomed by all the Lynes family: what does Matthew's great-granddaughter – Ellie – have against her, and what might his sinister clinical psychiatrist granddaughter – Maggie – be prepared to do to prevent Matthew and Emma being together?

When, out of spite one evening, Ellie gives Emma coffee instead of her usual tea, Emma suffers an extreme reaction and her heart stops for a few seconds. In those moments Emma discovers that coffee heightens all her senses, and she can detect the emotions of others around her in colour, revealing their deepest feelings – a form of synesthesia.

As questions of mortality and faith interweave, the bond between Emma and Matthew grows even stronger, but they accept that they must wait until his wife dies before they can have a life together.

After Christmas, and very reluctantly, Emma goes to meet Matthew's wife, Ellen – a frail and disabled elderly woman with a core of steel – and learns how a lifetime spent with Matthew will be one that demands the sacrifice of normality, and be full of obfuscation, concealment, and lies.

Blaming Emma for coming between Matthew and his wife, and destabilized by her presence over Christmas, Maggie reveals – in a threatening and vitriolic confrontation – that she has been in charge of assessing Kort Staahl's mental state since his vicious attack in October, and is determined to get rid of Emma. It is only a matter of time before ticking resentment explodes.

Just as Emma settles down to the new term teaching at Howard's Lake college, and looking forward to the history conference in the summer, she receives, without warning, a writ of prosecution issued on behalf of Kort Staahl. Emma is accused of defamation per se – a serious offence – and goes to trial worried that the spotlight will fall on Matthew as a key witness, and shocked that Maggie is involved as a witness for the prosecution. But there is more to the trial than at first seems. Part way through, Matthew's wife dies and, as he buries her a few days later, Henry's first wife – Monica – appears at the graveside, revealing that she instigated the trial in revenge against Matthew. Her sudden appearance after an absence of forty years drives her daughter, Maggie, ever closer to the borders of madness.

The following day the trial resumes with Maggie teetering on the edge of sanity while under fierce cross-examination on the witness stand. Emma fears she will reveal who Matthew is and, in one last desperate effort to protect his secret, she doses herself with coffee in an attempt to connect with Maggie emotionally using her newly discovered ability. She succeeds, but suffers a near-fatal heart attack. The trial is cancelled and, as winter turns a corner and Emma recovers in hospital, Matthew puts aside his past with renewed hope.

Emma has every reason to believe she can look forward to a future with Matthew as he is finally free to ask her to marry him. She in turn reveals the nature of her relationship with Guy Hilliard – her supervisor at Cambridge – and the reason she has found it difficult to forgive him and trust any other.

In England after the funeral of her beloved Nanna, Emma takes Matthew back to where his story started at Martinsthorpe, enabling him to face his traumatic past. Here he meets Joan Seaton and sees for the first time, in the mutilated tomb of his father, the fear and hatred in which he had been held by his community in the seventeenth century.

While most of Matthew's family accept the forthcoming marriage, not all are reconciled. Nor can Emma and Matthew be certain how her overprotective parents will react.

Family feathers settled, the families unite to celebrate the marriage in Maine. On a picnic by the river a few days before the wedding, Emma's niece and nephew – Flora and Alex – go missing, and only Matthew's swift intervention saves Flora from drowning. It is a close call: in the attempt to save her, Matthew suffers a severely broken shoulder, but will Emma's family notice?

As the couple start their married life together, Emma wants

to begin with a clear conscience, and slips the journal – which she took from the library the previous autumn – back where it belongs.

The history conference, at which Emma is expected to be the keynote speaker, looms. Without the odious Dean's knowledge, she has prepared her postgraduate students to deliver their research in her place. To her disgust, Emma discovers that Guy Hilliard is visiting the States and means to attend the conference. Although everyone – including her best friend, Elena Smalova – seems charmed by him, Emma doesn't trust Guy despite his claim that he's there to seek her forgiveness. Worse still, she discovers that Guy is dating Ellie – Matthew's great-granddaughter – bringing him within the family fold. She tells Matthew of her fears and tries to warn Ellie, but the young doctor refuses to believe her.

The conference begins amid a deepening heatwave. Despite the successful presentations of her students, the Dean makes it clear he won't let the matter lie. Moreover, one of her students has been manipulated by Guy, who gave her Emma's work to present as her own. Emma is livid, but trying to put her fears aside distracts herself with her grandfather's academic diaries, which Nanna had recently left to her. She discovers that her grandfather had been close to tracing Matthew's secret, aided by one of his students. Alarmed, she and Matthew spend a frantic night searching the documents for clues until they decipher the name "Vir" and realize that her grandfather's protégé all those years ago had been none other than Guy. The implications are clear: Guy had known who she was long before she had met him at Cambridge, and his continued presence at Howard's Lake college could be no coincidence.

Furious at the long-held deceit and alarmed by the ramifications, Emma confronts Guy at the conference. They arrange to meet at her home after the conference dinner that evening. Wracked by anxiety, Emma forewarns Matthew.

Guy holds a deep-seated grudge against Emma and her grandfather for thwarting his career early on. He shakes her belief in her own academic prowess, hinting that the only reason she gained a place at Cambridge was because he gave her preferential treatment. Not only that, but the Dean has offered him Emma's position at Howard's Lake college. Just when Emma thinks it can't get any worse, Guy tells her that he knows that Matthew is not all he seems. Petrified, Emma panics. She dashes from the room to get Matthew's sword, and is only prevented from going back to kill Guy when Matthew intercepts, saying that he will kill him himself. She comes to her senses and prevents him, but on returning to the study finds not only Guy gone, but photographs of Matthew as well.

Emma suspects he might have located the journal. It is now early morning. Matthew has left to find Ellie, and Emma hurries to the college where she indeed finds the journal missing. All it would take is the time for Guy to read the journal to discover Matthew's true identity and gain all the evidence he needs.

As a summer storm approaches, Emma races to Guy's hotel in an attempt to retrieve the photograph and journal, but Guy is one step ahead. She realizes she is running out of time and options. Guy says he is a speaker at the conference, but will give her the journal in exchange for her sleeping with him. She has no intention of doing so, but is prepared to do something much worse. As she readies herself, a mobile call saves her from taking the ultimate step. Buying time, she tells Guy that she will leave her husband and go with him, but that Matthew is looking for her and will kill him if he finds them together.

Offering to drive him to the conference, they set out, but the storm breaks, forcing them onto another route. As they drive,

Guy tells her that he knows who Matthew is and that he intends to reveal his identity at the conference. Emma believes she has no choice, but in the split second before she makes the decision to take his life, the car is forced off the narrow bridge by an oncoming truck, sending them into the torrent below. Matthew has been following them, and is able to free Emma from the submerging car, but Guy has been fatally injured in the crash.

Confused and ridden with guilt, Emma tries to come to terms with Guy's death and her part in it. To complicate matters, Ellie reveals that she is pregnant.

Matthew reassures Emma that all will be well and, as the book draws to an uneasy but positive conclusion, he and Emma place the journal in a secret place where it will remain – for the time being – hidden.

PART

I

Tyger Tyger, burning bright
In the forests of the night,
What immortal hand or eye
Could frame thy fearful symmetry?

In what distant deeps or skies
Burnt the fire of thine eyes?
On what wings dare he aspire?
What the hand dare seize the fire?

And what shoulder, & what art,
Could twist the sinews of thy heart?
And when thy heart began to beat,
What dread hand? & what dread feet?

What the hammer? What the chain?
In what furnace was thy brain?
What the anvil? What dread grasp
Dare its deadly terrors clasp?

When the stars threw down their spears
And water'd heaven with their tears,
Did he smile his work to see?
Did he who made the Lamb make thee?

Tyger Tyger burning bright
In the forests of the night,
What immortal hand or eye
Dare frame thy fearful symmetry?

William Blake

The technician leaned in, squinting at the screen. "Can you improve the resolution?"

Her colleague tapped in a few adjustments and leaned back to let her get a closer look. "Well, what d'ya think?"

"Looks similar, doesn't it? Been doctored, perhaps?"

The young man shrugged. "Dunno. Don't think so. Looks kosher to me."

"Bring up the first image again, Steve. Magnify..." He did as asked and she tilted her head, her brown hair swaying, and narrowed her eyes. "They're good frontal images – clear. You know, they are very alike. If it wasn't for the difference in age of the photos, I'd say you've got a match. Have you run it through photogrammetry to check? Where did you get them?"

He jerked a thumb over his shoulder. "Found the memory stick at the bottom of the filing cabinet. Been there years by the looks of it; must have fallen free of its file. Thought I'd take a look. There's a couple of documents on there with lecture notes for a conference or something, and these two photos."

"No dates on the images?"

"That first pic looks like it was taken in the thirties – look at their wedding kit and hair – taken with a Graflex Speed Graphic, four by five-inch plate, by the looks of it – American job – very popular with photojournalists in the 1930s. The other's contemporary; taken with a really sharp, quality lens. The only names I could find were in the lecture notes. A bloke named Hilliard – Guy Hilliard – wrote 'em..."

"And the other?" she asked, reaching for the phone.

Steve sifted the loose-leaf papers on his desk and found the hurriedly scrawled notes in blue biro he'd made earlier. "Yeah, here it is. The other bloke's name was..." He pulled at his lip as he tried to decipher his own scrawl. "Lynes. Dr Matthew Lynes."

Aftermath

"She's still not talking." Caught by the stiff breeze from the mountains, the kitchen door slammed shut behind me, echoing Ellie's action of a moment before. Her rejection compounded my guilt. "I don't know what else to do; I can't find any other way of saying I'm sorry." I slumped onto a chair by the table, and fanned myself with the pad of fine paper on which Matthew had been writing when I interrupted him. His pen lid sighed and clicked as he replaced it.

"It's early days yet – it's to be expected. Ellie didn't have the opportunity to come to terms with Guy's death, and sudden bereavement is doubly traumatic because of its very nature." He laid the pen in front of him, quietly, and at odds with my own mood. I slapped the pad down on the table.

"You don't need to remind me. If I could change what happened I would."

Matthew rose and pushed his chair back. "I know you would." He came and stood behind me, putting his arms around me and kissing the top of my head. "Time will help heal Ellie. She has a baby to think about and, when he is born, she will focus all her love on her child rather than embellishing her grief for his aberrant father."

I bent my head back until I could see him. "Are you speaking as a doctor or as her great-grandfather?"

"Both," he smiled. "Yes, time will heal Ellie. And you."

I wish I could be so sure. Now August, weeks had elapsed since the crash that had taken Guy's life, but Ellie's resentment of me still burned as fiercely as my guilt. The police investigated the accident thoroughly, of course, and I had been interviewed; but whether as a consequence of my remorse or because Ellie's brother, Joel, had some hand in moving the investigation on, they found me blameless. I wish I felt so. His death left matters unresolved in more ways than one.

I avoided campus. Banned by the Dean's decree, I wallowed at home unable to shake myself free of the accident and the part I played in it until, one day, Matthew came home from the med centre and found me listlessly scanning the internet in his study. With a disconsolate wave of my hand, I indicated the laptop on a small table.

"I can't find any work on here. Shotter has been as good as his word and I'm under investigation by both Cambridge and the college for falsification of qualifications. No other institution will touch me now. I'm going to end up doing nothing more than providing specialist editorial advice for academic publications and marking undergraduate essays for correspondence courses over the internet."

"Is that so bad?"

"I miss my students and I want my reputation back."

"Emma, I think you should go and talk to the Dean."

I prodded the keyboard in frustration, barely looking at him. "What's the point? Shotter won't give me my job back – Guy made sure of that." A stab of anger was followed by a twang of contrition. "I don't know if I have the heart to fight any more, Matthew."

Pushing the laptop to one side, he crouched down in front of me, forcing me to look at him, and cradled my hands. "Sweetheart, I'm worried that if you carry on like this for much longer, you'll find it difficult to pull yourself out of this despondency..."

I snatched my hands from his. "You said it will take time."

He captured them again, and this time held on firmly. "Yes, it will, but you have to make an effort to help yourself – nobody else can do it for you. Guy was the author of his own doom; if he hadn't died that day, we would have had to ensure it on another. He would have exposed us, Emma, and we wouldn't be sitting here now, debating it." He bent his head and I watched as the crimson air around him, which mirrored his emotional state, gradually turned mauve, then blue as he controlled his temper. "Guy took your job. Guy scuttled your career. Guy made Ellie pregnant. Guy is dead, Emma – and nothing is going to change that fact, including your self-flagellation."

We had spoken about this before – around and around endlessly – and he listened with utmost patience until I talked myself to a standstill, yet found no resolution. But how could I find healing when I held myself responsible? How could I absolve myself when I could barely look at my image in the mirror, let alone my conscience? On the night Guy took the photographs and revealed his motives for destroying me and all that I loved, Matthew had warned me. He warned me as I removed his rapier from its scabbard and went in search of Guy with the express purpose of killing him. He warned me, as he took the sword from my hand, that I could never reverse the taking of a life, and in doing so, made ready to take it himself as he had done many times before in his long past. But the events of the following day rendered his entreaty pointless, and Guy still died by my hand.

Several days after the crash I could bear it no longer. One morning I woke to see the triptych on my bedside table next to me. I sat up, lifted it from its place and closed the doors over the image of Christ. I secured the gilt hook and carefully laid it in its bed of faded purple silk in the old rosewood box and hid it in my chest of drawers.

Matthew did not comment when he noticed it missing, but I saw the look of swift disappointment and the flash of concern. Now, weeks on, here we were again, head-to-head with my obduracy.

He held my fingers more lightly now, sensing a shift in my reasoning. "Emma, the Dean wants to see you. There are things you need to discuss."

"Well I don't want to see him."

"Please…" he insisted, and I saw that this represented a small concession in the circumstances.

Two days later, I screwed up my courage and hobbled my pride enough to make an appointment to see the Dean. I hadn't been back to the campus since the day of the accident, but it had changed. Or I had.

Matthew kept me company to the atrium and there left me outside the Dean's office. The last time I stood here I had been in a position of power as I faced Shotter down. That had been before Guy resurfaced from the dregs of my past in an attempt to steal my future. I raised my hand to knock. The door opened.

"Come in, come in." Rather than Shotter's portly figure ensconced in his kingdom of intrigue and tradition, Siggie Gerhard greeted me in a lightweight floral two-piece, plump-armed and benevolent as always. I scanned the office for the Dean, but she was alone.

"Where's Shotter?" I asked cautiously, once I had returned her warm embrace.

"He's not here," she replied with her gentle Germanic

inflection. "Come and sit down by the window; there is a bit of a breeze and we need that in this heat, no?" She pulled Shotter's chair from behind his desk and jerked it over the frayed edge of the rugs and across the smooth planks to the open window.

"I'll stand, thanks. I want to get this over with as quickly as I can and I grovel better on my feet. Where is the bloated toad, anyway? I thought he would be eagerly waiting to rub my face in it."

Siggie took a hanky from her pocket and dabbed at the perspiration at her greyed hairline. She sat next to the open sash, leaning her elbow on the sill to catch the breeze.

"As I said, he is not here. Now, come, sit down and tell me what you have been up to. We have much to discuss." She patted the chair next to hers but I continued to stand. Across the room on the opposite wall, the row of photographic portraits of the current academic staff served as a sharp reminder that I was no longer one of them. Siggie saw me looking.

"There have been a few changes here over the last few weeks." She passed the desk on which stood a tubby vase full of vibrant sunflowers on her way to study the pictures, stopping when she came to the newest face in the line-up where mine should have been. Guy's derisive gaze challenged the camera and I felt my gut twist.

"Ah, yes – I met him only briefly. His death is a tragedy for some, but not for others, perhaps?" She lifted the photograph from the wall and examined it closely, then put it face down on the side table next to her. I twitched. She went over to Shotter's desk and opened the left-hand drawer.

"Siggie!" I exclaimed. "What are you doing?"

She removed a framed photo and took it over to the now empty place on the wall and hung it there. I recognized it instantly as my own. I gave a nervous glance at the door, outside of which I could now hear the low rumble of male voices. "For goodness sake, Siggie, the Dean will have your guts for garters!" She leaned back to check the angle, and straightened the frame.

"No, Emma, I do not think so. Stephen Shotter has no say in the matter. There," she said, admiring the result. "I think that is an improvement, don't you?"

I sat down with a bump. "Why?" I asked, as she joined me by the window again and lowered herself onto the chair, arranging her blowsy skirt in such a way that it didn't catch under her legs.

"Eh? Oh, Shotter, do you mean, Emma? He is one of the changes I referred to. He... overstepped the mark, I think you would say. I do not know the details, but there have been questions about his integrity and his suitability to lead the college."

"Why?" I asked again, but bewildered this time.

"I think you should ask Matthew. I believe he knows more about it than I do. Meanwhile, for some reason I have been asked to be Dean, although why a professor of psychology is considered suitable for the role I am not certain, but... there you have it." Her soft, plump hands rose and then fell with a gesture of resigned acceptance. "Now, one of my first tasks is to ensure continuity of staffing and I find we are short of a professor of history for the fall semester. I wish to offer this position to you, Emma – if you have not already found alternative employment, that is?"

Siggie would know I had nothing planned for the autumn term, as indeed I suspected she knew a great deal more about my situation than she let on. Outside on the lawns sweeping around this side of the college, a few research students sprawled in the shade of the trees, oblivious to the internal wrangling in my mind.

"And the investigation, Siggie? How can you justify the employment of someone suspected of falsifying her qualifications?" I had not intended the note of resentment that coloured my voice to make itself known, but it did. She sat back and took a moment to survey me.

"It has been brought to my attention that Guy Hilliard might have had a reason to discredit you, and his activities could be said to have been – how shall I put it? – not worthy of a man of his supposed reputation. Are you aware that he took one of the college's most unique and valuable documents? Yes, that is so," she said as my head shot up. "He took a seventeenth-century diary from the library shortly before his death. We have found no trace of it and must assume he took it with him on the morning of the accident and it is lost to the river."

So they thought the journal lost and Guy the one who had taken it. The irony was so delicious, so tart, it stung my eyes, and then I saw her looking oddly at me and I realized that my breathing had changed, becoming shallow and halting because I couldn't draw enough air into my lungs as I tried to laugh but found myself crying instead. I covered my face with my hands.

"There, there," she said quietly, and put her arm around me in much the same way my mother would. "There are two types of monsters: those like Staahl, who can be locked away, and those in your mind. You cannot escape the mind-monsters, Emma, you can only face them and deal with them one by one. You are not yourself at the moment; take some more time off. My advice is that you and Matthew get away from here for a little and sort out whatever is bothering you." I hunted for a tissue and, failing to find one, dragged my hand across my eyes instead.

"Siggie, the fall semester starts in a few weeks…"

"Don't worry about that; your students will wait until your return, and you will return, won't you, Emma? You will accept the position?"

I looked into her kind, shrewd eyes, then away in case she could read mine. "Yes. Thank you, Siggie, I will."

* * *

"Good," Matthew said when I went to find him in his laboratory. "Then justice is done."

"Did you get rid of Shotter?"

"Me? Why would you think I had anything to do with that?"

"Because Siggie said as much. Did you tell her to give me my job back, too?"

"No, I didn't. I don't have that authority and she is quite capable of making her own judgment on the suitability – or otherwise – of potential staff. If she is offering you the position, it is because she thinks you are the best person for the job. Period." On a computer keyboard, he tapped in a rapid series of numbers, clicked enter, pursed his lips as he read the result, and typed some more.

"And Shotter?"

His mouth lifted at one corner and, without taking his eyes from the screen, said, "Ah, well, I might have pointed people in the right direction." With a last look at the figures, he turned his back on the computer and, folding his arms, leant against the work surface. "Siggie is right in one other respect: we could do with a break. I promised you a proper holiday after the trial, and our honeymoon could hardly be called restful." He pushed away from the workbench to stand indecently close to me. "Do you think, if I asked her nicely, she would give me time off for good behaviour?"

I raised a weary smile. "I don't know about *good behaviour* – I don't think I have the energy to be anything but *good* – but I think Siggie would insist you accompany me, to prevent me doing myself a mischief."

"Wise woman," he said. "In that case, pack your bags and sun lotion; we're going on holiday."

Facing Demons

I picked up a water-worn pebble and turned it over in the palm of my hand. "I hoped I might find some peace here." I lobbed the stone into the water and watched it be consumed by the restless surface of the sea. "But I won't, will I? I can't escape my conscience." We walked along the shore for a few yards before I stopped and picked up another stone – smoothed grey as a gull wing, about the size of a small hen's egg, but flat, with a vein of quartz in the shape of a slanted cross. I ran my thumb across the face of the stone. "You said as much, Matthew, that night I wanted to kill Guy. You said you could never take back so irrevocable an act and it would be something I would have to live with for the rest of my life. As you have."

He didn't answer and we walked on again, finding our way around the larger boulders that edged the beach – all grey or black under the featureless pewter sky. I found no peace in it, but a quiet beauty that gave me the space to think. I had done a lot of thinking since we arrived on New Zealand's North Island.

"The difference," I continued, "between you and me, is that you killed for a purpose – in the line of duty – an act of war."

"Do you think that makes it better?"

"No – well, yes, perhaps. You went into battle knowing why you were there. Whether fighting for Parliament or the King, both sides fought for a cause and you all understood that death might be a consequence of war." For days now we had walked and talked and walked until – too tired to think any more – I could sleep. A spine of rock, rising out of the greywacke stones from the water's edge to the cliff, blocked our path like the backbone of some great extinct creature. He made a cushion out of his jacket for me and we sat in the shelter of the rock. He lifted his arm and I leant against his solidity, drawing on the comfort he gave.

"Emma, you told me shortly after the crash that you wanted to kill him, but at the point of impact you changed your mind. You told me it was an accident. Don't you remember?"

I thought back to the bridge and the twisted remains of the barrier that had given way to the nose of the truck before my own car was pushed through it and into the river below.

"I couldn't kill him, Matthew, but I hated him. He died because of my hatred. He died because of me."

"No!" Matthew said with vehemence. "No, Emma, he died because a steel reinforcing bar entered the left ventricle of his heart, and pierced his lung. It was no act of malice on your part. However you felt about him – and by God's sweet name, he deserved everything he got after what he did to you – however you felt, you were not responsible for his death."

"But I am partly responsible for his life," I said quietly. "By my actions I brought about his death before... before..." I crushed my fist against my mouth as I felt my chin quiver. "Before he could repent," I finished. I heard Matthew's exclamation but could not look at him.

"Is this what it is all about? You are concerned for his *soul*? Emma, the man's spiritual state was not yours to worry about. You are not responsible for anyone else's other than your own."

"But I am, Matthew, don't you understand? I did the worst thing I possibly could – just as bad as killing him myself: he had no time to make peace with God. Whatever he did in life, I had no right to condemn him to eternal death."

"He made his choice…"

"And I gave him no chance to change it!" Angrily, I thrust my hand into a pocket of gritty sand and crushed it into a loose ball. "The men you fought – the men you killed – knew the possibility of death and had time to repent before it became reality. You don't have to carry the burden of that, but I do."

"Don't I, Emma? Do you really think killing came so easily to me?"

"I didn't mean… But you don't talk about it."

"No." He rose and walked long-limbed the few yards to the edge of the sea. Insistent waves lapped at his feet, testing his resolve with foam-tipped tongues. "They say the more you kill, the easier it becomes," he said, with his back to me, "but it doesn't. One life, or many, the effect is still the same. Or at least, I have found it to be so." He turned around. "If this were a physical pain you harboured, I could reach inside you and take it. If I could do what you did for me, and provide some balm for your emotional hurt, I would. But I can't. I'm sorry you have this burden, Emma; I would have done anything to prevent it being so."

"Including killing him yourself?"

"Yes, if I had to – if I could find no other way."

"How do you live with your conscience, Matthew?"

He gave a short grunt of a laugh. "Because I have no choice in the matter." He crunched across the shingle-strewn sand to sit beside me again. He took my clenched hand in his, turned it over, and opened my fingers. "I can find no peace in death; it is denied me. For the meantime, I have to make do and find it in life." He traced the cross on the stone I still held in my palm. "And you must do the same." He closed my fingers over the pebble.

"I don't know how," I whispered.

He looked at me with earnest concern, face softening, eyes gentle. "Yes, you do – you told me once, not long ago, that I am forgiven – do you remember? That God has forgiven me and what I need to do is to accept that, and forgive myself. I can live with what I have done because I have repented. It is what you believe, Emma – not in theory, but in fact. Make it real."

"I don't deserve forgiveness."

"No, nor do any of us. Your remorse – mine – is worth nothing unless you make it real."

I had shrunk inside myself, taken refuge, but I could not escape the truth of it, because it lay at the very heart of me. The wind gusted, tearing at my hair and whipping strands into my eyes.

"I know what I have to do, Matthew. I just don't know how to do it."

He pulled my hood over my head and secured my hair inside it. His hand lingered, his gaze also; and I, trapped by both, felt a shift in me. He too sensed it.

"It is already done," he said, and pressed his lips to my forehead, sealing it. "It is time to move on."

It didn't happen immediately, but in layers – one by one dropping away, until one day, sheltering from a sudden downpour in a tin shack of a church, hail rattling on the roof like claws, I remembered a verse my friend Tom had left me in those dark days between Guy and my new-born faith.

"I've never been alone with this, have I – spiritually, I mean?"

Matthew looked up from studying the map he had spread over a side table to dry.

"No, I don't believe you have."

With my head tipped on one side, I surveyed the simple cross made of wood sitting on the plain altar table with its starched white cloth. "I think, although I always knew it in my head, perhaps I didn't feel it in my heart."

Matthew folded the map, tucked it in his pocket, and picked up his motorcycle helmet. "And do you now?" he asked.

I spent longer considering the question than I think he expected, and he crossed the worn planks scrubbed clean by years of feet and mops, to sit beside me on the wobbly pew. I looked about me, at the love and devotion sewn into the embroidered kneelers, and the blue pressed-glass vase filled with unfamiliar wild flowers.

"Yes," I said. "I do."

We spent the next weeks on the Harley we hired continuing our journey south and west, skirting the Tasman Sea, then into the mountains and fiords of South Island – so different to those of Maine – staying in isolated lodges for a few days before moving on to a village B&B the next. The bike gave us access to areas so remote we felt at times that we were the only inhabitants of a pristine planet in an age before knowledge stained it. In that time, I found the understanding I had been looking for, and the peace that came with it.

When we landed in Portland's jetport in the middle of the night after a long and convoluted journey, Henry greeted us.

"And how's my favourite step-mom?" He hugged me warmly, then stood back at arm's length, initiating an inspection. He nodded his approval. "Better for your vacation, I see. I should think I'm the only septuagenarian whose step-mom is less than half his age and can double as a supermodel."

"Flatterer," I laughed, and hugged him back. "I don't think I'll ever get used to being your..."

Matthew cleared his throat beside me as an airport security guard passed within earshot. I lowered my voice. "... Step-mother," I completed as he went beyond hearing range.

Henry turned to Matthew. "Dad," he said, clasping Matthew in a bear hug. "It's been strange not having you around; can't say I like it much. I guess we've not spent this long apart since the war."

Matthew returned the older man's embrace. "It's good to be home, son. Is everything all right with the family? How's Ellie?"

Looking suddenly grave, Henry fingered his beard. "We had a bit of a scare a couple of weeks ago; she started spotting after riding Lizzie. We ran a CBC, and ultrasound showed the foetus still viable – and a boy." He threw a quick look in my direction. "She's pushing her luck – working double-shifts – you know what she's like, but we can't get through to her. Maybe you can."

"Maybe. You ran the tests yourself?"

"I did, then destroyed the samples. The data's been encoded and uploaded on to E.V.E; I thought you'd want to see it."

"I do, thanks. Good work." Matthew noticed me smothering a yawn. "We'd better fetch the luggage and get Emma home before she falls asleep on her feet."

In Henry's comfortable car we headed north and west away from the sharp lights of Portland and into the strengthening night of the woods of Maine. Resting my head on Matthew's shoulder, I asked sleepily, "Why did Henry need to destroy Ellie's blood samples?"

"For the same reason she will have a home birth – as a precaution. Her blood carries genetic markers and we don't want it getting into the wrong hands."

Henry's eyes briefly met Matthew's in his driving mirror – the two so alike despite the care Henry took to disguise the similarity.

"Well, at least you don't have that problem with me," I said, bringing Matthew's arm around my shoulders and kissing his hand as he momentarily caressed the side of my face. Matthew looked out of the window into the darkness.

"No, indeed," he replied.

Birthday Boy

"It's no good, Pat. I've tried, really I have, but the blessed things won't cooperate." I flung the oven gloves on the side and scowled at the soggy flat objects in the little baking tins. They glowered back, palely. I regretted ever suggesting preparing lunch for our friends in celebration of Matthew's birthday, and rather thought that Pat might too. She tut-tutted in her motherly way and peered at the semi-cooked batter over the tops of her glasses.

"Emma, did you pre-heat the oven?"

I looked at her askance. "Of course I did! They wouldn't cook otherwise, would they?"

"*Pre*-heat, Emma – that means heating the oven for at least twenty minutes before you put them in. Didn't you read the recipe?"

I had – sort of. She had given us – me – a wonderful cookery book which I read with great diligence, but this morning I had received a really interesting article exploring the transition from feudal to absolutist monarchies in Europe, so I lost track of the time – a bit. My eyes slid away from hers.

"You could have chosen something simpler than roast beef and Yorkshire puddings, sweetie. Or you could let Matthew cook."

That would have been the easiest solution, it was true, but it was the first birthday of his that we had shared and I had been determined to do something resembling traditional British cooking for our friends, and I wanted to do it myself. I had failed on both counts. Now, as everyone waited patiently in the drawing room, I could almost hear their stomachs growl from where I stood. The door from the hall opened, bringing a gale of laughter as Matthew appeared still chuckling and carrying a tall-stemmed wine glass. He looked immensely cheerful, but then he wasn't hungry.

"Whatever it is, it smells good," he remarked, pouring a third of the contents of his glass down the sink, and then peering over my shoulder. "Ah," he added when he saw the flaccid goo. "Well, who needs Yorkshire pudding when there's plenty of beef and vegetables?" He hesitated. "There is, isn't there?"

I managed to get that right at any rate; I mean, how hard can it be to cook frozen peas? And the beef did smell – meaty. He saw my dejected look and kissed my flaming forehead.

"I'll give you a hand putting it together, if you like. Our guests didn't come here to test your cooking ability; they came for our company. They'll love whatever you produce."

I pulled a face. "That's good, because they'll need iron stomachs to eat this."

Pat lifted the beef from the oven before it burned any more, swapping it for the upside-down pudding. "Did you want gravy for the beef, Emma?"

I groaned. "Gravy! I forgot."

Pat and Matthew probably exchanged looks at that point, but I was too busy rummaging in the cupboard for a saucepan, muttering furiously to myself, to notice. Matthew leant down.

"Emma, there'll be plenty more opportunities to master the art of gravy-making." A stack of saucepans collapsed noisily and I said something I shouldn't. "There's no reason why you should be good at cooking," he persisted.

I emerged with a saucepan. "You are," I waved it at him, "and you don't even eat." I picked up the recipe book, peered at the index, and found *sauce*. I squinted at the wavering print before me. "Does that say 2 or 12 dessertspoons of cornstarch? What's cornstarch?"

Saul leaned forwards, nursing his glass and, in his soft melodic voice, continued with his gentle interrogation. "I understand your fascination with forms of punishment, Emma – I see it all the time in my line of work – but I don't understand why you think its study as necessary to your research."

I internally sighed. The same old misconception that had dogged me for years and which had been trotted out by the defence team as justification for Staahl's vicious attack on me.

"I don't study methods of torture as much as the persecution of groups and individuals it was used against, and I certainly don't get a buzz from it. Torture and interrogation are just part of the bigger picture that enables me to gain perspective. Nor am I interested in brutality for the sake of it; there are countless examples of *that*. I'm only interested in institutionalized interrogation such as that employed by the Inquisition for a specific purpose."

His kind face wrinkled into perplexed, olive folds. "But what of the victims of such violence? Does this not concern you also? Are you not at risk of diminishing the crime by giving a voice to the perpetrator – I would say, almost justifying their purpose by rationalizing it?"

"Of course it concerns me as a person – acutely – and I believe that there can be no justification for its use. But that's missing the point. Torture was just the mechanics of a machine driven by the hopes, desires, *fears* of the men who applied it. People get too involved in the mechanics, but the study of interrogation in itself does not define the reasoning behind it any more than a knowledge of a car engine tells you where the car has come from, or where it will go. Yes, the research is distressing – sometimes more than I can bear – but it is as relevant now as it was five hundred – a thousand – years ago, because what drove men then still drives them today, both in the persecution of belief, and in the persecuted. The power of suggestion, of rumour and what derives from it – that is what I'm interested in: people's *motives*, not necessarily their actions."

"We are at different ends of the perspective, then," Siggie enjoined. "We make it our work to understand the repercussions of persecution – I, in how it affects the psyche, while Saul assesses the culture of despotism and its impact on society."

I tore a grape from the branchlet on my plate. "And Matthew picks up the broken pieces and fixes them."

"Tries to," Matthew said, refilling Elena's empty glass, "and not always succeeding. Thankfully, it doesn't constitute a substantial element in my work, but when it crops up, it's hard to forget." He didn't need to refer directly to Staahl because, from their faces, everyone knew what he meant. "I don't think the value of Emma's work in relation to the modern world can be underestimated just because she focuses on the past. As she says, the relevance lies in what it tells us about people's behaviour – and that never changes."

"No, it does not!" Elena almost snorted. "It is the same always. In the Soviet Union there was persecution of all faith, a war on the culture of religion. It was a sys-te-matic attempt to wipe religion from society by the Soviet regime, but it failed, and it will always fail, because people want to believe."

Making his way through the selection of biscuits and cheese, Matias had been listening quietly to the conversation; now he took up the baton. "As I see it, the trouble is that people also need to belong, and that's when conflict arises. In the same way as a rogue cell is attacked and eliminated by healthy cells, in society, people turn on individuals or groups who don't appear to conform. The same goes for religious groups, as well as individuals..."

"Like Eckhart," I murmured, although that wasn't the first person who came to mind, and I saw Siggie's eyes flash towards Matthew in the split second it took for her to realize I had seen. She covered her tracks by continuing the conversation.

"Ah yes; Colin Eckhart is an easy target."

Elena had always been particularly unsympathetic towards the awkward professor. "But he is rude; he does not look at you when he is speaking, and he stands too close." Her hands flew in the air in exasperation. "And he doesn't listen; he just goes on and on about what he wants to say."

Siggie nodded. "As I said, an easy target. It is simpler to condemn the differences than to try to understand and accept them, I think."

Elena huffed. "I do not condemn him..."

Matias put his knife down on his plate and hurrumphed a laugh. "You haven't exactly gone out of your way to be friendly though, have you, kitten?" She glared at him. "Well, you haven't, so it's no good looking at me like that. Last week you even went the long way around the quad just to avoid him, and what's the poor man ever done to you?"

"I do not like the way he looks and talks – and he walks like this..." She hunched her shoulders and swayed them from side to side. "Like a bear. He makes me feel uncomfortable."

Saul drained his glass and set it carefully in front of him. "And seeing someone's differences as reason to exclude them is only a short step away from the gas chamber."

Elena looked as if she didn't know whether to be upset or

cross, but before she could decide, Matthew interceded. "But there is a world of difference between not understanding a person's differences, and intolerance – and an even greater one before intolerance becomes persecution. When it comes to it, there are always those who become petty tyrants because it is easier, or because they are frightened, or because they enjoy the sense of power and purpose they think it gives them; but there are many more who will oppose that tyranny given half a chance. Elena would be the first person to stand up for Eckhart if she saw him targeted, wouldn't you?"

She looked at him with grateful dark eyes. "Da, I do not like to see people bullied."

"I'll remember that next time you have a go at me," Matias grinned at her. Everyone laughed, relieved to have an excuse to lighten the atmosphere, which had become increasingly loaded with unvoiced tensions.

Elena trotted into the drawing room on her ridiculously high heels, eyes agog. "Emma, Matias showed me around the rest of your home; it is *bea-u-tiful.*"

Matias smoothed his unruly hair back in place. "Yes, but I did ask Matthew first, in case you were wondering. You'll be glad to know that Elena made me leave the silver, but I was tempted by that very convincing copy of the Wilson landscape you have in the hall. It'd look very nice on the wall above my desk." He made an artist's square from his hands, imagining it in his apartment. He dropped his hands as a thought occurred to him. "It *is* a copy, isn't it?"

It wasn't, but I didn't know how to answer convincingly. With a genial grin, Matthew handed him a glass. "I'll be sure to count the spoons when you go home."

Matias made to throw a punch, then seemed to remember

what had happened the last time he tried and slapped Matthew across the shoulder instead. "You do that," he said. "While you're at it, I've got my eye on your wife – bigamy isn't exactly a crime if you don't marry one of them." He dodged as Elena and I launched an attack simultaneously. A couple of months ago, a remark like that would have stung; now Matthew and I merely beamed. Siggie lowered herself gingerly into an upright chair by the sofa and I saw Matthew take note.

"Better come and see me at the med centre about your back first thing in the morning and I'll see what I can do."

She attempted to shrug, but it obviously hurt. "It will wait."

"No, it won't," he insisted. "Tomorrow – or I'll come looking for you."

"Your husband can be very stern, can he not, Emma? I think he would have made a better Dean." She leaned back with care, apparently found she could do so without it hurting, and relaxed a little. "I have heard good things about your students from last year; their research has been well received and I believe two of them wish to take a doctorate?" I nodded. "But they will only do so if you supervise them. That speaks for itself, I think. And how are your new MA students getting on?"

I thought about my little group of graduates, eager to get their research underway.

"I think they'll make a good team. Do you know what happened to Hannah?" I asked, as Siggie accepted a cup of tea.

"I am afraid the college cannot let the matter of plagiarism go. Hannah has a case of academic fraud to answer. She says she will appeal, but we have your original research to verify the evidence, and it is conclusive. I am sorry, Emma. I know you wanted her to face a lesser charge."

I recalled Hannah's stubborn anger in our last tutorial and, later, her triumphant presentation to the conference of my work as her own. "She is as much a victim of Guy Hilliard as I was, Siggie; I can't help but feel sorry for her."

"Perhaps," she said, "but she had a choice, and she made the wrong one."

A gust of cooler air invaded the room as the door between our drawing room and the Barn opened. "How did lunch go?" Henry asked as he and Pat joined us, picking up a cup and saucer from the tray.

"The beef was dry and the carrots were raw." I handed him the jug of milk. "The gravy was perfect, though."

"Well, that's something," he said, sitting down.

"Pat made it."

Pat gave a dismissive wave of her hand and resumed her conversation with Siggie.

"Ah." Henry took a sip from the cup, winced, then took another. "This is... interesting."

"Coffee substitute," Matthew said.

"Roasted barley, chicory root, carob, and added spices," I informed him. "No coffee allowed in the house in case I suffer another heart attack and really put the kibosh on the day."

"I like it," Elena volunteered. "I think it is good for you, Dr Lynes."

"Call me Henry, please," he said. "And I'm looking forward to trying that bottle of Cabernet Sauvignon you gave Matthew for his birthday – if he lets me share it, that is."

Matias drew up a chair next to Saul. "So how many does that make it, Matthew – thirty-four, thirty-five...?"

"Thirty-three," I said firmly, having agreed his age with him that morning.

Matias sucked his cheeks. "Really? What, again? I swear you were thirty-three last year. Either that or I'm losing it – early onset Alzheimer's, perhaps."

"Not that early," I shot back and, although he jested and we all laughed, Matias weighed up Matthew, taking in his appearance of youth in his lean, toned frame, unlined face, hair neither greying nor receding, unlike his own, and unchanged since he had met him some six years previously. At first I suspected he might be jealous, but the speculative look he gave him spoke not of envy, but interest. "Well," he said eventually, and almost to himself, once the conversation had moved onto safer ground, "all I can say is that doctors get younger every year. Whatever you're on, I want it." And he tossed back the remaining contents of his glass, and set it down.

"You will have to do something about looking your age," I remarked that evening, thinking back to Matias's comment as I tugged my brush through my hair without due care and attention. Matthew closed the last of the bedroom shutters against the dark and took my brush from me.

"What, four hundred and two years old? I hardly think my appearance as a corpse would help our situation. Do you?"

"Don't be facetious," I retorted. "You know what I mean."

He pulled the brush through my long hair, encountering a knot halfway down. Working at it gently, he said, "Apart from growing a beard, adopting glasses or wearing contact lenses – all of which would make me look more like my son, which would defeat the object – there's not much that I can do. I can't put on weight – or lose it – and the only lines I'll ever have are the ones I had when I... evolved."

"Lucky you," I murmured. "I've put on weight since we married. It's not fair – you make me eat." With one hand Matthew chucked the hairbrush on the bed, while the other pulled me close against him, his lips mouthing the lobe of my ear.

"And it suits you," he said, his other hand joining the

exploration of my new curves under my pyjamas, "especially here," and he drifted his hands over my hips; "and here," they met in the middle over the plane on my stomach, where they hesitated, then stalled.

"What is it?" I asked when, to my disappointment, his hands resumed their journey but were now less seductive and more reflectively absorbed.

"Mmm? I was contemplating our future here. I think that until it becomes more obvious that I haven't changed, we would do as well to stay where we're settled."

"But Matias..."

"Leave Matias to me; he's no threat to us. Now," he said purposefully, sliding his hands around my waist and manoeuvring me towards our bed, "I believe you were in the act of beguiling me, you wanton."

Later, when even the owl – which had taken up residency nearby – drifted towards sleep, replete after a night's hunting, Matthew rested his hands over the moderate bow of my stomach, singing quietly to himself. Even in the near-dark of the room I recognized the signs of contentment in the upward lift of his mouth as he leaned over and placed a kiss on the soft skin below my tummy button. The air – pale blue and vivid – hummed vibrantly around him. I reached down and touched the muted gold of his hair.

"What are you so happy about?" I asked sleepily. He kissed me again and lifted his head.

"How are you feeling?"

It had been a long day and an even longer night. I lay back against the pillow and wriggled comfortably, and my eyes involuntarily closed. "I'm fine." Then snapped open. "Why?"

4

Great Expectations

Stay, O sweet, and do not rise;
The light that shines comes from thine eyes
John Donne

"You're pregnant?" My sister exclaimed so loudly on the other end of the phone that everyone in the UK – let alone her husband – must have heard. "Golly Moses, Em; that was quick." I ignored the implication inherent in the unrestrained laughter that followed her lewd comment. "Have you told Mum and Dad yet?"

"I tried phoning but they must be out."

In the diminishing sound of breathing, I heard my sister look away at the kitchen clock above her oven, then back again as she brought the phone close to her mouth. "Yup, it's past two – they must be visiting Nanna at the cem. Hey, Em, Nanna would have been well pleased with your news, wouldn't she?"

The thought of Nanna in her pale lemon cardigan, with her eyes sparkling behind granny specs, brought a poignant, painful realization that she wouldn't share this with us. My emotions had been all over the place in the last few weeks since Matthew had divined my pregnancy; it had taken me this long to tell my family. I cleared my throat of its tightness.

"Well pleased?" I said starchily, because I didn't want her detecting the quaver. "Since when have you said 'well pleased', Beth?"

"Since I have two nine-year-old kids who go to the local school, Em. Hey, they'll have a cousin. How many weeks are you?"

I swiftly calculated. "Six now."

"You can tell so soon? Golly, I was at least eleven weeks gone with Flora and Alex before I knew."

"It helps having a doctor for a husband."

"Yes, it must do." She paused. "Emma, are you all right? You don't sound very... well, very happy about it all? It takes a bit of getting used to, I know, and don't let my three put you off." She waited for me to tell her that they didn't, although the thought of Archie and his wailing was enough to dissuade anyone from having children. Beth handled motherhood like a pro and it was one area in which I thought I could never compete.

"I realize Arch hasn't been the easiest baby, Em, but they grow out of it. He's so much better than he was now his teeth are through. Or are you scared of the birth? Is that it?"

I couldn't tell her it was everything to do with babies, but most of all my fear I wouldn't do my child justice as a mother, so I just said, "Yes, something like that."

"Well, it's a good thing you have Matthew to look after you. Ask for pethidine or gas and air – no, no – go for an epidural. They do those in hospitals in the States, don't they? Best thing I ever did when Arch was born, I can tell you."

"Mmm. Look, Beth, I'm really flogged out..."

"You must be; it's tiring carrying. Do you want me to tell Mum and Dad for you?"

"Yes, please."

"Oh good. I want to see the look on Dad's face – he'll be a

picture. I bet he thinks you're still a virgin." And she roared with laughter again.

I replaced the receiver feeling strangely deflated, and wandered through to the kitchen to put the kettle on. Waiting for it to boil, I opened the back door to the courtyard and stepped out into the sun. It felt unseasonably warm, with only a hint of the winter to come in the shade of the buildings. The remote mountains growled with unseen thunder, but above the house and as far as I could see, the sky remained impervious to the distant threat.

I crossed the stone setts to the wooden bench by the tack room next to the garage, which Matthew had installed for me to catch the last of the afternoon sun. I sat, feeling lousy and grousy all rolled into one disjointed muddle. Days after he had told me, I detected the first signs of pregnancy in the tenderness of my breasts, and then in the queasy sensation on waking. If Matthew was ecstatic, I felt less than thrilled, and unprepared for parenthood. If his joy made my lack of eagerness all the more apparent, Elena's enthusiasm shone a spotlight on it.

"You have something to tell me!" she had sung, skipping into my tutor room without bothering to knock, plonking her bag on my desk and flinging herself into a chair. Aydin rescued a book before it fell on the floor.

"I go now, Professor?" he asked, handing the book back and closing his laptop on which we had been discussing his doctoral proposal.

"Thanks, Aydin; we'll continue with this on Thursday. *Güle güle.*"

He smiled patiently at my poor attempt to say goodbye in Turkish.

"*Evet*, Professor, that is good. *Allahaısmarladık.*" I peered at him, trying to remember the few words Matthew had taught me. "It means I say goodbye when I go, yes? *Allahaısmarladık*." And he bowed his dark head slightly, the light catching his scalp through his short, thinned hair, and then again to Elena, who bounced up and down in the chair impatiently.

"Have you told Aydin your news?" she squeaked. "Matias told me at lunch. He said he knew something was up because Matthew keeps singing to himself and when he thinks no one is looking, he goes on the internet and looks at baby sites. When Matias caught him, Matthew said it was for his niece, but Matias kept bugging him until he dropped the beans and then he confessed and it is *wonder*ful!" she finished in a rush. "Isn't it, Aydin?"

I wasn't sure whether Aydin had caught the gist of anything Elena had just said. He hugged his laptop looking bemused. "Why did Dr Lynes drop beans? Why is this good?"

I started stacking books to one side of my desk, feeling a little nauseous again now lunch beckoned. "Elena means spill the beans, Aydin. It is a colloquial expression meaning to admit or confess something. Matthew told Matias that I'm pregnant, nothing more." I caught a slight downward tug of his mouth. "Don't worry, it won't affect my supervision of your doctoral programme or anything."

He met my eyes and I saw sadness there before he covered it with a smile. "I do not worry about my work, Professor." He held out his hand. "I am happy for you; a child will bring much joy, I think."

I watched Aydin pick up his bag and sling it over his shoulder, an unspoken grief dyeing the air around him purple. It occurred to me, as Elena chatted away, that I knew nothing about Aydin – neither about the life he led, nor about the one he left behind – and how easy I found it to become so embroiled in my own concerns that I forgot about those of others.

* * *

That had been a week ago. Now, as I made myself a mug of tea and added a teaspoon of sugar (pregnancy was playing havoc with my taste buds), I took myself back outside with the welcome diversion of a book. I read several pages, then put it down when the words swam unsteadily and the dates blurred, and wished I had taken Matthew's advice and had my eyes tested. I knew why I hadn't; it made me feel old and I wasn't ready for that just yet.

From the converted stables where Dan and Jeannie lived, a door opened and then shut. Ellie was pulling on riding gloves, and was halfway across the courtyard before she looked up and saw me. She did a double take, averted her head, and strode purposefully into the tack room. She reappeared minutes later with her heavy saddle over her arms.

"Ellie, what are you doing?" I called, when she made to walk past without acknowledging me.

"What does it look like? I'm taking Lizzie out for a ride. She and Ollie are going to their winter livery by the coast tomorrow." She stalked past and into the shadows of the arch, and then out into the sun again as she made for the paddock. I stood up, shading my eyes from the sun.

"Ellie!" I called. When she didn't respond, I ran after her, panting and out of breath. "Ellie, wait!" She stopped, regarding me with disdain as I tried to control my breathing. "You shouldn't ride – not after the last time. The baby…"

She shunted the weight of the saddle onto one arm and hooked a loose strand of hair out of her eyes. "What do you care about my baby?" She turned her back and walked on, crushing the dying grass under her booted feet. I tried to catch her, but her strength and stamina made my best efforts seem paltry, and I ran to keep up.

"But Matthew said…"

She flung the saddle over the fence. "What is it to you whether I have this baby? You would rather he were dead, like his father, so don't tell me you care what happens to his child." She clicked her tongue sharply and the pretty cream mare at the other end of the paddock looked up and trotted over, followed by Matthew's big Morgan stallion, bronzed in the sun and lazily flicking late flies with his tail.

Ellie vaulted elegantly over the post and rail fence, barely encumbered by her now-evident pregnancy, which her riding jacket could no longer conceal. She heaved the saddle onto Lizzie's back. I stayed on my side of the fence, gripping the rail in my frustration.

"Ellie, it doesn't matter what I think or feel. Henry and Matthew told you specifically that you're endangering yourself and the baby by going riding. This is ridiculous…"

She ducked under the horse's belly, tightening the girth straps and adjusting the stirrup length. She swung into the saddle. Sensing tension, Lizzie darted forward a few steps, shimmied sideways, and then settled. Ellie wrapped the reins lightly around her hands and stared down at me with an imperious air worthy of her aunt.

"What do you care?" she repeated. "I'm a Lynes – didn't you know – I'm *invincible*." Bitterly, she jerked on the reins, pulling Lizzie's head around and, kicking her flanks, drove the horse into a gallop. I watched them ride the shallow grassy slope into trees branded with the colours of an inferno, and out of sight. Ollie pushed his head through the rails and nuzzled my hands, looking for attention. I stroked his soft nose.

"I can't blame her, can I, Ollie? She thinks she's lost everything."

From the paddock, I could see the quadrangle of buildings sitting solidly on their slope above the river, and my own home

– four-square and handsome – rising above the Stables and the Barn – safe, solid, protective. From here, the distant sound of the river lay encapsulated by the stony banks, languid now that the mountain snow had long-since melted, depriving it of their swift legacy. I had not forgotten it had nearly drowned Flora earlier in the year when melt-water fed the spate, nor did I forgive it. One slip and my young niece had been consumed by the water. I searched the landscape for any sign of horse and rider, but saw none. One slip. I walked slowly back to the house feeling aimless and despondent in equal measure, unable to focus on the long list of tasks I had written for myself that morning.

The buildings were resoundingly quiet. Pat and Henry were taking a vacation, the occupants of the Stables were at work, and Matthew had been called to an emergency operation in town which only he would have the stamina to perform.

I waited.

I ate my mid-morning sandwich to curb nausea, dutifully drank my milk, and waited for the sound of boots on stone, the click of the tack room door. I stood up, went into the courtyard and under the arch to search the swelling hills again, with eyes screwed against the sun.

I waited.

By two, my restlessness had become anxiety. I tried Matthew's mobile but had to leave a message. Dan's wouldn't even do that, and Jeannie's – I discovered when I heard its ringtone from somewhere in the Stables – had been left at home. I phoned Harry.

"Your sister's taken Lizzie out but she's been gone hours. I can't get hold of Matthew, and Dan's not answering his phone. I'm really worried about her; can you get home? Where are you?"

I heard him apologize to whoever he was with. "Baltimore," came the short reply, "in an interview. I'll try to contact Dad, and if I can't, I'll take the next flight back. Hey, don't worry. Ellie's tough. Really tough."

But not indestructible. That element of the Lynes gene had not been tested to its limit. Although Matthew had pushed the bounds of endurance many times in his life, and his family bore some of his attributes, how far these would go in protecting Ellie and her unborn child remained to be seen. And I didn't want this to be the occasion on which her claim to durability was proved wrong.

I went out once more. A mordant wind lifted the heads of the dying grasses in a brief salute before it failed, and in a line over the mountains, banks of cumulus mustered over the far peaks, gathering like an army to advance on a valley too encumbered with the torpid atmosphere to move in defence. Even the luminous autumn colours, spreading like fire over the thickly wooded slopes, drowned under the weight of the static air. My skin prickled. Away in the paddock, an agitated Ollie snickered.

3:20.

I came to a decision. Running upstairs, I rifled through my wardrobe to find my short coat and riding boots, unused since Matthew's birthday and, donning them, came back down again and across the courtyard to the tack room. Matthew's saddle was slung glossy and heavy over its saddle tree; next to it, the bridle and bit. I lifted the leather headgear, drew the secured straps free, and turned it over in my hands. I recognized the bit, knew – roughly – which piece went where, but I had never paid enough attention when Matthew was tacking-up Ollie to be confident enough to do it myself. I attempted to lift the heavy saddle but felt my stomach strain, and rapidly let the saddle drop back, waiting for the twinge to pass. Now what? Next to the tack hung the spare stirrup leather Matthew used instead of a bridle when he took Ollie out bareback. I removed it, weighed up my chances of staying on the horse's back with only the strap as security, considered them slim, and decided I had to try anyway.

Ollie eyed me sceptically as I approached but, whether out of habit or curiosity, jogged towards me when I imitated Matthew's click, and let me stroke his blaze as I flung the stirrup leather like a necklace around his neck. Thunder rolled across the valley and the horse flinched. I glanced over my shoulder: the clouds breached the lower hills, spilling over the further ranges in swelling knots and in its wake, premature darkness. Still warm, the air bristled. Ollie sensed it; I felt it. He skittered a little, but steadied enough to let me mount him from the fence rail, balancing precariously for a second before swinging my leg over his back. I tried to remember the elements of bareback riding Matthew had taught me in the spring – finding my seat, letting the horse dictate my movement as he made a steady pace towards the trees where I had last seen Ellie.

Once beneath them, I realized I had no indication which way to go and decided to follow the faint trail through the thick undergrowth we usually took, kneeing Ollie's flanks to keep him on track. Trees crowded thickly either side of the trail – stands of birch with silvered trunks and acid-yellow leaves, red and scarlet hornbeam, oak, and a purple-leaved small tree I didn't recognize. In this shifting illuminated world, nothing seemed real other than Ollie's snorted breath in the untouched air. Without warning, he veered off the path. Caught unawares, I clung to his mane and gripped his sides with my legs to stop me from falling.

"Ollie, no, this way!" I urged, tugging his mane and prodding with my right knee, but the horse kept stubbornly on in a direction I didn't recognize. "Ollie, whoa! You're going the wrong way!" I tried to halt him but on my third attempt gave up. He seemed to know where he was going, tracing a path invisible to my inferior senses. The ground rose steadily, strewn with boulders and broken branches, occasional vivid red blueberry scrub and low limbs that whipped against my hair as I ducked to avoid them.

The bare-branched trees became sparser as we edged around a rock outcrop and I was shocked to see how far the weather front had advanced across the sky in the short time it had been obscured from us by the trees. Now only a sliver of blue remained. Stripped of their leaves, the exposed branches linked fingers through which I could make out clearer ground ahead. Ollie needed no prompting. With a sense of urgency, he picked up his pace. I hugged his neck, keeping low on his back as his hooves struck stone beneath fallen leaves, sliding a few inches on the uneven ground, but always in the same direction until, quite suddenly, he lifted his head and let out a high whinny. Then I heard it too – a scream, but not human.

Straining his neck, Ollie pushed forward into the clearing. Ruby-robed, a crimson tide of blueberry scrub cut a swathe across the clearing from which dark boulders jutted like curses.

I saw Lizzie first – a pale cream mound that heaved and thrashed as we approached, and then lay still. There was no sign of her rider.

"Ellie!" I called, then more desperately; "E-llie!"

By a tumbled rock and almost obscured by scrub, an arm raised, waved, then disappeared as it fell back. I slid off Ollie, found my feet, steadied, and stumbled over the tangled ground, with bushes dragging at my legs.

Ellie lay at an angle against a rock, leg twisted sideways, her booted foot crammed between boulders. I didn't need a medical degree to see she was in trouble. Protruding like a stump, the shin bone in her left leg warped the smooth fabric of her riding trousers. A dark stain spread from the distortion, travelling a little way up the channels the corded fabric made. Ashen-faced, eyes darkened by pain, Ellie licked her colourless lips.

"Lizzie fell," she said, her voice coarse. "I think she's badly hurt."

I glanced towards where the mare lay, the bridle clinking as she lifted her head. Ollie stood close by, occasionally nudging her with his nose.

"Let's see to you first, Ellie; I can't help Lizzie." I moved closer to get a better look at her leg.

"Don't touch it!" she shrieked. "It's a compound fracture."

"Yes, I can see that," I said quietly. "Tell me what I can do. Are you cold?" I took off my jacket, but she threw her arm out, pushing it – and me – away.

"You can't do anything, you're not a doctor. Get help."

I looked at her skewed leg, the damp scratchy ground, and nodded. I took out my mobile and punched 911.

"Don't be so stupid," she said, her lip curling despite her pain. "You can't get a signal here – do you think I haven't already tried?" Only then did I see her own phone lying beside her. "Anyhow, you can't call emergency services."

"Why not?"

Again, that derisory lift of her lip. "And how would you explain this?" She waved a limp hand at her leg. "The bone's already setting."

I remembered Ellie and Henry re-breaking and setting Matthew's shoulder after he had smashed it on a rock in the river. "Right, I'll go and get help. I'll be back as soon as I can." Leaving the jacket within hand's reach, I picked my way across the ground towards Ollie. He saw me coming, shied and stamped. I made soothing noises, took the stirrup leather in one hand, and led him to an outcrop from which I could mount. A rumble of thunder, closer than before, had his eyes rolling in terror. Lizzie screamed and Ollie jerked his head free, and ran. I watched him go until convinced he wouldn't return, and then trudged back to Ellie. She looked at me as if I had done it on purpose.

"Sorry."

She moaned, tossed her head from side to side and flung her arm over her eyes. "Sure you are," she replied caustically, when the pain abated.

"There must be something I can do…"

"You've done enough already," she spat, the glow of resentment and spite she exuded hardly discernible from the furious reds of the vegetation around her. She shivered.

I stuffed my hands into my jeans pockets and watched Lizzie struggle to stand – a pathetic, heart-rending image of desperation – but her legs gave way and she fell back, the saddle slipping further to one side. I hated seeing her suffer. I hated not knowing what I could do to help the animal. I went over – warily so that I didn't startle her, calling her name softly – so close that I could see the whites of her eyes and the pain and fear mirrored in them. I sang to her – a lullaby from my childhood – and undid the loosened girth strap from her belly, and the buckles of her headgear. Then, still singing, I pulled the saddle free of her back, and the noisy bit from her head, and rested my hand there instead. For a clear minute she seemed calmer, but a flash of lightning sent her juddering and I backed away in case she lashed out with her legs. The dull air cooled – quite suddenly – as it stirred under a freshening wind and the first, sluggish drops of rain began to fall. Slowly at first, as if testing our resolve, then quicker, heavier, until they pelted the ground like battering rams.

I tugged the horse blanket from under the saddle and ran back to Ellie. Spreading it over the taller of the two rocks, and securing one side with stones, I sat beside her, holding the loose end to make an improvised canopy over our heads. The wind yanked the blanket and whined, rain drove against my legs and the sky darkened until only the time on my watch told me it was not yet dusk. But it soon would be.

"Ellie, do you have matches, a lighter – anything I can use to signal with?"

"And why the heck would I have a lighter on me? I don't smoke."

This was going to be a long night. I couldn't leave her, but I didn't want the hours to roll by on waves of her vitriol, either.

"Ellie, whatever you might think of me, I didn't kill Guy."

She took her arm from her face. "Yeah? You sure about that? You might have fooled the police but I know it wasn't an accident. You wanted him dead; he hinted as much."

"I did – for a moment, no, well, two, actually – but when it came to it I couldn't – wouldn't – go through with it."

"You mean you were too scared to do what you wanted."

Staring through the rain into the darkness, I took myself back in time. "No, not scared. In the moment I would have done anything to protect Matthew and the family – and you – from what Guy was about to do. If anything, I was frightened…"

"Coward," she hissed.

"… frightened I wouldn't stop. I had so much to lose if I killed him, but Guy had so much more. At that final moment, I couldn't do that to him."

"So you say."

"Yes, Ellie, I do."

"So, what do you expect me to do – forgive you?"

"I'm not asking for anything."

"That's sure big of you."

"I can't change the past – any of it – but we have a future, and that is something we can do something about. I won't live in regret, Ellie, and I would like to think we can find some common ground, for the family's sake and our children's, if not for each other."

In the brief flash of lightning, I saw Lizzie writhe. Ellie must have seen her too, because in failing to hide a sniff, she brought her sleeve to her face and wiped it roughly. While the woman's defences were down, I placed my jacket over her and scrambled to my feet, and went with cautious steps over the rough ground to the horse. She had weakened considerably, barely raising her head as I approached. I laid my hand on her head, stroking and talking as the rain beat down around us, then risked a kiss on her soaking muzzle, bestowing a blessing.

When I returned to Ellie, her voice had become small. "She's dying, isn't she?"

I squeezed beside her beneath the sodden blanket, avoiding her leg. "Yes."

"I love her; she means the world to me. I don't want her to die." She tried to hold back a sob. Failed.

"Yes," I said again.

Ellie's levels of pain seemed to lessen even if the rain didn't, and I guessed that her leg must have healed enough to make it bearable. I couldn't shift the rock, though, and she remained skewered to the ground at an angle. By the time the rain stopped and the waxing moon played cat and mouse with the breaking clouds, not an inch of us remained dry. Less resilient than Ellie, the cold drove into my bones, making them ache. I sought refuge in sleep.

I woke to my hand being pinched.

"I heard something," Ellie said, her voice loud in the stillness. Immediately awake, I strained into the darkness. It must have been sometime before midnight, judging by the moon. "There!" she said, fingers clutching my arm, as sharp points of light danced and swayed between the trees. I heard faint voices calling.

"Here!" I yelled, my voice hoarse, struggling to my feet and nearly falling over loose rocks. "We're over here!"

The lights wavered, altered direction, converged, and from the silvered night we heard our names called.

"We're both here. Ellie's hurt," I said as a figure approached with a powerful torch. The beam struck my eyes, momentarily blinding me, then Harry's worried face became visible from behind the light. "Emma, geesh, we thought we'd never find you. Matthew!" he called over his shoulder. "They're over here. They're OK."

"Ellie's not," I said quickly, as Matthew emerged, moving with ease between boulders and scrub. "Her leg's smashed and she's been lying on the wet ground for hours." He joined Harry, already kneeling by his sister, making a swift assessment as she gave her own. He stood as Dan joined us, gave a brief description of her injuries, then came back to me.

"Are you all right?"

"Just wet and cold. How did you find us?"

"We didn't. I returned home to find Ollie loose in the yard with his strap on, and Lizzie gone. It didn't take much to work out what had happened and Harry confirmed it when he rang me. Ollie led us here. I doubt we would have found you until morning, otherwise."

"Lizzie…" I said, looking over to where I could just make out Ollie nosing her, making his bridle jangle. She struggled and screamed – a sound that seared my eardrums. "She's in dreadful pain. I couldn't help her."

"I saw," he said, his face grim. "I want to get Ellie sorted out and you home safe, and then I'll look after Lizzie." It was the way he said it, reminding me of the moments before I left Matthew and the river to look after Guy. He took a step towards me, blocking the writhing horse from view. "It's the kindest way, my love. I can't let her suffer any longer. Sometimes we have to do things that go against everything we believe. Sometimes we have to make that choice."

5

Of Dragons and Giants

"It's only for a few days." Matthew lifted Lizzie's now redundant saddle onto the wooden saddle rack. "Ellie specifically asked to see Maggie and it makes sense for her to stay here in her old room. She'll spend most of the time at the Stables, so I doubt you'll see her but, if you do, remember that this is *your* home and she has to abide by *your* rules." He used his thumbnail to scrape ingrained mud and blueberry scrub from the fine stitching. His hand rested on the glossy leather. "Anyway, she'll probably be too preoccupied with Ellie to give you any grief," he added without conviction. It wasn't just Maggie's imminent arrival bothering him; something else had kept him subdued since finding us on the mountain among the broken boulders.

"There wasn't anything you could do for Lizzie, Matthew; she was in too much pain. Ollie's going to miss her, though. We're all going to miss her." He didn't answer. I put my hand on his shoulder and tried to see into his face. "Does it remind you of losing Arion at Ancaster Heath?" At the mention of his horse's name, he closed his eyes, the muscles of his back tightening under my palm.

"It was the screaming – I couldn't stand the screaming. I'd forgotten what it was like, how I'd felt when Arion was shot from under me. I just wanted it to stop. I didn't think it would affect me after all this time. Ridiculous, isn't it? You'd have thought I would have become inured to such things by now. Obviously, I haven't."

"It's what makes us human. Lose our ability to empathize and we risk becoming so much less. I think we die a little when we forget to feel."

"I had to suspend that part of me in battle or I couldn't have faced it."

I recalled the moments before Matthew stopped me from killing Guy with his sword, anger expanding inside me until it cornered compassion. "Yes, I understand that now. I don't think I'll ever view war in the same way again. Talking of which," I gave a brief shrug, "I'll do my best to be patient if I see Maggie."

"Let's hope it doesn't come to that. We could do without Maggie's vinegar at the moment."

I managed a civil greeting when Maggie arrived, but avoided her thereafter.

Instead of turning right at the top of the stairs to go to our bedroom, I turned left and found myself outside her door. I had never seen inside the room she kept for her infrequent visits and the shut door felt like a bit of a snub. I sucked my cheeks. Perhaps the room needed airing. Or dusting. This was my house, after all, and I had the right – the responsibility – to know every corner of it. I took hold of the round brass handle and twisted. It was locked. From the direction of the kitchen I heard a door bang and then voices, and I scooted along the landing and into my bedroom before Maggie began climbing the stairs.

"I wondered where you'd got to," Matthew said when he came to find me some time later. "Are you feeling nauseous again?"

I waved vaguely at the laptop on my knees. "I thought I'd get some work done, but I was distracted by the view and then must have dropped off. This chair's very comfortable." From the bedroom window, full autumn colours lay in pools of copses or ran in ribbons along the river edge. Closer still, the orchard rusted.

His lips curled into a smile. "And there was I thinking you might be hiding from Maggie."

I pulled an innocent face. "No, no, of course not."

"I've some work I want to finish at the med lab this afternoon and I thought you might like some lunch before I go. Maggie's gone to see Ellie, by the way," he said, smiling sideways at me. "She's likely to be there all afternoon."

"In that case," I rose, stretching carefully, "I do feel a bit peckish."

Lunch helped settle the nagging nausea. I padded back upstairs to fetch my laptop and the little Italian treatise Matthew had transcribed for me last year when I was recovering from flu. Heading towards the stairs, something caught my eye: a shadow down the edge of Maggie's bedroom door where there hadn't been one before. The door was slightly ajar. I reached out to close it, but instead knocked. No answer. I checked over the banister, listened for any sounds and, curiosity singing, pushed the door open far enough for me to slip inside.

I'm not sure what I expected to find, but given Maggie's regimented attitude to her work and her immaculate grooming to the point of obsession, it wasn't this. A single bed lay pushed against the far wall as if irrelevant, and in the centre of the room, piled high with folders and skinned in dust, a table and chair. Document boxes stacked to one side looked abandoned as if a job once started had been left unfinished. Spanning the mantle shelf were framed photos of her family, and above them – on the wall over the fireplace – were scattered a dozen or so pictures of... cats. Curiosity overcame guilt. Tiptoeing, I examined the photographs, a secret history, a snapshot of Maggie's world. Among the portraits of Ellen I would have expected to see were those of her father in his youth, of Dan and his family, several of Ellie and two of Maggie as a tot and another, older girl – Little Ellen? She looked about eight years old, vibrant and alive. Maggie trotted along beside her, holding a child's bucket and spade and laughing. It must have been about two years before the crash that took Little Ellen's life and shattered the family, rendering Maggie an emotional orphan. Their mother, Monica, present only as an aside – stirrup trousers moulding to long legs, carmine-lipped, silk headscarf over curls, dark glasses mirroring the sky – she looked away from the camera at something distant and unseen. Apart from Dan and his children, there were no other recent photographs, and Maggie's life appeared to have stopped nearly fifty years ago, terminated along with her sister. Next to the picture of a smiling Ellen with the two young girls was a single votive candle in a clear glass holder in the shape of a cat, and a box of matches. It made me uneasy, intruding like this on an unspent grief.

As I made to leave, my eye fell on the manila folders on the table: hospital records – dozens of them. What were they doing here? Didn't data protection apply? Anyone might walk in and see them. I lifted the corner of a folder: medications, psychological assessment, somebody's history. History. That was it. Giving in to curiosity and putting my laptop and book down beside me, I sifted through the documents on the table, then bent and removed the lid of a box and frowned at the chaos. Folders had been dumped in no particular order, corners scuffed, pages unfiled. I couldn't help it. I checked a loose page, found its folder and popped it inside. Then another. Halfway through the first box, I stopped short. Staahl. Kort. It took a moment to register and another to quell the urge to throw up at the sight of his name. Breathing carefully, I removed the thick file, and sat cross-legged on the floor. I had that feeling, like standing on the clifftop, knowing it's dangerous, yet compelled to lean forwards and peer over the edge. I counted to three and opened the folder and was immediately confronted by Staahl's grey gaze. I gagged, controlled myself, and turned the page. I shouldn't have been surprised, but to see my name in the profile notes felt like an act of aggression, making me complicit in this man's insanity. I baulked, disassociated myself from the text, and read on.

Over the course of several months, Maggie had peeled Staahl's psyche like an onion, removing layers of madness until she found the core of the man. He'd been born in the west of Holland near Leiden, just over a decade after the end of the Second World War, the fourth and last child of a former professor at the university. Staahl had been the youngest by eight years, but other than the age of his parents at his birth – his mother had been nearing forty – nothing of remark stood out about his childhood other than a bout of truancy in his early teens.

"Tell me about running away," Maggie had asked. "Did you think about how your parents would miss you? Worry about where you were?"

"Why would they do that?" Staahl had responded, according to the annotated transcripts.

"What about friends?"

"Other children bored me. I preferred my own company."

"Would you describe yourself as a lonely child?"

He had thought about this for some time before answering. "I wouldn't say so. My oldest brother found a young rabbit. It had been caught by a cat and he gave it to me."

"Did you have a good relationship with your brothers?"

He had seemed surprised by her question. "My brothers?" He shrugged. "I don't know what you mean."

"Are you in contact with them now?"

His lip had curled. "Ernst and Johann send me Christmas cards. Peta died of tuberculosis some time ago."

"And do you miss him?"

"Should I?"

Bit by bit she picked away until she revealed the foundations of his childhood. When Leiden University was shut by the Germans in the winter of 1940 after the rectorial address protesting the exclusion of Jewish professors and the ensuing student protest, his father had found work with the German regime, identifying Jewish families and arranging for their arrest and deportation.

"And how do you feel about your father's involvement with the round-up of Jews?" Maggie asked him.

"It was the best position he could get at the time and it was better than starving. My oldest brother was about two then, with another on the way. They were always hungry, they said. There were Jews everywhere; they had to be controlled."

Maggie had recorded his lack of expression, of remorse. "Tell me about your mother."

"So that you can tell me she is the source of my problems?"

"Is she? What happened to her?"

He hadn't answered, but instead went on to explain that she had been a linguist and taught English and translated documents, but that she had stopped when she married.

"Did she resent giving up her career?"

Apparently he had shrugged. "She used to read *Beowulf* to me as a child," he sidestepped. "She liked to read stories of dragons and giants, of maidens in distress." I could imagine him lavishing stress on the final syllable. Maggie had underlined the word and then circled it twice.

"When did your father first start hurting her?"

Staahl didn't seem surprised she knew, or perhaps he assumed it was normal in most families; whatever the case, she had asterisked his reply.

"I used to go to sleep listening to her crying and I knew I wasn't alone. That's very comforting when you're young, Dr Lynes, to know your parents are nearby. Were your parents there for you when you were growing up?"

Maggie ignored his attempt to draw her in, and instead asked, "Did she stay to protect you, or because she was too frightened to leave?"

"Neither. She stayed because she wanted to. She was always so grateful to him; she loved him. Were you loved as a child, Dr Lynes?"

"What happened to your mother, Kort?"

I imagined Staahl's blank eyes focused on Maggie's face as she recorded his responses in tiny script, and he described his mother withdrawing from the world bit by bit until she had slipped into the river one night and disappeared altogether. "She always liked the Koornbrug bridge; she said the water was like music." He had laughed. "Did you know the canals are full of rats, Dr Lynes? During bad winters they would come into the streets foraging for food. I would go with my father to kill rats. We would kill dozens. Dozens. They had to be controlled." Like Jews. He made no differentiation. Wind whistled in the chimney making my skin crawl. How could he have managed to go masked for so long without detection?

I read Maggie's next question. "How did you feel when your mother killed herself?"

"It was a nuisance at first, but then we had a woman cook and clean and another who took in the laundry. The cook made a better *filsoof* than my mother. Do you know what that is, doctor?

Philosopher's stew – made of whatever was left over. I liked her stews."

I skipped pages detailing a series of failed relationships and his more recent past, until I came to a page that stopped me cold.

"Why did your father not return to Leiden University after the war?"

"They wouldn't take him back because of his war record, the hypocrites."

"Why do you call them hypocrites?"

"Because they wanted to do what he did but were too afraid. It takes guts to follow your instincts. People conform out of fear. They fear judgment."

"Judgment? Whose judgment?"

A slim smile. "God's. People's. Their own."

"Does God judge you?"

"What is God but the manifestation of people's guilt? They assuage their desire to hurt others all in God's name, but it is in the nature of Man to inflict and receive suffering because only then are they truly free."

"Free of what?"

I imagined the flash of temper. "Haven't you been listening? Guilt. Haven't you understood? Guilt shackles us to the earth. Don't you feel the weight of it, doctor? Wouldn't you want to be free of it if you could?"

"And the people on whom you inflict pain..."

"Inflict pain? I didn't say I inflict pain. I share pain. I grant the beauty of suffering."

"As you did to Emma D'Eresby?"

At this point Maggie recorded he closed his eyes and exhaled slowly through his teeth ending with, "Mmm, Emma... She understands the darkness. She wants to be free – you can see it – so much uncertainty, so much guilt."

"So, you were helping her when you shared the pain?"

"Helping her?" He blinked. "Yes, of course; she wanted me to help her. Only I understand what she needs to be free."

Maggie had resumed the interviews in December around the time Matthew must have received my note telling him I knew who he was, and just before he went to England to find me. I detected a change in her questions, and they became pointed and, I would have said, leading.

"Tell me about your relationship with Dr D'Eresby."

He did – at length. In infinitesimal detail he told her about the times we met, what I'd said, how I'd looked, how I had responded – his perverted understanding so warped that I didn't recognize myself in the woman he described as being infatuated with him. At last he came to the night of the All Saints' dinner, describing the lilac note he thought I had left for him, the steps he took to ensure we could be alone, the preparations he made to act out the fantasy he believed I shared, and Matthew's untimely intervention that prevented him from setting me free.

Unable to read on, I closed the folder with shaking hands and waited until the wave of sickness passed and my heart beat normally again. On the cover was a scrawled comment: Patient 105. Preston Falls. ME. I replaced the folder where I had found it. As I straightened, I nudged a slim folder with my elbow and it slid to the floor, spilling papers. I bent over to pick it up and put it back on the table face-up: E. D'Eresby. My name shouted from the cover. I always suspected she had compiled a mental dossier on me, but I hadn't expected it to exist in reality. A ribbon of anger coiled from me. I scanned the pages in mounting fury, thumped the folder back on the table, snatched up my laptop, and stomped out of the room uttering oaths under my breath.

* * *

"Why didn't you take it?" Matthew asked when later that evening I told him what I had found, still fuming and not in the least bit repentant now about snooping in Maggie's room. "She shouldn't have done that. It's unethical and disloyal."

"Not in her eyes. She was protecting you and the family from a gold-digging harlot. Oh, and a deviant one at that. Did you know that she believed every word Staahl ever said about me?"

From the expression on his face, he did. "She might have mentioned it."

"It wouldn't surprise me if she left that door unlocked on purpose." Which didn't exactly excuse my intrusion on her privacy. I hunched my shoulders. "Well, I'm not going to let it lie."

I didn't need to. The following morning as I finished breakfast, the kitchen door swung open.

"I think this belongs to you," Maggie said without preamble or pretence at niceties, and she deposited the little Italian treatise on the table by my hand. I sucked my teeth, equally annoyed she had managed to intercept my own planned ambush and at leaving such incriminating evidence in her room. This could go one of two ways.

Opening the book, I turned to the title page. "Good morning, Maggie. Thank you. I wondered where I had left it. How was Ellie yesterday?"

"As if you care what happens to her – to any of us. You were in my room…"

"Yes, I was – evidently. You really shouldn't keep patients' files unsecured; anybody might walk in and find them." I rose and took my plate to the sink. "By the way, I'd appreciate it if you would give me the file you compiled on me. Your notes are incautious – anyone reading them would be surprised to read that I 'relentlessly pursue the undead', which is a horrid way to describe Matthew's current state, if I might say so, and your assertions that I enjoyed being mutilated by Staahl are patently untrue. I don't want your incoherent suspicions falling into the wrong hands and damaging the family. I'll burn the file. Do you want me to come upstairs with you now while you fetch it, or would you rather give it to Matthew when he gets home?" I met her eyes without flinching.

She left the kitchen without replying and moments later returned with the folder. As I took it, she held on, the manila cardboard a no-man's land between us. "Did you find the notes interesting?" she cooed.

"They were as I expected."

"And those on Kort Staahl?"

Ah, so she had intended me to find them. "Ditto." I tugged and she let go of the folder. "One thing, though," I said as she turned to leave. "What happened to the pet rabbit?"

She paused with her hand on the door and looked back at me, her eyes slits. "He ate it," she said and let the door close resolutely behind her.

Unmasking Monsters

Sometimes I had to admit to being my own worst enemy. Trees rising in guard-red plumes gave the secure facility a semblance of grandeur, the modern glass-fronted exterior more akin to a corporate headquarters than a psychiatric unit, but it couldn't disguise the sense of threat I felt in approaching it, nor the all-pervading dread on entering the lobby.

At reception, I swapped my bag for a visitor's pass, and a security guard escorted me to the visitor's room where a member of the nursing staff greeted me and rattled through a list of dos and don'ts I barely heard over the jangling in my head. I sat at a table wondering for the millionth time why I felt compelled to do this, when I heard the familiar suppressed exhalation through closed teeth that had my hair rising along my arms and me fighting the impulse to run. I glued myself to my seat as Staahl was led to the chair opposite and sat down. I didn't – couldn't – look at him. He spoke first.

"I didn't know who they meant at first when they said I had a visitor. It took me a moment to realize it must be you, despite your change of name. So, you are married now," he stated. I covered my rings with my other hand as if that would somehow protect my new life from contamination. He followed my movement with interest. "It explains why you haven't been to see me. I've been expecting you, Emma; I've missed our little chats. I'm pleased to see you." Was he? His voice maintained the monotone I recognized from our few, memorable encounters. "I'm glad you were able to find the time to visit. The term must be well underway and I expect you have new students to teach." A fly buzzed and settled on the table between us and began cleaning its legs. "I miss my students. I teach literacy to some of the other... clients. The psychiatrists believe it will help me to develop empathy." If they did, they must have been disappointed, as Staahl remained as colourless and empty as when I'd seen him as I lay on the floor of the porters' lodge on the brink of death. A year ago. A year ago to the day.

I had nothing to say. "Yes," I managed, my throat rigid with nerves.

The air moved; he must have nodded. "They tell me I have a mental illness and that is why I am here, to help me recover. But I don't feel ill." He looked around the bland room, at the burly nurse waiting nearby, and then back at me. "I have the most attentive care from the doctors. They say I am a complex case, but I sometimes think that they don't know what to do with me. I'm told the medication helps, but it doesn't feel like it. It blunts my thought processes, dampens my desire to learn. You must understand how frustrating that must be for me, Emma – to not be able to think clearly, not be able to feel. Perhaps you could speak with them...?"

"No," I said hurriedly.

"Then why are you here? Have you come to ask my forgiveness?"

Was he joking? I risked looking at him but found his grey, expressionless eyes probing and sincere. Fine lines creased his skin as if he had had life sucked out of him, leaving a husk, and he had aged.

"No," I said again. Then why had I come, I asked myself, if all I was going to do was sit here like a mutton chop? I focused on the fly. "I... I needed to see you," I said at last. "I want to know why you thought there was a connection between us; why you did what you... did."

"Ah," he said, his gaze dropping to the inch of scar showing on the inside of my left arm. Feeling exposed and vulnerable, I pulled my sleeve over my wrist. Staahl linked his fingers on the table and leaned forwards, disturbing the fly. I drew back into my chair, and he smiled with the same expression of regret I had last seen in the atrium a year ago. "I've been told that I hurt you, but how could I hurt someone already suffering as you did? You wore guilt like a mantle when you should have been able to accept the part of you that longed to be free to express your innermost needs."

"What needs?" I asked, despite myself.

For an instant, he looked puzzled. "To understand your desires you must first conquer your fear." He tapped his forehead, making a hollow tokking noise. "Instead you kept them subjugated by that," he indicated my cross, "and bred guilt. I wanted to show you the way to freedom, to release you. I wanted to consume your fear."

In being here I confronted nothing more than his madness. There had been no rhyme nor reason behind his actions other than the delusions of his mind. What had I expected? A full-frontal confession, his remorse? Or merely the chance to see the man inside the monster and, in understanding him, kill it? I took my time before answering.

"You're right in one respect. I did feel guilt, but it wasn't as a result of my faith, but because I didn't trust God enough to sort it out for me. I tried to rely on my own resources, but how could I lean on something that was broken and waiting to be mended?"

Tilting his head, he viewed me with a relentless eye, before a breathless sigh slipped out. "And are you mended now?"

"Yes," I said simply. "I am now."

"Then you're here to forgive me?" he asked, a touch incredulous.

"I wasn't," I admitted, "because I didn't know how. I let you become a monster because you frightened and hurt me, but you're not, are you? You're unwell, that's all. I saw it at the trial, but I didn't fully understand."

Curiosity broke the featureless plane of his face. "On that last day, before they took me away, there was a light – in my head. It was too bright, like a searchlight, and I couldn't escape it."

I remembered the chaos of emotions in colours as I slipped from life, demanding my attention, begging for recognition, and then a presence – colourless and devoid of light. I had recognized Staahl before he went berserk and had to be taken, screaming, from the courtroom.

"That was you," he stated. "I thought I was mad." He tracked the progress of the fly as it sought invisible sustenance from the yellow-grained wood. "So you came here today – on this special day, a day we will always share – to understand me better. And do you understand me now?" The fly launched, circled, and landed close to Staahl's manacled hands lying exposed on the table.

Did I? "I don't think I'll ever understand what drove you to do the things you did, but I realize now that you didn't hurt me out of malice. I never shared your fascination with pain and darkness. I studied torture because I wanted to comprehend the motives of the men behind such acts and in doing so find the light and their humanity. But sometimes the light isn't there to be found, is it?"

Staahl didn't answer immediately, seemingly intent on the progress of the insect towards his outstretched fingers. "A fly doesn't think; it follows its instincts free of guilt and shame. Man is obsessed with rules that restrict his true nature." He watched the fly and with a sudden sweep of his hand brought the palm, *smack*, down on top of it, making me jump back. The nurse darted forward, but stepped back again as Staahl examined the oozing corpse with intense interest. With a flick of his tongue, he consumed it, savouring before swallowing. I stared in fascinated horror and he gave a slow, thin smile. "That will give my psychiatrists something to talk about at their next case meeting." He closed his eyes, the balls darting back and forth beneath the crêped lids. "I've had a lot of time to think since being in here. It's so much quieter than the state prison they put me in at first. I thought I would go mad. I could hear the other men ranting like lunatics. It is disturbing being surrounded by the insane, but Dr Lynes helped me come to terms with who I am, and I found it comforting to know that she understood what you mean to me. You mean a lot to her, Emma, do you know that? She mentioned you a great deal, although I couldn't understand why she felt it necessary to attack you during the trial. I think she was on the verge of a breakdown,. Don't you?"

"I think I'd better go." The chair scraped across the hygienic floor as I made ready to stand. Staahl opened his eyes.

"Thank you for coming to see me. I knew you would."

"When you were a boy, why did you eat your pet rabbit?" I asked on impulse.

"My *konijn*?" His expression became almost dreamy, then he fixed me with his blank stare. "It hated captivity; I set it free."

I sat in the car, hands on the steering wheel and engine running, staring at nothing in particular, until a security guard rapped on the window.

"Can I help you, ma'am?"

The window rolled down and I released the breath I seemed to have been holding forever. "No, thank you, I'm really quite all right. I'll be off in a minute. I'm not in the way, am I?"

"No, ma'am. Just as long as you're OK."

"I am, thank you." And as I said it, I realized how true it was with a certainty I hadn't felt for so long I'd forgotten what it felt like. I smiled. "Thanks, I am."

7

Blood Sinister

Henry popped his head around the back door and knocked. "Apologies for disturbing you at work, Emma, but have you seen Ellie recently? She's not answering her cell."

My finger hovered over *send*. "She dropped by to leave something for Matthew and then I saw her heading out after lunch, Henry. She must have left, oh..." I checked the time in the corner of the screen, squinting until it came into view, "... about an hour ago."

"Did she say where she was going?"

"No, she didn't. Is everything OK?"

He came into the kitchen, knocking clods of late winter snow from his boots, and sat down next to me at the table, looking tired. "She was supposed to see me for her health check and have her bloods done. That's the third time she's missed a date."

"And she's not forgetful."

He shook his head. "No, she isn't. I don't know why she's avoiding the tests. She knows how important it is to monitor her health in these last few weeks of pregnancy. Did she say anything to you?"

"She was a bit twitchy, but I put that down to her feeling like an overripe watermelon. She wanted to get some baby things in town, but I thought she had arranged to go with Jeannie. Can't the tests be done when she gets home?" I hauled myself, with my own growing bump, to my feet and went to find my new glasses left next to the kettle.

"It's not just a question of the tests, Emma; she's taking risks with her health that might impact on us all."

Cradling my stomach, I leaned against the counter, chewing the end of my specs. "How so?"

"If she goes into premature labour, or needs greater facilities than we have here, she'll have to be hospitalized. They'll do all the procedural checks as routine, and it'll only take someone with sharp eyes and half a brain cell in the phlebotomy department to spot the anomalies in her blood."

"I didn't realize it was so obvious."

"Obvious – no, but it would flag up questions we could well do without. They wouldn't know what they were looking at and would be obliged to run further screening. It's a risk we can't afford to take. Ellie's the first Lynes girl to give birth, and we don't exactly know what to expect."

"Hence all the health checks. So what will you do if there is an emergency?"

Henry slapped his hands on the tops of his thighs and stood up. "That's just one bridge we'll have to cross if we come to it. Until then, I'd better find my errant granddaughter and give her a transfusion of common sense."

I laughed. "Perhaps a transfusion of Matthew's blood wouldn't go amiss. There's plenty of common sense in him."

"If only we could. Unfortunately, that wouldn't be a good idea."

"Why not?" I asked, still smiling at the idea.

He stopped by the back door, one hand on the latch. "I thought you knew," he said, suddenly serious. "His blood's incompatible with ours – with everyone's. One drop is enough to kill."

* * *

"Rex is a bit frisky," I mused later that evening, balancing my tea on my bulge and watching the minute unpredictable ripples as the baby moved.

"Rex?" Matthew came back into our bedroom, towelling his hair into random sheaves.

"T-Rex – you know, like the one in *Jurassic Park*." The baby conveniently kicked, and the surface of the tea wobbled. Removing the cup, Matthew sat on the bed next to me and placed his hand on my stomach, smiling as his offspring wriggled beneath his palm. Light played through his hair as he replaced his hand with his lips, giving him a halo of gold. Everything about him seemed so benign and nothing hinted at a darker secret. "Matthew, why is your blood so dangerous?" He looked up, eyes cobalt in the light of the bedside lamp. "Henry said it would kill anyone who had a transfusion of it."

"Did he? Yes, he's right in that respect. Do you remember me telling you about the experiments I did a long time ago when I tried to save people's lives by giving them my blood?"

"Yes, you said they died."

"I didn't know then about the negative immune response – no one did. If you try giving someone incompatible blood, you run the risk of them going into shock, sometimes developing septicaemia, and worse. Since then we've discovered how diverse combinations of blood types can be – millions of variations – although we tend to classify them into main groups for practical reasons..."

"Such as giving transfusions?"

"Among other things. Most people fall into these groups, but a number have such rare blood types that they have to be on a register of rare blood groups in case of an emergency."

"And you're one of those people?"

"Sort of."

"Sort of" didn't rate as an explanation, but he picked up the damp towel and took it back to the bathroom without expanding his answer. I waited until he returned.

"Well?"

"Well, I have a rare blood type all right. Unique, in fact."

"As a result of what happened to you?"

"I don't know, perhaps – probably – but all the Lynes blood throws a marker that appears specific to the family; it's just that mine alone seems wholly incompatible with the rest of humanity. It's a pity; I once hoped to use it to do some good." There, that slide into self-doubt that still haunted him, that aching vulnerability.

"You do what you can, Matthew, and it's more than many. You have nothing to atone for in being who you are; it was beyond your control."

"I suppose it was." He checked the shutters and closed the curtains, and climbed into bed, tucking the duvet around me. "Sorry. This baby has made me rather more introspective than usual. It's made me realize how reserved I had to be around Ellen when she was carrying Henry, and how I don't need to be with you. Back then, I had no idea whether I could father a healthy child, but I couldn't share my fears with her; it wouldn't have been fair."

"But Henry is fine – better than that – he's inherited some of your benefits, and this baby will as well, won't he?"

"Yes, of course he – or she – will. You'll both be fine."

It was the way he said it: you'll both be fine. I pursed my lips. "Me? I didn't think I wouldn't. Why shouldn't I be all right?"

In reaching for his book, he knocked my little triptych, now returned to its rightful place by the bed. He righted it with the merest sideways glance at me. "No reason at all. That's what I said: you'll be fine."

Precious Cargo

Snow melted in clumps, leaving brown-patched earth and a tangle of lank grasses exposed to the lengthening days. I loved the snow – I loved the predictable winter here in Maine and the frost-nipped mornings and biting, clean air. I drew in lungfuls until they burned – but the ice could be lethal underfoot, especially when carrying precious cargo, as I did.

If I was honest with myself and peeled away the layers of cultural expectation placed on me, I had to admit to having my doubts about motherhood. It wasn't that I was adverse to the idea, but Matthew's unbounded enthusiasm left my own wanting, and my lack of experience with young children was in marked contrast to the ease with which he conversed with my nephews and niece.

"It'll be different when it's your own child," he assured me. "Don't judge yourself so harshly. You'll get a chance for some practice when Ellie's baby arrives."

"I doubt she'll let me near it. She tolerates me, but that's about it. She knows I find it difficult because it's Guy's child."

"But you're on speaking terms now and that's a start."

"And what if I get something wrong? I might end up hurting it – him," I corrected myself.

He gave me one of those ever-patient looks, accompanied

by a sigh. "Babies are tougher than they look, and are far more forgiving than you're ever likely to be on yourself."

I had smoothed my hands over the plane of my stomach, trying to imagine the child growing inside me and detecting any sign of attachment I thought I should have. Matthew must have guessed my thoughts because his hands joined mine. "You'll grow together over the next few months, just wait and see. Talk to him, tell him about your day and your work. Get to know him."

And over the winter as the nausea grew and faded and my body swelled, my detachment waned, and now, carefully negotiating the icy patches stubbornly clinging to the shadows by the garage, I protected Rex – as we now referred to him – from every slip or bump. He was no longer a stranger; he was part of me – of us. We were a family.

My mobile rang in the depths of my bag and I apologized to the shop assistant and dived in to find it. The taut voice on the other end sounded unnaturally thin and scared. "Emma, where are you?"

"Maggie, is that you? I'm in the baby shop in town. What's the matter?"

"Is Matthew with you?"

"No, he's…" I was interrupted by her stifled moan smothered by a booming tannoy message and a metallic clatter echoing down the phone. "Maggie, what is it? Where are you calling from?"

"Augusta," she rushed. "In the central hospital with Ellie. She collapsed and went into labour. She managed to call me, but…" She was interrupted by a man's voice and I heard her answer in the affirmative. She became agitated, urgent. "I must talk to my grandfa… Matthew. It's important. I can't reach him on his cell."

"It'll be switched off; he's in surgery this afternoon. Is she all right?"

"They did an emergency delivery yesterday morning. She only came round a few hours ago and was able to give them her name and my number. It took me several hours to get here. Matthew needs to know. He said he wanted to know if anything happened. He said…" her voice began to rise unnaturally and I broke through her escalating panic, doing a rough calculation.

"Have they taken blood samples from the baby yet?"

"Does it matter? What does it matter?"

I raised my eyebrows in apology and, turning away from the assistant, took myself to an alcove in the shop away from inquisitive ears. I spoke more calmly than I felt. "Maggie, it is imperative that they don't get hold of blood samples from Ellie or the baby. Matthew said they do routine screening after twenty-four hours. Do you understand what that means?"

I heard an intake of breath, imagined her swallowing her fear. "I… don't know if I can stop them."

"See if you can find out. If they haven't, delay them any way you can." I thought quickly. "Do what you can, Maggie. Perhaps Ellie can refuse to give permission – she knows what's at stake. I'll go to the Memorial myself and find Matthew."

It wasn't far, but the traffic dragged precious minutes into an eternity. By the time I pulled up in front of the hospital, my mounting anxiety had drained colour from the face staring back at me from the rear-view mirror.

"Ma'am, you can't stop there!" a uniformed man in blue baggy trousers informed me as I dragged my cumbersome form from the car.

"It's an emergency," I said, clutching my stomach and feeling that it wasn't so far from the truth as my muscles screamed at my unaccustomed haste. I made it through the doors before he could stop me and leant against the reception counter, puffing and feeling like a bloated sunfish. "Dr Lynes... please... get a message to him. It's urgent."

I received a doubtful frown. "Ma'am, Dr Lynes isn't in obstetrics..."

"No, but he is my husband. Please see if he's out of surgery; it really is very important."

He appeared minutes later, still pulling on his jacket, his hair all over the place and worry embedded in his eyes.

"It's not me," I said, before he could ask. "It's Ellie. She's all right, but she went into labour and she's in hospital in Augusta. The baby's fine and Maggie's going to try to hold up any tests, but she doesn't have any authority to stop them, does she?"

"No, she doesn't and nor do I. I'm only her uncle, but I do have some contacts there. Ellie can refuse them..."

"She's only just regained consciousness, Matthew. Won't they have run the tests automatically?"

"I would," he admitted. "I'd better get up there and see what I can do to pull those bloods. Sweetheart, can you contact Dan and let him know?"

"Done that." I tugged his sweater down at the back and neatened his collar. "They won't let you in looking like a scruff-bag."

Flattening his hair back into shape with his hand, he gave me a half-smile that faded almost as soon as it appeared. "I'd like to see them try to stop me. I'll call you at home when I have any news."

"OK, but I'll be back in a couple of hours; I want to get the buggy sorted out first."

"I'd be happier if you went home now."

I glanced up at the changed note in his voice. "Matthew, I want to get the buggy ordered." And feeling an obstinate niggle and because I jolly well felt like it, said, "And then I might pop to college and see if Aydin's finished his assignment."

"He can email you…"

"Or I might see if Elena wants to go out for a pizza."

Matthew took in the stubborn set of my jaw and sucked his teeth. "All right," he relented. "Do whatever you must, but when you get home, make sure you lock down all the shutters and doors."

I stuffed my hands in my pockets feeling this was all getting out of proportion. "Come off it. No one's likely to come after me. Anyway, it'll take ages for the blood analysis to come back – if they pick up anything unusual in it at all, that is. After all, they won't be looking for *freaks*, as Joel so subtly put it once, will they?"

"They won't fail to see the anomalies. They won't know what they are at first, but when they do they will want further tests done. We don't give them anything – *anything*, Emma – that makes us out of the ordinary. Please, do whatever it is you feel you have to, but then get home, lock yourself in, and keep safe." All his customary humour had evaporated, leaving tension thrumming his vocal cords. He didn't press his point; he didn't need to. He simply said, "I must go," planted a kiss on my forehead, and left, leaving me feeling adrift and ever so slightly thwarted.

The security guard was surprised to see me getting back into my car and squeezing behind the wheel. "False alarm," I mumbled, and then to ameliorate my previous abrupt behaviour, "Thanks for letting me park here."

Back in the baby shop and with a distinct lack of enthusiasm, I inspected and bought the buggy – a robust, rather glamorous three-wheeled stroller far removed from the cumbersome thing I remembered from my own childhood – and then considered going to college. I felt cross inside, manoeuvred, resistant to what amounted to an order to return home. It rankled – a feeling I hadn't had since Dad last gave me a command, and I hadn't expected to experience it with my own husband. Obedience had never been one of my virtues; I would have made a lousy wife in the seventeenth century. Accepting the receipt and pocketing my bank card, I tutted to myself, and the assistant's mouth turned down. I left rapidly, having profusely apologized, and, glowing with embarrassment, found my way back to the car.

My temper hadn't improved by the time I approached the range of buildings making up my home. The only light evident in the gloaming came from the Barn. As I passed along the drive, it was abruptly cut off as Pat closed the last shutters against the night. She must have been given the same message. I mooched into the kitchen through the back door and chucked my coat over a chair. Despite the temptation to throw all the doors and windows open to the world and yell, "Come and get me!" I shut each one systematically, locking the bars into place. Like a prison.

I had never felt that way before.

I had spent so many months wanting to be here with Matthew that even if acutely aware of the dangers the family faced, I never stopped to imagine what it might be like in reality. What were the chances that anything would come of Ellie's reckless disregard for her own safety? This was so far-fetched, wasn't it? Wasn't it? Fear fluttered and settled leaden in my gut against which Rex kicked, making my stomach heave.

Pat placed the mug of tea next to the plate of plain toast and I smiled in gratitude. "Thanks. I never know which is worse: to occasionally throw up or constantly want to pee."

She sat opposite me at the table with a watchful, motherly expression I supposed I would one day learn to adopt. "It gets worse towards the end, believe me. Every fifteen minutes with Dan – but he was a big baby and kept kicking my bladder. You think it'll go on forever and then one day your life changes. It doesn't feel real until you hold your baby, and then you don't want to do anything else."

"That's just about what Matthew says." I nursed my mug, rotating it between my hands and watching the concentric ripples shudder, disturbing the tranquil surface.

"What's the matter, sweetie? You seem a bit out of sorts. Ellie and the baby will be fine, you wait and see. Dan and Jeannie are bringing them home just as soon as they can, and Matthew will stay only as long as he has to; he'll want to get back to you the moment he's sorted this little problem out."

"So you think this battening down the hatches is an overreaction?"

She eyed me with a keen look. "No, I didn't say that. Has something rattled your cage?"

I gave a brusque laugh. "Cage just about sums it up. Don't you ever feel trapped by what might happen – this having to be ever-watchful and on your guard?"

"I'm used to it, I guess. Do you?"

"I didn't, or at least not in a way that made me feel crowded in, but Matthew sort of… ordered me home." I broke off because that last bit made me sound critical of him and disloyal, and I intended neither. "I think it made me feel hedged in, and I'm used to doing what I want, when I want."

She clapped her hands and laughed. "Ah, well, that comes with the territory. Once you're married you have to give a little and take a little until you know each other well enough not to need say anything. Sometimes you have to bend like prairie grass. The wind'll blow but your roots'll hold you firm and you'll be the stronger for it. I expect Matthew wanted you home safe."

"I expect he did," I said drily.

"And Ellie should have known better. I don't know what's gotten into her lately."

"Perhaps she's testing her boundaries," I mused, recalling her throwaway remark about being an invincible Lynes and Matthew's own reflections on his reckless youth. "Anyway," I said, draining my mug, "pregnancy certainly makes you restless. It's played havoc with my thought processes. Maybe Ellie's finding the same." Collecting Pat's mug, I went to the sink and ran the tap. She joined me with a clean tea towel.

"If she goes about shaking trees when she doesn't need to, she might stir up a nest of red wasps and Heaven knows what might come of it. We don't want any sort of trouble, do we? We've all had enough of that recently."

I sobered at the memory. "No, we certainly don't. This all seems so ordinary that sometimes I forget how different Matthew and his family are. And then I remember what's at stake." I gave an involuntary shudder and Pat took the mug from me as it chinked against the tap.

"That's why we take precautions, sweetie. Prepare for the worst and hope for the best," she quoted with a smile. "Lock your doors and windows and say your prayers."

"That shall be to you better than light and safer than a known way," I murmured half to myself, then rallied and regained my humour. "Let's just hope that Matthew's intercepted those tests."

"And drummed some sense into that granddaughter of mine."

"Once he's stopped being the proud great-great grandfather," I pointed out, to which she laughed.

As it was, Matthew didn't return until the early hours. He phoned some time before, principally, I guessed, to check I was safe, but was cagey on the phone when I asked if he had been successful. "Can you be overheard?" I asked, and he had said, "I'll tell you about it when I get home," and ended the call.

I lay drowsing until I heard the distant sound of his car

and the discreet click of the front door as it shut, and then his quiet movements around the house as he systematically checked the doors and shutters of each room. Finally, he slid into our bedroom, went through the same routine, and only then noticed me watching him in the dim light from under the door.

"I'm sorry, did I wake you?"

"I couldn't sleep." I wriggled upright against my pillows and switched on the bedside lamp. "Well?"

He dragged his sweater over his head. "There shouldn't be a problem. If the CDS... sorry, Child Development Services – contact her about retesting, Ellie will state her religious objections to more samples being taken. That's her only plausible opt-out."

"Retesting? So they had taken samples?"

"They had. Unfortunately there was a mix-up in the system and the baby seems to have developed the blood profile of an octogenarian smoker with severe gout." He smiled and a little of the tension left him. "At least it will keep the lab busy long enough for Ellie and Charlie to leave in the morning."

"Charles? Is that his name?" I lay back against the pillows. Charlie – Guy's son. *Guy's* son.

Matthew stood at the end of the bed, his shirt unbuttoned. "He's a sturdy little chap; he looks just like Dan did at that age."

"Not like Guy?"

Removing his shirt, he turned away. "No, not like Guy."

I woke to the distant whine of a drill and, on venturing downstairs in my PJs and dressing gown, found Matthew on his knees by the front door, shirt sleeves rolled to the elbow, revealing his muscled forearms.

"What on earth are you doing?"

He removed the screwdriver from between clenched teeth. "A bit of DIY." He lifted a planed panel of wood he had leant against the front door and held it against the sidelight, and proceeded to drive screws into one of the heavyweight hinges.

"*More* shutters, Matthew?"

He tested the panel, adjusted the hinge, and looked up. "These will help insulate the house. You shouldn't have to suffer a Maine winter just because I don't feel the cold." And he swung the shutter into place, plunging the hall into gloom.

Who was he kidding? I pulled my dressing gown around me, feeling a chill that came not from the thin frame of the door, but from within me. "I thought you said the blood tests shouldn't be a problem?"

He put the screwdriver on the floor next to him before answering. "It's time I reassessed our security. These sidelights and the fanlight above the door have always bothered me – there's little security in them. These should do the trick." He swung an iron bar I hadn't noticed until now, its newly sawn ends catching the light. It clunked into place, securing the entire width of the door and its flanking sidelights. "I'll paint it and do something with the ends so it won't look so utilitarian. There," he said, standing back. "What do you think?"

I didn't answer him; I couldn't, and by the time he looked around all he could have seen was my retreating back as I climbed the stairs to our room.

9

Meadow Rose

I grew used to the subtle changes in my surroundings, of course I did, just as I adjusted to the sudden shift in the family locus when Ellie returned, bringing with her the scrap of life Guy had bequeathed in the form of his son.

"Emma, they've been back almost a week."

"I know, I know. I didn't want to overwhelm her with visitors." How feeble an excuse was that? Matthew believed it no more than I did.

"Ellie needs your support. She doesn't have a husband to…"

"I know!" I snapped, regretting the sudden hurt in his eyes. "Don't you think I don't know that?" I said, more evenly. "Do you think I don't know the reason there is no one her child can call 'Dad'? I'm aware of it every minute of every day." I felt him near me, his arms go around me, his closeness reminding me just how alone Ellie must feel.

"Go and see her – not just for her sake, but for yours. Don't let Guy drive a wedge between you and this child. Charlie deserves to be loved and accepted in his own right."

I hovered, feet away from the minimalist crib resembling a huge scooped-out egg in which the baby lay, asleep.

"Go ahead, pick him up."

"I don't want to disturb him."

Ellie sprang to her feet, lithe as a hind, all hint of a traumatic birth healed and forgotten. "He'll sleep right on through." She picked him up. "Isn't he adorable? He's so good and he hardly cries at all." The baby's face screwed into multiple folds as he neared waking. "Here," Ellie thrust him into my arms. Holding him gingerly, I looked at him. How could she translate this little thing into love? What could she see that I didn't?

"He's... nice," I ventured, wondering if that was the right thing to say.

"Isn't he?" she beamed. "And he just loves the bear you gave him. What is it called again?"

"Paddington."

"Oh, sure. Paddington. He'll love the cute case and boots when he's older. And he'll want to wear that hat." She laughed and he stirred. I gave him back to her before he woke, and she crooned a few bars of a tune. I waited. I waited for her to turn mournful eyes on me and remind me of what I had done to her – to her son – to Guy. But she didn't; instead, she settled back in the chair her parents had bought for her to nurse him in. I shuffled.

"Come and sit down; I bet your back's hurting, isn't it?" she observed. "That'll be the oestrogen and relaxin flooding your joints. It helps make them more flexible, but it can be a pain." She laughed at her own joke, adoring her son.

"Yes, Matthew said it might happen." I remained standing. Behind me, the back door opened, letting in cool night air and Jeannie, carrying a bag of nappies. I greeted her frown with a cautious smile. "I'd better be going," I said, moving out of the way.

"Sure, OK. Come and see Charlie again soon, won't you? He's growing so fast he's already on the next size of diapers."

I left her exchanging baby news with her mother, and slid open the secret door between the Stables and my own home, re-entering a world I knew and understood. Leaning against the kitchen table, I released the tension I had been holding for the past half-hour.

"How did it go?" Matthew asked as he entered the kitchen balancing a load of firewood on one arm and making me start.

"Ellie seems to have forgotten what happened." I shook my head in disbelief. "It's as if Guy never existed."

"She has a reason to look forward to the future. She's moved on."

"And you're saying I should do the same?"

"I'm saying that she's let go of the past – all of it – and it is something both you and I could learn from." ·

I glanced at the newly reinforced kitchen door and discreet sensors placed in the corners of the room, blinking watchfully. "Do you think we can ever fully escape our pasts, Matthew?"

"I don't know, my love, but it will do no harm to try."

Early summer heat blossomed, bringing out mayflies that danced in striated beams of the strengthening sun outside the window of my tutor room. I missed it already, my den of knowledge, the intrepid exploration into the past. I would miss my students and their eager quest for the unknown, their unquenchable thirst. Packing my bag for the final time this semester, I straightened as the nagging ache set in my lower back.

"You will be glad when this little fellow is born, no?" Siggie stood in the open doorway surveying the stacks of books waiting to be packed in the gaping boxes on the floor by my mahogany bookcase. She bent down and picked up Horrox's *The Black Death* with its cheerful crowned corpse. "I see you are taking some light reading for your… confinement, I think you historians say. How many weeks is it now?"

"Two, and I feel ready to pop. Honestly, Siggie, how do women go through this time after time? He keeps dancing around. I bet he'll be into aerobics or something. You're really having a good time today, aren't you?" I addressed my vast bump, patting it with a degree of resignation. "I was hoping to get a paper written, but all this wriggling is a bit of a distraction." Rex gave an almighty roll that felt like grinding and I bent over, breathing through the discomfort.

"You get some rest," Siggie advised. "You'll need it when this baby puts in an appearance."

"Thankfully, Matthew's had more practice than I have. We'll job share."

"Has he? I didn't think he had any children with his first wife."

I mentally thumped myself and blamed my soggy brain for my loose tongue. "He helped out a lot when Dan's three were born. He's been more involved than I ever was with my nephews and niece."

"Ah, I see."

I fervently hoped she didn't. Slips like that were nothing in themselves but could add up over time, filling in bits of the enigma that made up Matthew's life. Finishing loading my laptop, I gave a vague smile. "We'll sort it out, and I'll be back to work soon, never fear."

"My dear, you have the entire summer to enjoy your baby, so enjoy him."

I totted up the weeks. "Golly, so I have. Mmm, that's quite a long time."

She smiled, embracing me. "History will wait for you. Go home, rest and be thankful for your child. I expect Matthew is looking forward to becoming a father, no?"

"Gosh, yes. He's buying a crib at auction today. It's very pretty

– early seventeenth century, English, with this lovely canopy carved with pomegranates…" I shut up at that point, aware of her looking at me curiously.

"You know, my dear, I sometimes think that you two belong to another era. You have been born out of time." Shaking her head and smiling, she tucked her arm through mine and, in this companionable way, walked me from my room.

"Ah, ah there you are!" Colin Eckhart scuttled along the corridor towards us, the hem of one trouser leg undone and catching dust as he went.

"Colin, you were looking for me?" Siggie greeted him. "How can I help you today?"

"I do-don't want to see you, Dean," he stuttered, looking beyond her shoulder to the window at the far end of the corridor. "I wish to see Professor D'Eresby."

"Emma is just about to go home to begin maternity leave; perhaps you could email her…?"

"No, not at all, Dean. I have something for Professor D'Eresby." His eyes swivelled in my vague direction, and he held out a book-shaped parcel wrapped in paper covered in heraldic shields. "It's a book for your lying-in: *Soussan's Cooking and Conformity in Medieval Europe: The Birth of the Modern Housewife.* Mrs Eckhart thought it would a… amuse you."

I remembered to close my mouth. "How… I mean, thank you so much, but how did she know…?"

He blinked rapidly behind his heavy spectacles. "I tell Mrs Eckhart everything about you," and suddenly beamed.

The orchard beckoned, soft sifting petals winnowed from the branches by the light breeze. Warm earth and long spring grass beguiled, and in the sheltered nook where the land dipped towards the southern sun, wild roses sprang, revealing the first shy blooms. Breathing in this melody of scents, I carefully lowered myself to the ground and pressed my sore back gratefully against a trunk, and placed the unwrapped book beside me. In the last year since Matthew had planted the orchard for my wedding present, the sylph stems had broadened, arching above me, the new green leaves sharp points in the blue, blue sky. Out here deadlines and expectations were as insubstantial as the gossamer webs floating on the wind. Out here there were no locks and bars, and I was five again and playing in the orchard of my youth – a faraway memory of sunshine and happiness I might very well have dreamed. Here, I felt free. Closing my eyes, I hummed a few bars from Handel's *Messiah*, stroking my bump in time to the melody and imagining Rex quietening in response.

"I thought you might be out here."

I opened one eye as Ellie dropped gracefully beside me. She swapped Charlie to her other arm and swept hair from her eyes with her free hand. "What's this?" She picked up the book and turned it over, reading the blurb. "A history book, huh?" She put it back in its bed of grass without meeting my eyes. "Guy would have liked to read it."

"It was not really his cup of tea."

"Wasn't it? I suppose you knew him better than I did." When I didn't say anything because a sudden twinge distracted me, she went on, "Charlie wanted to see Ollie. He smiled when he saw him; he thinks he's a teddy bear." She looked thoughtful for a moment. "Ollie misses Lizzie, you know."

"Will you get another horse, Ellie?"

"I don't know. So much has changed in the last year, hasn't it?"

It had. It was my turn to look away. As if she read my thoughts, she said, "I met Guy a year ago – a year ago yesterday.

I remember it so clearly. He came into the med centre saying he'd hurt his back." At the break in her voice, I risked a glance at her. She had pressed her lips together as she looked at her now-sleeping son. "I think about Guy every day and I wonder what he would say about Charlie. I wonder what we would be doing now – whether it would have worked out." She looked away and inspected the distant mountains.

"I'm sorry, Ellie. I'm so, so sorry."

She brought the baby to her lips and kissed him softly. "Yeah, I know you are. I can't say it's been easy, but it can't have been for you, either. I've never said this before, but I think I knew Guy wasn't playing me straight – although I didn't want to admit it at the time. I did love him…"

"I know you did."

"But not everything he said added up, you know?" She met my eyes. "You were right about him, Emma."

Rex tumbled inside me, catching me unaware, and I yelped and squirmed.

"You OK?" Ellie asked.

I laughed weakly, feeling nauseous and bruised. "Whew! That was quite a beating. I have another couple of weeks to go of this and I'm not sure I can stand it." I hugged my bulge. "You, young man, are making your presence known, but you don't need boxing gloves to do it." I exhaled slowly. "Sorry you were so rudely interrupted, Ellie. You were saying?"

"Sure, that's OK. I was only going to say that I should have known from the beginning Guy wasn't to be trusted."

"Why?"

"When he came to the med centre that day complaining of a bad back, I couldn't find anything wrong."

"Why didn't you tell him?"

"I guess I should have, but I liked him and he made it clear enough he liked me. I told him to come back for further tests although he didn't need them." Her skin flushed from her neck to her feline cheeks. "You probably think I'm stupid, right, but I chose to ignore those warning signs, to ignore you."

"I don't think anything of the sort. Guy was clever and persuasive. He did to you what he did to me. All we can do now is not allow him to be a shadow in our lives."

"Is that how you've felt about him all these years?"

"Yes," I said quietly. "I didn't know how to let go of the hurt."

"And now?"

"And now I think I have – finally, and with help."

"Now you have Matthew," she stated.

"He has definitely helped," I agreed, "but I needed to be healed from within."

Her brow creased for a few seconds, then cleared. "Oh, you mean by God. Yeah, sure, I can see it must help if you believe in something; it gives you a sort of focus, doesn't it?"

"Um, well, I see him as more of an active participant in my life, Ellie, but it took me a long time to let him in. I can be a bit dense like that – and obstinate." I wriggled as a spasm shot across my lower stomach. And then another. "OK, OK, young man, settle down. Ouch! Oh!" I felt colour drain from my face.

"What is it?"

"I think my waters broke." I looked down at the soggy fabric of my dress, frowning. "He can't be, surely? He's two weeks early."

Ellie took one look and became suddenly businesslike. "Have you been having regular pains?"

"Yes, but I thought they were Branston Picks, or whatever they're called. Ow…" I screwed my face as another one hit. "And they weren't this bad."

"Braxton Hicks," she corrected. "Can you walk? We need to get you back to the house."

She held on to my arm and I tried to get to my feet, but another spasm, sharper, longer, more intense, floored me. I sank back to the ground as pain like barbed wire seared across my lumbar region. "I don't think I can," I squeezed through clenched teeth.

"Can you count the contractions?"

I nodded, unable to speak, then shook my head as another wave spread.

"Was that another one?"

"Yeeesss."

"Do you have your cell on you?"

"Nooooo."

She muttered something that became irrelevant as pain swarmed again. She darted a look towards the house, standing serene in an emerald sea. "Don't leave me!" I begged. "I don't know what to do."

Coming to a decision, Ellie laid Charlie on my discarded jacket and, rolling up her sleeves, knelt in front of me. "I'm going to examine you."

"What?"

"Emma," she said firmly, "I'm a doctor. I need to see if you're dilated at all."

She lifted my skirt and at that point I didn't care what she saw or did because it took all my concentration to ride the next tsunami of pain. I heard her sharp intake of breath and a subdued exclamation. "OK," she said briskly, "you're already about eight centimeters dilated…"

"I can't be!" I squeaked.

"… and you're gonna want to push real soon."

I did.

"Matthew..." I puffed. "I want Matthew..."

"Sure you do, but you've got me instead. Ready to push?"

I lost track of time between the increasingly intense peaks and the brief respite of the troughs, one following the other relentlessly, until I thought there would be no end to this cruel transition to life. I might have sobbed in despair and exhaustion had I not needed every ounce of energy to focus on pushing and heaving and breathing. The heels of my hands became embedded in the soft earth, crushed grass staining my palms already tattooed with stems and grit. An ant explored a drop of sweat trapped between my thumb and forefinger, a tiny fly swung in the cobweb of hair loosened about my face, and on the sunny face of the gentle slope, the first wild rose bloomed. All became irrelevant as Ellie urged and cajoled and encouraged, but nothing she could say or do compared with the urgency of my body to eject my baby and be free of this pain. Ramming my back against the tree so it shuddered, I strained. Too quick, too fast; I'm not ready for this.

"He's crowning!" she exclaimed at one point. "Don't push, pant, that's it – you're good at this. OK, push – keep it going, it's not long now."

"What... choice... do I... have?" I groaned, feeling as if I was being split, ingesting the pain, beyond fear, unable to articulate my plea for help, but knowing I was heard anyway as petals – delicate as snow – fell around me.

"Push – pushhhh hard, c'm on, PUSH!"

With an almighty effort, I drew on the last of my reserves.

Collapsing on my side in an ungainly heap in the crushed sward, I drew air in short chunks. "How is he?" I gasped, struggling around. Ellie was making rapid movements, her face drawn into furrows of concentration. She didn't answer. No sound came from the baby – no gasp of life, no cry. "Ellie?" Panic swelled. "Ellie? What's wrong? My baby, give him to me!" I reached for the bundle, partially obscured by her bent form. She knelt upright, and with first one arm, then the other, took off her shirt and wrapped him in it like a shroud. My heart imploded. "Why isn't he crying? Ellie!"

She pulled the cloth from the little face. "Because she's too busy looking. See?" Grinning, she held out the baby swathed in the pink and orange shirt, and placed her in my arms. Dark eyes stared unfocused, and the small, creased face worked, her mouth opening and shutting like a fish.

"A girl?" I whispered, hoarse from effort. "My girl?" The baby snuffled at the sound of my voice and from her puckered mouth a small cry wound into the air. Speechless, I could only hold her, stunned.

"She's perfect, Emma, there's nothing wrong. We'd better get you back to the house and clean you both up. Are you still getting contractions?"

Was I? I became vaguely away of continuing discomfort, and nodded.

"Good, you need to deliver the placenta. I'm going to take Charlie to Gran and then get some help. Think you'll be OK for a few minutes, Emma? Will you be all right?"

I blinked up at her. "She's perfect."

She grinned again. "Yeah, she is; you did great. And she's my first delivery." She inspected her hands, smeared in blood and amniotic fluid, with a degree of pride.

"You did an amazing job, Ellie. Thanks – thanks for everything."

A car engine tore to a halt beneath our bedroom window, and seconds later the front door slammed open, shaking me from a drowsy state between waking and sleeping. I heard incautious steps taking the stairs two at a time and then Matthew appeared at the door, his fair hair wild. He skidded to a standstill by my bedside.

"I'm sorry, I'm so sorry I wasn't with you," he rushed, words tumbling. "How are you? Are you all right? Ellie said there was no time to get you back to the house – you didn't have any pain relief, it was too quick." His face creased with remorse. "I should have been there. I could have helped you with the pain..."

"We're fine; Ellie did brilliantly. I'm not certain about it being quick, though; it felt like ages."

"Thirty-seven minutes, Ellie said. She couldn't do anything about the tearing... I should have been there," he said again. His colours fluctuated between emotions so rapidly they almost merged, until he caught sight of the little bundle tucked in beside me, almost out of sight, and then he became a vibrant, ecstatic blue. With a degree of difficulty, I lifted the baby. He took her, and carefully cradling her in one arm, parted the cotton blankets from around her sleeping face, his eyes widening in wonder. "She's so beautiful," he said, softly. "My daughter." He leaned down and gently kissed her forehead, his lips murmuring against her skin. "What have I done to be so blessed?" He swallowed, controlling himself, and smiled awkwardly. "It's a good thing we have a crib now, but we don't have a name." He perched on the edge of the bed.

"All the ones we came up with were for boys," I pointed out.

"What about naming her after your Nanna?"

"Eleanor? She would have been chuffed to bits, but don't you think there are enough Ellie-type names in your family to confuse us as it is?"

"Possibly," he admitted.

"But her second name – and the one she preferred – was Rose. There were roses growing beyond the orchard," I mused, remembering the palest pink blooms. "It's rather fitting."

"The wild meadow roses on the south slope? They flower early there. Rose. I like that. Rose. Rosie." He rolled the name about a couple of times to try it out. "And she has your pink-toned hair." He smiled as I winced. "It's beautiful – as are you." He leaned down and kissed me, lingering and tender. I didn't feel very beautiful. Bits of me ached, others stung, and parts of me were bulging rather alarmingly as my milk began to gather. And I was tired – dog tired. He caressed my cheek and laid the baby beside me. "You'd better get some sleep while you can and I'll go and set up the crib. I think you'll both like it."

"I'm too big for it," I mumbled, eyes shutting despite myself, and he chuckled, stroking my cheek until consciousness – into which images and voices strayed – blurred. As I drifted, indistinctly and from a great distance, I heard the door open and then Ellie's voice asking quietly, "Matthew, do you want me to run the tests on the placental samples?"

And his reply, so casual I thought I must have imagined it, "No, thank you; I'll run them through E.V.E. myself."

"Oh. OK. Sure." Was that surprise I detected, or merely the effects of an overtired brain? It didn't matter, it couldn't matter, because all I wanted was to let myself go into the realms of sleep where I could be at peace and rest.

Secrets and Ties

Pat frowned at the cradle on the simple shaped stand that let it swing gently with the lightest push. "Why couldn't you just get something new? It'd be more hygienic. And why does Matthew like this old English oak, for pity's sake! A coat of paint would at least brighten it up." The glossy surface of the wood, polished smooth through generations of use, gleamed reassuringly in its antiquity.

"Oh, you know us, Pat; why have something new when we can have something old instead? It's the ultimate in recycling." I stroked the pretty carved scrolls of the canopy. "And Matthew's made certain it's clean, don't worry." Holding Rosie carefully, I eased forward on my pile of cushions to put her in the crib, trying not to wince. Henry stepped forward.

"Here, let me take her for you. I suspect," he said, smiling at her sleeping face, "that Dad likes the thought of continuity. He's collected antiques for as long as I can remember." He placed her gently in the cradle, and straightened. "Someone once said that people surround themselves with the things that make them feel safe and reflect their idea of family. His parents died when he was young, after all; perhaps all these antiques are his way of creating a home he never knew. I know I liked them when I was growing up, although my mother wasn't as keen. He kept most of them in his study – his little bit of home, he once said to me. I never did get that, seeing we *were* home. Still," he rocked Rosie in her crib as she began to stir, "home and family are everything to my father. He's over the moon with this new addition, and I can see why."

"Thanks, Henry," I smiled. "And thank you for her toy otter; she'll love it – it's so silky and squishy." Rosie wriggled a little against the otter, signalling contentment.

"That's our pleasure. Dad thinks he's the most fortunate man alive, but I have much to be grateful for: within a few short weeks I've become both a great-grandfather and a brother for the first time. How many men can claim that? There now, this clumsy old man has woken her up." He shook his head, tucking the quilted blanket Pat had made around Rosie's wriggling legs.

"Go on with you!" Pat exclaimed. "You're as soft as Matthew when it comes to your family."

"And you're not, Pat?" I laughed, regretting it as my healing torn skin tweaked.

"I may well be. Now, I'll look after Rosie at any time when you want to go out. I dare say there'll be shopping for baby clothes you'll want to do before long; she's such a big girl, and growing."

"I'll probably buy online and Mum's sending a parcel. It should be here soon."

"Oh, so you don't want to go to the stores?" She wore a hopeful look, and I remembered not to be so selfish.

"I might have to go to college, though. Would you mind if I left her with you then?"

Pat's disappointment melted into a smile. "Sure and I'll be glad to, sweetie; just let me know when."

"As soon as I can walk without looking like a penguin," I said a trifle caustically, as I inched off the cushions into a standing position resembling a rheumatic tree. Everything sagged, or it felt like it, and each movement was soreness magnified. "Yes, next week. She'll be three weeks old then and I should be more mobile and have mastered this feeding business."

"Is she still not feeding?" Henry asked, switching to doctor mode.

"We're getting there," I replied, more cheerfully than I felt.

"Next week? If you're still experiencing discomfort, are you sure you're up to driving? I can take you if you wish." Matthew watched Rosie snuffling at my breast.

"I want to get out and I've work to do. I said I'd meet up with Aydin and Josh for a supervision to check progress on their doctoral theses, and it won't take long. Come on, Rosie," I urged, feeling increasingly hopeless. She had seemed so hungry a few moments ago, but now she turned her head away and cried. "Why won't you feed?"

"Have you tried putting a pillow under your arm?"

"I've tried that."

"Perhaps she's sensing your tension," he suggested.

"Perhaps you should try feeding her yourself," I bit back. I sucked my cheeks. He stood up without commenting and picked up the shawl from where it had fallen to the floor. "Sorry. It's just that I'm worried she's not getting enough to eat."

He draped the shawl around my shoulders. "She must be; she's content and she's thriving."

"But she barely feeds for more than a few minutes, Matthew; how can she survive off that?" Illustrating my point, Rosie twisted away, her face screwed up in disgust. I felt horribly inadequate. "See? Perhaps there's something wrong with my milk? Or... or she knows I don't know what I'm doing."

"There's nothing wrong with either your milk or you. I don't know why she isn't feeding, unless..."

"What?" I pushed when he didn't complete his thought.

"... unless it might be that she doesn't need as much." He avoided my inquisitional stare, but couldn't disguise the transient fluctuation in the colours that surrounded him indicating he was hiding something from me.

"You said she is perfectly normal, Matthew. You said the tests showed nothing out of the ordinary for a Lynes."

"For a Lynes in the first generation, no. The differences were less marked with succeeding generations. I must have forgotten how Henry was at two weeks, although Ellen was less inclined to discuss those matters with me, such were the times."

"Didn't you have to train Dan and his children to eat more so that they appeared normal?"

"We did. That must be it," he said. "Anyway, there's nothing wrong with Rosie, nor how you are with her, so stop worrying."

"It's a bit difficult when Ellie's so at ease with Charlie. She seems to instinctively know what to do. That gene's missing from me."

"That's because you're overthinking everything. Disengage this for a bit," and he tapped me lightly on the forehead, "and start thinking with this," and he touched his fingers lightly to my heart, "and between the three of us we'll figure it out."

By the following week, it became clear that Rosie wasn't suffering as a result of my feeble attempts at nurturing, and the unfamiliar routines of waking at all hours to feed her a few mouthfuls of milk became the norm. Nor did she object when I bathed her. On seeing her bare tummy as I dried her, I couldn't resist kissing her petal-soft skin. She wriggled. "Did that tickle?" I asked. Her arms and legs jerked in response, and I kissed her exposed tummy again. She made an odd little noise and I looked up to find her mouth twitching, her eyes wide and bright. "Matthew!"

I called. He came into the bathroom with his sleeves rolled up and her clean baby suit in one hand. "Look at Rosie." I nuzzled her with my nose. "She's smiling."

"Hey, baby girl, are you smiling at your mummy?" he said softly, and she responded by moving her head in his direction and waving her arms, making excited little noises in her throat. "I do believe she is. Now we know how to keep her entertained through her christening."

"I don't think we can ask the vicar to blow raspberries to make her laugh," I said, doing just that and being rewarded with her wonky smile. "It might set a precedent. At least Mum and Dad will get to see her like this when she's tiny. They're so used to seeing Beth's three almost every day, and they'll miss Rosie growing up." My voice wobbled without warning and I sniffed back a watery laugh. "Ugh, these hormones. I can't listen to music without it setting me off."

Matthew put his arms around me and I welcomed his steady strength. "They'll settle down soon, and we'll make sure your parents see Rosie as often as we can and for however long we are able." *Until such time as my agelessness becomes evident*, he might have added. He didn't need to; we were both acutely aware of time running out. "I'd better get back to your father and finalize the christening arrangements. You go and have a sleep; I'll look after Rosie."

I pushed myself away from him before his tenderness set off an unwelcome round of tears. "I think I'll drop in on college and see how things are going; I promised I would." I reached for a clean nappy, ignoring the sudden twinge in my womb.

"What was that?" Matthew said, sharply. "Are you in pain?"

"Nothing some fresh air and exercise won't sort out." I whipped Rosie's nappy on like a pro. "She's clean, fed – sort of – and all yours for an hour or so. I'll be back soon."

* * *

If I expected the campus to have changed in the last three weeks since I last saw it, I was mistaken. It swam in a milky mist the sun failed to break, students milling in the way they do the planet over. One or two raised their hands in greeting when they saw me, otherwise nobody seemed to notice that my world had been turned upside down.

I made my way across the quad to my rather bare tutor room with a degree of caution to avoid the sloshing sensation inside, and the occasional stab in my nether regions that accompanied my progress. Months of pregnancy had left me breathless and I flopped into my desk chair, sweating, to await Josh.

"Holly's got a job at the museum as a curator," he told me in an exchange of news, long legs, as ever, stretched out in front of him as he lounged inelegantly. "She's keeping me in the manner to which I am accustomed while I get my PhD," he added, in a most appalling attempt at a British accent.

"Beans on toast for every meal, then?"

He grinned. "Yeah, something like that. Anyway, she was offered this job and it was too good to pass, so…" he shrugged. "Can't afford hair dye, but we're kinda happy with that." He looked it and his naturally dark hair suited him. He had grown up in the last year and, I suppose, in a way, so had I. People change, don't they? Things move on.

A little ache tugged away, reminding me that Rosie was growing older by the second and I wasn't with her to witness it, an odd feeling and one to which I wasn't accustomed. I steeled myself and thought about work, but in around the edges Rosie crept, finding my weakness, undermining my defences. I missed her, but first, I had promised to see Aydin. I looked at my watch, calculating how long it would be before I could see her again.

Aydin looked much the same as he ever did when he arrived

carrying an oversized carrier bag. I had been resting my eyes for a moment or two when he knocked quietly, and I probably looked as awake as I felt.

"I am sorry to disturb you, Professor."

"No, not at all, Aydin; come in and sit down. How's the research going?"

"It is well, thank you. I will email you. I will not be keeping you long, but I wanted to give you this." He held out the big plastic bag, from which a few large leaves poked. I peered inside.

"Thank you. What is it?"

"It is mulberry tree – for your little girl. It is traditional gift for a girl in Turkey. It is for your… your… o-chard."

"How on earth do you know about my orchard?"

"Professor Smalova told me. She tells everyone about your daughter and your house and your o-chard. She says your daughter looks like her anne."

"A-neh?" I queried, thinking that I must have a quiet word with my garrulous friend before she let something slip I might regret.

"Mother," he said. "Yes, she is like you." Beaming now and jerking his thumb in the direction of my remaining posters with the demons leering out at us, he said, "In Turkey, pregnant women must avoid looking at such things, but I do not think this superstition can be true. Professor Smalova says that your baby is *çok güzel* – very pretty. It is not possible for her to be a monster when her parents are good."

"Oh, Aydin!" I laughed.

"I do not joke. There are monsters in this world. They are out there," he pointed through the window at the mist-swathed trees, "and they are in here," he rapped his knuckles against his head. "We make monsters – they are not born. You and your husband do not make monster." He rattled the stake supporting the sapling, making the leaves shake. "You plant good seed and it makes good tree. Its fruit will be good because you are good – inside you are like the sun – you... you shine."

Taken aback, I could only blush.

"Now, I leave you because you will want to get back to your *küçük Gül* – little Rose – and you look tired. I think you will need rest, no? But I give you this first," and he pressed a small, rough object into my hand. I squinted at the fragment of pottery – about three inches long – with an incised shape along its length. A hole had been drilled through one end. "I cannot give you gold as my custom say I should, but I can give you this. I found it at Miletus when I was a boy. I did not know its... sig-ni-ficance then. It is better than gold, is it not?"

I nodded, speechless, as I traced the flowing outline of a fish with my finger. I felt a sudden need to be with Rosie and Matthew with a yearning that squeezed my heart.

"I did not mean to cause offence..."

I found a hanky in my sleeve. "You haven't, Aydin. It's one of the most special things I have ever been given. Thank you. And thank you for the tree. Rosie will love it, and I'll make sure she knows it's from you when she's old enough to understand."

"You are most welcome." His eyes warmed, losing their customary guardedness. "I hope that I might be honoured to tell her myself one day."

The staff car park seemed miles away as I trudged slowly past the med centre and accommodation blocks, carrying the tree. It felt insanely heavy for its size, and I shifted it to the other hand, feeling my insides object to the sudden movement. Despite the early promise of sun, mist had thickened into fog, and droplets clung to my hair, making it curl damply against my neck. Safely tucked in my trouser pocket, the little fish pressed comfortingly against my thigh, yet the waistband pinched and I wished

I'd worn my maternity skirt instead. My legs were filled with porridge, but my head felt as if it would take off if it hadn't been attached at the neck. Forcing my legs to move, I reached the car feeling bloated and increasingly uncomfortable. I fumbled my keys from my bag and dropped them.

"Hey, Emma!"

Leaning against the car, I suppressed a groan. "Sam. Hi."

He bent and picked up the keys. "You dropped these." My hand shook slightly as I took them from him. He ran a hand through his thick, dark hair. "That glad to see me, are you?"

"Sorry; must have overdone it a bit. How are you?"

"I was going to ask the same. You're a mom now, huh? A little girl."

"Elena told you?"

He grinned. "Who else! You gave birth in a field, she said, and Lynes wasn't there…"

"In an orchard," I corrected, crisply, "and, no, Matthew wasn't there, but he would have liked to have been had she not been two weeks early." Needing to sit down and wondering where this was leading, I unlocked the car, but Sam didn't appear to be in a hurry to leave. He held the door wide, looking relaxed and amiable. "Sure, it's tough him missing out. I was there for all three of mine; wouldn't have missed it for anything. Been a hell've a year for you both and that would've made up for it a bit. Still, she's safe and that's all that matters, isn't it, Freckles? You and she are safe. Tell him we'll catch a beer sometime, you know, hang out."

Sam. Being nice? About Matthew? "Uh, yes, I'll do that, Sam. I'd better go."

"Yeah, you sure look pale. She keeping you up at night? You'll need more rest than you think in these early weeks. Is she colicky?" I began to shake my head, then decided I'd better not in case it came off or I threw up. "That's lucky. I'll let you go. Take care." He planted a kiss on my cheek, and waited for me to climb into the car before shutting the door and tapping the roof in farewell.

Resting my tacky forehead against the steering wheel, I gathered myself for the journey home.

Tap, tap.

I opened the window and Sam peered in, brown eyes molten with concern. "You sure you're OK? I'll drive you home if you like, no sweat."

Gripping the wheel, I formed words through numb lips. "No, thanks; I'll be OK."

"I haven't been drinking or anything. I'm off the hard stuff now. On OJ big-time." His attempt at a joke was lost on me.

"No. Thanks." I started the engine.

"Well, if you're sure…"

I pulled away and, in the rear-view mirror, saw him watching me disappear down the drive until I lost him in the fog. From somewhere a horn sounded and I slammed on the brake, the seat belt constraining my violent forward propulsion. Jerked back in my seat, I sensed something inside me snap – like the feeling you get when an old rubber band gives way under pressure. *Stupid idiot*, I castigated myself, feeling more nauseous now.

With greater urgency than before, I stepped on the accelerator and headed on the back roads home, avoiding the traffic. I made it over the narrow bridge in one piece, not caring now that it and I were bound by Guy's death, because that seemed a lifetime away and irrelevant. My pulse galloped, perspiraton running freely down my neck and gathering beneath my arms and stickily between my legs. Head pounding, I turned onto the road heading towards the mountains and Rosie and home.

Around a wide bend not a mile from home, a car headed

towards me through the fog, flashing its lights in warning. I swerved back onto my side of the road and came to an abrupt halt. Like a nightmare, Guy's face appeared in my windscreen, mouth gaping, blood oozing from his ears and nose. I could smell it – fresh blood, fresh… blood. I felt sick again.

Staggering from the car, I threw up into the long grass by the roadside as the other car slewed to a halt yards from me, the engine left running. A hazy figure emerged.

"Emma!"

I looked up as Matthew reached me. His gaze dropped to my legs, face paling in the mist, and I glanced down to see what he saw: a dark stain had appeared down the front of my trousers. Confused, I reached and touched it lightly and my fingers came away wet and red. My mouth opened, words slurring. "I… I… don't think I'm very well…"

"Henry!" Matthew bellowed, lifting me from the car and carrying me, boneless, towards the house. "Henry, I need your help!"

I heard the Barn door open and Henry call across the courtyard. "Dad, what is it?" Footsteps and then, "Sweet Heaven! There's blood everywhere. Has she been in an accident?"

"She's haemorrhaging. I had a call from Sam Weisner saying he thought she shouldn't be driving. I found her weaving all over the road."

Henry opened the kitchen door, and chairs clattered as Matthew kicked them away from the table. Clearing it with a sweep of his arm, he laid me on the surface. I floated above it, cushioned by oblivion. Through a filter, distant voices debated, first Henry, alarmed, "We need to get her to the hospital."

"We don't have time; she's already lost too much blood."

"Dad, she needs an immediate transfusion. We don't hold blood here. If we leave now…"

"She'll be dead by then." Matthew rolled my sleeve out of the way, exposing my arm to the air. "Get me my bag, Henry."

I wasn't dying; how could I die?

"What are you going to do?"

"Get me my bag." I sensed his hesitation and Matthew's growing urgency. "Now, Henry!"

I couldn't leave my baby. "Rosie," I mumbled.

Matthew leaned close, speaking swiftly. "Pat and Ellie have taken the children for a walk." He was shoving his sleeve above his elbow, knocking the overhead light in his haste. It swam above me. My insides felt hollow, my feet and hands a creeping coldness. Henry returned carrying the medical bag, and handed it wordlessly to his father. I felt the familiar swab of something colder than me, and then a sharp stab. I moaned.

"Cannula," Matthew said, stretching out his own arm and baring it to the light.

Henry didn't move. "What are you doing?"

"We're wasting time. Give me the cannula."

"You'll kill her!"

Matthew held out his hand. "I haven't time to debate it. Give it to me."

Henry grabbed his arm. "You know what'll happen if you give her your blood. I can't let you do this…"

Shaking himself free and snatching the cannula from his son's hand, Matthew said under his breath. "She's dead if I don't." He met my eyes with grim determination. "Trust me, my love." I wanted to say I trusted him, but words had long-since evaporated as I began to shake uncontrollably. "Trust me." He looked over his shoulder. "Henry, I need you to hold Emma still."

Henry backed away into the shadows. "I can't be a part of this. It goes against every oath I've taken, everything I believe in as a doctor."

Teeth gritted, Matthew growled, "Then don't do it as a doctor, but as my son."

Henry stared into his father's eyes, blazing now, then swallowed, nodded, and stepped into the light. His hands burned as he pinned my arm to the table. "She's bleeding too heavily. There's no point giving her blood – you've got to stop the bleeding first."

"Wait," Matthew said. A ribbon of red wound through the narrow tube between us.

"It's pointless," Henry insisted. "Your blood's incompatible with every living creature on the planet. Dad, listen to me. The only chance she has is to stop the bleeding and get her to the hospital."

"Wait…" Matthew didn't take his eyes from me, as if looking for some sign, opening and closing his fist and driving his blood through my veins. I felt nothing at first and then warmth in the tips of my fingers. They flexed. Matthew and Henry's faces merged, blurred, then sharpened into focus as spots of clarity appeared in my vision, like fog clearing in patches. I blinked, struggled for air, and the weight in my chest lightened. My tongue loosened, became mobile. I licked parched lips. "Rosie…" I mouthed. I became conscious of the burning in my womb again and twitched to escape the pain.

"She's going into shock," Henry warned. "There's nothing you can do now. Your blood cells are attacking hers, releasing toxins – she's dying, Dad – you're *killing* her!"

The trembling in my limbs lessened, my body quietened. I felt the hard table under my shoulder blades, the grain of the wood beneath my fingers, despite the slick blood. The gold watch on Matthew's wrist glinted as it marked the seconds. Minutes passed. The light from the lamp became painful as it pierced my eyes. I turned my head to avoid it. Standing by my legs, Henry gave a sharp intake of breath and he released his hold on me. "She's stopped bleeding. How the blazes…?"

"Rosie," I managed audibly this time.

"Our baby's safe. You're safe."

"See. Her."

"Soon," he promised, and at that moment the kitchen door opened, letting in fresh air and animated chatter. "Look, here she is."

Pat screamed and her hand flew to her mouth, turning away as if protecting Rosie from the scene that greeted them. Still clutching Charlie, Ellie darted forwards. "What's happened? Matthew, Gramps, what's happened to Emma?"

Matthew had become wan, his hand limp against my own. "Too. Mush. Blood," I murmured. "Mat'hew, stop."

He grunted acknowledgment, and tugged the tube from his arm, the small wound dribbling, blood caught in the tangle of fair hair as he healed. Then more carefully, he removed the other end from my own, replacing it with his thumb. He swayed slightly. He looked how I felt. "Mat'hew?"

His colour began to return. "I'm OK, Emma."

"For Pete's sake!" Pat exclaimed, partially recovering. "What's going on?"

"Yes, Dad," Henry said quietly. "What just happened?"

Ellie took in the table flooded in blood, the pool coagulating on the floor by Henry's feet, the discarded tube. "You've given Emma a transfusion? Of your blood?" Her eyes rounded. "Matthew, she should be dead…"

"Ellie, take the babies home and then look after Pat, please; she's in shock."

"Yes, sure, Matthew, but…"

"*Now*, please, Ellie. I will explain later."

The door closed behind them, leaving Henry and his father

facing each other across the length of me. The pain inside had subsided to mere throbbing, my skin vibrated, my blood alive and humming to a different tune. Matthew grabbed a handful of tea towels from the drawer and began to mop me up. Henry hadn't moved.

"What will you explain, Dad? Why Emma spontaneously stopped bleeding, or why she didn't die? Or will you explain how you knew she wouldn't react adversely to your blood?"

I attempted to sit up, but Matthew restrained me. "Stay still."

"You knew – you knew before this happened. You weren't taking a risk, were you? You knew."

"I couldn't be certain; it's a miracle it worked..."

"You *knew*," Henry threw at him. "The only way I can see that she's survived is that it's a fluke, a million – billion-to-one chance she's compatible." He laughed roughly. "Either that or you share common genes..." He stopped, looking first at Matthew and then at me, colour draining from his face until his skin resembled the grey of his neat beard. "You... you said you didn't know where you came from. Dad, you've always claimed you don't know."

With my clothes sticking to the table and the iron stench of a butcher's shop filling my nose, I managed to struggle to a sitting position. "Henry..."

He stared down at me, nostrils flaring in temper. "And you know, don't you, Emma? You've known all along." He slapped the heel of his hand against his forehead. "What sort of fool does that make me? My own father keeps something like this from me after everything we've been through? After all these years?"

Matthew took a step towards his son. "I never meant to deceive you. I did it to protect you..."

"Like you did my mother? From what? From the *truth*?" His lips drew back from his teeth. "You're a hundred years old, for the love of God! What have you to hide that I don't already know?

Isn't it enough to have led a life hiding the truth of ourselves without you lying to us about our ancestry?"

"Henry, that's not fair!" I burst out as Matthew visibly blanched. "You don't know the circumstances. He would have told you if he could, but..."

He turned on me in a mixture of hurt and anger. "And you, Emma, he trusts you enough to tell *you*!"

"He didn't tell me; I found out for myself."

"How?"

"I... guessed – suspected – he wasn't as he seemed."

"How, Emma? What did you discover?"

I moistened dry lips. "It's complicated, Henry. I think... I mean, if..." But Matthew placed his hand on my arm as I struggled for words.

"I think," he said quietly, "that it's time I told the family the truth."

"All of it?" I whispered.

Matthew looked his son straight in the eyes. "Yes, all of it."

Revelation

I moved into a more comfortable position. Bits of me still throbbed from the after effects of the haemorrhage the day before, but it was nothing compared with the impending discomfort of the family meeting as they gathered in our drawing room, voices muted to a rustle. Uncertainty crowded their faces and lay in hunched shoulders. Matthew waited as each member of his family found somewhere to sit, but he had withdrawn into himself over the last twenty-four hours and raised his defences, so that even I found them difficult to penetrate. Rosie lay sleepy and warm in my arms, unaware of the rising tide of tension around her.

Ellie came in last from the Stables, having put Charlie in his crib, and she now sat next to her parents, flicking anxious looks between Matthew and me. Subdued, Henry stood by the window, arms folded, grim. Tight-lipped and sitting on the edge of her hard chair, Pat was beside him.

"Pat, Henry, won't you come and sit down here?" Matthew indicated the comfortable sofa which had been left vacant for them. When Henry didn't answer, Pat coughed to clear her throat.

"We're fine here."

Matthew looked at the assembled faces regarding him as if he were a stranger – a freak.

"Thank you for coming. Especially you, Joel – I know you had to get special leave – and Harry, having travelled all night to be here," he began. He laced his fingers, his knuckles white. "This isn't going to be easy, and I've spent your lifetimes trying to find a way of telling you what I am about to reveal now. Before I say anything, I want you to know that I have always tried to act in the best interests of all the family, and I regret any hurt I might cause you – especially you, Henry." He paused, gathered himself, and then, "I want to tell you what happened. I want to tell you my story from the beginning…"

Leaning with his elbows on his knees, Joel was the first to break the hush that had fallen on the room after the last syllable had left Matthew's lips. "You're *how* old? Geesh!" Jeannie didn't correct him for once, and instead looked at Matthew with new eyes.

Dan pulled his earlobe. "I had no idea."

"No," Matthew said.

"I can see why you didn't say anything before," Ellie ventured, when she found her voice at last. "I don't know what to think."

Harry said nothing, biting his thumbnail, absorbed in his own thoughts. Standing to shut the French window, Joel locked it and, shoving his hands in his pockets, leant against the frame. "The fewer people who know, the better our security, right? That's why you didn't tell us."

"Yes, to keep you safe, and… because I didn't know where – or how – to begin."

"But Emma knew," Jeannie said, with a hint of an accusation that Maggie had also adopted in her wooden expression as she fingered the head of her snake necklace.

"Emma bears no blame in any of this," Matthew started, but I stopped him, swivelling in my chair and facing his family.

"I know Matthew's history because I found out, otherwise he wouldn't have told me." And I explained, step-by-step, the path I had taken to trace Matthew back to the Lynes of New Hall and Martinsthorpe. "But he's incorrect in saying I have no part in this – I have. It was because of me that Guy Hilliard turned up, and he already knew some of the story. It didn't take much for him to piece the rest of it together." I saw Ellie's expression cloud. "We couldn't tell you – even you, Ellie. Guy would have winkled it out of you one way or another. This information is a time bomb."

"What we don't know we can't tell, right? It can't hurt us," Joel said. "Yeah, that's how it is in the Army – need to know, and all that."

"What I don't understand," Dan said, "is why Emma survived a transfusion of your blood."

"That's simple." Henry broke his silence at last. "They must be related. Isn't that so, Matthew? We didn't spot it when we did that first analysis on Emma's blood because we weren't looking for a connection, but you did. That's why you ran everything through E.V.E." Matthew's lack of response confirmed it. "All this time, all these months, you've known, but you kept it from us..."

"I suspected, Henry, but I couldn't be certain. When I met Emma for the first time – heard her name, discovered where she came from – I suspected the coincidence was too great to be one. Yes, we are related – separated by generations – but related nonetheless. My grandmother was Emma D'Eresby." Everyone's eyes fell upon me at once as if I'd sprouted gills. I felt I owed them an explanation.

"In the region I – we – come from, there's quite a lot of intermarriage between some families down the generations. It's not really surprising we're related. It kept land and property within the family and strengthened political ties..." I tailed off as Henry cut me dead with a look.

"You'll find you're the only one who hasn't been taken by surprise."

I dropped my gaze, unable to withstand the bitterness in his, and hugged Rosie.

"Then the genetic component that made us the way we are, and which you share with Emma, is the key?" Ellie asked Matthew.

"The genetic component, yes, but I still don't know why this happened to me in the first place any more than I did a hundred – two hundred – years ago. It was certainly triggered as a result of my uncle's attack, but I don't know what the scientific reasoning behind it is now any more than I did then."

Joel grunted. "Some fluke, you and Emma meeting like you did."

"Fluke?" I interjected. "No, I don't think so. I don't believe in coincidence."

Harry's head shot up and I found myself confronted by inquisitional eyes. "Are you saying this was meant to be?"

"I believe so, yes, Harry."

"And you think we should accept it at face value?"

"You know that I do." I noted the emotions of each of them: the doubt, uncertainty, denial – subtle, shifting colours echoing the confusion they all felt. Ellie voiced it, "So what now?"

Joel pushed himself away from the window. "We carry on, sis; nothing's really changed, has it?"

"Hasn't it?" Henry's voice, hoarse and cracked, came from the back of the room, and the subdued conversations came to a halt. "Everything's changed. You laid a foundation of trust on nothing but lies. I believed in you, Dad. I believed every word you ever said to me and it turns out to have been a lie."

Matthew held out his hands, palm up and offering atonement. "Henry, my love for you has never been a lie; you know that. You know you mean everything to me, and I've done everything I can to protect you and the family."

Henry nodded at Rosie. "You have a new family to protect with your lies now. You betrayed me, you've betrayed all of us. I hope you can live with yourself, because I can't." He about-faced in a wash of red-hued bitter disillusionment and, pushing past Joel's surprised form, flung open the door between the two homes, and left.

Smoothing her palms over her skirt, Pat stood up. She threw an apologetic look at Matthew and followed her husband, leaving the room to its emphatic silence. For what seemed like minutes, but was probably only a matter of seconds, we stared at the blank-faced door.

"Gee-*eesh*," Joel mooted.

Standing, Dan cleared his throat. "Jeanette and I have some work to be getting on with for Monday. We'll leave you to have some time to yourselves. Ellie, are you coming? Charlie will be waking from his nap." Riddled with anxiety, lips pressed into a bloodless line, she nodded. "Boys, you coming? Maggie?"

Harry followed his sister, but Joel hesitated, shoulders broadened by his military stance as he hipped his hands. "Gramps won't say anything to anyone. Nobody'll say anything."

Matthew didn't reply, so I said, "I'm sure they won't, Joel; they know what's at stake."

"Yeah, Gramps'll come around."

Maggie hadn't moved. She hovered by the door as if she wanted to say something, then took a last look and followed Joel through the door to the Barn.

I waited until the door closed behind her and we couldn't be overheard before turning to Matthew. "Henry's in shock. He probably didn't mean it the way it sounded. He'll think about it and want to talk more, but he'll forgive you, darling, you know he will."

Bleak-eyed and hollow-voiced, Matthew sat on the edge of the sofa, nails digging into his hands and his head bent as he stared blindly at the floor. "No, I don't think so. Not this time. He meant it – he meant every word of it."

PART

2

And I said to the man who stood at the gate of the year:
"Give me a light that I may tread safely into the unknown."
And he replied:
"Go out into the darkness and put your hand into the Hand of God.
That shall be to you better than light and safer than a known way."
So I went forth, and finding the Hand of God, trod gladly into the night.
And He led me towards the hills and the breaking of day in the lone East.

M. L. Haskins

The Gate of the Year

"Mummy! Theo's eating ants again."

I scooped him up, brushing panic-stricken insects from my son's cheek. "What are you doing, cheeky chops? Ants don't want to be eaten."

Twirling in her skirt, Rosie then lifted it over her head like a cape and peeked out. "I extept it's the formic acid; it tastes like lemons."

"I expect you're right," I said, fishing one out of his mouth with my little finger, damp, but alive, and wondering how my four-year-old daughter knew what ants tasted like. "Come on, Rosie, we'll be late."

"Of course, lemons might taste like ants," she mused, strapping herself into her booster seat while I secured Theo in next to her, still looking very pleased with himself. I wiped his chin free of dribble and what looked suspiciously like an insect leg, and gave him his bear instead. "Daddy says citric acid tastes like formic acid to humans, but they're chem'clly different." She walked her model T-Rex along the window edge. "I prefer lemons."

I had to ask. "Why?"

"They don't wriggle, like this," and she made her fingers scurry against her lips.

I grimaced.

"I hope you've given up eating ants, Rosie, or there won't be enough for the anteaters."

She squealed with laughter, setting her brother chortling. "That's silly, Mummy! Anteaters don't live in Maine."

We drove from the shelter of the courtyard through the big gates under the arch and out onto the drive that was no more than a track, through the long grass singing with grasshoppers. "Has Daddy been telling you about his adventures again?"

Bewitched by the passing sky, Rosie twiddled her fingers, her dinosaur forgotten. "Yes."

"Rosie, you remember you mustn't tell anyone else, don't you? These are our stories and they belong to us. They're not for sharing with your friends." She met my eyes in the rear-view mirror.

"I know, Mummy. Daddy's different." And not just her daddy. Her differences were becoming increasingly apparent, even for a Lynes. She barely slept now, and I had long since given up cajoling her to bed, only to find her with her father ensconced in his study in the early hours of the morning, poring over a book together, or him telling stories to make her eyes pop. Her rate of learning accelerated, and I never knew whether I would find her playing with Lego or learning Latin. It stirred an ember of envy that I had to firmly extinguish.

"But it's nothing to be worried about, darling," I added quickly. "Everyone is unique; everyone's different in some way or other."

"'Different is good'," Rosie said firmly. "Daddy said so. God made us 'cos he's the Lord and he made Heaven and Earth and the sea and *a-ll* that's in them." She made an expanding circle of her arms, encompassing the world.

"Did Daddy say that, too?"

"No, Rev'nd Baker said so last Sunday. Didn't you hear him?"

I screwed up my eyes, thinking back to the previous weekend, but it was lost in a blur of nappies and teething and sleepless nights. "You re'mber. He said that we are made in the image of God and then Theo pushed all the hymn books on the floor and everyone laughed." Almost everyone. I coloured at the memory. Her brother bounced and rocked in his car seat at the mention of his name, and Rosie leaned sideways and tickled his tummy. "I don't mind being different," she said. "Do you, Mummy?"

"Er, no – no, not at all."

"God doesn't mind if I'm big and fat like... like a watermelon..." she patted her tummy, "... or teeny-weeny like ants." She held up her thumb and forefinger to the sun and made a gap between them through which she spied the golden star. "God loves me just the way I am," she said philosophically.

"He does," I confirmed, warming at the thought. "We are made perfect in his sight."

"He doesn't mind if I'm clever..." she continued.

"No, he doesn't," I said, wondering where this was going.

"... so he won't mind if I stay at home with you and Daddy and Theo and Ollie."

In the mirror, I narrowed my eyes at my daughter. "But then you wouldn't be able to play with your friends in preschool and that would be a shame. You would miss your friends, wouldn't you?" I concentrated on taking a left turn down the tree-lined street leading to the kindergarten belonging to the school in its elegant red-brick building. Parents expelled tots and teens from the expensive-looking cars queuing either side of the road, and bundled them through the gaping mouth of the front door. I died a little every time I left her there. Finding somewhere to park, I remembered Rosie hadn't answered me. I switched off the engine and twisted in my seat. "You like seeing your friends. You like Jamie and Clara, don't you?"

Still staring into the sun, she seemed determined to capture it, but eventually said, "I wish people were more like Jesus," and her fingers compressed the burning orb until she blotted it out altogether.

Theo entertained himself by trying to pick the shiny sequin butterflies off Elena's bag, propped against the desk in my tutor room. Elena bent over her seven-month bump and peered at his head. "Emma, Theo has ant in his hair." She pronounced his name "*Teo*", Russian-style, which I rather liked. I looked up as she removed the ant from the fine blond strand and flicked it out of the window.

"Mmm, he likes ants. He had a handful for breakfast this morning."

She tutted. "You're weird." She seemed to like the word she had recently mastered, because she tried it again. "Weird, do you hear me?"

Closing my book, I put it back on the shelf and picked Theo up, checking for further stray creatures. "I hear you. Where do you want to go for lunch? I haven't long before I must go and pick up Rosie. These short sessions play havoc with my timetable. Hey, slobber-chops, are you hungry?" I nuzzled Theo's neck and he chortled good-naturedly.

"Can't Matthew go?"

"It's a bit of a long hike from New York," I pointed out. "Frankly, I wanted to go with him, and Rosie would have loved the Met museum, but he's doing some ghastly business-related work, and she would have missed school, so..."

"You're stuck with me instead," Elena finished, and companionably tucked her arm through mine, and the three of us trundled down the long corridor towards the stairs.

I hadn't needed much dissuading. The idea of any time spent

in the company of the odious legal representative was a thought too far. Anyway, Matthew needed to discuss family matters with George Redgrave, and no matter how hard he tried to contain the hurt, it seeped out of him every time he mentioned Henry, colouring the air around him until it bled.

It was difficult to remain morose in the face of Elena's chatter and the warmth of the late summer sun, and we ended up buying sandwiches to eat by the college lake, laying our jackets not far from where Sam had spread the picnic all those years ago. Squealing in delight, Theo spotted a duck. "Not near the water, young man," I cautioned, as he scuttled off on all fours. Elena watched him, unable to disguise the curl of wistful envy. I handed her a sandwich and bottle of water from the bag. "Are the test results back yet?"

Still watching him, she shook her head. *"Nyet."*

Distracted, Theo negotiated a spiky clump of reeds. "No news is good news?" I ventured, but she became glum, fingering the wedding band next to her engagement ring.

"Matias is so angry that this bad gene came from him, and he worries that the baby will be, how do you say... *deformirovannogo*. And lately, we – he – finds it difficult to... you know..." She shrugged despondently. "Has Matthew said anything to you?"

"No, but he wouldn't break patient confidentiality and tell me anyway."

"Matias is not his patient; he is his friend," she responded, a little fiercely, making Theo stop what he was doing and look around. Her chin quavered. "We want this baby to be healthy so bad, but I want Matias even more, Emma, and I am frightened there is something wrong with him."

"I know," I said hugging her, and feeling her distress. "Matthew will do everything in his power to help him. And I want to help you. I can't give you what you want, but I can give you hugs, my time and lots and lots of pizza."

She snuffled a laugh, her colours changing like a chameleon from distressed blues to sombre purples, becoming lighter as I fed her hope. Drawing back, she wiped her nose. "You make me feel better," she managed at last, then sniffed and frowned over my shoulder. "Should Theo be eating that?"

Theo had dozed off into one of his short, intense sleeps in the car on the way to pick up Rosie from preschool, giving me time to mull over Elena's fears. She never mentioned death, but it lurked behind her eyes and sapped the light from her. It had grown into a faceless monster, unknown, nameless and therefore without the boundaries of definition, free to stalk her waking hours and expand in the mirror of the night. Matthew knew more than he was saying, and it could only be a matter of time before the results came back. It put my own fears into perspective, for as it stood now, it was unlikely I would lose my husband to death. Had that made me complacent? Did I deserve his life?

The traffic had proved lighter than anticipated, and I parked opposite the school without the normal rugby scrum for places, and watched the drift of kindergarten parents towards the gates as they arrived one by one. Mostly women, they gathered in huddles, shooting thin-lipped comments between them like a pinball. I had no desire to join them – I wouldn't know what to say – so I stayed put and hoped that Rosie wouldn't be the last out again. Parents were discouraged from going in to collect their child; it stifled independence, we had been told from the outset. You could tell the parent of a new inmate; they hovered anxiously and alone for the first few days, until they were sucked into a group, or retreated to the anonymity of their car to wait instead. No newbies waited by the gates today, and only a few of us loners kept to our cars, ready to leap out and grab our children at the last possible moment to avoid having to do anything other than exchange a nod and a smile with other parents.

Late September sun heated the interior of the car, scalding the leather. I opened a window and leaned an elbow on the edge, welcoming the slight breeze that nudged the brilliant yellows of the trees lining the street. A bunch of children, ranging in age from about three to seven, scuffled out, accompanied by several staff. I spotted Rosie and waved wildly. She ignited into a smile, and heaved her diminutive dinosaur bag onto her back, giving her a purple hump. Being careful not to wake Theo as I lifted him from his baby seat, I slipped out of the car, ensuring the locks engaged behind me. I indicated to Rosie to wait with her friends, and dodged a car to cross the road. By the time I reached her, standing to one side of the gates, she looked rather subdued.

"Hello, darling!" In an attempt to save her dignity, I refrained from crushing her in an enormous bear hug, but she threw her arms around my middle, so what choice did I have but to return it? "Oo, I missed you," I said, swinging her around with my spare arm. "Did you have a lovely day?" She threw a glance at the retreating backs of her friends, their pigtails bouncing in time to their mothers' brisk pace.

"Can we go see Ollie when we get home? Please," she remembered to say.

"Yes, we can go *and* see Ollie, if you would like." I counted to three and took the plunge. "Rosie, would you like some of your friends to come over to play after school one day?" It didn't come naturally, but I was sure it was one of those dutiful things parents were supposed to do. Matthew had said that Ellen fed dozens of Henry's friends when he was a child. "They could come for tea," I added as a rash afterthought.

She thought about it for all of two seconds. "I want to see Ollie," she stated.

"Ollie. Not your friends. Right. Perhaps just once? I'm sure you'd enjoy it. Look, those children are calling to you. Go on," and I gave her a gentle push towards them. She walked reluctantly towards the group under my watchful eye, but before she reached them, one thin, freckled boy, a few years older than her and inches taller, called out, his words lost in the rustle of desiccated leaves from the street trees. The wind died and then quite distinctly I heard, "Dozy Rosie! Dozy Rosie!"

I saw her stiffen, her shoulders hunch and, without warning, she leapt, sending the other children shrieking as they split and ran. She lashed out at the boy, her small fist punching into his stomach and sending him flying onto his back. Her fists continued to beat the air as I pulled her from him before she did any lasting damage.

"Get her off! Get her off!" A gilded woman in white leather and a fake tan tottered towards us. By now a small crowd had gathered to watch, and seeing his mother, the boy began to cry. Rosie scowled at him in disdain.

Shaking her finger in my face, the woman spat, "I'll report her for this. She attacked my son. I saw her!"

Startled awake, Theo shied from her wagging finger. I shielded him from her spite, and tucked Rosie behind me. "Then you will have heard him taunting my daughter."

"He did no such thing! You should know better than to let your girl run wild. She's dangerous. I'll have her expelled. Children like her shouldn't be allowed."

I scanned the woman's waspish colours, broken with scarlet anger, and realized where her son had learned to bully. Apologies would count for nothing here. Picking up Rosie, I turned away, grateful to have her to hold, to stop me from shaking. "Don't you walk away from me," the woman shouted, but I did exactly that – anything, *anything*, to get away from those gawping faces and accusing eyes. "You're not fit to be a mother!" she yelled as a passing shot.

"Rosie, don't stick your tongue out at people, please," I said quietly, as we crossed the road. When we reached the pavement, I rearranged her twisted skirt and brushed the hair from her sombre eyes. "Has that boy said things like that before?"

"He's horrible," she said, subdued.

"I heard what he said. It isn't true. People say nasty things when they don't understand, or when they're unhappy inside."

"Like his mummy? She's all orange." She pulled a face.

"I expect so. Come on; we'll go home and take Ollie his carrot." I took her small hand and we wove along the crowded pavement back towards the car.

A dark-haired woman in sunglasses and a nondescript suit, and partially obscured by moving people, stood by the car. I picked up the pace. As we neared, she bent down to retrieve something from between the gutter and the wheel, and in straightening, bumped into me.

"I'm so sorry," I said automatically, but she walked away without acknowledgment and was lost to view among the other parents. "Oh, all right then," I scowled at her back, by now well and truly fed up with the afternoon's events.

Rosie's clear voice lifted over the heads of the pedestrians. "Mummy, that lady's rude."

"Shh, Rosie! She probably didn't see me."

"She did. I saw her see you."

Unlocking the doors, I hustled her into her seat. "Then perhaps she's had a bad day, or something's on her mind."

"But she wasn't wearing a hat!" my daughter objected.

I opened my mouth to explain the colloquialism, then decided enough was enough. Theo yawned, exposing pink gums and the tips of his first teeth. "I think we'd better get home. Ollie will be waiting in the paddock and Theo can find some more ants to chew."

The afternoon's drama was forgotten the instant Rosie spied her father on the roof of the house on our return.

"When did you get back?" I called up to him, shading my eyes from the afternoon sun. "And what on earth are you doing up there?"

"About an hour ago. You weren't back so I thought I'd take a look at that slipped tile. Hello, Rosie-posy, how's my girl?"

"I missed you, Daddy."

Matthew did a controlled slide to the edge of the roof, clung for a second to the eaves box, and dropped the thirty or so feet to the cobbled yard, landing lightly on his feet.

"Don't do that!" I exclaimed, when I found my voice.

Rosie jumped up and down on the spot. "Daddy's Spider-Man."

He picked her up and hugged her, then extended an arm to pull me close, and kissed his son's sticky cheek. "I wish you would use a ladder like any other person," I grumbled, but he grinned and ruffled my hair.

"I missed you all. Home is where my family is."

"Daddy, Theo says he wants a puppy."

"Does he, indeed?" He tried to look serious. "And I expect you would like a puppy, too?" She nodded vigorously, and I raised a quizzical eyebrow only to be met with his slight frown and shake of the head. I decided distraction would be more effective than an outright "no", which would only result in a flood of questions.

"Do you think Theo would like to visit Ollie now, Rosie?"

Rosie looked thoughtful for a moment. "Yes, but he would

prefer a puppy. Can we have a puppy, please, Daddy?" She turned blue orbs on her father.

"Sweetheart, we can't..." he began, already seeing her face fall.

"But we have a puppy," I pitched in. "Look at his fabulous fur!" And I ruffled Matthew's hair, making it stand in windblown sheaves of corn-gold. "He looks just like a Golden Retriever."

"Daddy's not a puppy!" Rosie objected, giggling despite the pout she tried to adopt as her father pretended to lick her face, but snuffled her neck instead, then rolled onto his back, dragging her with him until she forgot to object and plead in the tangle of laughter and limbs that followed.

The phone was ringing as we tumbled into the kitchen through the back door. Rosie dashed off to the study, and came back after a few minutes with the handset. "It's Granny," she said, with an air of importance reminiscent of the Annunciation. Depositing Theo on the floor, I took the phone.

"Darling, I am *so* sorry to hear the terrible news. Matthew must be devastated," Mum rushed, without further preliminaries.

"News? What news?"

"Rosie's just told me Pat and Henry are dead. I had no idea." Rosie, swinging her legs on her chair at the kitchen table, colouring in and humming to herself, appeared oblivious to the confusion she had created.

"Mum, no, they're fine. I think she must has dreamt it. Or something."

"Oh." A pause. "Well, that's wonderful, darling. So when she said, 'Daddy's mummy and daddy are dead', she meant...?"

I did a quick double take. "Er, I think she must have confused 'passed on' with 'moved on' – as in moved away. To Arizona. Where they now live."

"I see. Well, I must say, I'm relieved to hear it. We're very fond of them, as you know. We were a little surprised when you said you hadn't been to see them recently. I know you live a long way away, but still, Matthew doesn't want to let too much time slip by. Pat and Henry aren't getting any younger, and I'm sure they would appreciate a visit."

"Talking of which," I said brightly, "Matthew and I were discussing Theo's christening and wondered whether you would mind if we came home – to Stamford, that is – and…"

"Darling, that's a wonderful idea. We could have tea here – I'm sure Beth and Rob would like to cater for it. Your father will be so pleased." Brimming with enthusiasm, she chatted away quite happily until she came to a breathless stop. "I almost forgot. Rob wants a quick word; have you a moment?" I heard a fumbled exchange as she passed the phone over, and then, "Emma?"

"Rob, hi. Is everything OK? How did it go?"

"Just fine and dandy," my brother-in-law said in his soft Scottish burr. "The papers came through and they're all signed, sealed and will be delivered if the solicitor gets his finger out. How's it feel to be a partner in the catering and hospitality business then, Em?"

I laughed. "Not me. That's strictly Matthew's business. I wouldn't have a clue where to start."

"Ah, well," Rob sighed, "I know we've been a bit slow taking up the offer…"

"Four years slow," I pointed out, slipping my jacket off and draping it over the back of a chair.

"Yes, well, we didn't want to be taking your money, but to be honest it couldn't have come at a better time. We got the place for a knock-down price because we paid cash, and the kitchens are usable with a good scrub until the rest of the refurb work is completed."

I detected he still wasn't comfortable taking money from us. "It's a business partnership, Rob, not charity. Matthew will expect a good... return – if that's the right word – on his investment."

"Oh, aye, and no doubt you'll be visiting every so often to make certain your money's being well spent.'

"Definitely. Mum will want to see Theo's new teeth."

"And, of course, you'll be wanting a complimentary five-course meal."

"We wouldn't want to eat the profit margins." We both laughed, and I marvelled at how adept I'd become at skirting the issue of eating.

"We'll be as rich as Croesus before you know it and I can buy an Aston Martin like your husband's. How's it running, by the way?" Matthew had traded in his car for something newer and faster and still decided it wasn't fast enough, so had had it modified. It had caused quite a stir on campus, and I had spent a good week or so being plied with questions by curious students and envious staff (mostly men, I noted wryly) about engine capacity, which was pointless, given I didn't know, and cared even less. At least he had opted to have it sprayed his trademark cranberry, which I did like, although it hardly blended in and could be seen from miles away. Rob detected my lack of interest and thankfully moved the conversation on.

"Anyway, I just wanted to say thanks. Yes, yes, I know, it's business," he said quickly, as I began to interrupt. "But thanks, Em – to you both – for enabling it to happen."

"You're welcome. I'm glad we were able to, and I'll make sure I tell Matthew when he's finished mending the roof."

"Good," Matthew said later that evening in the study, once he had tamed Rosie's exuberance with a story from her favourite book, and Theo had dozed off in the crook of his arm, lulled by the soothing timbre of his father's voice. With care, Matthew placed the snoozing baby on a pile of cushions, Theo's leg twitching occasionally as he slept. "Beth and Rob have a solid business plan and will make the restaurant work, if anyone can. They just needed the means to do so." He stood, and from his document case he had left by the desk, took a wedge of papers to do with my sister's new restaurant. Opening the panel in the wall, he revealed the hidden safe, and then slid the rear section aside. From its depths, he removed the battered metal box. I expected him to make me go through the complicated procedure to open it, but instead he negotiated the subtle clicks and turns until we heard the small click of successful deactivation. He lifted the lid with care, releasing the smell of parchment and wax seals, checked the small bottles containing the chemicals and the detonator next to them, and began to sort the papers into a new folder.

I took the journal in its wrinkled leather bag from the case. The pages had survived remarkably well, but when I looked at it now, precious though it had always been, it came with a caveat. Unbidden, I saw the light fading from Guy's face as the water rose around him. "*Em'ma*," he whispered from among the pages. I closed the journal and put it back, jogging one of the cardboard sleeves as I did so. Deliciously antique writing peeped out at one corner of the folder and something fell onto the desk with a clunk. A key. I reached out to take it. "What's this? I don't recognize it."

Matthew intercepted, and popped it back out of sight in the corner of the box. "Just an old key," he said, and put the new folder on top, shut the lid, and replaced the box.

Theo's naps were getting shorter, just as Rosie's had done at his age. He began to croon as he always did before waking, and

Matthew picked him up. Together, we went next door into the drawing room where Rosie was chatting away to herself as she played. It reminded me of the earlier incident and it hurt. Matthew patted the sofa and I sat next to him, welcoming his stalwart presence. "You're a bit pensive this evening; are you all right?"

I lifted my shoulders briefly. "I'm OK. Glad you're back, though." I craned my neck and kissed him swiftly on the cheek, and took possession of his spare arm.

"Mmm. So what's bothering you?" Rosie busied herself on the other side of the room, building a complex structure from Lego, seemingly in another world. "Rosie?" he mouthed.

"Friends," I whispered back. "She doesn't seem to have any."

"Oh? What about those two in her group? Jamie and Clara, isn't it?"

I shrugged again and he looked nonplussed. Rosie, oblivious, pushed something small and almost round through a channel of bricks with her finger, squinting after it. She seemed to be telling herself a story.

"Has she said anything?"

I told him about the incident outside the school and we watched Rosie play, unable to express the creeping despondency we both felt. "We can't change her, Matthew, any more than you could yourself," I said eventually.

"Yes, I know, but she's the one who has to live with the consequences of it. Theo, too, in all probability."

"It's not so bad." I hugged his arm around me. "It could be worse. I'll keep an eye on things and have a word with her teacher if need be. Surely she's not so very different from other children of her age, is she?" We both looked at our daughter. On the other side of the room, things were getting exciting as Rosie's monologue accelerated and she began waving her arms about, helicopter fashion "What are you building, poppet?" I asked.

"It's a zig'rat," she said, slightly indignant that the higgledy-piggledy multicoloured bricks needed further explanation. "Nanna's zig'rat," she added, beaming. "She lives in there," and she pointed to the haphazard pyramid rising in the middle.

"Ah." I counted to three. "Rosie, darling, the ancient ziggurat of Ur was built for the *god* Nanna to live in, not your Great-Nanna. It was built about four thousand years ago," I added, helpfully. There followed a momentary pause as Rosie considered this latest piece of information.

"It might be Great-Nanna," she said, eventually. "Great-Nanna was very old."

"Yes, but not *that* old, sweetness. Nor was she a god."

Rosie pursed her pink lips. "Daddy's old. Daddy can live in there." She bent down and fished something from inside the cave-like entrance.

Smothering a smile, Matthew canted his head. "What do you have there?"

She hid her hands behind her back. "Nothing."

He did one of those disconcerting things I always forgot to do when challenged by our daughter's obstinacy: he didn't react. She squirmed under his scrutiny, and stepping carefully between the loose bricks, came up to us. The object rolled unevenly in the palm of her outstretched hand.

"Daddy's nutmeg! Rosie, you know you mustn't touch the things in the cabinet!"

"Emma, it doesn't matter…"

"And it's cracked. It wasn't cracked before. Daddy has had that for hundreds of years; it's very special." I saw my daughter's face crumple, and swallowed my dismay. "Rosie, I'm sorry. I didn't mean to be cross."

"Let me see." Matthew took the nutmeg and rubbed his finger over the hairline fault in the worn wood of the fruit. "There. It's only a crack in the outer case, just as it would have done if I had left it on the island to grow into a tree. No harm done." He lifted her onto his knees with his spare arm and she hid her face in his neck.

"Sorry," she said in a small voice.

He kissed her hair. "That's all right, sweetheart, but don't play with the things in the cabinet. If you want to see them, we'll show you, but there are pieces in there which are dangerous..."

"Like the big knife?"

"Yes, and some things which are very delicate..."

"The hippi-campus?"

"Like the glass hippocampus. But most of all, next time Mummy or I ask you something, tell us the truth straight away. There can be no room for secrets in this family." He closed his eyes briefly, his mouth forming a solid line. "Not any more." He smiled then, and put her on her feet and handed Theo to me. "Come and show me your ziggurat. What were you using the nutmeg for?"

"It's a ballista. It goes, wheeeeeeeeee spooosh!" The imaginary weapon of her fingers flew over her head and landed in the centre of the structure, scattering plastic bricks. "The Termites have won!" she declared in triumph. Newly awake, Theo bounced on my knee.

It took a moment for the penny to drop. "Elamites, do you mean, Rosie? The people who defeated Ur?"

"Elamites, belemnites, ter-mites!" she sang out. "The zig'rat is like a termite mound, isn't it? And *a-ll* the people run round like this." Her fingers now became little figures scurrying around the remains of the structure. "People build buildings and termites build mounds."

"And the ballista?" Matthew asked, puzzled.

"People go bash, bash, bash and break the things they build.

Why do people do that, Daddy? Why do people hurt the things they make?"

"I suppose," I said thoughtfully when we were finally alone, "that she does come across as a little... *different*, to the uninitiated." I yawned and pulled the duvet over me. "One thing's for sure. I'm going to have to work on her chronology, although Nanna would have thought it very funny to be considered worthy of a step pyramid. And I'm not entirely certain ballista were in use in that period, either." I stared at the ceiling, thinking. "Actually, they probably were."

Beside me, Matthew laughed softly. "And you think Rosie might be seen as different!"

I nudged him carefully in the ribs, and he had the grace to pretend he felt it. "I'm not the one teaching elementary science to a four-year-old."

"Point taken, although I've had to reassess the situation and up my game."

"Why?"

"She was getting bored."

Rolling over, I propped myself on one elbow and looked at him. "I'm not sure things are going to get any easier for Rosie at school. She laps up everything we teach her and just wants more. She plays it down at school, but she's finding it difficult to disguise her differences."

"Has she said so?"

"Not in so many words, but she doesn't always realize what might be viewed as unusual and what won't. At some point, someone is going to notice." I laid my hand on his chest, feeling the beat of his heart against my skin. "Matthew, there's going to come a time when we have to move on from here." His muscles tensed under my hand as he sat up, dislodging it.

"I'm on the verge of a breakthrough, Emma. I have Matias and Sung working on the project full tilt, and we are this close – " he held up his thumb and index finger with barely a sliver between them, " – to cracking the code. I can't leave my research now – I can't train anyone else to achieve what they do – not without years of work. And then there's E.V.E…"

"E.V.E. is just software…"

"It's more than that, Emma – much more – and without Henry…" He stopped and looked away. "Without Henry, I can't hope to re-establish the programs within a reasonable timescale."

"You don't have to pretend, Matthew. I know you don't want to leave just yet in case Henry decides to come home."

He exhaled slowly. "Just a while longer, Emma; give me a little more time and then… then we can move on and make a new life. In the meantime, perhaps we can get Rosie onto an accelerated curriculum at school so she won't get so bored. There might be children there she will get on with."

Elementary

The sounds of children playing swarmed through the open classroom window with the cooling autumn air, and the middle-aged woman rose and closed the casement. "They get noisy at recess," she explained, sitting down at the desk in front of which we sat.

"I expect they are enjoying themselves," Matthew remarked, mildly.

She tucked her greying sharp-cut hair behind one ear and produced a neat blue school folder with Rosie's name on it. She cleared her throat. "Rose," she began, avoiding our gaze. "She's an... interesting little girl."

"Interesting?" I said. "In what way?"

She ran her tongue over her teeth, adopting a professionally cool smile. "I'm glad you came to see me. I was going to call you. There are some issues..."

"She's having problems making friends," I intercepted, before she mentioned the recent incident with Bully Boy. "We were wondering whether there might be another friendship group she could join – in an accelerated class, perhaps?" The teacher's face sagged. "Not that she doesn't like being in this class, of course," I hastened to add. "It's just that she, well, she gets..." I floundered for a better word, "... bored, and we wondered whether she might find more friends in an accelerated learning group. There are such things, aren't there?"

Colour flared along the woman's neck. She opened the folder containing what looked like at least a dozen pages of typed and handwritten notes. "Rose does have some friendship issues surrounding play and socialization..." she said carefully.

"He was calling her names!"

"... and there are some concerns about her cognitive development." She let the implication settle in the following silence, broken only by the cacophony outside.

"Cognitive development? In what sense?" Matthew said evenly, giving me time to recover.

She gave a little cough. "Child Development studies have shown that children of working parents sometimes do take more time developing skills. It's to do with the amount of time spent reading and playing with them. Children develop at different stages. I'm sure it's nothing to be worried about."

"Can you be more precise?" Matthew continued to smile, but I detected a certain coolness about it. So did she. Small pucker marks appeared around her mouth as she pursed her lips.

"I'm sure you are aware that the school expects a certain level of attainment, and there is competition for places..." Matthew's expression hardened and the teacher hurried an explanation. "Rose is withdrawn in class. She doesn't mix with the other children and can't complete quite basic tasks..."

"Such as what?" I butted in.

The teacher glanced at a list in front of her. "Simple colour coding, a Draw-a-Person test, matching pairs – and she was unable to respond to visual prompts: she couldn't identify a picture of a bug."

"Did you ask her to classify it?" I said shortly. "She's been able to correctly identify dozens of subspecies of dinosaur since she was three, she can write whole sentences, and was building a ziggurat only the other evening."

"Excuse me?"

"Ziggurat. A stepped pyramidal structure, built... oh, it doesn't matter. The fact is she can do all these things and you're saying that she has *cognitive* difficulties?"

"That and other... challenges. Mrs Lynes, we haven't seen Rosie do any of the things you mention. It's only natural for parents to be anxious about their child's progress and to see things that are, well, frankly not there. The truth is that Rose is very withdrawn in class and sits and talks to herself and stares out of the window. She won't even answer questions. Sometimes I don't think she's even listening."

I leant forward, ready to argue, but Matthew put a hand on my arm. "What do you suggest?"

She gave me a quick, worried look before answering. "My advice is that we look at a remedial programme for Rosie. It'll take things more slowly and allow the therapist to work with her at her own pace."

I almost choked. "Therapist?"

"For her eating disorder. She refuses to eat with the other kids and she's been caught spitting food out when she thinks no one is looking. It's the recommendation of our Child Development specialist. I know it can be a shock," she said, gently, "but with early intervention, it's amazing what can be done."

We waited for her outside, standing apart from the other parents where we couldn't be overheard.

"I don't believe it!" I fumed, ramming my hands into my pockets.

"It certainly doesn't ring true," Matthew agreed.

"You don't seem very upset."

"Upset? Why should we be? It's hardly an accurate assessment of our daughter, is it? I'm more concerned that they referred her to a Child Development specialist."

"Why?"

"Because the data might be collated and entered into the system. We should have been consulted and then we could have prevented this. One thing's for certain: she can't stay at the school. Still," he said, "before we act, we'd better have a chat with Rosie and see what she's been up to." The school bell shrilled, heralding a multicoloured stampede of children. "Here she comes now."

Rosie shot out of the door, instantly recognizable by her Red-Setter hair and determined expression, and headed towards the school gates. Before she had gone more than a few steps, she turned around at the sound of her name, and a couple of older children of about eight or nine emerged from the building. They called to her and she stopped, uncertain. Clearly, through the general end-of-day commotion, came a mocking chant. "Lazy Daisy, crazy lady, out, out, out..."

Her face clouded and she dropped her bag. Her fists bunched.

"Oh, no..." I started forward, but Matthew was already ahead of me.

"Rose!" At the sound of his voice, she lowered her arm. He reached her, and bending down, spoke. She nodded and took his hand. He turned, and fixed her persecutors with a steely eye, said something short and to the point, and they scarpered along the pavement, bags banging against their legs as they ran.

"They laughed at me."

Matthew lifted her onto the wooden climbing frame he had built beside the orchard, from which I could keep an eye on her from beneath the shade of the summer trees. "Who did, sweetheart?"

"The children did. When I first went to school, Miss Thompson asked what the moon is and I telled her."

"What exactly did you tell her?"

"I said a moon is a sat'llite that orbits a planet and that Earth has one moon, but Jupiter has lots and lots and I like Io best because it looks like a marble, and Amalthea because it's orangey-red like a berry." She imitated popping something into her mouth and scrambled to the top of the frame in seconds. "I said our moon reg'lates the tides and luna cycles and luna means moon in Latin and I like Latin, but Miss Thompson said nobody likes a know-it-all and the children laughed at me and I said my daddy told me and he and my mummy know lots of things." She crossed the balance beam, hopped onto the slide and emerged moments later at the bottom. "But she asked me a question, Daddy," she added indignantly, "and I answered it."

I removed the piece of chipped bark from Theo's dribbly fist and put him in the baby swing by the mulberry tree. "So, now when you're asked a question, you pretend you don't know the answer, is that it?"

"Yes." She danced over to the monkey bars, skimmed up a pole, and began swinging from one to the next.

"Rosie, what do you like best about preschool?"

Dangling from the middle bar with one hand, she paused. "Going home," she said, letting go and landing lightly. "Can we go and see Ollie now, please?"

"Harry!" she squealed when we entered the courtyard to find him sitting on my bench soaking up the sun, and ran to meet him.

He swung her in an arc. "Hey, Chipmunk! How's my favourite great-aunt?" She giggled as he tipped her upside down. "And is Ottery behaving himself?" He addressed her toy otter. She wrinkled her nose at him.

"He's always doing this," she said, making her otter dance on Harry's chest.

"Hi, Harry," I greeted him.

"Emma, how are you?" He hugged me warmly, pulling a face at Theo in my arms and making him laugh. "And how's my little man? Not so little, huh? Whew, you've grown," he said, taking him from me, and then lighting in a grin as he saw Matthew. "Thought I'd stop by and catch up, if that's OK with you both?"

Matthew embraced him. "You know you are always welcome. Come inside and tell us your news."

Matthew gave Theo a piece of cucumber to gnaw and cool his gums. "So, you were just passing. Colorado via Maine: a bit out of your way, isn't it?"

Harry put his glass down on the table, leaving a moustache of milk across his lip, and wiggled his eyebrows at the children. "Yeah, well, I've been to see Gran and Gramps."

"Ah." Matthew's expression gave nothing away of the sudden flush of painful regret that ripped through him. "How are they?"

"Gran misses Maine; she doesn't like the Arizona heat."

"And Henry?"

Harry borrowed Theo's discarded bib and wiped the milk from his lip. "He's OK."

"Would you like to elaborate?"

He folded the bib several times, then glanced at Rosie, who listened with wide-eyed interest.

I lifted Theo out of his high chair. "Rosie, please take Theo and read him his favourite book; he likes it best when you read to him."

"I want to hear Harry's story," she objected.

"Rose," I warned, and she reluctantly slid off her chair and hefted Theo into her arms, his legs dangling. Harry waited until the kitchen door swung shut.

"He hasn't said so, but Gramps is still kinda mad at you." He paused, rotating the empty glass on the table in front of him. "He's stopped dying his hair grey, won't wear glasses or contacts any more, and he's shaved." He glanced up. "He looks like you, Matthew – just like you."

Matthew didn't respond, but twisted his worn signet ring until it sat true on his finger. He pressed the pad of his index finger onto the deep engraving, examining the resulting light imprint of his family coat of arms. "Has he said anything else?"

"He hasn't mentioned you. Gran won't say anything, of course – she won't be disloyal – but she misses the family and seeing the children – and you, Emma; she really misses you. But Gramps won't change his mind. I've tried talking to him, but he changes the subject, and if I press him, he just gets up and walks out."

Matthew nodded, his mouth raised in a scant smile. "He was stubborn even as a boy." He took the remains of Theo's tea to the sink, and began washing the plate. "I could always talk him around, but then in the past he always trusted me and listened to what I had to say." He leant his hands on the edge of the sink and bowed his head, water flowing pointlessly. Harry and I swapped worried looks. Rising, I went over and switched off the tap and placed a tentative hand on his back.

"Matthew?"

"Four *years*, Emma. He won't even acknowledge my letters."

"Give him time, darling..."

He rounded on me, taking me by surprise, his eyes flaring. "Time? I have time, but with each year that passes, his grows less, until..." He brought his temper under control, but it stemmed not from anger, but frustration and guilt. "Four years. He's not seen Rosie since she was barely a month old and he's never even met his brother," he finished, in shades of despair.

"Daddy?" We hadn't seen Rosie come into the kitchen and now she tugged anxiously at his sweater, her scattering of freckles coppery in the afternoon sun. Wordlessly, he bent down and picked her up, his face hidden in her vibrant hair. A crash came from another room.

"Golly. Theo," I said, and rushed to find him. A strange twanging sound came from the study. Theo looked around as I opened the door, his hand raised. He smiled his gummy grin. On the floor in front of him lay the lute-like cittern. He thumped it with a stout hand, making the wires vibrate tinnily. He gurgled, dribbling.

"He's teething, huh?" Harry came in and sat cross-legged next to us on the floor. "I don't think I was as good-tempered when I was cutting teeth."

I wiped my son's chin. "I doubt you were as bad as Joel makes out."

"I think I probably was." He plucked a string, sending a thin, clear note into the air. "Matthew taught me to play the cittern. I thought it was a strange instrument to play, but then…" He shrugged.

"His grandmother taught him when he was a boy. Citterns were all the rage when she was young."

He ran his fingers across the strings, thinking. Theo bounced and waved his arms in response. "That must have been, when… fifteen-o-something?"

"Something like that."

"Strange." He picked up the instrument and balanced it on his knee. "It's strange, but now that I know his story, I find I don't have the same doubts I used to. Remember? When we were decorating that Christmas tree?"

"I remember."

He nodded, and played a few notes. "Joel and Ellie are OK with it; Dad, too. Mum not so much. She pretty well freaked out. You know how she always thought we were abnormal? Yeah, well, now she thinks Matthew's some kind of monster." He plucked hard at a string, sounding a harsh note like a broken piano wire, and Theo's mouth opened in an exaggerated "o". "Sorry, little fella." He strummed softly, picking up a melody I'd often heard Matthew play in the early, sleepless hours before dawn. "Your dad's no monster. I was thinking about it, and it occurred to me that Matthew's as much part of creation as I am. I reckon he's not cursed by this life, but blessed, whatever he might think sometimes." He coloured slightly under his tan. "That's what I think, anyway."

"And I think you're right, Harry. Who are we to second-guess God? 'God moves in a mysterious way His wonders to perform. He plants His footsteps in the sea and rides upon the storm.'"

"I don't know that. Is it Old Testament?"

"Er, not exactly. William Cowper, an eighteenth-century English poet."

Harry smiled and shook his head. "I should have guessed it would have something to do with history. I wonder if Matthew ever met him?"

I grinned. "It wouldn't surprise me."

"I didn't. I'd left England by then." Matthew moved from where he and Rosie stood by the door. "I see you can still play, Harry."

Harry held the cittern out to him. "Not as well as you, Old Man."

Matthew smiled, losing the lost look of moments before as he took it. "I've had a good deal more practice. Rosie's coming on, though, aren't you, sweetheart?"

I made room for Matthew and Rosie to join us on the floor.

"Theo wants to learn too, by the look of it." Theo obliged my maternal pride by grabbing the end of the cittern and trying to chew it. Matthew removed it from his grasp and instead showed him how to pluck a string. He watched, enthralled. A ribbon of envy scrolled out of Rosie.

"Perhaps you could show Theo how to play, Rosie?" I suggested, and she agreed with alacrity, balancing the cittern awkwardly across her stretched-out legs. Harry watched the children for a few moments. From the pocket of his jeans he pulled a mobile phone. "Would it be OK if I take a photo of Emma and the kids? Pat would love to see them – Dad, too. I'll make sure you're not in it," he added, as Matthew hesitated.

"Go ahead, but don't print them out or send them a soft copy. We made that mistake before. Keep them on your phone and then delete them as soon as you can."

"Sure. No one else will see them." Harry took several shots of the children and me bathed in soft evening light. He then handed the phone to us. "Thought you might like to see some of Charlie; he's grown so much in the last few months." He had indeed. We hadn't seen him since Easter and the slim little boy gazed thoughtfully at the camera with dark eyes, his oak-brown hair curling on his forehead. He looked more like Guy than Dan now.

"I guess it's better he doesn't look much like a Lynes," Harry commented. "He won't have to find ways of making himself look different." I couldn't find anything to say, and Matthew filled the awkward gap.

"Hopefully we'll see him before too long. I've asked Ellie, your father, Joel – and Maggie, of course – if they'll join us for Thanksgiving. Do you think you can make it this year, Harry?"

His smile broadened into a grin. "If Emma's cooking, try and stop me!"

"I'll put the oven on," I muttered. "The turkey'll have to climb in by itself. I expect Matthew will end up doing most of it."

Harry laughed. "With an invitation like that, I couldn't refuse."

In a single elegant movement, Matthew stood. He retrieved something from his desk and slipped an envelope into Harry's hand. "Henry doesn't answer my letters and I don't know whether he even opens them. If you see him, please give this to him and do whatever you can to make sure he reads it."

Harry looked down at the heavy cream envelope decorated in Matthew's fine script, his good-natured features sombre. "Sure. I won't leave until he does."

"Thank you." Matthew clasped his shoulder, straightened and conjured a lighter mien.

"Now," he said, "tell us what you've been up to."

14

Special Delivery

"I'm so pleased for you." I hugged Matias and got a bristly kiss in return. "Matthew told me; I hope you don't mind. What a relief. Now perhaps you can get on with life and look forward to this little chaplet's arrival." I patted Elena's bump as I passed her. "And all those sleepless nights, sicky bits on your shoulder, colic, nappies…"

"Cheers." Matias accepted the beer and sat down on the sofa, making it wheeze. "I'm having second thoughts about this; can we send it back?"

Elena flicked her fingers in a dismissive gesture. "Don't be silly, Matias. Emma, what is nappees?"

"Diapers," I clarified. "It's so hot for late September. Sit down and take the weight off your feet while you can."

She slid a sly smile in her husband's direction. "Matias has been doing a lot of that lately."

He stretched his arm out along the back of the sofa and closed his eyes. "I have to get some training in, you understand. It's never too soon to start. I'm baked – and it's not just this heat. That husband of yours must have been a slave driver in another life."

"No, not that I'm aware of," I murmured.

"Well, he certainly knows how to crack the whip when he wants to, that's for sure." He opened one eye and peered at me.

"Do you know how many times I've run the data on the gene sequences through that wretched program?" I took a sip of iced tea and shook my head. "No, well, neither have I. I've done it that often I'll be doing it in my sleep next. What the heck is he looking for? Has he said? Because he sure hasn't told us. Sung asked him outright the other day, and Matthew just smiled and gave him another sequence to analyse. Even Megan's seeing him in a new light, and it isn't favourable. What's he playing at?"

"Haven't a clue."

"Matias snores," Elena giggled. "He sounds like a pig." She imitated him and prodded his stomach with a painted nail. Matias grunted, looking put out.

"I wouldn't mind so much, but Matthew makes me feel old just looking at him. Bet he doesn't snore," he grumbled. "He doesn't even look tired." I was saved from finding an answer as the shrill tone of the doorbell cut through the limpid afternoon heat.

The scent of dry earth and shrivelled grasses accompanied the gush of warm air as I opened the door. A man in a brown uniform and plain peaked cap held out a parcel. Sweat darkened patches beneath his arms.

"Matthew Lynes?"

"No. I mean, he's not in, but he lives here."

The man's eyes roamed the shaded hall behind me before coming back to rest on my face. "Delivery," he stated. "Sign here." He produced a handheld gadget with an electronic signature box. It smelled new and plasticky and the smooth black surface felt hot in my hands. I did a quick squiggle and exchanged it for a parcel the size of a shoebox.

"Ma'am," he said, and returned to the waiting van puking fumes into the overheated afternoon air.

I left the parcel on Matthew's desk and went back to my friends. "Package for Matthew," I said.

Matias squinted at his watch. "At this hour?"

"Must be a special delivery. You're empty; want a top-up?"

He proffered his glass. "Bet it's more supplies for these darn tests he's been running. Careful, Em, or he'll start experimenting on you; you know what these science types are like."

Elena snorted, spilling drops of cordial on her maternity dress. "You like experimenting with me."

I held up a hand. "Too much information, thanks. I have a paper to write on 'Cardinal Sin and the Rebirth of the Reformation' and I don't need any such distractions."

Elena smirked. "Da, you've already made two little distractions. Do you think you'll have a third?"

"Golly, girl, Theo's only seven months old, give me a chance."

"I want lots of babies," she declared. "They will all look like their father – little teddy bears. Cute, just like Theo." She bounced my son on her knees, kissing him when he laughed.

"Even the girls?" Matias said with a grimace.

"*All* of them," she declared, wrinkling her nose at the baby.

"Now I know there's another man. Emma, keep an eye on Matthew or I'll be doing a paternity test as soon as the umbilical's cut. Mind you, I wouldn't mind some of his DNA; might stave off old age." He winked and I pretended to find it amusing, but my insides wound up in knots at the thought of it. I should have been used to it by now, but the truth was that comments like this were becoming increasingly frequent and I wondered how much longer they would remain jests before they became barbed.

Matthew was reluctant as ever to discuss moving on when he returned home later that evening.

"But Matias has noticed you haven't aged. How long can we keep this up?"

He shuffled through the pile of post on his desk, not looking at me. "As long as we have to."

"He keeps mentioning it, Matthew. He makes it into a joke, but even so, it's as if he's probing."

"Matias is no threat to us, Emma. I'll ease off the workload."

I felt like slamming my hand on his desk. Instead, I bit my tongue and counted to three. "It isn't the work, Matthew, you're not listening to me. He's tired, yes, but it's more than that: he's curious – about you, your work…"

He faced me, his eyes reflecting the deepening blue of the evening sky. "Emma, I hear you." His gaze dropped to the package on his desk. "What's this?"

Annoyed by the diversion, I growled, "Special delivery. For you," I added, although his name was clearly written on the plain wrapping.

He frowned. "I haven't ordered anything."

Still put out, I gave an impatient shrug. "Perhaps it's from Dan. Or Henry."

He picked it up, fingering the tape sealing the edges. He put it back down without opening it. "Who delivered it?"

"What? Oh, I don't know – a bloke in a brown uniform."

"UPS?"

"No. I don't know. Maybe. What does it matter?"

"Did he have a badge, any form of ID? Think, Emma. Did he?"

"No. He didn't. Why?"

"Did he come into the house?"

"For goodness sake, Matthew, he was just a delivery man! He rang the bell, I signed for the parcel, and then he left. That's all – nothing else – nada."

"Perhaps you're right," he muttered to himself, staring at the package.

"About which bit?"

"Perhaps it is time to move on." He picked up the parcel. "I'll open this later," he said and walked out of the room with it tucked under his arm.

Portland

"Mummy, why is that lady not wearing any clothes?" It was the sort of thing I didn't particularly want to hear sailing on the ocean of hush in the muted gallerias of the museum. Amused visitors turned to watch as I hurried back, Theo struggling in my arms, to find Rosie staring at a splendidly robust young woman. "Is she hot?"

"I expect the artist thought so." I put Theo down and he contented himself playing with my bootlaces while his sister and I contemplated the painting together.

"She's fat," Rosie stated, twirling in the pink tutu, fairy wings, and stripy purple tights she insisted she wore on our educational day out in Portland, despite my reservations and the freezing weather.

"It's the artist's expression of beauty – it was fashionable during the eighteenth century to be well covered."

"I like the clouds," she said, thoughtful, inspecting the dove-grey, Rubenesque cumulonimbus in the background. "She should put some clothes on or she'll get a-ll chilly when it rains." She did a theatrical shiver. "When is the eighteen cen'try?"

I held up my hand, spreading my fingers and counting. "We live in the twenty-first century, so we count back: twentieth century, nineteenth century, eighteenth century. How many is that?"

"Three-tieth century," she replied promptly, proving she had inherited Matthew's mathematical nous, even if she had a way to go with the nomenclature. "Did Daddy meet her?"

"Shh!" I warned, laughing nonetheless, and reduced my voice to a whisper. "I doubt it very much. Come on, I need a cup of tea. There's a good display of historical glass in the café downstairs. We can sit by that." She seemed distracted by something and I followed her stare, but saw only a few people milling in the way people do when in such places – abstractedly and in their own worlds. "What is it, Rosie?"

She did a pirouette. "Nothing," and danced off towards the stairs, with Ottery tucked under her arm. I started to follow, but Theo had found my mobile in my bag. "Not that, young man," I said, trying to retrieve it from him. "Yuk, Mr Sticky Paws." I made a grab for the phone but Theo lobbed it before I could get a grip. It clattered to the hard floor, and slid out of sight behind a screen. "Little monster. Hang on, Rosie," I called. "Theo, no!" To my horror, he had located my purse, and proceeded to tip the contents on the floor. He watched, mesmerized, as shiny coins spun and rolled. I groaned. "You just had to do that, didn't you?"

Rosie trotted over and stood with her hands on her hips, wings quivering. "Theo, that wasn't helpful for Mummy," she scolded, and he grinned. By now we'd gathered a bit of an audience, and my face flushed with embarrassment and the effort of bending over with a baby without my jacket riding up my back and displaying too much. Rosie scrabbled around gathering coins with the help of a middle-aged woman and her son, while I thanked them, and went to find my mobile.

"Ma'am, are you looking for this?" A man with oddly long legs and a navy-blue jacket appeared from behind the screen, and held out my phone face down. He had hard eyes, like grit.

I hesitated, scanned his colours, but they were indistinct. He smiled – the sort you do when you want to reassure someone.

"Ma'am?"

I took it from his outstretched hand. "Yes, thank you." I turned it the right way up; the face glowed, bright and alive. My surprise must have shown because he added, "Just checked to see if your name was on it so I could contact you – say I'd found your cell." His expression remained inscrutable.

Or he could have left it at Reception.

"Right, yes, well, thank you again," I said. He jerked his head in acknowledgment and made for the stairs, looking neither right nor left, and descended them with rapid steps. I watched until he disappeared, oddly rattled, then pulled myself together. "Come on, Theo, let's get that tea and feed the monster."

I popped him into a high chair near a display cabinet of mouthwatering glass in tints of the sea. "Stay with Theo and I'll go and queue. Would you like anything to eat or drink – other than sweets, that is?"

Shaking her head, Rosie wriggled onto a chair, swinging her stripy, sparkly legs, and I went to the long counter, holding my breath past the coffee machine as it coughed fumes in my direction. "Tea, please, and could you possibly warm my son's baby food? Thanks." I perused the display of cakes. The chocolate muffin looked tempting; it would complement the tea and I might persuade Rosie to try a little.

"You're English, aren't you?" a voice said.

I turned to find a woman of about my age with an oddly blank expression in the short queue behind me. "I'm sorry?"

"I just love the English accent. It's so quaint." If she did, neither her face nor her voice betrayed it. "I bet you get that a lot."

"Oh. Right. Thanks. Yes, I do." I took my cup of tea and wished the baby food would hurry up and heat. At the table, Rosie was playing pat-a-cake with Theo to the amusement of couples nearby.

"Whereabouts in England do you come from?" the nondescript woman asked.

"The East Midlands," I said, not really wanting to be drawn into a conversation, nor wishing to appear rude. I found my purse and made ready to pay.

"I went to London once. To the theatre," she persisted. "I saw *The Mousetrap*, you know? Agatha Christie wrote it."

I handed the notes to the man at the till. "Oh. Yes," I replied over my shoulder, tucking the change away in my purse. I felt a tap on my arm. The woman held out a photo of herself squinting in bright sun, taken outside St Martin's Theatre in the West End. I smiled vaguely.

"Lovely. I must get back to my children. It's nice to meet you." I thanked the helpful chap behind the counter and, picking up my cup and Theo's jar of food, extracted myself. But a gloved hand gripped my arm and the scalding tea slopped.

"I am so sorry!" she exclaimed, grabbing a handful of paper napkins and beginning to mop my wrist and the sleeve of my jacket.

"It really doesn't matter," I said. "Please, just leave it!"

She took a step back, her eyes shifting beyond me and towards the range of display cabinets. I spun around. A glossy-haired woman, her dark hair drawn into a tight ponytail, stood in front of the table where Rosie and Theo sat, blocking them from view. She bent towards them.

"Hey!" I called in alarm, the tea forgotten. Whether she heard me or not, I didn't know, but the woman moved away, disappearing between stands of tourists. Rosie was unwrapping something gaudy. She lifted it to her mouth. "Rosie! Don't touch that!" I rushed towards them. Too late, her cheek bulged, the white stick protruding from between sticky lips. "Take that out. Now!" Plucking the sweet from her surprised mouth, I dropped it on the table and began wiping residue from her lips with a tissue. "What do you think you're doing! You know you never take anything from strangers. Ever."

Her mouth quivered. "But she wasn't a stranger, Mummy."

I stopped. "What do you mean?"

"She was that lady we saw at preschool, the one that bumped you and didn't say sorry. She was nice today. And she made Theo laugh."

Heat drained from my face. "How, Rosie? How did she make him laugh? Did she touch him? Rosie, did she touch Theo?"

"She tickled him, like this," and she leaned over and scrabbled her fingers under his soggy chin. He chuckled and blew some bubbles. "Ewe, Theo, you're all dribbly," she giggled.

Alarm bells jangled and my stomach crunched. I hoiked Theo from his high chair. "Get your wings, Rosie, we're going home."

"But Mummy, I need to…"

"Now. Quickly." I couldn't say why, but urgency pressed in from all corners, and every face seemed turned towards us. The Mousetrap woman had vanished and there was no sign of the other.

By the time we reached the car, I was running and breathless, Rosie catching her toes on the pavement as I hauled her along beside me, the wings flapping from one hand.

"Mummy, please, I need…"

"In the car." The locks clicked shut and she climbed into her seat.

"Why do we have to go?"

I checked the mirrors and pulled away from the pavement. "We just do. I have things to do at home."

She fell into mute contemplation of the sleet-grey sky and I concentrated on negotiating the road system. Only once we had left the confines of the town and the perspiration had cooled on my skin did I look around and see the downward turn of her mouth.

"Rosie, I know you were looking forward to seeing the rest of the paintings…"

She traced a drop of rain on her window, her eyes glistening. "I wet myself." From his baby seat, Theo gnawed his fist and was beginning to whimper from hunger. Feeling stupid and a failure, I stopped at the first convenient spot, and helped Rosie out of the car in the privacy of the open door.

"Here, darling," I said, peeling off her wet things and wrapping her in a blanket. "It doesn't matter; it's my fault. You tried to tell me but I didn't listen to you. I'm sorry, baby." I folded her to me, feeling her arms wind around my back, her cheek wet against mine. A car passed, and then another, chipping loose stones from under their wheels as they sped by. "I think we'd better get home; it's starting to sleet."

She nodded and climbed back in the car while I collected her damp clothes and found a corner in the back to put them. I heard another car approaching and scooted into my seat as it neared, and quickly shut the door so it didn't have to swerve further into the road to avoid me. As it passed, I caught a glimpse of a high black ponytail and stony face, but not enough to be sure. I swivelled and followed the tail lights until they vanished around the bend. It had neither slowed nor stopped and the driver gave no indication that she was in any way interested in the car pulled over by the side of the road. But then why did I consciously have to slow my breathing and release my grip on the steering wheel? I realized Rosie was watching me with a worried frown, so I made an effort to smile.

"Right, the road's clear; let's go home," I said brightly. "Perhaps it's snowing there."

"And you're certain it was the same woman you saw by the car at preschool in September?"

"I didn't get a good look at her, Matthew, but Rosie's sure it was her."

Matthew's eyes flicked towards Joel, and the young man picked up my car keys. "I'll go check the car out." He left, securing the kitchen door behind him. Joel had arrived shortly after I told Matthew what had happened in Portland, but we had wasted little time on pleasantries.

"And this other woman – the one who distracted you in the queue?" Matthew asked.

"Distracted me? What, on purpose? So you think they are linked?" My skin ran cold and I shivered.

"Quite possibly." He lifted Theo into his arms. "You're freezing. Let's go through to the study; the fire's lit there."

By the time Matthew had checked on Rosie playing in her bedroom, Joel had returned. He held up a small, rectangular, matt black object, splattered in mud. "Behind the wheel arch," he said, his face grim.

Matthew turned it over in his hands. "One of yours?"

"It's a common enough model, but not one of ours. I checked your car as well, but it's clean."

"Why would anyone want to track me?" I asked, feeling a bit sick. "Isn't it illegal, or something?"

"Without a warrant, yes, and even that's issued only for a short period. But this must have been on your car for the last month, so…"

"It's below the radar," Matthew muttered. "As for why, it can only be to know where you are because they wanted to intercept you, which they did this morning. What did the woman in the queue look like – any distinguishing features?"

"Not really. She didn't smile and she looked sort of… plain. The other woman had mid-length dark hair – very glossy – and a sharp jaw."

"Unnaturally shiny? As if it's been dyed, or a wig?"

"Um, well, it might have been. I don't know."

"And the car that passed you on the road. What did it look like – the make, colour – anything?"

I swallowed. "I didn't notice anything unusual about it; it looked kind of… ordinary." I felt about as useful as fish bones on a Friday. After a bath and a cuddle, and with Matthew's gentle questioning, Rosie had provided far more detail with all the perspicuity of a child. He had also checked both children and, apart from Theo's copious amounts of drool, found nothing suspicious. Our son was now happily exploring the study floor at speed.

"And this is the first time you've thought you were being followed?" Joel asked.

"It's the first time I've noticed," I said, "but then, I wasn't looking before. Anyway, we left immediately. I don't think we were followed and I might have been mistaken about the car."

Matthew ran a hand down his face. "I doubt it." Neither he nor Joel spoke, but a brooding presence filled the space between words. I looked from one to the other.

"What is it?" I asked. "Did I do something wrong?"

"You weren't to know…" Joel began.

"Don't soft-soap me, Joel. If I've done something that's endangered the family in any way, I need to know."

He raised his brow, briefly pursing his lips. "Emma, they spooked you. They wanted you to think you were being followed, and the moment you took the children and left, you confirmed their suspicion."

"Suspicion of what?" I said, aghast.

"That you have something to hide."

"Well, I... I couldn't just... stay there!"

"Sure, why not? What reason has an ordinary, law-abiding citizen on a day out with her kids to suspect she is under surveillance? People with nothing to hide don't run, Emma. You ran."

I flapped my hands in guilty frustration. "I didn't know. I didn't think. But why were they watching us in the first place if they didn't suspect something?"

"That," Matthew said, "is a very good question. As is why they wanted samples of our children's DNA from the saliva on the lollipop and Theo's dribble."

"Is that what they were after?" Joel asked. "It figures, I guess."

Alarm combined with exasperation made for a potent mix. "No, it doesn't!" I exploded. "None of it makes sense. Why did they want their DNA? What are they looking for? What does this mean, Matthew, and who, for goodness sake, are 'they'?" Both men stopped and looked at me as if considering me properly for the first time since Joel had arrived. Matthew spoke first.

"They are likely to be anyone who might take an interest in what we have to offer, or see what we are as a threat."

"A threat to what?"

"National security."

"You're joking! What possible sort of threat are we, let alone a four-year-old and a baby?"

"It's not a question of any discernible threat posed by the individual, Emma, but whether our particular strengths could be used against the State by an organization ruthless enough to develop and exploit them. That's what will concern them, and if the State can use our anomalies to develop their own arsenal in the fight against terrorism or rogue regimes, then all the better."

"But if they're on to you, Matthew, we've got to go – leave now – tonight."

Matthew shook his head. "No, that's the worst thing we can do right now."

"Because only someone with something to hide runs?"

His mouth twitched. "Quite. In the meantime, we'd better take precautions. I'll up the security at this place and advise the rest of the family to do the same. As for our cell phones, we'll keep what we have because they are registered with a network, but we'll have a back-up just in case."

"In case of what?" I asked.

"In case they are using our cell phones to keep tabs on us."

"They can do that?"

"Yeah, sure they can," Joel said. "Every time you use your cell for a call, to text, or browsing the web, you leave a signal that's traceable. We – they – can listen in to conversations, know your whereabouts, who you've talked to, what's your favourite takeout. Smartphones hand all that info on a plate."

"So I'll simply not use it," I said, reaching into my bag.

Matthew shook his head. "That would register as a change in behaviour, which is as good as saying 'I know you're watching', which is the last thing we want."

"Then… then I'll switch the blasted thing off, or remove the battery," I said, cross at being thwarted by something as mundane as a wretched phone.

"Which will also alert them. Who does that nowadays? Just use it as normal, but restrict your calls to asking me to get some diapers at the store and any other day-to-day stuff. You know the sort of thing. For anything else – for emergencies – we'll use burners."

"Burners?"

"Yeah," Joel answered. "Burner phones. They're not registered to a person or network so are more difficult to trace. Ideal for single use – like if we have to contact each other in a hurry. But nothing else – nothing routine that forms a pattern of behaviour that can be traced to you."

"And damn your constitutional rights," I uttered under my breath. Joel raised a quizzical brow, but Matthew obviously remembered the conversation he and I had shared before my trial. He clasped the tops of my arms as he bent his head to look at me directly. "Emma, we always knew this was a possibility."

I squeezed my fists, making my knuckles crack. "I know."

"Joel will replace the tracker where he found it. With any luck they will think your actions today were just those of an overanxious mother, that's all, but we need to warn the rest of the family. If they have tags on us – whoever they are – they'll be watching the others. You, too, Joel."

Unlocking his arms from his broad chest, Joel gave a sharp nod. "I'll get on to it. We need to know who's set this up, and if it's one of the agencies, I'll track it down."

"Can you get anti-surveillance devices? And we should establish a perimeter – something that will buy us some time if it's breached."

"I know the system – uses physical sensors at the outset, with thermal cameras and GPS for accuracy, and video to confirm intrusion. Set up monitors in the kitchen and it'll give you what you need to make a quick decision."

"Good."

"And I'll pick up a couple of automatic weapons just in case of…"

"No!" Matthew brought the flat of his hand against the table with a crack, making the air shake. "There will be no guns."

With a puzzled frown, Joel said, "Hey, I know you don't like them, but they'll as sure as hell be armed, and…"

"I said no guns."

"Why?" Joel demanded. "You always taught us to defend ourselves in whatever way we can. You could stop 'em before they get up too close, buy that time you said you need. They're the ones doing the attacking. *They* are the enemy."

Matthew levelled a stare at him. "And does my enemy suffer any less because he is my enemy? Killing is too easy as it is. No guns, Joel. No. Guns."

It looked as if Joel might push the point, but instead he lifted his hands in acceptance. "OK, sure. If that's the way you want it."

"I do," Matthew said. "It might also make them less inclined to open fire on us. Bullets are indiscriminate in whom they kill." His glance fell on the baby, and a shiver of fear cooled my skin. "Now, there's much to be done and we'd better get started."

The tension left Joel's shoulders and he relaxed into a half-smile. "Yeah, there is. I'll see to it." Theo had crawled to Joel's legs and now hauled himself upright on his wobbly pins. Joel bent to pick him up. "Hey, little fella. We can't have your mom and dad running around the country missing Thanksgiving, can we?" He bopped foreheads with the baby, who gave his customary laugh, his eyes crinkling like his father's and making my heart lurch.

"As for Thanksgiving," Matthew said, "this gives us all the more reason to gather as usual. We'll make a show of our normality, but we'd better start making preparations."

Joel grimaced. "Just in case, huh?"

"Indeed." Matthew smiled – a tight, restrained smile. "Just in case."

"This is it – this is what it's always been like for you, isn't it? This watching and waiting and running."

Joel had left us with a promise he would be in touch as soon as he learned anything, and now Matthew looked around the study as if trying to record this moment before it passed into history, like all the other moments before. The brass lantern clock I had given him as a wedding present marked the minutes before he replied.

"This feels different. Perhaps it's because the children are so young, or that we're settled here. Or that for the first time in my life I have someone without whom I cannot face tomorrow." He canted his head and gave me an odd look filled with pain and regret and longing. "For centuries I've searched for the reason for my continued existence in the hope I can find a cure for this life. But now I don't want to. I want to live, Emma; I want to live for you and our children, and our children's children. And I'm scared. God forgive me, but I am scared that something or someone will take me from you." He looked away and, hearing the break in his father's voice, Theo grizzled. Matthew picked him up and hid his face in his son's baby hair, murmuring softly to him until he settled. Only then did I realize how vulnerable Matthew felt and that I – we – were the reason for that vulnerability. My heart twisted in bittersweet joy.

"Daddy?" Rosie must have slipped into the study unseen, as pinch-faced, she now tugged at his arm. He knelt down, and held her to him. Clasping Ottery, her thumb found its way to her mouth.

"It's all right, sweetheart. There's nothing to be worried about." He kissed her hair and then her brother's forehead, and stood up. "What have you been making upstairs? Would you like to show us?"

"A castle," she replied, taking her thumb from her mouth with a soft "pop". "A castle with walls and a moat and a... a gatehouse where no one can get us. Come and see."

"That's good, Rosie," he said, his eyes meeting mine over Theo's head. "That sounds perfect."

16

Exit Strategy

When everything you've taken for granted suddenly seems to be coming to an end, it brings things into focus. You develop an awareness, as if the mundane veil of the everyday slips, and for the first time, you see what you have to lose, what is at stake. Faced with an uncertain future, you cling to the familiar, while all the time noting each indicator of change – and dreading it. This weight that now fell on us – as thick as smog, and as dulling – sucked joy from our lives as we went about projecting an image of normality, and I felt so disjointed, all at sea. And yet life went on around us – hope, and light, and joy.

"I left it over there." Elena waved a hand in the direction of her desk. "On top of the other papers, I think. Wait, I will look."

"Stay there," I motioned, and she flopped back into her chair. I sifted through the pile of articles as she watched me wearily.

"I do not know how women stand this. My ankles, they swell, and I feel like a *morzh*, a… a wal-rus. Matias says I look beautiful – like his little Russian doll – but then he does not have this to carry around…" She indicated her pronounced bump. "Well, maybe a little," she relented, with a hint of an impish smile. "He eats enough for two…"

"Are you taking my name in vain again?" Matias asked, pushing the door open wide with his foot while balancing a cup on top of the plastic crates he carried. "Emma, sorry, didn't know you were here, or I'd have brought you some tea."

I found the article, took the tea from the crates before it spilled, and handed it to Elena. "Thanks, but I'll get some later. I'll leave you two in peace."

Plonking the crates down, Matias wiped his forehead with his sleeve. "Don't go because of me. We don't see enough of you as it is, and it's likely to be less in the future."

I looked at him sharply. "Why?"

"When this little one is born, I mean," he said, patting Elena's stomach. She grimaced and pried herself from the chair. "I want to go the bathroom again," she moaned. "Don't go away, *da*? I want to know what you think of my article."

I flipped the magazine open, found Elena's piece, and began to read as Matias stacked her books and folders into the crates. I read the first page, then the second, aware he kept throwing me glances. "Like to borrow my reading glasses?" he offered.

"No, thanks, I'm fine." I read on, engrossed in popular culture in Soviet society.

He snapped the plastic lid on one of the crates and eased off the next. "Wearing contacts nowadays, then? Or have you had laser surgery?"

"Oh, no, neither." I pulled at my lip, thinking, and turned the page. So many similarities with my own period of history. How little people changed.

Matias had ceased sorting and stacking. He nodded slowly. "Yeah, I noticed you don't seem to have sight problems any more." I fumbled and dropped the magazine. Matias cocked his head. "You OK, Emma?"

"Yes, fine. Why do you ask?"

"You seem a bit twitchy – Matthew, too. Only, Elena and I... we wondered whether everything's all right between you.

Demanding job, marriage, kids – it can get on top of you." He continued when I didn't answer. "Must be tough teaching Rosie at home – not much time to yourselves. You can talk to ol' Uncle Mat if you ever need to – expert in all things extraordinaire in the bedroom department, if you know what I mean."

"Has Matthew said anything?" I asked, bending to pick up the magazine from the floor, and buying thinking time.

"No, but then he never does, which is why I thought you might."

"Oh."

"He seems more edgy and he's upped the pace in the lab again – everyone's feeling it. He's really pushing to get this project finished. I'm guessing something's on his mind. Not seen him like this since, well, since that trouble you had, you know, when you went back to the UK to recover from the attack. He was devastated when you left, Em, like his whole world had collapsed."

My throat tightened at the memory of the pain I'd unwittingly caused. I coughed lightly to loosen my vocal cords. "No, we're fine, really. The project's important to him, Matias. You know what he's like – can't rest until it's done. I'm sure it's nothing more than that."

"If you say so." His voice softened. "Just remember, if you ever need someone to talk to…"

The words blurred on the page in front of me. *Don't cry; for goodness sake you mustn't cry.* "Yes, thanks."

"Because you two are the closest thing we have to best buddies. I mean it, Emma; we don't want to see you fall apart." I felt his hand on my shoulder, heard the concern in his voice, and I wanted to tell him, I wanted to share the burden. But I couldn't; it wouldn't be fair. They had their lives to lead and deserved to do it in ignorance and peace, no matter what happened in our own. Blow, I'd miss them.

"Hey, it's all right." He put his arms around me, a little awkwardly at first, and then more firmly as he felt me shake. "I don't know what's going on, but I don't like to see my friends in trouble. If you need anything, you know where to come, don't you?" He held me at arm's length, his rumpled face kind. "Promise me?"

I sniffed, not meeting his eyes, and nodded to placate him, and hearing Elena's voice greeting a student outside her door, quickly reassembled my features into a smile. "I must go and leave you to it," I said, swiftly kissing her cheek as she came in. "Great article, by the way. And thanks, Matias." I squeezed his arm as I passed.

"Don't you forget now," he warned as I collected my things.

"I won't," I said.

"Good afternoon, Professor."

I looked up from my laptop. "Aydin, hello. Didn't you get my message about this afternoon's tutorial?"

"*Evet*, but I wanted to see you, if you have moment. I have had response from government. They say I am to be granted citizenship after all."

I surprised him by flinging my arms around him. "That's brilliant news – the best. Now you can complete your doctorate without interruption. Oh..." I stopped as a thought struck me.

"Professor?"

"It's nothing; it doesn't matter." But it did. Who would supervise his thesis, if not me? It had taken him years to get this far and he had only narrowly missed being deported. "I'm sorry, Aydin."

His face drew into a frown. "I do not understand..."

I opened my mouth, but decided my news would spoil his special day. Telling him about our plans to move could wait until after Thanksgiving. "I'll tell you another time. Nothing to worry about." I smiled. "Are you celebrating your new status?"

"Of course! It is Thanksgiving and I have much to be thankful for. You will have celebration too?"

"We will." I switched off my laptop.

"How is my little *gül*? And Theo?"

"Very well, thank you, and Rosie's mulberry tree is twice as tall as she is. I've made you some jam, as I promised. We had loads of mulberries; it's been a good year."

"That is good," he beamed. "I think your fish is looking after you."

Fingering my fish that dangled ever-present from my keyring, I said, "Yes, it is indeed."

Finished for the day, I packed my laptop and swung it over my shoulder. Andrew Marvell queried me with his sidelong glance from the print on the wall, demons leered, but God grasped Man firmly by the hand. "Don't let me go," I whispered. "Please, don't let me go."

It felt almost pointless, braced as we were on the precipice, yet I had to behave as if nothing had changed. And it hadn't. Over the last weeks, my students had still come and gone, I'd marked assignments, given feedback and suggested new paths of enquiry. I smiled and greeted colleagues, went to the occasional staff gathering with Matthew, where we acted out a normal life as normal people do. But I was aware all the time that we might be subject to scrutiny, watched for moving shapes within shadows, a pursuing car, until I suspected even those whom we regarded as friends might be secretly watching us, whispering, taking note. It made me twitchy.

My back flinching like fleas, I entered the library's central void and heard the door close serenely behind me, sealing the lies outside. My bastion against the world. Inhaling the bookish balm, I went straight to the history section as always and selected a few titles at random, spent a few minutes leafing through them, and then made to leave. Thanksgiving was fast approaching and the library was unusually busy as young minds became focused on completing assessments before the break. In the queue to check out my books, I heard a grating hack behind me as phlegm was cleared from a congested throat. Someone leaned close, enveloping me in the scent of stale tobacco and aftershave. My hackles rose.

"Well, well, look who we have here: Professor D'Eresby. Or is it Mrs Lynes? Always said you'd end up married, with kids, and someone else's name."

"Good afternoon, Madge," I replied stiffly, reluctantly acknowledging the leathery Head of Anthropology squinting up at me. "How's the cough?"

"Don't be like that, Emma, my dear. Haven't seen much of you recently. Avoiding my company, or has Matthew been keeping you busy looking after hearth and home like a good hausfrau?"

"And why would I want to avoid you, Madge, I wonder?" I said, unable to resist the caustic twist.

She rasped a laugh. "Good to see that marriage to your dull doctor hasn't blunted your wits after all. Or do you wear the trousers? I'm sure Sam would be willing to fill them." Several students and at least one lecturer were taking an unhealthy interest in our conversation, and had inched closer.

I rolled my eyes. "Give it a rest. Have you nothing else to talk about?"

Her whip-thin eyebrows arched. "Bit touchy, aren't you, my dear? Not getting enough sex, or is Matthew finding his entertainment elsewhere? You know you can rely on me for utter discretion." The queue was moving forward at the pace of a doped slug. The student in front of me had mislaid his ID in one of his bags and was now sifting through each file – thoroughly – to find it. "Or perhaps he's got you pregnant again to ensure you don't stray."

This was getting intolerable. I had almost decided to dump the books and walk away when I saw a familiar figure come through the doors. To my intense relief, he spotted me at once, raising his arm and waving wildly. Madge didn't bother hiding her displeasure. "What does the fool want?"

I counted to three. "I don't know and I don't care, but I find his company amiable, informative and honest, so, if you will excuse me... Hello, Professor!" I returned Colin Eckhart's greeting as he bumbled towards me through a group of second-year students, scattering them grousing like pheasants.

"Ah, Professor D'Eresby! Thursday. Fifteen-hundred hours precisely. I thought you might be here." His pedantry might once have irritated, as might his suggestion that I was predictable. Now, however, I welcomed the brown velvet jacket and stout figure others found comic. Madge eyed him with open dislike, to which he appeared oblivious. "Mrs Eckhart and I are ce... celebrating Thanksgiving. We're having a... a Pilgrims' Supper – authentic seventeenth-century dishes cooked on an open fire – Mrs Eckhart is an authority on historic cuisine."

"What an excellent idea; I've never thought of doing that." I ignored Madge's disdainful grunt.

He pushed his glasses back up his nose. "Mrs Eckhart would like you to join us. And Dr Lynes as well, of co-course."

"I'm sorry, Professor, I would have loved to come, but I'm expecting Matthew's family for Thanksgiving. I'm really sorry. Thanks for inviting me," I said, as his face fell.

"Yes, yes, well, well – another time perhaps." And he poddled off towards the elevator to the history section.

"Another time," I said softly to his retreating back. Why, oh why did it feel like I was saying goodbye? I expected Madge to make some snide remark, and looked around, but she and her spleen had left without me noticing. She was one person I wouldn't miss.

"Good afternoon, Professor," a dry voice said beside me. The queue had moved on and the librarian held out her hand for my books.

"Hi," I said, giving them to her and watching her scan them into the system, then as something to say, "What are you doing for Thanksgiving?"

"It is not a day of celebration for my people. In fleeing their persecution, your people brought it to mine." She said it without malice, but I felt the accusation all the same.

Taken aback I said, "They didn't mean to. Men like Nathaniel Richardson wanted a new life free of the hate and fear they saw where they came from. They didn't want to impose it on anyone else."

"I don't expect they did, Professor, but it followed just the same."

I detected impatient rumblings in the queue behind me. "We all seek freedom from the things that haunt us, don't we, whatever the source, but sometimes we can only find that freedom inside ourselves. Sometimes..." I stopped because in that moment the truth of it struck me.

"Professor?"

I canted my head to look at her thoughtfully. "We're all pilgrims in some respect, aren't we? We're all searching for something, but sometimes it's already found; we just don't see it."

"Emma, a moment, if you please." Siggie caught up with me as I left the atrium and made my way towards the staff car park along the paths blown free of leaves by a chilly wind. In the distance,

I could see Rosie kicking her way towards me through soggy piles of umber and gold and garnet, Matthew with Theo on his shoulders a little way behind. Siggie's own colours fluctuated uncertainly, although she smiled brightly enough.

"I won't keep you, my dear, I can see you are keen to go, but do you know why I might have received a phone call about your employment here?"

"From Cambridge? I thought all that was sorted out years ago."

"No, from somewhere else; he didn't say where, only his name – Kowalski – and he was more interested in how long you've known Matthew."

My husband had swung Theo from his shoulders and was now encouraging him to take steps, but every now and again he shot a quick look in our direction. The breeze crept around my shoulders and found its way down my spine.

"Why on earth would anybody be interested in our relationship? How ridiculous! He could always have asked us," I exclaimed, although it sounded hollow to my ears and probably to hers.

"That is what I said to this man, but he was unable to give me a satisfactory answer. Anyway, I wanted you to know, because I do not like questions being asked about my staff without proper authorization, which is what I told him."

I tucked my blue scarf into my jacket and folded my arms in front of me, a defensive gesture which she probably noted. "What did he say?"

She lifted her shoulders and let them drop. "He said he would get it." In seeing Matthew and the children, and waving to them, she might have missed the colour flee my face. "Ah, what a delightful picture your family make. Living the American Dream, eh?"

She didn't wait for Matthew, but waved again and returned the way she had come, escaping the cold.

"What did Siggie want?" Matthew asked when I joined him.

"Someone's been asking questions about us." Rosie was throwing leaves over Theo, who laughed and rolled in the heaps as he rapidly disappeared beneath them.

"I take it they didn't give a name and designation?"

"A name – if it's a real one: Kowalski."

Matthew raised a sardonic brow. "I doubt it; Kowalski's the Polish equivalent of Smith. Nonetheless, I'll pass it to Joel to check out. Has anyone been following you?"

I now knew the telltale sign of surveillance. "I don't think so."

"Well, we have been followed. He's by the cars pretending there's something wrong with his engine. No, don't look around."

"You should offer to give him a hand, Matthew," I said drily.

"As much as it would delight me to do so, he mustn't know we've seen him. Joel was very specific – make no contact whatsoever. We're just having a wonderful family time together, aren't we?"

I took the hint and gathered a handful of leaves, throwing them into the air for Rosie to chase. She ran after them, then bounced back towards me. "Mummy, look what Daddy gave me!"

Something golden dangled on a stout chain around her neck. "A nutmeg, Rosie?"

"Daddy's nutmeg." She giggled. "Daddy says it'll be safer around my neck than in my hands. And look, it's in a little cage all of its own." She held it on its chain for me to see – the gilded nutmeg rattled in an intricate cage of gold imitating blades of mace.

"It's very pretty," I said, somewhat puzzled.

"Daddy says I'm carrying hope around my neck." She twirled around, scooping an armful of leaves and throwing them above her, and then pounced on her brother.

"I think we've given our shadows enough of a show today, don't you?" Matthew slid his arm around my waist while keeping one eye on the figure in the car park as he kissed my ear. "Time we went home. We have more DIY to do."

The small device in Matthew's hands remained mute as he moved steadily around the dim kitchen. Finally, he switched it off and placed it on the table. I eyed it. "What does it do?"

"It detects multi-frequency signals from surveillance devices. We're clear for the moment at least." He looked around the room. "We'd better get the shutters closed."

"But it's still light," I protested. "Don't shut out the light."

"It'll be dark within the hour. Let's stick to our normal routines. Anyway, I have some tasks that need doing for which I don't want an audience."

I hugged my arms around myself wondering who might be out there watching, and how long we could maintain this façade of normality when inside I felt myself crumbling a little more each day.

"I'm going to phone home."

"You are home, Emma," Matthew said quietly. "This is our home."

"It doesn't feel like it sometimes," I said, more to myself than to him. He began to close the shutters, double-checking that the bars sat securely in the sockets.

"Careful what you say on the phone," he called after me. "Keep it…"

"Normal. Yes, I know."

"Is everything all right, Em?"

"Yes, of course it is, Dad. Why shouldn't it be?" I bit my tongue hearing the prickly tone in my voice. Dad heard it too, but chose not to rise to it.

"It is nearly midnight, or had you forgotten the time difference?"

"I counted backwards instead of forwards – again. Sorry." Idiot.

"Maths was never your strong point, was it, Em? Your headmaster never did understand how someone so bright could fail to master basic mathematics."

"No."

"But then, nor did I." He paused, and down the echoing phone line I heard the long case clock in the hall strike. "I gave you a pretty hard time over it, if I remember correctly. I am sorry, Emma. I'm sorry for all I put you through." He waited for my response and I had to breathe deeply to control the tremor in my voice, but it still came out in a squeak.

"That's OK, Dad."

"It's in the past, hey, Em? It's history."

"Yes, Dad, it's in the past."

We went on to brighter memories, but all the time in the back of my mind came Ellen's warning that a time would come when the only contact with my family would be by telephone as Matthew could no longer disguise his lack of aging, and that which had been so distant a prospect now became a creeping reality.

"And how is Rosie getting on at school?" he asked.

"Ah, well, um, she isn't at school. She's at home."

"Not very well, is she? Poor little lass."

"No, I mean we've taken her out of school, Dad. She wasn't, er, ready."

"Oh?" I heard his disappointment and the effort he made to disguise it. "Well, children develop at different rates, don't they?" he said, in an attempt to be positive. "I'm sure she'll come to it in time." He cleared his throat. "We haven't seen you for quite a while now. Your mother was wondering about this visit you mentioned? The twins are growing like Topsy, and Archie's been at school for a couple of years already – not that it matters, of course. Rosie is that much younger and she's bound to catch up."

"Yes, she will."

"So, a visit is on the cards then, Em? For Theo's christening?"

A visit home? If only things were that simple. And now that the prospect of seeing my family seemed beyond reach – at least for the time being – I felt their absence keenly.

"I think we've left it a bit late to book the church so close to Christmas, but I'll see what I can do," I promised vaguely.

"Right-o," my father replied, with forced jollity. "Love to all." The line went dead except for the persistent whine like the top note of a scent – barely discernible from the background noise of nothing – and then a tiny click and the noise ceased. I replaced the handset, fighting the temptation to yell at whoever had been listening, and went to find Matthew.

He read my expression as I went back into the kitchen, and simply nodded. He spun Rosie into his arms. "Hey, kids, shall we play a game?"

"Horses!" Rosie shouted.

"How about hide-and-seek?" His eyes slid to the pantry, and he quirked one brow.

"All right," I said, taking the hint and capturing Theo as he crawled under the table. "The three of us will hide and we'll see if Daddy can find us."

"Daddy must hide his eyes," Rosie demanded, covering her own. He did as bidden, and we skipped out of the kitchen and into the hall, stifling laughter. Rosie headed for the stairs, but I pulled her back, shaking my head and indicating the dining room door. We sidled into the darkened room and waited.

"Coming, ready or not!" Matthew called. "Where are you?"

Rosie opened her mouth, but I issued her with a warning look and she promptly shut it. We heard the kitchen door swing open, footsteps in the hall. Taking Rosie's hand, I tiptoed across the dining room to the door to the kitchen, cautiously opening it and, seeing the room empty, made for the pantry.

"But, Mummy..." she whispered.

I held a finger to my lips and, opening the pantry door, we slipped into the space lit only by the light from the kitchen. She began to slide the door to the Stables open, but instead I pointed to the floor. At the far edge of the great stone slab, I pressed down hard with my foot. Rosie's mouth opened in surprised delight as the cantilevered slab tipped open, revealing the steps.

"Where are you?" we heard Matthew call from the hall, and without hesitation, Rosie hopped down the steps into the dark void under the floor. I followed with Theo clinging to me, just as we heard Matthew come back into the kitchen making loud stamping noises with his feet.

"Mummy, why...?"

I whipped a hand over her mouth and kissed her head. "Not. A. Word," I breathed. Above us came the sound of doors opening and closing, chairs moving, a loudly muttered, "Now where are they?" Quiet until that moment, Theo suddenly found his voice. He babbled his excitement.

"No, Theo, he'll find us," Rosie moaned softly as we heard footsteps above us, and then the slab opened, letting in the light and Matthew's cheerful greeting.

"Ah, there you are! I thought I heard you."

"The-o!" Rosie protested. "You gave us away." She pushed past me and stumped up the steps to her father, pouting.

"But I didn't hear *you*, Rosie-posy; you were as quiet as a snowflake. I do believe you would have won the game."

"But we didn't, Daddy. You caught us like... like mice in a trap."

"Matthew, how can I keep Theo quiet if I have to? He doesn't understand what's at stake, and the more I try, the louder he gets." To illustrate my point, from his cot on the other side of our bedroom Theo danced up and down in his baby suit, waving Bear and singing his "*da-da-da*" song and blowing bubbles.

Matthew sighed as he rose from our bed. "Let's hope it doesn't get to the stage where we have a need for silence." He went across to the cot and picked Theo up. Father and son regarded each other, each holding the other's gaze, each so alike. Matthew smoothed Theo's pale sand hair and the baby put his hand to his father's mouth, wrinkling his nose and smiling. "Da-da-da," he patted. "Da-da." Wordlessly, Matthew kissed the pudgy fist and laid Theo down, tucking him in with the cot blanket Pat had made for Rosie. From where I was lying, the hand he briefly laid on his son's head made it look as if he was bestowing a blessing, and he murmured something too quiet for me to hear.

"What are we going to do?" I whispered, when he slid back into bed beside me, pulling my blue cashmere rug over my shoulders to keep out the November chill. "I don't think I can stand this game we're playing for much longer. It was easier with Guy, and even with Staahl, because I could put names and faces to them. But these... people – whoever they are – are nameless and faceless, Matthew. We don't know who they are or what they represent except that they are 'the enemy'. They won't just go away, will they? They've never been this close before."

"No, not for a long time."

"So...?"

"So I want you to be ready to leave in the first week of December. Pack the barest minimum for you and the children.

Everything else can follow at a later date – it's how we've done it before. I have passports and identity documents in the leather case in the wall safe – you know how to access it."

"You make it sound as if you won't be there."

"I'll be there, but you must know what to do in case I'm not. We go about our daily business as usual – I'll work at the lab, you in your tutor room, but we take it in turns to be at home so the house is never empty. One of us must be able to get to the safe. Keep our cell phones on at all times and we can have a call signal if anything happens. In that way, we will have an exit strategy, and I can get back to you." I shuddered and he drew me close to him, absorbing my fear. "It's only a week until we leave and nothing is likely to happen in that time. The main thing is to make them think we suspect nothing."

"I'll make a hair appointment for Christmas, book Theo in for the jabs he doesn't need…"

"That's it – nothing's changed. Meanwhile, the family will join us for Thanksgiving in a few days and we can alert them to our plans. It's not safe to say anything except face-to-face; our calls are being monitored and our internet accounts will have been hacked." He grunted a laugh. "Now that is something that's changed in the last couple of decades."

"And where will we go?" I barely dared ask, whispering now that Theo had dropped into sleep.

"Somewhere safe."

"Is that even possible in this day and age?"

"Anything's possible, my love. All things are possible."

There was comfort in certainty, that sense of relief that, no matter how much you feared the future, your path was known even if the outcome was not. Like getting the dentist's verdict after weeks of toothache. As much as you dreaded the operation, it was so much better than the not knowing. We would leave this life and embark on a new one. It had been inevitable, one way or another. Our home was where we were, wherever that might be.

"Will you tell me what you have planned?"

"It's better you don't know."

"You don't trust me?" I said, my voice rising, indignant and ready to argue.

He cradled my face between his hands and burrowed into my eyes, his own flickering with their tiny flames. "I trust you with my life, Emma – my life." His voice dropped, soothing, mesmerizing, until I felt beguiled by its warmth and melted by its honey tones. "Emma…" he murmured. "'Lie with me and be my love, and I forever thine…'" He kissed my eyes, my lips, his mouth curving at my response.

"… then tell me…" I urged before I forgot what it was I had been cross about, but his lips found the contours of my neck and my fingers his hair, until my fear faded, ready to go wherever he led.

Army of Ghosts

There's only so much you can do, so many preparations you can make, to sever the ties that bind you to your present life. Over the following days I found myself spending time among the things to which I had grown accustomed – running my fingers over the bronze statue of the horse, listening to the delicate tick of the clock, nudging my children's cradle and watching it swing back and forth in ever decreasing arcs until it came to a gentle halt. On the odd sunny day, I muffled myself against the cold and sat under the bared limbs of my orchard and listened to the wind singing in the branches. But now, with three small bags lined up on my bed, I wrapped my triptych in the children's christening robe and placed it with Matthew's translation of the Italian treatise at the bottom of my flight bag. In a silver box in which I kept locks of baby hair and Rosie's milk teeth, I put the sapphire earrings and two rings Matthew had bought me at the birth of each child, and the little pebble from New Zealand. I wore only my Nanna's old pearl earrings and the plain cross my father had bought me, and kept the jade necklace Mrs Seaton had given me, on which Theo liked to chew to cool his sore gums. It seemed fitting, somehow, to leave the States as I had entered it. I crammed my blue rug on top of the few travelling clothes, but everything else would have to wait until the house was packed up and the contents moved to storage once we had disappeared. One day – when the hunt died down and the trail ran cold – Matthew said that a removals firm would turn up at the warehouse, empty the containers, and the contents would vanish like the owners had done before. Perhaps then, Matthew would be reunited with the tokens of his past, wherever we were living, whenever that might be.

Engrossed in my task, I hadn't heard him come into our room and I jumped when I noticed him leaning against the door frame, his arms crossed on his chest, quiet eyes watching.

"I've nearly finished. I just need to find some room for Theo's Bear. He can't sleep without it. He... he..." I rammed my fist into the small pile of clothes and nappies. "There's no room. I can't fit everything. I can't fit their *lives* in here."

"Leave it – I'll finish the packing." He put his hand over mine and found it shaking. "We'll get through this, Emma. We will pack up and move on. It's what we do; it's what we've always done."

"I haven't, Matthew. I was born and brought up in the same house. Nobody ever threatened me, nobody hunted me. When I left my front door in the morning I knew I would see it again that evening – and my parents, and my sister, Nanna... Grandpa." I hung my head, sucking air through my teeth, willing myself to calm. "The clock would always strike, Tiberius would purr... they were markers of normality, Matthew. I took all those things for granted."

Drawing me to him, he held my head against his chest, rocking me slightly to the beat of his heart. "We are the markers in each other's lives and in the lives of our children. We carry our memories in here," he kissed my head, "... and in here," his chest made a solid *tok* as he tapped his heart. "Do you think I would hesitate over one single thing in this house if my family was in danger? Would you?" I shook my head beneath his hand. "So, I'll finish the packing and you find Bear, and together we'll make some sense of this mess."

* * *

I switched off the mobile and went to find Matthew in the kitchen. "Snow's delaying flights out of Toronto, and Ellie and Charlie can't make it. She sent her apologies."

"It's probably just as well. They're better off over the border at the moment."

I eyed the vast turkey, stuffed, trussed and ready to go. "We can't hope to get through that dinosaur."

"No, but Joel can, and so can Harry, and between them they'll polish off half the bird at least. Theo'll have a go as well, won't you, my boy?" He ruffled his son's hair and was rewarded with his Churchillian chuckle.

Resting her chin on the table and not to be outdone, Rosie piped up, "I want some turkey, Daddy."

"Do you indeed, young lady? This bit?" He pointed to a gargantuan leg. "Or merely the whole thing?" She wriggled and squealed as he caught her up by her dungarees and turned her head over heels, blue eyes sparkling, her hair dangling. Anyone looking at them would think nothing of it, but his brooding blues gave him away. Still, he was doing a lot better than I was.

"I'm going to campus to see how Elena's doing." With a flick of my hips, I pushed myself away from the kitchen counter. "I'll get back before the others arrive."

Matthew righted Rosie and put her on her feet. "Emma, you could phone her."

"No, I can't. Not for what I want to say."

In the hall, I reached for my scarf, and as a second thought took Matthew's blue one off the hook instead, and wound it around my neck. The toes of my boots nudged Theo's little bag next to his sister's and my own. They looked innocuous enough, waiting there. The door opened behind me, letting an oven-warmed draught fill the cooler space.

"At least keep your cell on, as we arranged."

"*They'll* be listening," I said bitterly, reaching up to the car keys on the hooks by the coats. "They are *always* listening."

"Of course they will. And don't take my car," he said as my hand hovered over his keys, "It's skittish in snow. I don't want you involved in any accidents."

Collecting the pot-bellied cactus in its orange pot from the windowsill in the kitchen and tucking my bag beneath my arm, I kissed the children and my husband. "I won't be long. I'll be back in time to help lay the table and do the veg."

I picked up my shadow at the intersection where our road joined the highway, although why they bothered with a tail I couldn't imagine, given they knew where I was and where I must be going. I resented this intrusion, baulked at our lack of privacy, and would have liked nothing better than to tell them so, vociferously and without restraint. I wanted to confront our ghosts, unmask them, and in doing so strip them of this power they had over us. Except that I mustn't. So I drove as if blithely unaware of the car behind me, or the one which took its place a few miles later that followed me to the gates of the college, where it stopped, as usual, to wait.

"I didn't expect you!" Elena threw her arms around me, her bump leaving a considerable air gap between us in which my jade beads swung. "I thought you have family coming for Thanksgiving today?"

"We have, but Matthew's doing the cooking and I wanted to see how you are." I looped hair behind my ear. "And I wanted to give you this." I handed her the cactus she had given me all those years ago when I was recovering from Staahl's attack and before I knew Matthew's secret. "I think it might need repotting."

Arched brows gathered in a frown. "Why do you give me Mr Fluffy? Don't you want it any more?"

Stuffing my hands in my pockets, I raised my shoulders slightly. "Well, he's been a good friend to me over these years, and I thought you might like his company while you're on maternity leave."

"Sure. OK." She rotated the tubby little cactus in its garish pot, inspecting it. "And then I give it back to you, *da*?"

"Consider it an early Christmas present," I said, not meeting her eyes.

"Why? Will you not be here for Christmas?"

"Don't be daft, of course we will." I laughed, but it didn't ring true.

She put the stubbly cactus on the sofa table.

"I think there is something wrong. Matias says so, too. He has known Matthew for ten years and he says he's never seen him like this."

"Like what?" I whipped.

"Like that. He says he acts as if he has something on his mind, but when Matias asks him, Matthew is..." she struggled to find the word, "... e-va-sive. Yes, and he is more impatient. That is not like Matthew."

I sank onto the sofa next to her. "No, it isn't."

"We thought there might be trouble between you, you know? But there isn't, is there?" She clasped my fingers in her own. Her rich brown eyes widened. "You are saying goodbye, aren't you? You are leaving."

"Matthew wants to move closer to Henry in Arizona. Nothing's decided yet, but Henry and Pat are getting older..."

I let her fill in the rest, and she might have done in the past, blissfully indifferent to my lie, but she knew me better now. She put her arms around me.

"Emma, I am going to miss you. We are going to miss you all."

"Don't say anything to anyone. Please, Elena – it's very important."

"I will say nothing," and she zipped her lips and smiled through the beginnings of tears.

I stood, shrugging my coat over my shoulders, and rallied a smile.

"Anyway, we're not going yet. We have to find somewhere to live, get the house on the market, you know the sort of thing – and that could take months if the housing market is sluggish. We'll probably still be around to see this little one crawling." I patted her bump gently. "Well, at least long enough to celebrate the day he's born." I gave her a lingering hug. "Take care and God bless. God bless you both."

I left her standing in the doorway and made it to the bottom of the stairs leading from the married apartments before letting go. It wasn't that I wouldn't see her again, just that the next time we would both know that our friendship was on the clock, and the finality of it hurt, like grieving.

Leaning against the wall, I waited until I had gained mastery over my emotions, ruefully reflecting that motherhood made me more prone to crying, and pushed the door open into lightly falling snow. I stopped dead. There, by the corner of an accommodation block, stood a man hunched into a dark winter jacket, the collar turned up over his chin and a hat pulled down to his eyes. He beat his hands together to keep warm, and stamped his feet. Long skinny legs in grey trousers made him look like a heron. It was the first time one of them had shown themselves so openly. Without hesitating, I took a left towards the Humanities faculty, keeping to the path and making it look as unhurried as possible. I nipped into the foyer, crossed to the other side, and opened the door to the quad.

"Professor!" I looked around. Aydin descended the stairs towards me, his work case in one hand, a bottle bag in the other. He held out the bottle, beaming. "Professor, I am glad to see you. As a citizen of the United States of America, I give you, Happy Thanksgiving!" His face straightened. "Professor, are you ill?"

I shook my head, dashed a harried glance at the rear door. "Aydin... I am so sorry... I can't..." I caught a glimpse of a rapidly moving figure nearing the building. "I'm sorry," I said again, "I must go." And I left him with confusion scored across his brow.

Quickening my pace and blinking snowflakes from my lashes, I bequeathed dark prints in the thin snow. Across the quad a door yawned open, and another man stepped out. I recognized him as the failed mechanic from the staff car park. He started walking towards me. At that moment, from the med centre I heard my name and without thinking, turned. Matias grinned and waved. His smile wavered, then dropped and he took a step forward. With a slight shake of my head, I swivelled and walked purposefully towards the door at the far end of the cloister, ducked right towards Matthew's office, along the corridor and out into the med centre reception. From there I could see the two men still in the quad, heads together, then they split, one pulling his mobile from his pocket, the other making for the cloister and the atrium.

I legged it through the rear staff door and made for the car park with the first lights from the flats bleeding onto the thickening snow. A figure emerged from between the few parked cars left there and I darted sideways to avoid it, but a thickly accented voice called out, "Professor!"

"Aydin, I can't stop." I looked over my shoulder, but the path behind me remained clear. "I have to go." Hoiking my keys from my pocket, I fumbled the lock button. "I'm in a rush. Must dash. Family's waiting."

"Something is wrong." He broke off, looking back towards the medical facility, and I swung around. The long-legged man had rounded the corner and was now making his way towards us. I swore under my breath and yanked the door open, flinging my bag onto the passenger seat. Aydin held the door. "You are in trouble?"

"Yes," I said simply.

"I help you."

"No! You mustn't get involved. Please, Aydin."

"I have seen trouble. I know trouble. You go." He slammed the door shut and turned as Heron-legs reached the top step to the car park. Snatching the bottle from the bag he still carried, he lurched towards the steps, swaying and gesticulating wildly. I threw the car into reverse, scattering gravel, then into drive. The man ran down the steps, mobile to his ear. Breaking into song, Aydin collided with him, blocking his way. Heron-legs tried to push past him, and the last thing I saw in my rear-view mirror was Aydin's raised fist bearing down on the surprised man's face.

Think. I must think.

I went the long way home, checking my mirrors every few minutes. No other car appeared to be following me, but then why should they, given the tracker installed behind the wheel arch that gave my location away? It was time to be rid of it. I drove through thickening snow until I felt calmer and managed to persuade myself to stop for petrol. It looked normal – unrushed, innocent.

Checking no one was behind me, I drew up outside a gas station and joined a queue for last-minute fuel. Pretending to drop my bag as I opened the door, I crouched between cars, fumbled under my wheel arch, found the tracker, dislodged it, and whacked it under the neighbouring car. I wiped my hands on my trousers and climbed back in and set off at what I hoped looked like a leisurely pace, only picking up speed when beyond the village and out on the country roads climbing towards the foothills and home.

I recognized Joel's 4x4 parked outside the front. I drove into the courtyard with relief, and saw Dan's Audi pulled neatly to one side in the garage beside the Aston Martin. Harry's practical Ford, tucked by the Stables, gently gathered snow. I reversed next to Matthew's car and stilled the engine. The silence of snow filled the courtyard, crowding my ears with whispers, curling kisses melting against my skin. No sound of pursuit came from the long drive, nor from my home in front of me – the shutters not yet closed against prying eyes.

Halfway across the courtyard and taking care not to slip, I saw a light switch on in the Barn, and movement behind the glass. The back door opened. "Henry!" I exclaimed, starting forward.

"No, Emma, it's me." Dan stepped into the snow, residual light reflecting from his glasses. "I'm sorry, I didn't mean to startle you; I was collecting something for Mom. It's good to see you." He crunched across the freezing snow and hugged me warmly. I looked beyond him into the Barn's kitchen.

"So, Henry and Pat…?"

He shook his head. "Perhaps next year. And Jeannie sends her apologies, but, well…" he faltered, looking embarrassed.

"It's all right, Dan, you don't have to explain. I'm glad you could make it at least." A gust of laughter escaped the kitchen on a wave of turkey-scented air. "Is everyone else already here?"

"They are. I collected Maggie on the way. Are you all right, Emma? You're looking a bit grim. Has something happened?"

"I'm not entirely sure, but I think things are about to change."

"How many?" Matthew asked, worry gathered in corrugations between his eyes, and the long-necked silver serving spoons he had been about to lay, forgotten in his hand.

"Two men that I saw – the one in the car park we spotted the other day, and the other with long legs. He looked familiar, but I can't place him."

Joel came around the side of the table. "They'll be working teams of two with the women you saw in Portland. They're not cooperating with my agency as far as I've been able to find out, but that's nothing new. Their surveillance is standard practice, though, which makes it easier for us to avoid when it really counts."

"I haven't done a good job of it so far."

"You've done OK." He riffled his short hair, thinking. "What's surprising is that they've blown their cover so obviously."

Matthew rested his knuckles on the polished wood. "Wanting to flush us out?"

"Yeah. Maybe."

A table fork glinted askew. I straightened it unconsciously. "Perhaps I shouldn't have left like I did. It made me look suspicious."

Matthew shook his head. "And if you hadn't, who knows what might have happened? You say it looked like they were going to intercept you?"

"I thought so, yes, otherwise I wouldn't have scarpered. It was Aydin who delayed Heron-legs. I hope he's OK. The other guy looked pretty angry."

I heard a distinct tut from Maggie. "If you hadn't stopped to talk to your student, you could have left without incident."

Dan shot her a look. "That isn't helpful, Maggie."

Her lip curled. "It's not the first occasion she's put us in jeopardy, and this time she's involved a stranger. Her self-interest knows no bounds."

"'Acid for blood'," Joel drawled in an undertone meant for his brother's ears but was clearly audible to the rest of us. Maggie paid them scant attention.

"Trusting her was a mistake from the beginning. She's brought this upon us. All she's ever done is divide us and draw attention to the family. If it weren't for her, my father would still be here. If it weren't for her, we'd..."

Matthew brought his open hand down on the table, making the water in the glasses shudder. "Margaret, if you have nothing constructive to add, don't say anything at all. Feel free to leave at any time." She writhed under his steel glare and her hand jerked to her throat where the snake necklace coiled. She dropped her gaze. Matthew drew breath. "It looks like the game plan's changing."

"Whose game plan?" I asked. "If it's not Joel's agency, then who has something to gain from tracking us, and who has the authority to do so?"

Joel answered. "It's a prelude, Emma. Tracking is only a means to an end..."

"What end?"

"That," Matthew said, "will depend on who's sanctioned the operation. Joel believes this has the hallmarks of agency surveillance, but it's unlikely they're working autonomously."

"Which means?"

"Which means they are working with, or for, another agency. Which brings us back to your question: who has something to gain?"

"Well, who does?" Harry asked his brother.

Joel hunched forward in his jacket. "I've been digging around, and the most likely agency interested in what we've got to offer is the SSC – Soldier Systems Center. They're responsible for R and D – Research and Development," he added when he saw me frown. "It's for the Army: specialized clothing, equipment, body armour, that sort of stuff, but also human performance."

Harry whistled. "What, like endurance?"

"Yeah, bro'. They take volunteers and see how they perform under environmental extremes – heat, cold, altitude, that sort of thing."

"I can see why they'd be interested in us," Dan said.

"Sure, Dad, so can I, but they're not."

"What do you mean?"

"I mean I have a contact who has... contacts, and she hasn't been able to trace the source of the operation – no orders, no mark, nothing. They've never heard of the Lynes family. The SSC's not it."

"They dropped my surveillance some time ago," Dan pointed out.

"Mine too," Harry said. "What about you, Maggie?"

"The last I recall was over a month ago. I haven't seen anything since then, but then I'm not the focus of attention, am I?"

I disregarded her snipe, even if I could still sense the shards of glass she sent on splinters every time she looked at me. "So they're only interested in us, Matthew." I swallowed. "You, me and the children." He had become increasingly withdrawn over the course of the conversation and now he stood obliquely, radiating clouds of doubt and something I wasn't used to – fear? "Matthew? Do you know who's hunting us?"

Resting his fingertips on the polished surface of the table, he studied them. "I don't know for certain, but I had knowledge of an organization – neither associated with the military, nor dependent on it for funding – that was established by the government specifically to coordinate scientific research for military purposes. It was mostly research into advanced technology to support weapons development, but not all. One section concentrated on the effects of viruses, nerve gases, famine and glut – that sort of thing – using volunteers. But there were also rumours of experimentation of a different – clandestine – nature."

"Like the sort of thing that went on at Porton Down, you mean?" I asked.

"Worse." The faint tick of the clock from his study marked the seconds in which his colour flared and faded. "Much, much worse."

"Matthew?" I asked tentatively. "How do you know?"

"Because they tried to recruit me." Pale afternoon light filtered through his lashes and reflected off indigo eyes. "Anyway, the unit was disbanded after the war along with the agency – or so it was believed."

Dan lifted an eyebrow. "You think it – or something like it – is behind this surveillance?"

"Possibly. Probably."

"Could it be your research they're interested in?" I suggested.

"It might, although it has no military potential as far as I'm aware."

"But if you've been seeking to reverse the effect of whatever made you this way, might they not be interested in exploiting the same mechanism to recreate the effects?" Dan persisted.

"Geesh, you make it sound like *Universal Soldier*, Dad," Joel snorted from the fireplace, where he outlined the pommel of the medieval sword with a finger.

"Is that what you've been working on all these years?" Harry asked. "A way to reverse what you are? Who we are?"

"I did, among other things." Matthew took my hand and held it between his own, his finger tracing the lions on my engagement ring. "But not now. I am what I am, but it's taken me this long to accept it, and now I will use it to protect you all for as long as I am able. You might as well know, one of the reasons I wanted us to be together today is to tell you that we plan to leave here in a few weeks. It's time to move on."

"Where to?" Dan asked. "I need to give Jeanette some warning."

Matthew looked at each of them in turn. "I'm not asking you to come with us. You will all have a home with us if you want it, but it will be safer if you go your separate ways – sever all contact – for now."

Strangled dismay erupted from Maggie's throat and she started forward, knocking a chair. "I can find work anywhere where you are…"

"No, Maggie, it's too risky. You all move on – take on new identities and new lives for as long as it takes for them to lose sight and forget us."

Harry hooked his thumbs in his pockets. "Yeah, we've prepared for this enough over the years – just didn't expect it ever to happen, you know?"

"I know," Matthew replied evenly.

"And now?" Dan asked.

"And now it is time to eat and give thanks for what we have. We have time to talk over the details of our move later, but for now I hope you're hungry."

Joel did a drum roll against his stomach. "I thought you'd never ask, Old Man. Hey, Emma, what have you been cooking? Smells good."

"Nothing to do with me, Joel. Ask Matthew. I didn't even make it back in time to do the veg. I'd better go and fetch the children."

Rosie had trotted ahead down the stairs with Ottery and I had Theo in my arms clutching Bear, when Maggie came out of the bathroom, patting her hands dry on a handkerchief. She made to walk past without acknowledging us.

"I'm sorry, Maggie," I said to the back of her head. From two steps below me, she stopped and turned around, curious despite herself. "I'm sorry we couldn't be friends. I would have liked to have known you better, but it seems that we'll be going our different ways soon and I don't know when we'll next meet. For Matthew's sake, and that of your family and our children, I hope one day we can find common ground." Balancing Theo on my hip, I held out my hand. She looked at it with cold eyes, then at me, and proceeded down the stairs without saying a word. I let my hand drop. "Ah, well," I spoke into Theo's hair as he sucked my jade beads, "we tried, didn't we? At least what's said can't be unsaid, and perhaps she'll remember it one day when it really matters."

"In your best bib and tucker, Uncle Theo?" Dan chuckled, putting the cornbread on the table next to the golden turkey. I took Bear from Theo's hand and tucked it down beside him in the high chair pulled up to the table.

"Hey, buddy," Joel whispered in a theatrical flourish from next to him, "this turkey ain't big enough for the two of us."

"It sure isn't big enough for you, bro," Harry enjoined, puffing his cheeks like a bullfrog.

Like old times. I had to smile, despite the circumstances.

Ranged around the glossy table, candles the only form of lighting except for the new flames exploring the logs in the fireplace to brighten the snow-dull day, we took each other's hands and bowed our heads as Matthew said the Grace of his childhood and gave thanks to God for bringing us safely together. So much had changed since I had heard him recite it that first Christmas when we had all been together and when only I knew the foundations of his past. The truth had caused so much pain, had driven the family apart, and yet Matthew had found some peace within himself, even if it had come at a price. We all felt Henry's absence, missed Pat's homely wisdom, but there was a wholeness here also, where I guess it had always been, unstated yet understood, in Matthew's grounded presence.

"Mummy, I'm not hungry," Rosie said a touch plaintively, when I put a teaspoon of peas on her plate next to the smallest helping of turkey and vegetables possible.

"I'm not, either," Matthew said, "but we'll pretend we are."

"Like when I had to have a sandwich every day at preschool even when I didn't want it?"

"Exactly. I'll show you how to make it look as if you've eaten something."

"I gave Lewis my sandwich. He said my mummy makes the best sandwiches…"

"That's a first," I murmured.

"… but then my teacher said I mustn't give my food away and I must eat it all myself."

"What did you do then, Rosie?" Harry asked, helping himself to more gravy.

"I sticked it under the table like this," and Rosie demonstrated, making the silver candlesticks rattle as she slammed her little hand on the underside of the old table.

Stifling a smile, Matthew steadied a napkin ring as it headed for the edge. "That reminds me of being told to eat spiced smoked eel when I was about, oh, seven or so. It was one of the first times I had been allowed to join my father, grandmother and uncle at the table and I thought myself very grown up as we had important guests, although I had to wear a high lace collar and it tickled like spiders." He scurried his fingers across Rosie's hand and up her arm and she wriggled and laughed. "All went well until a dish of eels – a gift from one of the guests – was served. It took one mouthful for me to know I didn't like eel. My grandmother told me to eat what was on my plate – one of these very plates we have here." He tapped the silver sixteenth-century dish in front of her. "Well, I couldn't – I wouldn't. Luckily for me, we had a hound who would sit next to me hoping I might drop some food…" He looked sideways at his daughter and she clapped her hands to her mouth.

"Daddy, that was naughty! Did your granny see you?"

"No, but my uncle did and he thought it very funny because he didn't like eel either, although Horace, our dog, certainly enjoyed it. But I did like cowslip tart with nutmeg grated over the top and I ate all of that."

"Not this nutmeg!" Rosie wiggled it on its stout chain. "I won't let anybody eat this nutmeg."

He kissed the top of her head. "Quite right, Rosie-posy. You keep it safe." It was the first time he had spoken so openly about his childhood in front of his family, and now that he had done so, it was as if something inside him was released, so when Harry said, "Is this the same uncle that you had… problems… with?" Matthew answered, "William. Yes, it was," and went on to talk about him in greater detail than I had ever heard before.

Joel indicated the swords hanging on the chimney breast. "Is that the sword he attacked you with?" Everyone had finished eating except Theo, who continued to munch steadily through the little pile of peas in front of him, picking them up and inspecting them one by one with round eyes.

Matthew rose and, going to the fireplace, removed his sword. "No, he used a main gauche – that's a parrying weapon – while this is my rapier, given to me by my father."

"Isn't that the one you used to cut your wedding cake?" Dan asked, holding his hand out to Joel, who inspected the notched blade. Matthew nodded. "It is, but it was used for the purpose for which it was made prior to that. I cleaned it thoroughly, in case you were wondering," he grinned. "And that is the Lynes lion on the pommel, and that…" he said, his face becoming animated as he pointed to the old print in the gilded frame next to the medieval sword still hanging above the fireplace, "… is New Hall, our family home. That is where I grew up, where generations of Lynes lived and died before me. That is where I come from. That is who I am." His face shone, almost indistinguishable from the light shining from within him, infusing the air with a palpable vibrancy until the room tingled with it.

"I can't get my head around it," Joel said, shaking it. "It's something else knowing your great-grandfather's four hundred years old, but that he's also English! Geesh, and it's Thanksgiving; is nothing sacred?" Laughter rippled around the room with the exception of Maggie, who maintained a profound silence.

"It's what Dad always wanted to know," Dan said quietly, "where we come from. He knew Ellen's history, of course, but not yours."

The light faded from Matthew's face. "I know, and I would have done anything to be able to tell him and to have them here with us today."

Maggie had remained mutely observant as usual, only speaking to accept or decline a dish passed to her, or speak quietly to her brother. Now, however, her voice cut across the normal hubbub around the table and the occasional sing-song from Theo. "So you never knew your mother," she stated, fixing Matthew with expressionless eyes.

"I have only the vaguest memory of her, yes. My father, grandmother and uncle brought me up, Maggie. They – and Nathaniel Richardson, our steward – were the constants in my life – that and my God – until my uncle betrayed us. I cannot overstate the importance of my family and my faith in sustaining me through these years. Without them, life would have been unimaginable." He held her gaze until she dropped it, and she made no further comment.

I stood, breaking the awkward pause. "It's getting late. I

think I'll make a start on cleaning these." I began to gather the small silver dishes with the Lynes coat of arms. "Get Matthew to tell you where they came from; that'll make your heads spin."

The last dish had been put in its soft bag, and joined the rest of the silver in the big trunk secreted under the floor of the pantry, and Dan and Harry were playing horses with the two children, with Maggie looking on with an almost wistful expression. Her colours had changed over the course of the meal, becoming muted, softer, flexing and changing as she listened to the conversations – something I'd never observed in her before. I couldn't easily interpret them, but I noted their confusion, and wondered whether she was experiencing the self-doubt and inner reflection that seemed to elude her before.

Excited squeals echoed from the drawing room, but the dining room was a pool of quiet. Bear had become lodged between a table leg and the high chair and I was bending to extract it when I sensed a change. Like a quiver in the density of the air. I straightened, looked around. The only movement came from the fire burning low in its grate. Light spread in a narrow arc from the door into the kitchen. I tried to find the locus but saw nothing in the room. There it was again – a blind movement, felt, not seen. Puzzled, I went to the window and squinted outside. Snow had stopped falling from scattered clouds, and the intermittent sun glazed my breath against the glass.

I started as a low voice warned, "Move away from the window." I stepped back against the wall, knocking my hip in my haste as Matthew swung the shutters across the window and secured them with the heavy iron bar. From the hall, I heard the bar being dropped across the front door and similar sounds from the rooms above my head. All noise of play had ceased. "The sensors have picked up movement at our perimeter."

In the moment it took for me to absorb what he said, he had

closed the shutters on the other window, thrusting the room into darkness.

"They're here?"

He strode back across the room and took me by my elbow, propelling me towards the hall. "Get the children. We're leaving."

"But..."

"Now, Emma."

He disappeared into the study, leaving me standing. Footsteps from the hall heralded Dan carrying Rosie, wide-eyed and anxious, and behind him Harry with Theo clinging. Maggie hovered by the study, fingers plucking at the skin between her thumb and forefinger, pecking air in little gasps. The snake necklace quivered at her throat. Matthew reappeared with the battered case and the document folder. "If any of you have a cell phone, leave it here. We can't risk being traced." He put his on the hall table. I found my burner phone in the bottom of my bag and left it next to his.

Dan patted his pockets. "I got rid of mine some time ago."

"So did I," Harry said.

Maggie put hers on top of mine. "What do I do now?" she asked, eyes staring.

"What we've practised, Maggie," Matthew said. "You go with Dan and drive north-west to the designated area. You remember where that is?" She nodded. "Then you will know what you need to do next. Go!"

"What will you do? Will you be there? How can I..."

"Margaret, there's no time to debate this." He turned to his grandson. "Your car shouldn't be tracked, Dan, but take the alternative route just in case. Harry, take Emma and the children – you know where to go..."

"No!" I said. "Matthew, we go together or not at all."

"It's me they're after, Emma. They'll follow my car and it'll give you and the children time to get away. I'll meet you at the airstrip if I can, but I have to get back to the lab and destroy E.V.E. It has data on it that I can't let them find."

Harry was dragging his coat from the hooks. "You'll lead them straight to it – that is if they're not already there waiting for you. I'll do it. They won't follow me if they think you're somewhere else. I know the codes and I know the drill. Better still, I'll take the Aston and they'll think it's you – buy you some time."

Feet thundered overhead, and Joel all but tumbled down the stairs.

"Six of them – at least – about three hundred yards and closing. They have door breakers, Matthew. It won't take them long to breach our defences. We could fight them off..."

"No – only as a last resort. I don't want anybody hurt. Get going, Joel; you know what needs to be done."

Joel grabbed his jacket and found his keys as Matthew lifted the heavy bar from the door. He nodded once, opened the door and Joel sprinted down the steps to his car. He was gone as Matthew slammed the bar into place. "We'll leave from the back. Harry, are you ready?"

"I'll go to the lab, then head south and warn Gramps. Dad, can you contact Ellie? I'll let you and Mom know I'm OK when I cross the border."

"Take care, son." Dan embraced Harry, smiled briefly at me and placed Rosie in Matthew's arms.

Matthew picked up the case in his free hand. "We need to move. God speed, all of you. Maggie, go with Dan..." He looked around. "Where is she?"

"Maggie?" Dan called. He checked the study, the drawing room, the doors crashing open as he yelled, "Maggie! We must leave *now*." He returned to the hall without her.

"Has she already left?" I asked, and as if in answer, from the courtyard came the faint roar of a powerful engine. I checked the line of hooks by our own coats. "Matthew! Your keys have gone."

Subduing oaths, he ran to the kitchen and flung the door open, sprinting across the icy flags towards the furious tail lights as the Aston Martin tore through the massive gates now standing wide, and out into space beyond. He stood for a second, fumes hanging in the air, then his head jerked around, listening. He turned, and ran back towards us. "Get inside!" He slammed the door shut and bolted it. "Maggie's taken my car and left the courtyard wide open – she's in no fit state to drive. What the hell's she playing at?" He thumped the counter in frustration. "We've got to get out of here or we'll be trapped."

"Two're approaching the front," Harry warned, watching the monitor.

Matthew viewed the screen for a few seconds then swore again under his breath. "They have stun grenades."

"Grenades?" My heart lurched. "They won't attack us, surely? The children…"

Dan thrust keys into Matthew's hand. "Take my Audi – it's fitted with Charlie's booster seat. I'll go in Emma's car. The tracker will cause enough confusion to give you a few extra minutes before they realize she's not in it."

"I took it off my car earlier. I… I didn't want them following me," I stuttered.

Dan paused, then gave an odd grin. "I'll make sure they follow me," he said, and shrugged his jacket on, checked the monitor for signs of movement and then, taking a breath, said, "Good luck," and he and Harry ran for the cars.

Theo began to whimper. Still in her father's arms, Rosie said, "Mummy, Theo wants Bear."

"Emma, we haven't time," Matthew began, but I was already

making for the dining room. I snatched up the bear, tucking it into Theo's rompers. An almighty crash splintered the air and I dropped one of the bags, swinging around. Retrieving it, I ran back to the hall to seize the first coat that came to hand, as the front door reverberated with a second crash. Matthew grabbed my arm and dragged me from the hall as daylight broke through cracks in the wood. We made for the kitchen door, but a quick glance at the monitor revealed dark figures hugging the shadow of the walls.

"Take the children. Get to the car." Matthew flung the pantry door open. "Rosie, go with Mummy."

"Daddy!"

The flagstone rose and yawned and I threw the bags ahead of me and ran down the steps as he lifted Rosie down to me. "Rosie, remember the game," he said, and then to me, "If I'm not by the observatory, leave. Don't wait." A resounding blow shattered the remains of the door. "I'll distract them. Go!" And Matthew shut the flag, cutting him from view. Moments later, the air cracked, punching our ear drums. Rosie covered her ears, and Theo's mouth opened beneath my hand. I clamped it firmly and warned Rosie to stay quiet. I swallowed to clear my ears and found them whining. The small space choked with dust. In the ensuing silence, I stretched to hear any sound other than our own breathing and persistent ringing. "Remember the game," I mouthed to her. Above, faint at first but becoming louder, steps – rapid, heavy-footed, booted – muffled voices. Then a shouted warning, furniture overturned, glass breaking, running. A succession of deafening bangs punctured the air somewhere in the direction of the dining room and, through minute fissures in the planks of the kitchen floor, a savoury smell, redolent of winter evenings... Thin at first, it grew and blossomed: smoke. Theo began to fret against my hand. "Shhhhhh," I said, although my heart thrust against my ribs in an attempt to escape.

Taking my hand from his mouth and gathering the bags over my arm, I backed towards the rear wall in the darkness. I felt the hard outline of the trunk of silver, then the crumbling surface of rough bricks. I found the loose brick, removed it, and pulled the iron-cold lever. A rush of cool air – free of smoke – greeted us, and Theo began to kick and squirm, building himself up to a full-throttled scream. "Please..." I begged into the nest of his hair. Bending in the low tunnel, stumbling blindly against the damp bricks, I led the way, protecting Theo's head with my hand, Rosie's little breaths marking her passage behind me as she clung to the hem of my sweater. And all the time I listened for sounds of discovery and pursuit, for a triumphant cry from unknown voices as Matthew was cornered and subdued.

I could taste fuel in the back of my throat before my eyes adapted to the thin lines of dull daylight filtering through the garage floor. Stopping beneath the heavy wooden inspection hatch, I listened for any sounds above me. Theo's fingers wound in my hair, tugging, but he had stopped struggling and seemed to be listening with me. Faint noises came from within the house, but no nearer than that. My finger against my lips, I pointed up towards the hatch, making my fingers walk, and Rosie frowned and nodded. I gave her her coat to put on, and her bag to carry, and wriggled Theo into his snow suit. Putting him down, I listened again, heard nothing, and holding my breath, slid the inspection hatch along its rails, grit grating. Cautiously, I raised my head until my eyes levelled with the garage floor and became accustomed to the stronger light flooding through the open doors. Tracks in the drifting snow marked where the Aston Martin had slid and fled. Dan's dark blue car stood at the other side of the garage. Anyone standing in the courtyard or in the kitchen of my home would see us cross the empty space. It was a matter of timing. I knelt in front of my daughter. "Rosie, we have to get to Dan's car, but we mustn't be seen."

"Like fairies," she whispered.

"Like fairies," I confirmed. "When I open the door, you must run like an otter as quick as you can and into the car without making a sound. Listen and do exactly what I say. Do you understand?"

She hugged Ottery. "And then we find Daddy?"

"And then we find Daddy," I confirmed again. I checked the courtyard for signs of movement, snow lodged and freezing in the cracks, outlining the grey setts in a grid. "Ready?" I lifted her, Theo next, and climbed out last, keeping low. Counting silently to three, I pressed the button on the keys. The lights flashed orange as the locks released. "Run!" We crossed the garage floor and I opened the car door. Rosie scrambled in across the driver's seat to the other side and I all but threw Theo into the back seat and the bags after him, had the keys in the ignition and the car in reverse before the first shouts came from the Barn. "Hold on!" Shunting the gears of the unfamiliar car, I shoved my foot on the accelerator, lugging the car door shut before the entrance to the arch could tear it off as we plunged through it. The drive was clear in front of us, but it wouldn't be for long. "Rosie, get into the back seat and strap yourself and Theo in."

"I can't lift him."

"I know; just do the best you can."

"Mummy!" she wailed. "Our house is smoking... Mum*my*!"

"I know, Rosie." I concentrated on not skidding on the freezing patches of snow. New flakes were beginning to gather, obscuring the tyre marks of the fleeing cars. I left the hard track at the point where the drive bent and dipped out of sight of the house, the tyres sinking slightly into the softer ground, tussocky grass cloaked in snow brushing the underside of the low-slung chassis. The silver dome of the obsolete observatory came into view. There was no sign of Matthew. "Where are you? Where are you?" I uttered, peering at the low building, when he appeared out of nowhere, slamming against the car in his haste. He wrenched my door open, tossing the case in first.

"Move over!" Matthew took my place and, not hesitating, flung the car forwards around the observatory and towards a stand of young trees. "Buckle up," he warned, and without slowing raced into the thick of them, the car jolting in the bumps, sliding over exposed tree roots, low branches whipping and scratching like nails. The car launched over a bank, hung suspended for a few seconds, before hitting the road at an angle. Matthew straightened the car and I tasted blood in my mouth, a flap of broken skin where my tooth had cut my lip. I swivelled in my seat.

"They're OK," Matthew said, and a glance in the back confirmed it, Rosie white-faced, Theo bewildered. Only then did I see the soot-blackened skin on the back of his hands, smeared under his jaw, and the charred sleeves of his shirt. "Stun grenades," he said, shortly.

"The house?"

His mouth tightened and I saw in the rear mirror a thickening column of smoke rising above the retreating trees.

"We have our lives," he stated. He took the corners tight, speeding up as we came out of each curve, gradually increasing the distance between us and our burning home, handling Dan's car with precision, despite the deteriorating road conditions. I squeezed between the seats and checked Theo was secure in the child seat. The powerful engine upped a notch. "This should buy us some more time; they'll think we're heading for the border and by the time they find we're not, we should be clear."

"Where are we going?"

"We're leaving the country, but not for Canada." He checked

the car clock, barely taking his eyes from the road through the falling snow, now thickly whipped by a keen wind. "This weather'll make it harder for them to track us, but we must get to the airstrip before dusk or risk its closure. Joel should be almost there by now. The road forks up ahead. We take the left road further into the mountains and away from the border. They won't be expecting that. What the...?" He swerved to avoid a dark car parked part way across the road. Ahead, sharp blue lights pierced the muted colours of the snow-ridden sky.

"Matthew! They've set up a road block!"

He slowed, taking care not to over-brake as a uniformed officer flagged us down. "Stay calm. There's an ambulance over there; someone's come off the road. Looks bad, God grant them peace." He reduced the car's speed until it crawled at an agonizingly slow pace past a group of people gathered around a gurney balanced at a precarious angle on the slope. As we passed, a blood-red chassis, the sleek bonnet bent in a corrugated snarl, lay rammed against a boulder. A broken doll of a woman, blank eyes staring from her stark, white head, bent awkwardly on the deflated bed of the airbag.

Like before. Like a lifetime ago.

Matthew let out a low moan, and colours of anguish filled the car with metallic grief. I felt his pain in the heart of me, a palpable weight, leaden, plumb-dead.

"That policeman's staring at us. He's coming over." I grasped his arm. "Drive, Matthew, you must drive!" He came to, shaking his head and accelerating away as if escaping the image of his dead granddaughter. We drove on some miles before he spoke, his throat tight with pain.

"I didn't think... I never thought I'd see her like that... like her sister..." He swallowed. "Why did she do it? Why didn't she do what I asked?"

I stared blindly through the driven snow, seeing that first fatal crash that welcomed me to Maine, and Matthew – unknown to me then – bending into the twisted car to close the eyes of the dead woman, as if she mattered, as if he cared. He carried with him more experience of death than anyone – and now this.

"She wanted to help, Matthew. She thought they would follow her and give us a chance to get away."

"She didn't need to do that – to do anything."

"Yes," I said quietly, "she did." I pulled myself back to the present. "Do you want me to drive?"

He cleared his throat, glanced into the rear-view mirror and shook his head once. "It's not far. We need to be ready. Rosie, do you have the document folder I gave you?" She held up the brown leather folder she had been clutching all the way. "Good girl. Give it to Mummy, please. When we get there, you might have to run very fast. Do you remember when we played our running games and how Thompson's gazelle evade cheetah?" Rosie made her fingers scuttle in a zigzag motion in the air. "That's it. When we get to the airstrip you'll see our plane waiting there and I want you to be a gazelle and run towards it as fast as you can."

"Will you be Chasing Cheetah, Daddy?"

"Let's see who can get to the plane first," he evaded, "and then when we're airborne, you can help me fly."

Rosie clapped her hands. "I'll win! I'll win!"

"Emma," he said more quietly, "I'll get us as close as I can. I'll carry Theo. Get to the plane. Joel'll be there to help you on board."

I looked behind us at our son. "You think they'll be waiting?"

He took longer than I hoped to answer. "We've done everything we can to hide our trail – the plane's registered at another airfield, the flight plan falsified – but somehow they knew we would take this route."

Aghast, I looked at his grim face. "How? Why?"

"Did you see the black car we nearly ran into where Maggie was?"

"Yes, but... You said yourself the car's skittish in snow. It was an accident, Matthew, it must have been."

"Was it?"

I felt sick. "They must have followed the car."

"Maybe." He didn't sound convinced.

I stared blindly at the maverick snow, seeing Maggie's twisted form instead. "You always meant to use the Aston Martin as a diversion, didn't you? That's why you insisted on keeping the colour and make. For someone keeping a low profile, I always wondered why you had such a distinctive car. You were going to draw them away from us if anything happened, weren't you? That would have been you lying in that ditch, Matthew, not Maggie. She knew, she must have done." Wind buffeted the car, sending dry snow scudding against the windows.

"She must have guessed, but in using this route she's ambushed our head start. They'll know it's not me in there and they'll widen their search pattern. Still, with any luck we can use this snow to our advantage. My eyesight's better than theirs in low light, and the wind will cover our tracks. Hopefully they won't be able to find us. Nonetheless, once in sight of the plane you'll have to run as fast as you can, because that's where they'll focus their attention once they realize we're not heading for the border. Do you think you can do that?"

"I'll try."

"Let's hope there's no reception committee," he said grimly.

"Amen to that," I agreed.

He increased speed and I clung to the door handle, bracing myself against the turns. Something slid from my shallow coat pocket and rattled to the floor and disappeared under the seat.

A car's rear lights dawdled in front of us as it negotiated a blind bend. "Hang on, Rosie," I warned as Matthew overtook with no more than an inch to spare. A sign whipped by.

"That's the airstrip. There's an old logging track to the north of it. If we can throw them off our trail long enough, we'll make it into the trees. We're losing the light and they won't spot us in this snow." He checked the mirrors. "Get ready; we're nearly there."

I forced a light tone. "Rosie, do you have your running legs on?" She kicked her legs in acknowledgment. The car slowed, veered off the road and was between trees on a track only Matthew could see, as dark trunks squeezed what little light there was from around us. He switched off the headlamps and we trundled forwards across the uneven ground.

"Over there," he said, "can you see? Landing lights." Specks of light danced between trees like fireflies, becoming brighter as we neared the perimeter. The outline of a jet appeared between flurries of snow, and my heart lifted. He slowed the car where the line of trees thinned, and stopped just short of a sturdy fence. Matthew scanned the airstrip over the top of the steering wheel. "This is as close as we get. It looks clear. Let's go."

My foot tapped against something in the near-dark. "Hang on." I fumbled in the footwell and retrieved a thin, smooth case. In horror, I stared at the mobile in my hand. "How long has that been there?"

The muscles in his cheek twitched. "It's irrelevant now; they know we're here." With a quick snap he reduced the SIM card to pieces and lobbed the phone into the thickest part of the woods. Without further comment, he climbed out leaving me gaping like the idiot I felt.

"Matthew, I'm so sorry," I said, following him. "I didn't know…"

He opened the rear door and handed me the document

wallet. "I should have checked a long time ago. Rosie, climb out – quickly now."

"How do we get past the fence?" I shivered, craning my neck and squinting through the snowflakes. Matthew backed out of the car with Theo in his arms.

"It's a deer fence; it's not meant to keep people out. Hang on to Theo. Rosie, come here." He lifted her up as high as he could reach. "Climb the fence."

"Like my climbing frame," she whispered, using the wide wire entwined with last summer's growth as a scrambling net.

"Careful!" I implored in a hushed undertone, but she was up and over and down the other side, jumping into the long, snow-covered grass.

"You next, Emma. I'll hand you the bags, and then follow with Theo and the case."

I made it to the top, balancing carefully, and Matthew passed the bags. I dropped Rosie's dinosaur rucksack to her and she swung it onto her back, and then let my own fall with a soft *thlump* into the snow. I lifted my leg over the wire, but my coat button caught. I tugged. "Wait…" I looked down, and something indistinct caught the corner of my eye. I strained into the dark of the woods. "Matthew!" I hissed, but he had already followed my gaze.

"Move!" he said and, with Theo under one arm, started to scale the fence.

I yanked at my coat and all but fell the rest of the way as the button detached and spun into the air, releasing me. I scrambled to my feet and grabbed the bags as a 4x4 emerged from the woods, stopping behind the Audi, illuminating us in search beams of headlights.

From the top of the fence, Matthew shouted, "Get to the plane!"

Snow flicking from her heels, Rosie was already running towards the jet where the door had opened and a flight of short steps lowered to the runway. A figure appeared at the entrance, beckoning to her – Joel. His head jerked up and he shouted something indistinct over the hum of the engine, gesticulating towards the distant main gates. Car headlights bounced and bobbed towards the plane, becoming gleaming level eyes as tyres hit the smooth surface of the runway and sped towards us.

Caught in the lights, Rosie hesitated, her mouth falling open. "Run, Rosie, run!" I cried, gasping for breath, and she spun around and dashed towards the steps. From the perimeter fence behind us strong, thin beams of light jerked wildly in the gloaming, as black-coated figures climbed over and advanced at a steady run, spreading out like spiders on a web.

Snow stung, my teeth ached, my lungs fought for air, but Rosie had made it to the base of the steps and Joel ran down to meet her, scooping her up and retreating into the plane. Jumping a runway light, I had reached firm ground with a hundred paces to go and with Matthew barely a dozen yards behind me, when something moved in my peripheral vision. Too late I heard Matthew's shouted warning, and was knocked sideways. Winded, I lay for a moment face down, snow rammed up my sleeves, burning my cheek. "Emma!" I heard Matthew yell as a hand grabbed first one of my wrists and then the other, and started to secure them behind my back. I kicked up and back and heard a grunted exclamation as my heel engaged with something soft. My hands free, I clambered to my knees, then to my feet, but an arm hooked around my neck, pulling me down and anchoring me. I began to choke, and Staahl's face flashed unbidden in my memory. A heavily haired wrist lay exposed and I sank my teeth into the flesh, tasting iron. He screamed an obscenity. Spitting blood, I wrenched away, swinging my bag and clouting the man on the side of his head with a wooden thud. He fell to the ground and didn't move, his humanity hidden by a mask. Faceless.

For a moment I stared at him, then shouted commands came from nearby and I swung around. Figures, similarly masked, surrounded Matthew in a tightening circle. He held Theo close in one arm, all the while moving to find a weakness in their offence.

"Emma, get to the plane!" he shouted. He made a sudden rush towards two men as their attention wavered, then darted sideways between them, his speed and agility taking them unawares. One of the figures spun around and raised his arm towards Matthew's back. A sound like angry wasps zipped through the air. Matthew grunted in shock and fell to his knees. Recovering almost instantaneously, he leapt to his feet, his arm protecting Theo's head. "Don't fire! Don't hurt my son! You want me, don't you? Let my family leave."

From behind the line, a long-legged man in a thick coat pushed through the cordon now preventing Matthew from moving either left or right. I recognized him from the college, despite the handkerchief held against his face.

"There's nowhere you can go, Dr Lynes," Heron-legs said in a voice muffled by swollen lips and a broken nose, and in that instant I realized where I had seen him before: the museum in Portland. "We just want to ask you a few questions. No one need get hurt." He dabbed at his lip, motioning to the men, and they began a cautious advance towards Matthew. Heron-legs held out his hands, palm up, a bloodstained handkerchief limply flapping in truce. "Come now, Dr Lynes, just a few questions, then you can go home with your family." He smiled the colour of lies.

"He's lying, Matthew!" I cried, remembering Maggie's dead-eyed stare. "He has no intention of letting you go. Joel! Help him!"

Illuminated by the fierce headlights, and trapped, Matthew threw a desperate look at me, then addressed Heron-legs. "For the mercy of God, let them go."

"What are you waiting for?" the man snapped to the waiting men.

"Sir, the boy..."

"We'll take him too. Go on!" One of the men came within reach of Matthew, and raised his arm to fire. Theo, terrified and struggling, began crying. Matthew moved suddenly towards the armed man, lifting from the ground and raising his foot as he leapt, bringing it down on the man's leg. The sickening snap was audible from where I stood, still rooted by fear. Without warning, Matthew changed direction towards me, and several of the men raised their arms, and points of light danced on the snow before focusing on him: not guns – Tasers. Fury boiled through me. The unconscious man lay some feet away, an object in the snow next to him. I made a grab for it and began to run towards the circle. Too late, Matthew was hit in the shoulder, narrowly missing Theo. He staggered, regained his balance, but encumbered, he couldn't protect himself and was hit again, his body convulsing from the current.

What caution was left to me evaporated in intense rage, and I reacted without thinking. I fumbled the button and fired the Taser wildly, managing to hit the man closest to me in the neck. He fell forwards, writhing stiffly, but by now several men grappled with Matthew, who held them at bay with one arm, becoming rapidly overwhelmed. Several Tasers sent him reeling, and Heron-legs managed to grab Theo as he fell. Theo screamed, eyes wild with terror.

"Don't you dare touch my baby!" I yelled, and threw myself at Heron-legs, succeeding in dragging Theo from his clutch as he registered surprise at my strength. Thrashing out with my bare fist, I felt bone give way, fresh blood warm on my skin, and I wanted to hit him again, beat his face into a pulp for touching my child. Vengeful, spiteful anger clouding pity, obscuring judgment.

"Emma!" I heard Matthew call me back to my senses. Tearing wires from his body and free to move at last, he charged the group of men, knocking them sideways and running back towards the wooded perimeter, drawing the men away from us – away from the jet.

Struggling back to his feet and holding a gloved hand to his bleeding nose, Heron pointed after him. "Don't let him reach the trees!"

Matthew's voice carried over the snow-laden wind. "Get to the plane, Emma."

"Matthew! No!"

Several Tasers hit him in the chest, bringing him to his knees. "Go!" he gasped, pain searing his face.

"Leave him alone!" I screamed, beginning to run towards him. "Let him go!"

Matthew rose to his feet, diving at two of the men and sending them sprawling before they realized he had moved.

Heron-legs roared, "Take him down!"

"Emma, protect the children! *Leave*," Matthew implored. And then he stopped fighting. He simply stopped, raising his arms sideways – sacrificed, crucified. I saw what he was doing, and blood drained from my heart.

"No, Matthew, no!" I screamed. "Fight them. *Run!*" But he just stood there and someone came up and kicked him viciously behind his knees. They buckled and he sank to the ground, his arms extended as if at the block. He raised his head, staring straight at me, and from nowhere, but as clear as if he had spoken it aloud, "Emma, you promised me..." Men closed in, Tazers raised and pointing. Matthew called out, "Joel, get them out of here."

From behind me, I heard heavy booted feet running, and then Joel was tugging me after him, back towards the waiting plane.

"We have to go, Emma."

"I can't leave without him."

"We have no choice," and he nodded towards a group of men who had broken away from the cohort and now made their purposeful way towards us. He took Theo and we made it to the steps, but he had to almost carry me into the jet. "Get buckled in," he said shortly, climbing into the pilot's seat. I strapped Theo in next to Rosie.

"Mummy, where's Daddy?" she asked, eyes dark, hair sticking in strips to her whey-skinned face. I didn't answer her. I couldn't, because from the window against which I rammed my face as the jet lifted into the air above the stationary vehicles, I saw Matthew raise his head, illuminated by the car headlights, and watch us leave him to be dragged to his feet and manhandled into the waiting van.

18

Exodus

"He made me swear – he made me promise." Stricken, Joel's blue eyes darkened with anguish. "Don't you understand? I couldn't help him." Crushing Theo to me, I looked away. "Emma, geesh…" Joel rammed the heel of his hand against his forehead. "Why didn't he fight? Why didn't he just… kill them? He could have done it."

I felt a tug at my arm. "Mummy, when's Daddy coming?" Rosie climbed from her seat and onto my knees next to her brother, wrapping her arms around my neck. I heard her, felt her wriggle to get comfortable, and saw the dark purple confusion surrounding my children, but it didn't seem real. Numb, detached, I watched the frosted moon silver the shredded clouds beneath us. Somewhere, far below in the scalding night, Matthew faced our worst fears alone.

"He could have killed them, Emma," Joel insisted, "gotten away."

I rested my head against the seat back and closed my eyes. "He didn't want to kill anyone, Joel. He's had enough of killing. He wanted us to escape, that's all. He wanted us to be safe." I opened my eyes and looked at him wearily. "It was always going to come to this. Sooner or later his past was bound to catch up; he just wanted to make sure none of us would be there to suffer with him."

"He made me promise to protect you and the kids first." Joel's face crumpled. "There's nothing I wouldn't have done to save him, except break my word. Why did he make me promise, Emma? Why did he have to do that?"

"Because he knew you wouldn't leave him and because he didn't want you doing something you would regret for the rest of your life."

From the cockpit, muffled voices crackled and Joel pushed to his feet. "I filed a flight plan north-west; that's Canadian air traffic control wanting verification. We mustn't disappoint." His mouth twisted bitterly.

"We're going to Canada?" I addressed his retreating back, although it hardly seemed to matter any more, so I barely heard him when he said, "No – we've been over Canadian airspace for some time," as he climbed into the pilot's chair, and seconds later, the plane swung around the face of the moon, heading on a new, unscheduled trajectory into the darkness.

Rosie shook me awake. "Mummy, Theo's hungry."

I blinked in the low light of the cabin, disorientated, coming back to reality with an unpleasant lurch. At some point, Joel must have taken off Theo's snow suit, and now, strapped into his seat, Theo chewed Bear's ear furiously. What little milk I had left after the trauma of the past day was sucked dry by the pressurized cabin, and I had nothing to give him. He struggled at my breast, but came away fretful and unsatisfied. The lockers yielded food that would keep hunger at bay for the time being. I fed and then changed him in auto, barely noticing what I did. In the children's bag, I found the spare nappy I had put there, just in case. I frowned at it: did I ever really think it would come to this? I shook myself free of the leaden gloom. "Rosie, are you hungry?"

She wobbled her head and settled back in the cream

upholstered seat, sucking her thumb and watching with huge eyes. Dark circles ringed them, and the cabin lighting made her face unnaturally pale. "When is Daddy coming?"

Concentrating on washing Theo gave me time to compose my answer. "When he can, darling."

Hearing me awake, Joel spoke over his shoulder. "We'll be landing soon. It's a short strip and might be a bit rough."

"I've been helping," Rosie said. "Joel says I'm a good flyer."

"The best," he said. "Emma, this is under the radar, but if we get a reception committee, you're my co-pilot, right?" That reminded me of flying back home to Maine with Matthew, and the memory of it hurt.

"Right," I managed, turning away so Rosie couldn't see the pain screwing tears from sore eyes.

"And if we're intercepted, we're landing to check an engine fault and to refuel. You have the passports?" he added. "Just in case?" Did I? I hunted in my bag, stained and damp from snow, and retrieved the document wallet. Inside, I found four United Kingdom passports – mine, Theo's, one for Rosie... and Matthew's.

It didn't matter where we were, or where we were going. A car drew up on the tarmac of the private landing strip. All I knew was that Matthew wasn't with us, so when a turbaned man in a sweater and black jacket and matching beard said, "Morning, love. Take the bag for you?" I could only answer stupidly, "You're British."

"It's been a long flight," Joel explained, lifting Theo in next to Rosie.

"I ain't got a baby seat, mate," the driver frowned. "Not that far, though. Reckon it should be all right."

"This'll have to do." Joel slid my travel bag under the baby, whose chubby legs – now back in the snow suit – dangled over the edge.

"Where are we going?" I asked, covering the children with my blue blanket, and waiting for Joel to get in the front next to the driver. He remained standing and I knew then he wasn't coming with us.

"I have to go back, Emma – see if there's anything I can do, you know?" His skin looked dull beneath the fair stubble lining his jaw, creases of worry running in a sharp V between his eyes. I embraced him for a long moment without answering. His grip finally loosened and he released me. "If I hear anything, I'll be in touch. You sure you're gonna be OK?"

I nodded. "We'll be fine – they've got what they want. Just take care – please. I don't know what sort of reception you'll get. If they were prepared to do that to Maggie..."

"Yeah, well, someone'll have to pay for that."

I rested my hands on his forearms, feeling the tension in the heavily muscled arms. "Joel, no. Matthew wouldn't want you to take revenge – he wouldn't want that on your conscience. Anyway, there's the rest of the family to watch out for now he's... gone." I let my arms drop.

He cleared his throat uncomfortably. "This guy knows where to take you. Matthew said if anything happened... you know... then there's everything you need in here – everything," he emphasized, rapping the battered metal case. "You better go. Keep a low profile, right? Keep off the grid."

"They have Matthew – they don't need us," I said.

"Sure, but you can't be too careful. Stay out of sight; stay low; stay safe."

"You come a long way, duck?" the driver asked the rear-view mirror as we drove from the airstrip.

A long way?

"Yes," I replied, "I have." He waited for me to elaborate but gave a little shrug when I failed to supply any more information. I'd come a long, long way, further than I ever thought possible, and now I travelled with all I had left in the world into an unknown future. In the dim light of the car, Rosie and I held hands and I stroked Theo's head until he fell asleep, his baby lips parted from which soft snores came. Outside, a gentle drizzle misted the windscreen against which the blades swept in even strokes, too dark to see where we were, or where we were going. I leaned forward. "Where are we going?"

Drizzle had given way to a lean dawn parading the horizon in slivers of silver by the time the car drove down a long drive, past contorted gates and under the broken gatehouse arch to come to a standstill in front of the ancient façade. The angry ticking of a blackbird broke the steel silence of the morning.

The driver jerked a thumb at the weathered oak door. "Seen better times, ain't it?" He hunched into his padded coat and sniffed the November air. "Sure you don't want me to drop you and the kids somewhere else? My cousin's got a place in Leicester. It's not much but it's better than this and it's cheap."

Rosie let go of my hand and skipped up the broad steps leading to the door and gave it a shove. It remained obdurately shut. On the tips of her toes, she reached up and knocked, the taps absorbed into the great door.

"Rosie, Mrs Seaton won't be up yet. It's very early; we'll wait." I turned to the driver. "Are you sure this is the address you were given?"

He scratched at his beard. "This is it. Look, love, I can give my cousin a call and at least you can get the kids something to eat." Rosie stooped by the wonky pot by the steps and reclaimed something from the crumbs of old compost, swathed in dead leaves and cobwebs. She held it up. "I found the key!"

The key. And why would there be a key under the pot? "We'll hang on here, thanks," I said to the man. "I don't expect we'll be long." Rosie was already trying to feed the long iron key into the keyhole, smearing her fingers in rust. The driver eyed me with a degree of doubt.

"If you say so. Here's me card if you change your mind." He handed me a card with his contact details and a bent corner.

"Thanks..." I checked the card, "... Mandeep, but I don't have a mobile."

"No mobile?" He shook his head, patted his pockets and held out his. "You need to call someone?"

Hesitating, I took it from him and found my hands shaking as I dialled the only person I could think of. I spoke swiftly, circumventing the inevitable flurry of questions after the initial dumbfounded silence, then handed back the phone. "You've been very kind." I mined my bag for my meagre emergency stash. "I'm afraid I only have a few dollars."

He held up his hand. "All been paid for." He chucked Theo under the chin and waved to Rosie, and left us in a cloud of diesel fumes with the blackbird scolding from a nearby tree. There seemed little point waiting any longer. I went up to the gnarled door and knocked loudly. Then again, straining to hear any answering movement from inside. Rosie waved the key at me.

I sighed in resignation. "Might as well. Daddy must have arranged this with Mrs Seaton." At the mention of him, my stomach curled into a tight fist, grinding from my belly button through to my spine. I pushed it away, concentrated on the here and now. "Perhaps we can take Mrs Seaton a cup of tea to make up for the intrusion."

With Theo balanced on one hip, I worked the key in the lock, shedding shards of rust and dislodging a spider. Pushing the door open, I peered around the edge, but Rosie nipped through the crack. "Don't trip over the cat," I heard myself say automatically, although there was a marked absence of life in the porch, but she was away. I left the battered box by her little bag she had dropped by the door and went into the panelled cross passage of the inner hall. It was bare except for the old Gurney radiator, its metal fins cold to the touch and home to feathery webs that blew like pennants in the draught from the door. On our right, the stairs dog-legged out of sight. I stood at the bottom, feeling like an intruder. "Hello?" I called, waited a moment and then, "Hello? Mrs Seaton – Joan – it's Emma Lynes."

There was a tap-tapping of feet running on the landing above, and Rosie's little face appeared through the heavy balusters of the bannisters. "Mummy, there's nobody here."

"There must be. Hang on. I'll check down here." I went into the great hall with Theo struggling to get down. The tatty sofas were still there by the fireplace and a standard lamp with a wonky shade, but the fireplace was empty bar a few charred sticks and the remains of a pigeon's nest. I let Theo explore the expanse of the medieval hall and went through the door behind the dais into the Jacobean room beyond. The rooms were empty with neglect, bordering on dereliction, with no sign that anyone had been there for some considerable time. Retracing my steps, I went into the kitchen. The tap no longer dripped, but ivy explored a cracked pane of glass, and the room smelled terminally damp. Propped against an old milk bottle was an envelope. At some point a mouse had nibbled the edge, and small, black droppings littered the table. In the dim light, I read the thin letters: Mr and Mrs M. Lynes. Clippings of paper fell like confetti as I unfolded the letter, the centre as pierced as a doily by tiny teeth. I read it, hearing Joan Seaton's sparrow voice.

> *No. 5 The Mews*
> *Castle Hill,*
> *Stamford*

My dears,

Such excitement. I wish I were here to welcome you to your new home, but time has taken its toll on both it and me and, whereas you will inject some life into its old bones, I am afraid that this carcass will have to stay put and wait for you to come and visit me.

I feel that you know the Old Manor already and it is fitting that you should become its custodians. My husband would have been delighted to have a distant cousin take on the place, Matthew, and I know your dear grandfather would have approved, Emma. It is high time it heard the sound of children's voices again and perhaps one day little Rose will have a brother or sister to keep her company. I do so love the photograph you sent of her first birthday – you both look blooming – but I would appreciate a photograph of Matthew if you have one to spare.

I have been unable to leave the house as shipshape as I would wish and, although I planned to leave the furniture for you, I am afraid that Roger insists on it being sold to cover expenses. I really did not have the heart to argue with a banker, as figures were never my thing, but I've left the few bits and pieces I think really belong to the house. I could not bear the thought of strangers having them and Roger won't notice their loss.

When you are settled and visiting your parents, Emma, perhaps you might spare me a few minutes. I would so like to meet Rose and to see you both again. Please do not leave it too long, however, as time is not on my side.

Until then, this is the first time in nearly eight decades that I have lived anywhere other than the Old Manor – what an adventure!

Joan Seaton

Perhaps it was the stress of the last twenty-four hours and jet lag from the flight, but all I could do was stare at the paper until the letters blurred. A crash from the great hall brought me to life. I ran back. Theo had pulled the standard lamp over and he now sat on his round bottom looking rather surprised. The remains of the bulb lay perilously near. I picked him up and wiped his fingers free of dust and grit. If he had cut himself, there was no evidence of it now.

"Mummy, there isn't anyone here," Rosie said a little crossly, emerging through the screens from the outer hall.

"No, you're right; it's just us." I looked around the unlit room, the tatty moth-eaten curtains and the broken spring in the sofa surfacing for air through threadbare chintz. The gallery above the screens looked unsafe, and a stain darkened the broad stone flags where I suspected a roof slate had slipped and let in the rain. My breath stood pale in the air when I spoke. "This is where we'll be staying for now."

"When is Daddy coming?" she asked for the umpteenth time.

"I don't know, Rosie, but we'll have to make the best of this, so that when he does, he'll have a lovely surprise."

Rosie flapped her arms sceptically, looking around her, then eyed me with all of her four years of wisdom. "Mummy, I won't have to go to school, will I?" School. Doctors. Dentists. Local Authorities. Telephone and the utilities – where did I start? If I registered for any of them, wouldn't our names come up on some database or other? Would someone come looking for us? What were we going to do for money if my credit card could be traced? "No, you don't have to go to school, darling."

"Good," she chirped, "then I can help make this castle booootiful." She twirled on the spot.

"Moated manor," I muttered absently, wondering how on earth I could educate her in sciences and maths and all the things in which she showed a propensity and at which I sucked. I felt an overwhelming desire to find a corner somewhere and curl up and hide.

"Moated manor, moated manor," she sang, the gilded nutmeg bouncing on its chain, and then suddenly stopped, looking thoughtful. "I'm hungry," she announced.

"Rosie, you can't be; you're never hungry!"

"Theo is, too." It was true, Theo had pulled my jade beads free of my jacket and was mouthing them hopefully.

A car rumbled uncertainly into the courtyard, stopped, and my sister climbed out, crackling amid a plethora of plastic bags. She dumped them at my feet. "This place isn't easy to find, is it? I went through Oakham twice before I found the turning from Brooke. What's going on, Em? What are you doing here?" She returned my wordless embrace. When I didn't answer because I couldn't, she said, "Golly, you look *terrible*. Where's Matthew? Have you two fallen out or something? Where're the kids?" She followed me through to the kitchen while I composed myself and gave her the ragged half-truths of a story I thought she might believe.

"OK," she said slowly, perching on the wheezy vinyl-topped stool in the kitchen, "and in the meantime you're supposed to live here, in this dump?" Huddled in the warm spot by the old Aga, we waited for water to boil in a small saucepan I'd found, to which I added a couple of the teabags Beth had brought with her. She viewed the resulting brew with suspicion. "If there's no running water…"

"The tap doesn't work, but the old hand pump over the sink

still functions. It should be potable if boiled." I waved a hand at the contents of the table. "And thanks for bringing the food and the nappies and the cleaning things. Oh, blast, toothbrushes…"

She dug in a carrier bag. "I thought of those – and the toothpaste and the soap. And towels. Oh, and here's my old mobile and lead; I've put a tenner on it to get you started. Yell if you need more." Her hands flopped on her knees, the cord dangling. "Oh, but you haven't got electricity, have you? You can't charge it. Really, Em, you can't live here. You can stay with Mum and Dad until you've sorted yourself out." I shook my head. "I know it's not ideal, but it's better than this."

"We're staying here, Beth. This is our home now." The idea felt alien, the word "home" stiff on my tongue. "And don't tell Mum and Dad – not yet. Give us a few days."

"What about getting Rosie to school or if Theo needs a doctor? And there's no heating. What about baths? Don't tell me you'll be lugging water for a bath by the fire. I know you're obsessed with living in the past, but this is ridiculous." She put her arms around my shoulders and gave a light squeeze. "Look, putting your pride aside, let me give Mum a call…"

"No, Beth."

"Em, come on, be sensible…"

"No." Pride didn't come into it. Pride was the last thing on my mind, but my husband had arranged for us to be here and this is where he would expect to find us, when… if. I closed my eyes, seeing the last urgent, desperate look he had given me. "We'll be OK. And Beth, please don't tell anyone else we're here."

Her dark eyebrows curled into a question. "Who would I tell?"

"Oh, anyone, I don't know… a neighbour, a teacher at the twins' school… you know."

Standing back, she became serious. "No, I don't, Em. Are you in trouble?"

I laughed hoarsely and flipped a hand at the kitchen with its peeling green walls. "What, more than we are now, do you mean?" I went to the window and ejected the intruding tentacles of ivy, replacing them with a piece of screwed-up newspaper to stop the steady stream of winter air cascading through the gap. "I just want us to be left alone without some... some... salesman turning up on our doorstep wanting to sell plastic double glazing or solar panels to a historic listed building." I turned to find her – purse-mouthed – summing me up.

"And I'm Madonna. You're a lousy liar, Em; I wasn't born yesterday. If you're hiding from Matthew..."

"I'm not."

"All right, for whatever reason then, I won't say anything to anyone, except Rob, but don't treat me like an idiot. Now, what else do you need?"

"A job. I haven't any money."

Her mouth slackened before she snapped it shut. "But you're loaded."

"We were. Not any more, or at least not that I can access."

"How?" she spluttered. "Why?"

"It doesn't matter. I haven't any more than a few dollars and a bit in my bank account here. But I can't get it, so I'll have to work."

"At least with your qualifications, Em, you should be able to get a teaching position easily enough. You could reapply to Cambridge, surely?" That meant PAYE – National Insurance contributions – application forms – security checks – becoming visible.

"Do you have any jobs going at the restaurant – for cash?"

"Golly, that's not like you; a bit underhand, isn't it?" She almost laughed, but saw my expression and sobered. "I'll have a chat with Rob. A job, huh? You don't have a car to get to work

– and what about the children? You can't afford childcare." She chewed her lip. "School's very handy for Rosie... no, no, all right, not school. Mum and Dad could look after them, I suppose. Gosh, Em, what are you going to tell them?"

A solitary crow left the branches of a tree and rose in ragged flight, calling. I followed it until it had crossed the width of the stone-mullioned window and disappeared from view.

"I don't know, Beth. I don't know any more."

She stayed as long as she could, injecting her warmth and brightness into the barren stone, chasing Rosie and playing pat-a-cake with Theo, but she was as overwhelmed by the enormity of the task as I was and, eventually, admitted defeat.

"I'll bring Arch's old playpen over for Theo and some Lego for Rosie, as well as anything else I can lay my hands on – winter clothes, for a start. The kids must be freezing. Look, Em, are you sure you don't want to come back with me? Mum'll crack bolts if she finds out you're here and didn't tell her."

"What, and miss the chance to live like lords? Cheers, but we'll rough it here. Thanks for the things – for everything."

"That's what family's for," she said simply, and gave me a hug.

Her absence made the house seem bleaker. Now fed and asleep on the high-sided sofa in some of Archie's old baby clothes, Theo looked content enough, and Rosie entertained herself going from room to room exploring. I pushed the second sofa against the first to create a makeshift cot, and went to find her.

She came running towards me down the long corridor, her cousin's trousers sagging at the waist. "I've found a secret!" she exclaimed, hitching them up.

I peered closely. "And you've found the biscuits!" I brushed her top free of crumbs and she giggled. "I'd better find you a belt. Now, what secret have you found?"

At the wide stone arch, decorated with intricate carvings curving over our heads, she stopped. "It's a secret door, Mummy. Why is it here? Can we go in?" In answer, I heaved the door open and we stepped into the heart of St Martin's church. It took a minute to adjust to the low light. Flakes of distemper littered the red and white floor tiles, and green mould grew up columns where light couldn't reach, but little else had changed. Rooted, my daughter seemed in awe.

"This is the church of St Martin's, Rosie, and it is very, very old. A long time ago, long before you and I were born, Daddy came to church here with his family." I picked her up, feeling her warmth against me, and together we went to the Lynes tomb. "This is where his mummy and daddy are buried. They are your grandparents." She didn't say anything and I wondered how much of this she understood and whether I should say anything at all. But it seemed important that she know, and perhaps more so because this was the only tangible link that we had left.

"Rosie, you remember what Daddy and I have told you about where he comes from?" Her fingers had found their way to her mouth, and she nodded. "Look up, darling," and I pointed to the window above us. She gazed at the family captured in glass, the fair-haired young man vibrant despite the dull day. Solemn-eyed, she removed her fingers.

"It's my daddy," she said.

"Yes, it's Daddy," I confirmed, a lump forming in my throat, my eyes burning. "And when we miss him, we can come in here at any time and here he'll be, waiting for us." I pointed again, this time at Henry and Margaret Lynes. "There, you can see his parents, your grandparents."

"Who is the sleepy baby?"

"Daddy's baby brother; he died."

Rosie inspected the window and then looked down at the

tomb. She reached out to touch the face of her grandmother, her fingers marking her high cheekbones, her neat nose, her lips. "Is Daddy dead?" she whispered. Her directness knocked the breath from me, her sorrow an all-consuming smoke, like a shroud. I held her tightly and she wrapped her legs around my middle.

"No! No, Rosie – he's not dead, he can't be!" I controlled my voice.

"Then why isn't he here?"

How could I answer when I had nothing to give? "We'll visit every day and ask God to bring Daddy home to us."

"Then are we going home?"

"We are his home, and this is where we live, and this is where he'll find us." My voice broke, the weight of his absence growing like a tumour. "Why don't you explore the church and see what else you can find?" Fatigue leaching any residual strength, I sank to the floor against the nearest column and closed my eyes. Behind the lids, figures from the window bowed and danced.

A branch of the yew tree brushed the window, jerking me awake. How long had I slept? I felt sticky and unkempt. Rosie was inspecting the Lynes tomb with thoughtful fingers. She held something up in the dying light of day. "Can we bring some more?"

I stood, shedding flakes of paint from my trousers. "What do you have there? Flowers? Somebody left flowers by the tomb?"

She waved the desiccated stems and they disintegrated in her hand. "They were on this plate." In her other hand she held a small dish. It looked familiar.

"Rosie, let me see that." It was heavy and dull with years and the metal cold and grimy. I used my thumb to rub away the dust. "Oh!" I almost laughed. "Look!" And in the centre a faint shape appeared. "*Divers goodes*," I murmured. "It's the missing dish. The Seatons must have had it all this time. How funny.

We've lost the other twenty-three and after all these years find the twenty-fourth. Daddy would laugh if he knew." I choked on the last word. Rosie peered into my face and I conjured a smile. "Come on, let's go back to Theo and give this a clean."

Family Matters

Beth's car trundled into the uneven courtyard, leaving tyre marks in the pristine frost. I went to greet her as the car came to a halt, the sun reflecting off the windscreen and mirroring my phantom reflection. "You're an angel of mercy," I called, wrapping my jacket around me. "I'm out of chocolate and in desperate need of clean clothe..." I stopped dead as the passenger door opened and my mother slid out, looking grim. From the rear seat, Dad heaved himself to his feet.

"Mum caught me in your room getting your things," Beth said, throwing me an apologetic look. "Once she finished interrogating me, she insisted on coming here."

Our mother took a long, hard look at the dilapidated house, the disintegrating gatehouse, the broken slabs of the courtyard, the slipped slates on the roof, and then turned her attention to me.

I cleared my throat. "Hi, Mum."

She unpicked my dishevelled form like a seamstress. "Your father says he had no knowledge of this," she stated, starchily. "Elizabeth tells me that you have been back in the UK for the last week."

"Sorry," my sister mouthed from behind her.

"And yet you didn't think to tell us," Mum continued. "Where are the children?"

My eyes shifted to the open doorway, from which came sounds of excited squeals and chasing. Without waiting to be invited, Mum stalked inside. Dad came up and I braced for the inevitable wire-brushing. Instead, he hugged me. "It is so good to see you – to have you home, Emma. I expect there's a reason why you're here?" I nodded. "Well, then, you can tel..."

"Hugh!" my mother snapped from the threshold.

He raised his eyes to Heaven and winked. "Perhaps it can wait until later," he murmured.

Arm shaking with fury, Mum pointed to the heap of broken furniture draped in worn-out curtains in the middle of the great hall, and the two children in various states of disarray among it. "*What* is *this?*"

"Rochester Castle," I began. Rosie popped her head out of the top.

"Granny, Theo is lord and I am King John and I'm going to siege it, but I need some pigs and some pickaxes." I thought I heard Dad grunt a laugh behind me.

"We were just sorting the furniture to see if we can salvage any," I explained, "but some of it is a bit too woodwormy and we thought we could burn it because I haven't had time to collect any woo..."

"What do you think you are doing? Look at your children, Emma – Rosie says she hasn't had breakfast, and she's hardly wearing a thing in this weather, and Theo, he's... he's filthy!"

I looked at my sooty son and my daughter's bare feet. "They were helping me clear out the bedroom and Theo climbed in the fireplace. Without a fire," I hastened. "It was a bit grubby," I added needlessly. "It'll wash off."

"With what?" she demanded. "Beth informs me you've no hot water or any modern conveniences. You haven't anywhere to wash your clothes and no electricity for a refrigerator – not that you need one, it's so cold in this place."

"Mum…"

"Be quiet, Elizabeth, I'm talking. What is more, I understand you're here alone; is that correct? Where is your husband?"

"He's not here."

"That much is obvious. Where is he? Have you left him?"

"Of course not!"

"Then he's left you."

"No!" I felt my skin burn under her microscopic stare. "He's away," I said, lamely. "He's with the… the government." *Don't ask me any more*, I begged, silently. *Don't make me lie.*

Dad's eyebrows lowered. "With the government, hey? A bit hush-hush, is it, Em?" I nodded so I didn't have to elaborate. "Well, I'm not surprised; I always thought Matthew must be working on something in R and D – never particularly forthcoming about his work."

"That is no reason for his wife and children to be living like this," Mum whipped, her toe rapping the galvanized bucket I'd found to put under the leak. "What are you doing here, Emma? Why aren't you in Maine?"

"Matthew didn't know how long he might be away, so he thought we would like to be close to, er, home – family."

Mum snorted her disbelief. "*Here?*"

"Well, yes – here. He knows how much I've always wanted to live in a historic building, and this became available. And it does have family connections."

"That's very true," Dad observed.

"And immaterial," Mum flashed. "Collect your things and you can come back home with us. We've plenty of space and the children can have Nanna's room. We can be back in time for lunch."

"Mum, there aren't enough seats in the car," Beth pointed

out, "and it's illegal to double up," she added before our mother could suggest it.

"Well, we'll bring both our cars and come and collect you tomorrow, first thing, won't we, Elizabeth?" Beth opened her mouth to answer, but Mum had already moved to a different tack. "Now, Emma, what about schools…"

The familiar tingle of obstinacy. "Rosie's not going to school, Mum. I'm home-educating her as we did in Maine."

"That was when you had a husband to support you." She must have seen the hurt blanch my face because her mouth softened and she adopted a more conciliatory stance. "Darling, you must see that it's hopeless; it's positively medieval. Beth said something about you not having enough money to pay for the utilities. That can't be right, surely." I avoided her eyes and removed what looked like a dead spider from Theo's dusty fingers before he ate it. "If Social Services find you living like this they'll impound the children, or whatever it is they do."

"Then they'd better not find out. We're not leaving."

She took a step back, her mouth becoming an angry line.

Dad intervened. "Penny, leave her. If Emma wants to live here, then let her. She knows where to come if she needs us. We'll get the utilities sorted out for you, Em; don't worry about that. Get you registered and an account set up, and at least you can get the lights working."

"Dad, no – thank you. We're fine as we are. I'd rather do that myself. I'll get a job and pay for them myself."

"A job? And how do you expect to work with two young children?" Mum demanded.

"I did," Beth murmured.

"You had a husband, Elizabeth, who didn't leave you to fend for yourself in what amounts to no more than a glorified slum."

That did it; my temper flared. "Under no circumstances criticize my husband. He would be here with us if he could." Jabbing the air to emphasize my point, I said, "This is where he wants us to be and this is where he'll find us. Enough. End of discussion. Now..." I counted to five, "... would you like a cup of tea?"

Rosie ran ahead across the inner courtyard, seemingly indifferent to the biting easterly that was feeding thin, high cloud over the sky. The sun seeped through, but brought no warmth. Dad pinched his scarf closer to his neck.

"Tough at this age, aren't they? Don't feel the cold like we do. At least you won't need a fridge for the time being." We walked through the door to the stone walled garden and into another world. "Well, well," he exclaimed, "I haven't been here for many years. The Seatons kept it immaculately – kitchen garden over there, cutting garden for flowers along here – and over there," he indicated with his head, "the soft fruit cages. All gone now, I see." He looked thoughtful. "The top fruit seems to have survived, though."

"Top fruit, Dad?" Any subject was better than the one we had left behind, and I dreaded him returning to his normal habit of probing. Mum might be a natural, but Dad had made Intelligence his career.

"Top fruit – apples, pears, plums – at the far end of the orchard. Had some old varieties, if I remember correctly. Will need a good prune now, of course." We traversed the stony paths now bearded in grass, and saw Rosie scrambling up a craggy pear tree. She wedged herself securely, and waved to us. Her grandfather waved back. "The siege of Rochester Castle, hey? That was a sapper job. Good one, too, by all accounts. No time like the present to be teaching them about the past, eh, Em?" He broke a twig from an apple tree and inspected it.

"Yes, Dad, but it's about all I can teach, apart from English and geography. Matthew... Matthew taught Rosie maths and the sciences – and music. And Latin."

He tapped the trunk, felt the bark under his gloved fingers. "I don't know much about music, and my Latin is a little rusty, but I can help out with maths and physics. Engineering, too, if you like."

I remembered his ill-tempered attempts to teach me basic arithmetic at the dining room table until I had writhed in frustration. "Er, well..."

"I expect Rosie learns best by example, doesn't she? We could dig over the kitchen garden together and do a little science at the same time. Make a game of it and give you a bit of time with Theo. How does that sound?"

"Perfect, thank you."

"It's what your grandpa used to do with you and Beth, and you both turned out all right. He taught me a thing or two, although I wouldn't admit it then. I only wish I had spent more time with you. Still..." he beat his hands together to drive some warmth into them, "... it's not too late for my grandchildren, if you'll let me."

"What about Mum? She's furious."

"Don't worry about your mother; she'll come round. She's just concerned for her little girl, that's all."

Rosie swung off the branch, humming "I Had a Little Nut Tree", dangled from one hand, then dropped the eight or so feet to the ground, landing lightly. She trotted off along a path, singing the rhyme to herself. Dad watched, curiosity creasing his forehead. Without taking his eyes from her, he said, "What happened in the States, Em?"

"I told you. Matthew's been seconded to the..."

He turned neatly on his heel with military precision. "My darling Emma, I spent a good part of my career in Army

Intelligence. I might be an old dog, but I know when someone is in trouble. You're jittery as Hades and it looks as if you haven't slept. Who are you hiding from?"

"I don't know, Dad."

"Then what is Matthew mixed up in?"

"Nothing. He's done nothing wrong."

"I didn't say he had. So, will you tell me why a man – supposedly seconded to the government – loses everything, necessitating his wife and children to flee the country of his birth?" I didn't answer. "I didn't swallow that story about him buying you this place because you like history." I continued to watch Rosie without comment. "Very well, then, I suppose I will just have to trust that you know what you're doing." He straightened his shoulders in his thick tweed coat. "In the meantime, there's enough dead wood in these trees to keep you warm. What do you say to Rob and the twins coming over and giving us a hand? It will be good to get the family together – help you out."

"I don't know…"

"Give them a chance to repay some of the kindness you've shown them. Rob'll be pleased to do it."

"I didn't know you knew about the restaurant!"

"I might be a bit of a duffer, but it wasn't difficult to work out. You get a nose for subterfuge – benign or otherwise."

I cast a swift look at him and he raised a sandy eyebrow to which I returned a half-smile.

"OK, but on one condition – no more questions."

He raised his hand in a salute. "Scout's honour."

I laughed. "Dad, you were never a Scout."

He was right. Weeks of surveillance had left me worn thin and jumpy. I managed to get all the window shutters working with the help of a chisel and mallet I found in an old chest of drawers that served as a tool store in one of the barns, but even securely locked down each evening, I lay awake listening to the unfamiliar night sounds and for footsteps and the creak of a door. Lying next to her sleeping brother in the bed we shared, Rosie listened with me, and to prevent my creeping anxiety infecting her happiness, I told her whispered stories of her father's past and the generations of history to which he bore witness.

After the initial shock of separation, the loneliness set in and, following that, a sort of equilibrium. My next biggest issue was finding a source of cash. True to his word, Dad, Rob and the twins turned up in wellies and jeans, and we set to clearing the orchard and reducing the surplus wood to useful logs we left against the wall to dry. While Mum and Beth looked after Theo, Rosie ran around gathering twigs with Archie, who at nearly six, took it upon himself to be her "big brother".

"Good luck with that," Rob commented as his youngest son watched open-mouthed as Rosie evaded his attempts to catch her by scaling a tree and lobbing tiny, withered crab apples at him from above. Rob leant on the tree loppers to watch. "You know, putting aside circumstances for a minute, this is a great opportunity for the kids to get to know each other." Depositing an armful of smaller branches on the pile, I joined him. "Emma, about a job at the restaurant..."

"It's OK. Beth told me you can't take anyone else on; we'll make do. Just admit that you don't want me anywhere near the kitchens."

"Your antithesis to anything culinary might have had something to do with it. No, seriously, it's just that we're fully staffed." He checked over his shoulder, but the twins and Dad were inspecting a gnarled apple tree sprouting mistletoe like a green beard speckled in pearls. "I know you're keeping a low profile, and Heaven only knows how you'll avoid being clobbered with council tax if they find out you're living here, but in case they do, this might come in handy." He unzipped his rough jacket and withdrew an envelope. "It's not as much as we'd like, but this is your share of the profits. Matthew said we were to keep it to reinvest in the business, but I guess he'd rather you have it. It'll tide you over Christmas if you don't eat anything." He smiled uncertainly. "There'll be more where that came from in time – when the business becomes established."

"Thanks."

"It won't buy you an Aston, or anything."

"Then it's a good thing I don't want one. I need some transport, though. I can't ask you to keep coming all the way from Stamford every time I need something. I can walk directly to Manton over the fields to get a bus, but I'll have to take Theo and Rosie and the ground's not suitable in places, and a taxi's out of the question."

"Not ideal, is it? Look, that cash'll get you a banger with a year's MOT and low insurance. Do you want me to find one?" He frowned. "What's the matter?"

"Yes, please, but I can't have anything traceable back to me. I daren't."

"Are you in that much trouble?" He exhaled slowly, making a whistling sound through his teeth. "All right. I'll buy it in Beth's name. That way you won't have to pretend to be a middle-aged Scottish bloke when you get pulled over by the police for speeding."

I smiled thinly. "I really don't want to involve you, but..."

"You can't see an alternative," he finished. "No, I know. See it as payback. We'd never have bought the restaurant without you. Now," he said, easing his long back, "we'd better get this finished so we can enjoy that banquet I know you have waiting for us inside."

CHAPTER

20

Between a Rock and a Hard Place

Send me some tokens, that my hope may live
Or that my easeless thoughts may sleep and rest
John Donne

How quickly we adapt when we have to. Over the next week, Rosie and I explored room by room, noting what could be salvaged, the general state of disrepair. We decided which rooms we would live in and turned the keys on the others which seemed to have served as no more than a repository for the generations of detritus Roger Seaton had spurned. Then we went outside to the great stone barns full of corrugated scrap and tarpaulins and mice, down past the trees to where the formal gardens and tennis court once stood, and further to the waterlogged scrapes that were all that remained of the fish ponds by the narrow river. Overgrown and unloved, the bones of the manor lay under matted grasses and a tangle of bryony, bramble and hop.

Bit by bit we unpicked the history of the house and, as it became more familiar, we found ourselves seeing past the scars of its past, and found in its worn façade and dusty demeanour a more friendly face. Devoid of electricity, we resorted to time-honoured methods of cleaning. Finding a broad-headed broom in the stables, we wrapped it in a bit of curtain and sprinkled the great hall's slabs of stone with water. And then Rosie sat astride the broom like a hobby horse while I pushed her around, leaving wet snail trails that Theo, thundering along on all fours, followed.

When they grew tired of cleaning and my hands and knees became raw, we cocooned ourselves in front of the fire in my blue cashmere blanket smelling of home, and I read to them tales of Alexander the Great, of knights in castles, of Peter Rabbit and Winnie the Pooh, until darkness fell and I could see no more. I found a certain peace in an existence stripped of complication, and manual labour drove out the gnawing hunger that life without Matthew left. Too tired to stay awake, I fell asleep after our prayers to the sound of Rosie's song. But all the while that aching loneliness, the fear of what Matthew might be going through, the dread that I might never see him again.

One night, hours before dawn, an unheard sound woke me. I lay straining into the dark, my heartbeat the loudest thing in the room. There, a soft noise outside the shuttered window. Scratching. Rosie looked around from where she read in the remaining light of the fire as I climbed out of bed and put my finger to my lips. I could sense her fear as, wide-eyed and numb, she watched me check the shutter bar. My daughter: not yet five years old and already world-wary and watchful. I glanced at Theo's sleeping form – no more than a bump of rumpled duvet in the bed. Innocent. Vulnerable. How could I protect them, guide them – be mother and their father? Who – on God's good earth – had the right to steal their childhood?

Anger swelled, and I found myself in the hallway, down the dark stairs; outside in the night, poker in hand, facing the unseen foe that snatched my sleep and threatened my children –

had stolen their father and my husband. My bare feet stung and slipped on the courtyard flagstone.

"Where are you?" I yelled into the night. "What do you want? Show yourselves, cowards!" Through the arch, mist clung to the contoured land, veiling the oncoming dawn and lank grasses stiffened with frost. Fumbling my way to the front of the house, I expected to see masked figures swarming, but instead a shape moved low on phantom wings, and soared in an arc towards the blank eye of the gatehouse. An owl. I watched it fly back towards my shuttered window and land lightly on the ledge from which it stalked the surrounding land with night eyes. I'd last seen an owl with Matthew. We had watched it from our bedroom window, his arms around me, bathed in moonlight as bright as day, safe and warm.

At the thought of Matthew, his absence grew, becoming a bubble of overwhelming loss. What did I think I was doing? What could I do? The futility of it all swamped my brief courage. The bubble swelled and popped. I dropped the poker and, sinking into the sedges lining the dry moat, raised my head and into the anonymity of the mist, howled out my loneliness.

"It's the best I could do for the money," Rob said, handing me the keys. "I got them to throw in new tyres and a tankful of petrol. I think the Scottish brogue gave me an edge in negotiations." I circled the scarlet Nova, inspecting it. "I thought the five-door would be easier for getting the kids in and out, and I've put Archie's old car seat in there for Theo." I opened the rear hatch and let it drop closed again, expelling a waft of stale nicotine a cheap air freshener in the shape of a tree couldn't disguise. "I gave it a quick vac, and it could do with a good clean, but I've checked it thoroughly – it's sound enough and it'll be economic to run." He shrugged. "Not what you're used to, is it?"

"If it'll get us to town and back again safely, then I don't care how old it is or what it looks like. Thanks, Rob, you've done a grand job."

He handed me the envelope of notes; it was considerably thinner than before. "That's all that's left after tax. I got the insurance a bit cheaper, though."

Tucking it away, I smiled. "You're a star. I owe you a mug of tea for that."

We took a bundle of wood each back to the house to feed the kitchen stove. From the great hall I could hear Rosie giving Flora commands to gallop. Rob fed wood into the Aga. "So, what are you going to do about cash?"

Centring the kettle on the hob, I crossed my arms and leaned against the chimney breast where warmed stone radiated gentle heat. "There're not many jobs I can do for cash and no questions asked, so I'll either have to sell my body or my jewellery – and since only one of them's moral, it'll have to be my jewellery – and hope that I can come up with another source of income before my options run out."

"Not your wedding ring, surely!"

"No, not that – never that. But the earrings Matthew gave me, and Nanna's gold watch should fetch enough to tide us over. I won't sell her earrings unless I have to, and never my cross."

"Won't last for long, though."

I gave a thin smile. "No, not for long."

He was right. Setting Christmas aside, the remainder of the cash was barely enough to pay for necessities, let alone the vital repairs to make the house weathertight. Several roof tiles had slipped, letting in sparrows and the rain. Come spring there would be a flock of them up there in the rafters, holding court in high voices.

Desperate times called for desperate measures. Among the

papers in the leather document wallet, I'd seen George Redgrave's contact details. Loathsome misogynist he might be, but he was also the family lawyer and was under strict instructions to help me if Matthew was unable to do so. Through him I might be able to release some of the wealth Matthew had tied up in businesses and shares and things about which I had absolutely no idea at all. But Redgrave did. I had a thirty-second window to find out before the call could be traced.

I prayed the battery would hold out long enough as I punched in the numbers on Beth's old mobile and spoke to an officious receptionist.

"Your name?" she asked in tones that made my toes curl.

"Lady Cordelia Flyte," I said stiffly, feeling obdurate.

Twenty-five seconds.

Redgrave was patently a snob if ignorant of the literary reference; he took the call immediately. "Lady Flyte," he drooled, "how might I assist you?"

"This is Emma Lynes, Mr Redgrave; I need your help."

Twenty seconds.

The ensuing pause echoed down the phone. "Lynes?" he stated. "You must be mistaken. I'm afraid I don't know anyone by that name."

"You hold my husband's account – Matthew Lynes. We visited you…"

"Ah yes," he hurried, "I do recall something." I heard a faint click, making my blood run thin. "I will need to look at my records. Where are you staying now?"

Fifteen.

Why wouldn't I be in Maine? Where else would I be? "Mexico City," I lied.

"Very good," he said smoothly. "Give me your contact details and I'll…"

I didn't let him finish. I stared at the mobile long after I'd cut him off and saw it shake in my hand. He hadn't asked where Matthew was; he assumed I wasn't in Maine. He knew – and if he knew, it meant he had been told. Who else had been listening?

"Mummy?" Rosie stood by my side holding a piece of paper.

"What is it, darling?"

"I've made a letter for Father Christmas." She held out the letter. "Can we put it in the chimley?"

Kneeling in front of her, I took the paper on which she had written, in green crayon, a list in oversized letters. Here and there, a beautifully formed letter stood out as palpable evidence of her father's late-night writing sessions. Figures in red decorated the edge of the paper, and above them a big yellow sun smiled.

"It's beautiful," I said, my vision swimming.

"Mummy, read it."

I rubbed the back of my hand across my lids, coming away wet. "My eyes are tired, Rosie; will you read it to me, please?"

"Dear Father Christmas," she read from the jumble of squiggly letters. "Please bring me my daddy and a puppy and make Theo grow quicker so he can play more." She pointed to a large green dot. "I put in a period."

I smiled, "So you did; well done. In England, we call it a 'full stop'. Who are these people?"

"That's Father Christmas, and that's Theo and that's you and that's me and that's Daddy. And that's Puppy."

"What's Daddy doing?" I asked, puzzling at the figure with his arms raised towards the sun.

"He's looking at Jesus," she said, as if it were obvious. "Daddy says Jesus is the Sun of God and we have to look to Him for all our hope, so he's looking at Jesus because he hopes to come home."

I pressed my lips together and breathed carefully to still the bulging emotion galloping up my gullet. Why was I being so wretchedly emotional all of a sudden? Must be PMT. "And what would Theo like for Christmas, do you think?"

She stuck her finger in her mouth thinking and swaying back and forth. "Theo would like... a puppy," she said firmly with a nod. "Can we put dec'rations up now? Please?"

Christmas and decorations were the last thing on my mind, but I would have to make an effort for the children's sake. "It would be fun to make some, wouldn't it? We could decorate the house as Daddy did when he was a boy – with ivy and holly and berries from the garden."

"Yes, yes, yes!" Rosie jumped up and down.

"But first I have something I must do. Why don't you get yourself ready and see if you can get Theo into his boots?"

I took the battered metal box from where I had hidden it from inquisitive little hands and secreted myself in the stone-lined pantry. We assessed each other – it with an unblinking eye and me with mounting caution. Matthew had made me practise unlocking the complicated mechanism until I could do so blind, and I did now, eyes tightly shut, listening for the telltale click and whirr of the locks deactivating the explosive device in the lid. Easing the lid open released the heady perfume of parchment and sealing wax and leather. I removed the contents and, leaving the box out of harm's way, took the documents through to sit by the fire in the great hall.

Setting aside the journal in its stained leather bag, I started to sort through the pile. I don't know quite what I expected to find, perhaps some cash stashed away between the neatly stacked documents, or a secret bank account I could raid. Instead, I unfolded page after page of title deeds going back centuries and each signed and sealed with Matthew's distinct antique signature: *Matthew Lynes* – his history laid out spanning generations and continents – land in countries that no longer existed, houses long since demolished and eaten up by motorways and shopping centres. Retrieving a loose scrap with a scribbled address that had fallen free of the rest, I looked in despair at the documents spread around me on the sofa. What had he hoped we could gain by keeping these, other than a record of his life in wax and ink – an elegant reminder of what had been? Only one seemed of any value: the title deed to the Old Manor and its lands. He had paid Mrs Seaton a fair amount for the farm, but it gave us little more than a roof over our heads and nothing with which to repair it. Matthew might have known what to do with this lot, but I hadn't a clue. I refolded the deed and chucked it on the pile. At least we couldn't be evicted.

Sounds of struggle and protest came from the hall. Rosie had Flora's old ladybird wellies on and was trying to persuade Theo into the boots Mum had bought him, but he sat stolidly on the floor with his legs thrust stiffly out in front of him and a look of deep resentment in his downturned mouth.

"Come on, Theo, we're going into the garden. Look, Rosie has her boots on." I wriggled a boot on one foot and stretched for the second. "Da-dee," he said, and fixing me with an accusing glare, dragged the boot off his foot and lobbed it as hard as he could. It struck me squarely in the face. My lip began to swell beneath my fingers. I looked at his stubborn jaw, his sister's shocked expression, and something inside crumbled. Without speaking, I left them, stumbling along the corridors until I came to the church. Closing the oak door on the world, I leant against it, not knowing why I was there but feeling the desperate need to escape.

From what?

From everything: from this house and its need to feed off non-existent funds. From my children and their dependency on me, when I failed them in so many ways. From Matthew, because every waking moment reminded me of what I'd lost and the torment he might be going through. And I resented it. I resented being in this ridiculous position. I resented years of looking over my shoulder, and obfuscation and lies. I resented the short time we had spent together – this reining in of my emotions, of the loss of hope and the futile stiff upper lip and the gnawing reminder of what I should be. Of the almost getting there only to have it taken away. I resented my failure. I resented the years spent in guilt. I resented God.

Collapsing against the Lynes family tomb, I looked up at the window above the altar. "Why?" I demanded of the crucified image. "What is this all for? Why do you give so much only to take it away again? Why bring us here when Matthew is… is locked away somewhere? Do you even give a monkey's what happens to us? What more do you want, when we've done all we can?" I curled my fingers into fists. "Don't you understand – I can't go on – I have nothing. Left. To. Give."

No answer. No sudden flash of insight. No peace.

I didn't even have the energy to cry. I pushed wearily to my feet. "I give up. You win. Have it your own way."

Rosie and Theo sat side by side on one of the sofas in an aura of deep blue melancholy. Theo had his boots on and his feet stuck out over the edge.

"I said Bear wanted to go outside so he had to put on his boots," Rosie explained. "Theo didn't mean to hurt you, Mummy."

"I know."

"Can we go out now? Please?"

I nodded, subdued, flat, and Rosie hopped off the sofa and ran towards the hall. I picked Theo up – a warm bundle in his padded suit. He regarded me sombrely, and putting his hand to my sore lip, patted it. "Mumma."

I returned a weak smile. "It's all right, baby, it's almost better."

Out under the wide sky, I followed Rosie without enthusiasm, helping her gather strands of ivy with bobbly heads of sloe-blue berries, and red-berried serrated holly. She then ran ahead to the walled garden to find mistletoe. I found her hanging upside down from her favourite pear tree, singing to Ottery. I popped Theo in the baby swing Dad had rigged for him, and went to cut mistletoe.

"'I had a little nut tree, nothing would it bear'..." Rosie sang, "... 'But a golden nutmeg and a silver pear...'" From across the garden a robin chided. It flew to the wall-head, cocking its bead-black eye. I cut a few sprigs of mistletoe, preoccupied, as Rosie started her song again. "'I had a little nut tree, nothing would it bear...'" The robin flew down to a nearby branch. "... 'But a golden nutmeg and a silver pear.'"

"Silver nutmeg, Rosie, and a golden pear," I corrected without thinking.

She swung back and forth in a halo of red-gold hair. "Daddy said 'golden nutmeg', like mine – look." I cast a sideways glance at my daughter, holding out her nutmeg necklace for me to see. I frowned.

"Yes, but the rhyme is 'silver nutmeg', darling. Daddy must have forgotten."

"Golden nutmeg, golden nutmeg," Rosie sang. "Daddy said I carried our hope in my golden nutmeg."

I stopped snipping. "What did you say?"

She ceased swinging, reached up to take hold of the branch, and did a neat somersault to the ground. "Hope in my nutmeg." She waved it at me and it rattled heavily in its cage of gold.

"Rosie, may I see it, please?" I helped her undo the catch. The gilded nutmeg lay solidly in my hand. Peering closely, I made out the fine line where the two halves of the cage around it joined.

Rotating the nutmeg, I pressed the cage gently. It remained whole. I turned it over and inspected the bottom, and back again to look at where it attached to the decorative jump ring.

"Are you trying to open it, Mummy?"

"I thought it might, but I must be wrong." I handed it back to her.

"Like this." With a quick twist of the jump ring the cage sprang open in her fingers and, beaming, she held out her hand on which the loose nutmeg rolled. "Daddy showed me."

I took the nutmeg and this time, without its cage, noticed how heavy it felt. Shaking it, I detected a distinct thud of something solid inside. Certain now, I pressed firmly where the casing naturally cracked, and the nut broke open. Instead of the nut-brown fruit, something refracting light tumbled into the long grass. Rosie pounced.

"Glass! It's pretty!" She waved it in the sunlight, splitting the rays. I took it and held it up to the sun, squinting.

"I think… it's an aquamarine. It's huge!" I swallowed. "Golly." Cleared my throat. "Wow." And I found myself laughing and, not being able to stop, collapsed into the damp grass, where the laughter became sobs that shook my body, sucking air in painful chunks.

"Mummy!" Rosie tapped my shoulder, peering past my loosened hair. "Mum-my!"

Gradually, I brought myself under control and pulled her to me. "It's all right, sweetheart. It's just that God has a strange sense of humour sometimes, and I just saw the joke. How could I possibly think that we wouldn't be provided for? How could I have doubted for one moment that he doesn't have us, right here, in his hand?" The pale blue, exquisitely cut stone, glittered on my palm.

"It's mine," Rosie said. "Daddy gave it to me."

I hugged her tightly. "Daddy trusted you to look after the nutmeg so that he could help us when we needed it. This stone is his way of looking after us even when he isn't here. We can mend those roof tiles now. We might even have a bit left over."

"But… my nutmeg…" Her lip began to wobble.

"Look, the halves fit together and we'll put it back in its cage just as before." I kissed her forehead. "You have carried our hope so carefully; Daddy would be very proud of you."

She brightened and, wriggling free, said, "Can we put the dec'rations up now, please?"

"Yes," I said, climbing to my feet and feeling my trousers sticking damply to my skin. "It's time we made this house our home."

CHAPTER
21

Father Christmas

Sitting in the window embrasure in a patch of sun, I nudged the stone and it spun on the deep sill, sending shafts of fractured light spinning like a disco ball. My attempts to sell it had proved worryingly fruitless.

"And you came by this, how?" the besuited jeweller had asked, holding it between thumb and forefinger like an accusation.

"My husband. He gave it to me."

He looked me over and I scraped my still-damp hair behind one ear and sat up straight. I'd left a trail of mud across their plush red carpet and my sister's old hacking jacket didn't help my image. The only respectable thing about me were my rings, which he had already sized up. He probably thought I'd nicked them.

"And you have documentation – proof of ownership, a GIA certificate?"

"No. What's that?"

"Verification that the stone is genuine... authentic."

"Well, it is, isn't it?"

He smiled in that condescending manner some men have towards younger women. "Without a certificate I would be taking a risk..."

"Are you interested in buying it, or not?"

"If you let me have your details, I'll get back to you."

Plucking the stone from the table and slipping it back into my pocket, I stood up. "Thanks for your time." And I left, keeping my face averted from the intrusive surveillance of their security system.

I now faced an unenviable truth: it must be worth a bit – I knew that much from my days browsing Bond Street jewellers – and I possessed the means to fix those tiles, feed my children over Christmas, and perhaps even put petrol in the car, but without authentication and giving my name and address, I couldn't sell the wretched thing. Anyway, with a frantic week until Christmas, most reputable dealers were putting off new trade until the New Year, and the less than respectable ones – well, I had hoofed it out of there quicker than I could spit. Perhaps I could take Dad along with me and lend an air of gravitas to the next meeting. He could always growl at them. On the other hand, I didn't want to have to explain to him why I was suddenly in possession of a large aquamarine. There was no other option but to put it away until after Christmas and hope for inspiration.

The lid of the metal case fell back, making the phials of explosive chemicals rattle and me flinch. Wrapping the stone in one of Mrs Seaton's old lace hankies, I dropped it in a corner. As I began to close the lid, a loose piece of paper, caught in the perpetual draught from a ropey leaded windowpane, floated haphazardly to the floor. Smaller than the rest, it seemed out of place, so I put it to one side as I relocked the box and took it to the pantry to hide.

The scrap was still there when I went back in. Flicking it with a nail, I read my husband's writing: Levi Dobranovich, and an address in Birmingham. Nothing more. Was it significant? Probably, but nothing indicated its relevance other than Matthew had thought it important enough to leave it there.

I left the paper under a pine cone and went to stoke the Aga to reheat my sister's lasagne and put the kettle on. The solid mass of chilled cheese and white sauce looked particularly unappetizing, and my stomach quailed at the thought of eating it. Christmas was going to prove interesting.

"But of course you're coming home to us for Christmas, darling," Mum had said on her last visit. "Beth, Rob and the children are coming over for the day. You can't possibly be here by yourselves – that would be quite miserable. Think of the children."

I had – endlessly – but an undefined notion kept niggling away in the nether regions of my psyche, compelling me to stay. "Thanks, Mum, but we'll have Christmas here. Perhaps we could pop over on another day?"

"That's silly, Em," Beth said when she heard of my decision. "You could have had a few days off, being mollycoddled, fed and *warm*. Golly, I couldn't survive without a hot bath. How do you shave your legs? And how you cope washing your hair under that hand pump I'll never know."

"We manage. It's quite fun, really – like camping."

"I hate camping. I always had my period the moment we arrived at the campsite. That reminds me – do you need any more supplies? You must be due."

"What?"

"You know – *feminine* products."

"Yes, I know, I know. Hang on..." I counted on my fingers while my sister waited impatiently. I looked up, aghast. "Oh, no, Beth – no, I can't be!"

"You're not pregnant, are you? Em, you idiot!"

I flumped onto the wheezy stool by the stove and must have looked pretty desperate because Beth wrapped her arms around me. "You are in a bit of a pickle, aren't you? It's not the end of the world, Em. Let Matthew know and then perhaps he'll cut short whatever he's doing. He won't want you struggling alone here if you're pregnant."

Pregnant. How on earth was I going to manage, with Theo still in nappies and needing less and less sleep as the weeks went by? Soon he'd be up all night like his sister and, although I didn't need as much food or sleep as I used to, I would still need to rest at some point. Matthew had always been there, taking advantage of the long nights to teach and bond with his daughter, whereas I barely managed to juggle everything without him with the two children as it was. A bubble of loneliness surfaced and popped in a sob. I quickly smothered it; there were plenty more where that came from if I gave them free rein.

Beth squeezed me to her woolly bosom. "I know, it's a bit of a shock, isn't it? I remember when I found out I was pregnant with Arch. You'll give Matthew a call, won't you?" I made an indeterminate movement with my head which she took for a nod. "Good, and that settles it – if you won't come to us, we'll come to you – bring Christmas lunch and everything."

I pulled away. "Beth, you can't!"

"Yes, we can. I've always wanted an Aga and Dad'll love playing Lord of the Manor. You can put him on that dais and he can wear a paper crown."

"I haven't enough chairs..."

"We'll bring some from the restaurant in the van. Any other objections?"

"I haven't any presents for anyone."

She flapped a dismissive hand. "Right, we'll be over bright and early. Make sure both ovens are hot."

"Both?" I queried, frowning at the range.

"Em, there are *two* ovens. You are hopeless; it's a wonder the kids don't starve."

* * *

Sharp blue skies replaced the moose-grey clouds of the previous few weeks and welcomed Christmas morning. Brittle frost limed long grasses and glazed the bronze leaves of last season's brambles as Rosie puffed clouds of vapour towards the rising sun. "Can Daddy see the sun?" she asked. Stacking logs into the sack, I checked her, but her colours were bright in the early morning light.

"I don't know, but it's the middle of the night in Maine."

"Yes, but the sun's always there even if we can't see it, isn't it? That's what Daddy says. Daddy likes the sun."

An image of Matthew raising his face to the golden disc crashed heavy-footed into my memory. I gave a wobbly smile. "Let's get this wood in and make the house cosy."

Cosy. That was one word that didn't quite fit the great hall in winter. Still, the fire helped if you climbed under the hooded canopy with it, and with swathes of ivy studded with holly and whatever berries we could find, the room looked homely and welcoming enough. We had improvised a tree and Rosie hung pine cones on cotton as baubles that Theo batted like a cat, and swags of ivy for tinsel. High up and out of reach, I draped the few remaining strands of bright red bryony scavenged from the hedges. The tree looked very... traditional.

"Shall we go and put Jesus in his crib in the church," I suggested, "and spend some time with Daddy before everyone arrives?" In the quiet of the church, we laid Jesus in his matchbox crib among the dolly-peg figures on the rickety altar, next to the cross made of plaited grass, while Theo explored, occasionally stopping to hoist himself to his feet. There, isolated for just a little while from our shattered world, we found peace and a sense of wholeness.

***

"Happy Christmas, Rosie!" Dad lifted her into the air with some effort. "I think you've grown since last week. Are you looking forward to Aunty Beth's turkey?" I slid a quick look in her direction but she had it sewn up.

"Mummy says I mustn't because I have a funny tummy." She patted her stomach, looking suitably disappointed. It was at least partially true. "I can have a teensy-weensy bit, can't I, Mummy?" She turned large, sapphire eyes on me.

"Better not just yet, sweetheart. Perhaps later."

"Dicky tum, hey? I hope it's not something you've eaten." He put her back down a little hastily. "That Gurney's making a difference, Emma; it's almost warm in here."

"And the Aga's belting out heat. Beth's been here all morning..."

"... slaving away," Beth said, appearing from the kitchen to greet our parents, wiping her hands on her apron. "We've got your thron... chair ready for you, Dad. The kids are in the great hall sorting presents if you want to say hi."

"Where's Theo?" Mum asked with her anxious face on.

"Helping," I said, giving her a hug. "Happy Christmas, Mum."

"Splendid," Dad announced, sitting back in his chair to give the cloth-covered table a final appreciative sweep. "Beth, you've worked wonders."

"Darling, Theo's only had a mouthful or two. Would he like a little more? And are you sure Rosie shouldn't have something to eat?"

"Theo had plenty for breakfast and Rosie's fine, Mum. It's better if she doesn't. Anyway, she's busy playing with the Barbie Flora's given her. She loves it." I smiled at my teenage niece, her bubble hair tamed into a neat bob.

"Wait till she sees the castle," Flora beamed. "You remember the one, Emma? You and Matthew gave it to me one Christmas." She faltered as she saw my face straighten at the memory.

"I do, Flora. That's really kind of you to let her have it." I crumpled my napkin, feeling suddenly hollow.

Dad cleared his throat. "Such a fine room, Em. You've made it much more comfortable. I was looking at the family tree a few weeks back. I'd forgotten that one of our ancestors lived near here in the sixteenth century in a place called New Hall – long gone now, of course. An Emma D'Eresby. Married a Lynes too. Same family Joan Seaton told us about that time – chap had a run-in with his uncle and had a narrow escape, by all accounts. Lynes and a D'Eresby. Extraordinary coincidence."

Beth, rosy with wine, raised her glass. "Em doesn't believe in coincidence, Dad. She would say it was 'meant to be'." She finished the last drops, chortling.

I wiped Theo's chin free of gravy, fighting the sticky hand that tried to push me away. "There's a stained-glass window in the church which has an image of her, Dad. The Lynes family is buried here."

"Really? I'd like to see that." Did it matter if he saw the resemblance between the stained-glass image and his son-in-law? Did part of me want to tell him, to remove the veil of lies we had drawn – by necessity – over our lives? *No more lies*, Matthew and I had promised each other all those years ago, when the uncertain future seemed more solid than ours did now.

The wind had gathered strength during the course of the morning and now sucked and blew at the chimney. Mum shivered.

"It's the ghosts, Granny," Alex grinned. "I bet this place is haunted. Seen any ghosts, Emma?"

"Alex, really!" Mum admonished. "Although I don't know how you sleep here alone at night, darling."

"I'm not alone, Mum."

"I know, but it isn't the same without... I mean, it's different, isn't it?" She changed the conversation. "It used to be so beautifully kept when I met your father here, girls. We had the most wonderful tennis parties, and the terraced lawns overlooking the courts had herbaceous borders to die for, or so your father thought."

"They did," Dad confirmed, looking wistful. "The Seatons had several gardeners to maintain it."

"And the winter ball. Hugh, do you remember? The music and the dancing – not that your father ventured much beyond a waltz – but we had such fun. The Seatons always had a magnificent Christmas tree covered in lights and decorations, and a big ball of mistletoe hung over there in the doorway." She indicated the door to the screens passage. "Really, one couldn't enter the hall without someone trying to snatch a kiss." She laughed, a little self-consciously, I thought, and had avoided looking at me throughout her reminiscences. There was nothing I could say.

"I like *our* tree, Granny," Rosie piped up, looking her grandmother dead in the eye.

Mum coloured. "Yes, of course, darling. It is a super tree – so clever of you."

"I think I'd better put the kettle on," I said, making the trestle shudder as I rose.

Rob began to collect the bowls. "Alex, Flora, give me a hand, please. Arch, grab the napkins."

Mum's colour deepened. "I didn't mean... but, how could Matthew leave you like this? What sort of husband lets his wife and children live in such a state? And at Christmas! He could at least have made an effort to be here for Christmas."

Biting my tongue, I said quietly, "He would be here with us if he could. Now..." My chair grated over the stained stone floor as I pushed it back. "Would you all like tea to go with the cake?"

"She doesn't mean to," Beth said, depositing plates on the kitchen table next to the remains of the turkey.

"I know."

"Mum's just worried about you."

"Yes, but she has no need to be."

"You can't blame her; you've hardly been yourself since you've been here. You're sort of... absent." How could I not be? I'd left part of myself in the States. "You've still not heard from him, then?" I gave a quick shake of my head. "Yeah, but Matthew'll be OK, won't he? I mean, if he's working for the government and it's all hush-hush and that sort of thing, they'll have to look after him, won't they?"

I half-heard her as from the kitchen window I watched Rosie take Barbie and Archie on a tour of the inner courtyard, chatting away and demonstrating the lifting gear on the covered well.

"Anyway," she said, becoming brisk, "staring out of the window all day won't get these dishes done. Is that water hot yet?"

I turned from the window and felt the side of the first kettle on the stove. "It's boiling." Steam spiralled as I poured water into the sink half-full of cold water. Leaving my rings on the deep windowsill and rolling my sleeves past my elbows, I reached for the sponge. Beth picked up her apron from the stool. "Alex, Flora – come and help, please. Rob, chivvy them along will you, love? Now," she said in a busy voice, "let's get started."

With hands already soapy, I plucked the apron from her and gave her a little push towards the door. "You've done enough today; it's my turn."

"Don't be daft, Em; you need to rest, and those hands of

yours wouldn't know one end of a washing-up sponge from the other. Mine, on the other hand..." She held out stubby fingers, red skin chapped and nails ridged. She pulled a face.

"All the more reason you go and sit down," I insisted, not rising to the sibling jibe. "I'm quite capable, so don't treat me like I'm completely useless. Can I have that second kettle of water, please?" She tutted and grabbed a cloth to lift the kettle. As Beth turned, kettle spitting, she skidded on the greasy flagged floor and boiling water shot from the spout over my bare arm. I yelped, recoiled, and Beth shrieked. Rob came running from the great hall, followed by the twins and my parents.

"Sorry; I'm so sorry," Beth gasped, face colourless, still clutching the kettle as I stood staring like an idiot at the scarlet skin of my arm. I covered it with my hand.

Rob grabbed my elbow. "Quick, put it under cold water!"

Beneath my hand, the pain was lessening by the second. "I'm OK, don't worry."

"Did you burn yourself?" Mum asked, trying to pull my hand away. "Does anyone have any lavender oil? Do you need a doctor?"

"No, really, I'm fine; it wasn't that hot – look," and I showed them my arm, a fading reddened mark where the water had scalded my skin.

Beth's mouth fell open. "But it was boiling..."

I rolled my sleeve down to my wrist. "Well, it couldn't have been. Come on, I want to get this lot washed up and put away. Alex, Flora, clean tea towels are hanging over the Aga, please." I located the sponge again and began cleaning the carving dish vigorously. Behind me, I heard Beth protesting, "But it *was* boiling, Rob..." as he led her away. In the foxed glass of the mirror above the sink, I met my father's eyes briefly before he, too, turned and followed them.

He suspected something – he had told me as much – and

part of me ached to share this burden of knowledge that now separated me from my kin. This is what Matthew had lived with for all the years of his changed life – this degree of separation. He must have known the risk of buying a house so close to my family. Did he too feel the need to return to his roots? Or was it that he never expected us to live here in my parents' lifetime – or even my own? Now that was a sobering thought.

Outside, the younger children played in the last light of the winter sun. Archie heaved a bucket onto its side and water gushed over their feet and they danced in the flood, laughing. I marvelled at Rosie's capacity to take life as it came. As I watched, her head suddenly jerked around, tilting to listen. Then I heard it, too – an unfamiliar car engine, growing closer. My breath caught in my throat. They had found us.

Rapping an urgent warning on the window, I beckoned her inside. She didn't move. "Rosie!" I shouted through the glass. She looked at me, but instead of making for the safety of the house, started towards the outer courtyard.

"What's the matter?" Alex asked, dishcloth in hand, but I was already running into the screens passage and to the back door. This is how they had caught us out last time – when our guard was down, the family gathered in celebration. It wouldn't happen again. It couldn't. Dad appeared from the great hall. "Emma, what is it? What are you shouting for?"

"Get inside, close the shutters and lock the doors!"

"What the...?"

I was in the courtyard where Archie was standing alone and confused. "Arch, inside," I ordered him. Evening light made silhouettes of the high walls, but premature dusk darkened the courtyard. And there in the archway to the outer courtyard, stood Rosie. Without warning, she dropped Barbie, let out a squeal and darted forward.

"Rosie, no!" I yelled, dashing towards the arch, hearing her swift footfall tapping across the flagstones.

"Daddy!" Her cry echoed around the walls. "My daddy!" I reached the archway in time to see her fling herself at a tall figure outlined by the setting sun and haloed in fire.

"Matthew!" I breathed. For blind seconds I couldn't move, but Rosie had drawn back, gazing up at the figure bending down to her. Her thumb found its way to her mouth. The low sun filling the gatehouse arch stung my eyes as I began to move towards them, and she looked around uncertainly as I approached at a run. "I want my daddy," she whimpered. My skin prickled. "Rosie, come away!"

22

Reparation

"Emma," a calm, quiet voice called.

In the broken light he looked like Matthew, sounded like him, but it didn't *feel* like him.

"Henry?" I queried. "Henry!" I made the last few yards at a run and flung my arms around his neck. Hesitantly at first, he returned my embrace, and then strongly, fiercely.

"I'm so sorry, Emma; we came as soon as we could."

I pulled away, looking around. "'We'?"

He pointed behind him through the golden arch and out of sight along the driveway. "Pat's in the taxi. She wanted to make sure we are – I am – welcome before she imposed on you."

"Welcome? Of course you're welcome! We've missed you. Matthew would be so relieved to know you're here, that you're safe."

He stepped out of the light, his forehead furrowed. "You can say that knowing how I behaved? My ridiculous... relentless... antipathy towards him?"

Laying my hand on his arm, I peered up into his face. "Henry, you are his beloved son. Matthew never held you responsible. He regrets not having told you everything from the start. He just didn't know how. He was always worried he would lose you."

"I should have known better than to blame him. I should have known…" He hung his head, guilt suffusing the air around him.

"We all should have known. Matthew said to me once that hindsight is a precious commodity in very short supply."

Henry's mouth lifted. "Yes, that sounds like my father."

From behind me, a small voice said, "He looks like Daddy."

"Rosie, come here; it's all right." I brought her to stand by me, my arm comforting around her slight frame. "Darling," I said carefully, "this is Henry."

Henry bent down to her again and his face softened into a smile and his voice gentled. "Hello, Rosie. I haven't seen you since you were a baby. I remember choosing that otter for you just after you were born. You are such a big girl now and look just as pretty as your mommy. I'm so glad to meet you again." He held out his hand, palm up, inviting. Rosie looked at it, began to extend her own small hand towards his, but suddenly withdrew it and retreated to the safety of my legs. Clinging to the folds of my skirt, sharp eyes assessed him for a long moment. "Are you my big brother?"

Henry looked surprised and then laughed. "Why, yes I am."

"Daddy told me about you lots. Have you come home?"

Henry looked up at me. "Have I?"

"Mum, Dad, we have visitors. Pat and Henry are here." I stood aside and Beth's jaw slackened and I heard Mum's little gasp as I watched confusion ghost their faces. Dad peered at Henry before convention spurred him to stride forward with his hand outstretched in greeting.

"Well, well, this is a surprise. Patricia, Henry, I think Emma believed you were Special Forces come to investigate the strange goings-on at the manor." He laughed. "It's so good to see you."

"Golly, Henry," Mum exhaled, her hand fluttering to her cheek, "I thought you were Matthew."

Henry fingered his smooth-shaven jaw. "I'm afraid not. We always did bear a strong resemblance. It's that obsession with youth – contact lenses and a bit of bottled sunshine." He ran his fingers through his thick, wheat-gold hair, identical to his father's. "Call it an old man's vanity."

"Well, I certainly wish I had your genes," Rob said, coming forward to shake his hand.

"So do I," Pat darted a laugh before that avenue could be explored further. "Years in the sun haven't been as kind to me. And there's Flora and Alex – and Archie! My, how you've all grown up. Oh! And this must be Theo." Her eyes misted and she pressed a hanky to her nose. "Look at me! Don't take any notice; I'm just a silly old woman."

"It's been a long flight," Henry explained as I led Pat to the sofa by the fire to sit by Mum and introduced her to Theo. He gave her one of his angelic smiles and promptly burped, and she laughed, but more joyfully this time. The years had left their mark in her overly sunned skin, and her hair – once carefully cut and coloured – lay steely and ragged about her slackened jawline. But she still smiled like the Pat I once knew, and mere minutes with the children had begun to loosen the tension her shoulders bore.

"A long journey? You've been living in Arizona, I believe; is that where you've flown from?" Dad asked.

"No." Henry covered his hesitation in settling himself down on a rickety chair by the hearth. "No, we've been on a bit of an extended tour of Indonesia, Papua New Guinea, East Timor – always wanted to see more of the world." His eyes briefly met mine. "We would have come sooner, but..."

Standing with his sturdy back to the fire, his feet planted firmly apart, Dad did his best impression of Lord of the Manor. "I expect communication was compromised in such remote regions. Certainly was in my day."

"Yes, we were out of contact for a time," Henry finished quietly, and there was so much left unvoiced in the way he said it. For all he looked unnervingly like Matthew now that he had shed the glasses and beard, the light I was so used to in his father was absent in the son. I could only guess at what they had been through to get here. I detected he would rather not say.

"You must be exhausted," I said. "I'm afraid there's not much lunch left, but there's plenty of tea and Christmas cake if you would like some."

"And bags of chocolate," Beth added, "if Em will share it."

Once I'd waved my family off later that evening, I went back into the great hall. Pat dozed with Theo by the fire and Henry inspected the silver dish – recently emptied of glittering chocolate coins by the children – in the remaining light of the Christmas candles. "So, you've heard nothing?" he said, without looking up.

"I hoped you might."

He outlined the faint coat of arms in the centre of the dish, and shook his head. "No. I've heard nothing since Joel got a message to us. We were on the road within an hour. Left everything behind, as I expect you have." I felt my face drain and he winced in apology. "I'm sorry, that was insensitive of me." He came over. "You had no other choice than to leave him – you couldn't risk them taking the children. It's what he would have wanted." He made it sound as if he thought Matthew were dead. He must have realized because he added, "Dad wanted you safe because it gives him something to live for, Emma. He won't give up – give in – while you are safe."

"Yes, but the fact is that we *are* here in relative safety and he is not. We don't know where he is, who has him – anything. I can't sense him, Henry. We always had this thing – this connection

– it's difficult to explain, but it's not there any more. I know I shouldn't despair, but I can't help it. And seeing you like this, so very much like him, makes his absence unbearable."

"If I'd known it would have caused you so much pain, we wouldn't have come."

"No," I shook my head with vehemence. "That's not what I meant. I don't want you to go. Stay for as long as you want. My home is your home, as it has always been and as Matthew intended." Henry turned away, and at first I thought I had somehow offended him, until I detected the sombre mantle clouding him, and the slight shake of the silver dish he held. "Henry?" I reached out and placed my hand on his. "I don't know how long we will be safe here, but Matthew must have believed it offers us a chance of some sort of normality – a future. Please, stay, and be part of it with us."

He glanced over to the sofa, where Pat still slumbered, then back to me. He drew breath. "The thing is, Emma, we've had a complete lockdown on our finances, all our assets. We tried to access them but they've been ring-fenced and we couldn't risk being traced, so we have nothing to offer you but Pat's baby-minding service and my hard labour to pay our way."

"And both will be very welcome. I don't want anything, Henry. I'm glad of your company; it's odd how tiring it is, hiding the children's differences, let alone mine, from my family."

He placed the dish back on the table, a keen interest replacing the doubt. "You've noticed changes, then, since the transfusion?"

Pat stirred, and I nodded to the window seat at the far end of the room. We sat in near-darkness, thankful of the shutters holding back bitter wind, and lowered our voices.

"Nothing much at first – I had more energy, perhaps, didn't need as much sleep. Oh, and my appetite shrank – not that I had much anyway. But over the years I've noticed I heal more quickly and I no longer need glasses to read. All small things in themselves, but..."

"... they add up to something significant," Henry finished, pinching his lips with his forefinger and thumb, thoughtful. "Dad must have been interested in the changes in you."

I couldn't help but smile. "He was very excited and it spurred new areas of research. He was on the verge of a breakthrough when we had to run. It was one of the reasons why we didn't leave sooner."

"And the other?" I didn't answer, and Henry said slowly, "He thought I might return, is that it?"

I gave a short nod of affirmation and Henry closed his eyes. Finally, he opened them again. "Had he... changed – at all?"

"Physically? No."

He looked into the shadowed corners of the room, up at the ceiling arching over our heads, picked out by the darkened beams like the skeleton of a fossil in chalk, at the high stone mantel with the shields carved upon it. "So this is where he came from all those years ago."

"Near here – at New Hall. You remember the etching we were given for a wedding present? It hung to one side of the dining room fire at home."

"I always wondered why you had that."

"Mrs Seaton gave it to us. She met Matthew once and I think... I think she knew. Anyway, this was her home. She sold it to Matthew, but I didn't know he had bought it until we came here. The Seatons held the manor for centuries; they were cousins to the Lynes – to you. Look, this is the Lynes coat of arms." Lowering my voice and taking a candle, I crossed to the fireplace and held its uncertain flame to the carved stone shield and waited for him to join me. When I glanced at him again, his eyes glistened.

"I never imagined... I never thought..."

I laid my hand over his again and this time he grasped it. "In the morning I'll show you around and then introduce you to your ancestors."

"It's very basic, I'm afraid, but it's probably the best of the bunch." Fragile winter light did the tatty bedroom few favours. The walls shed paper like sloughed skin, and a desultory moth broke into ragged flight from the remaining rug barely covering the wide elm planks.

Pat assessed the space, cluttered as it was with saggy cardboard boxes, the carcasses of generations of woodlice, and empty picture frames propped in the corner and gaping like mouths. "Well, it could certainly do with a good clean."

"I know it isn't what you'd choose."

"Emma," she said, looking earnestly at me. "This family has been separated too long for me to care where I lay my head. Just as long as we're together. Henry's not been himself since we left Maine, and Maggie's death and Matthew's disappearance wounded him far more than he lets on. It's like something's been broken inside him, you know?" I nodded. "Anyhow, it's good of you to have us in your home."

Home. Yes, I suppose it was home now. "Then I should warn you," I replied, "the kitchen was last updated a couple of centuries ago and I still haven't worked out how to use the oven."

"Sweetie," she hooted, "some things sure don't change. Don't you worry about it. I can cook sourdough on a campfire if need be."

"It might just come to that," I murmured.

Downstairs, Henry and Theo were deep in conversation, which seemed to involve a great deal of bottom-bouncing and chortling. Henry sat cross-legged on the floor holding Bear, and

Theo, pulling himself to a rocky standing position, jiggled for a few seconds, and then dropped onto his backside with a squeal. From the bastion of a sofa, Rosie watched, fingers in mouth, mute. Without looking at her, Henry said, "Rosie, I could do with some help. I reckon the orchard would be a great place for a see-saw next to the swing. How about it? There are some long planks in one of the barns, but I don't know which is the best. Do you think you could help me out?"

Regarding him with cobalt eyes, she took her fingers from her mouth, climbed from the sofa and ran across the great hall and into the screens passage. A moment later the back door thumped. Henry looked crestfallen. "She hasn't spoken to me since we arrived."

"You look like Matthew and she misses her daddy. She doesn't know you yet."

Theo climbed onto Henry's legs, and patted his chin. Henry smiled, his eyes crinkling in that good-natured way that reminded me so much of their father. "At least I've not blotted my copybook where my little brother is concerned." Theo slid off and rocketed towards the window on all fours.

"It isn't your fault, Henry. She'll come round. It's been a lot to adjust to in a short period of time."

He smiled again, this time with a laconic slant. "Ah, so you can still read emotions, can you?"

"Loud and clear. Don't feel guilty; she'll be better once she's had a run around outside. Like her father, a bit of sunshine perks her up and we've not had much this last month." I traced the lateral joints in the flagged floor on which we sat, debating how – or whether – to bring up the next subject. Henry made it easier.

"Emma, is something bothering you?"

I glanced at him from under my lashes. "Henry, I'm so sorry about Maggie."

He avoided looking in my direction and instead watched Theo's attempts to stand using the push-along dog Matthew had given Archie when he was about the same age. Eventually he said, "I couldn't go to her funeral – none of us could – so her family wasn't there to say goodbye. To die in that state, alone, frightened, pursued... what a waste of life." He looked at me then. "She was never really happy, was she? You knew that as well as anyone. Perhaps that's what makes her death so hard."

Theo succeeded in pushing the dog along a few steps, an ecstatic grin on his little face making the contrast between his happiness and Maggie all the more poignant. He patted the dog's back and promptly sat down with a thump. He looked over his shoulder at us, wondering whether he should cry. I smiled at him and he laughed instead.

"Henry, I've been thinking about Maggie a lot recently – why she took Matthew's car, what she must have been thinking and feeling. All I know is that she thought it was something she could do to buy us time, to give us a chance – something positive for once, after all those years of resentment. She didn't die in vain, Henry; she bought us enough time to get to the plane – she gave us that chance."

"Not for Dad."

"No, but for his children, and for me; she died in an attempt to help her grandfather. When had she ever been able to do that? When had she ever been in a position, either mentally or physically, to return some of the love she had been shown in her life? When I saw her last – back at the house – something about her had changed. I couldn't put my finger on it at the time – too much was going on – but on reflection, she'd had a change of heart – as if something inside her had woken up."

"It's a pity she died before she could benefit from it."

"She died believing she could help us, Henry, and in that gift, she found a sense of freedom and happiness I don't believe she had experienced in a very long time."

"Do you truly believe that?"

"Yes," I smiled, placing my hand to my breast. "In the very heart of me." I stood up and brushed myself down. "I think it's time Theo had something to eat; he's enjoying chewing that dog's ear too much."

Henry rose as Pat came bursting in carrying something heavy, face flushed. "Look what was in the corner of the bedroom!" she exclaimed, holding out a gilt picture frame, chipped gesso glowing white and a length of gadrooned moulding missing. I looked at the unremarkable seventeenth-century landscape: yellowing fluffy trees, fluffy ochre clouds, fluffy... cows. No wonder Roger Seaton had rejected it. "Gosh. Yes, er... thanks." I ran out of things to say. Her eyes gleamed and, slowly, she turned the frame around.

Henry spoke first. "Well I never!"

"I couldn't believe it when I saw what was painted on the back," Pat said. "Isn't he handsome!"

I found my voice, taut with emotion. "He... he didn't know what had become of it. He thought it destroyed, but the Seatons must have had it all this time. Perhaps they had the awful landscape painted to disguise Matthew's portrait on the other side – to protect it – to preserve his memory."

"Then we have much to thank them for." Henry wiped away dusty cobwebs strung across his father's face, revealing an inch-long slash in the canvas. His hand dropped to his side, the smile from his lips. "Nonetheless, it seems someone had it in for him, like the monument in the church." He moved his head slowly back and forth. "I hadn't realized until now what he meant when he said he had been driven from his home, his community. I don't think I wanted to understand."

Pat gave me the painting and I took it to the light, carefully removing years of dust with a tissue. Gilded hair touched his high-necked collar, the starched white material edged in lace over a restrained blue doublet – slashed with silk and buttoned in silver. Neither Puritan in sobriety, nor extravagantly flamboyant, he represented a more peaceful era before conflict erupted into which he would inevitably be drawn. But it was in the lively expression he wore and the intelligent interest in his eyes that I recognized the man I knew and, in that second, I felt the cord that bound us, unbroken, resonant across the acres that separated us and the oceans of time. I brought the portrait to my lips and kissed it, willing him to feel it.

"I don't know what I'd do if I were separated from my husband," Pat observed. We were alone once again. "Henry's gone to fix that see-saw for the children. He needs something to take his mind off things, as do you. It can't be easy being here without Matthew, nor seeing him every day in his son."

"I'd much rather you were both here – Matthew would, too." I looked down at the benign face gazing back at me. "I'd like to get this repaired, but it'll have to wait. The roof needs looking at first and I suppose we also have to eat." I leaned the portrait carefully against the wall.

A sound of scampering distracted us and Pat burst out, "What are you doing, little man?"

Theo raced towards us, a piece of paper clamped between his lips, a mischievous look in his eyes. He reached our feet and, laughing, I picked him up and balanced him on my hip. I removed the soggy paper, exchanging it for a kiss. "He's being a puppy. I suspect Rosie's been training him as a substitute, hasn't she, slobber-chops?" We rubbed noses like Eskimo kisses and he gurgled happily. "Now, what have you found?" I tilted my head to read the scrawled writing: Levi Dobranovich, and the address and telephone number. How apposite; I had quite forgotten.

Henry and I disembarked in a dismal street little more than a glorified alley, off a busy main road, on the outskirts of the city. The cold sun seemed to struggle to gain a footing here. Traffic fumes clung to the pores of the buildings, and cheap fascias in foreign languages advertised unfamiliar foods. Cooking smells, pungent and aromatic, drifted from the flats above the shabby shopfronts. I felt alien in these surroundings.

The taxi sped away, leaving us marooned. A man sat on a stool by a shop door, eyeing us. He hawked and spat. Keeping my head down, I checked the address and located a battered metal door between two shopfronts. It had neither a name nor anything that gave away what might lie behind it, only its street number: 294. The red eye of a surveillance camera stared down, high up and out of reach. Pulling my hood further around my face, I pressed a button on a little square plate set into the wall. There was a pause, then a click as something released, and Henry pushed the door open for me. He leaned close. "Looks can be deceptive," he said doubtfully. I certainly hoped so.

A narrow flight of stairs ran up directly from where we entered. Another door stood sentinel at the top, ajar. We brought with us the odour of the street and it lingered in the ill-lit stairwell. I hesitated. I had no option other than to climb the stairs.

Violin music, more at home in a street café in Vienna, drifted through the crack the open door made. I pushed it gingerly, hovering at the threshold. The furnishings were rich – almost decadent – and at odds with the threadbare world we had left in the street below: a swollen walnut bureau with ormolu mounts, a longcase clock in russet mahogany, and in the corner, a tall stove released a gentle heat. Thick curtains hung in deep swathes across the single window and the only illumination came from strong, clear spotlights carefully positioned above the table in the centre of the room.

"Come in, come in," a European accent instructed from beyond a partition. "I have been expecting you." A little man wearing a stained leather apron, and round as a tub, greeted us. He seemed old – very old, though what his age might be I couldn't guess. He was made smaller by his bowed back and he peered up through glasses thick as pebbles. He looked like a gnome and creaked like a broken gate.

"Mr Dobranovich?" I ventured, but the old man stared at Henry as if retrieving a memory.

Finally he spoke, his voice as shrivelled as his body. "You remind me of a young man I met in my youth."

Henry replied with caution. "I... don't believe we have met before."

"You look very like him," the man said in his strangely accented English that reminded me a little of Elena. "I have an eye for such things," and he tapped his forehead with a stained finger. He beckoned us closer and now that I saw him closely, I understood his appearance of extreme age. Skin, thinned by years, creased in fine lines that spread from his eyes and around his mouth into tiny rivulets, each one engrained with jewellers' polish like niello work. He held out gnarled fingers, and I hunted in my pocket for the stone, but instead of taking it, he lifted my hand to his mouth and kissed it in an age-old gesture of courtesy.

"You are most welcome, please, come – be seated, be comfortable." His voice – if thin with age – sounded surprisingly musical, and when he smiled his dark eyes shone with genuine warmth. He led me to the flamboyant, gilt-framed chair that dominated the small room, where he left me enthroned under the spotlights. He squinted up at Henry, interrogating him, and then indicated the plain chair next to mine at the table.

"Y-es," he drew out, "you look like him. I made a necklace in the form of a snake for his wife – a fine piece, one of my best." He drew a brass eyepiece from his leather apron so didn't notice Henry blanch beneath his tan, before recovering. "No matter," Levi continued. "You have something you wish to show me, eh?" I placed the stone on the black cloth in front of him, the complex facets spitting ice-blue fire. For a long moment, he studied it without touching, then he held it to the overhead light, turning it slowly and inspecting it from every angle through a jewellers' loupe. "I know this stone." He focused gimlets on my face. "Where did you get it?"

"It's not stolen!"

"My dear, I did not think it was."

I flushed. "My husband gave it to me."

"Your husband?" His glance flicked towards Henry.

"No! No, not Henry. It is real, isn't it? I mean, it is an aquamarine?"

"I must first ask why you think I might be interested in buying this jewel."

Taken aback, I answered, "Your name was among my husband's things."

"But he did not come here himself."

"He can't," I said a little sharply, and modified my tone. "He gave me the stone to sell if I needed to. And I do. I don't have any paperwork, or a GI-something-or-other and, no, I don't know if it's been mistreated, or coloured, or anything like that."

"It has not," Dobranovich stated. "It is a natural, Internally Flawless, blue diamond – unnamed – but of impeccable provenance."

"Oh, my giddy aunt!" I whipped my hand up no sooner than

the words had left my mouth. "I'm so sorry, I didn't mean to say that. A diamond! Are you sure? It's huge! You can tell all that just by looking at it?"

"Not with all my years could I tell the history of a stone by looking at it." He smiled as I writhed, feeling ridiculous. "I should know – I sold it to a young man many years ago. The cut is very distinct – unique, in fact – and the man looked just like you, sir. Yes, exactly like you. But I regret, I cannot buy this stone."

"Why not?" I flustered. "We've not done anything wrong…"

"I do not say that you have, but I do not have the means to buy it from you." He pushed the stone towards me across the table, his sleeve drawing back as he moved. Blurred, inked marks showed at the edge of his cuff as it rode up his forearm. Numbers. He saw me look, saw the realization in my eyes. He pulled his sleeve to his wrist. "That is so, young lady. I carry my history with me, and that of my people. Even had I half its value to give you – and that would be a great sum indeed – I would be robbing the man who gave me something of greater worth than this priceless jewel."

"He helped you escape?" Henry asked.

"I promised him I would never speak of it and I am a man of my word. I recognize the truth when I see it, and I see it in you. So, I ask you, sir, was it your father to whom I sold this stone?"

"Undoubtedly."

Dobranovich bowed his head. "Then I am honoured to be of assistance. I cannot buy this jewel, but I will sell it on your behalf."

"I don't want to be identified," I said rapidly.

"And no questions will be asked. I have clients who will respect your desire for anonymity."

"Thank you. Will it take long?"

"It will take as long as it takes. Although there is no need to doubt its authenticity, my clients will wish to send it to a laboratory for testing. If you would be pleased to leave a number where I can contact you..." He noted my hesitation. "It will go no further, I assure you. One last thing," he said, as he registered the name on the paper I wrote for him. "Did your husband also give you that lion-head ring you wear on your finger?"

"He did," I said, wary again. "Why do you ask?"

"As one persecuted, I have long understood the privilege of secrets," he answered and bent over my hand and lightly laid his lips to the ring.

Henry opened the door onto the street, pulling his hat down to cover his eyes and his scarf to obscure the lower part of his face. "Perhaps we should have asked for a receipt."

"It would have seemed rather churlish. I think we can trust him. Don't you?" We walked beneath the harsh glare of the street lamps down pavements slippery with the spray from passing cars. "Gosh, a *diamond*. I had no idea. I wonder if we'll ever get to hear Matthew's full life story." We approached a junction to hail a taxi. "Just when I think I know him, something else pops out of the woodwork."

Henry flagged down a cab. "Did Dad never mention Levi to you before?"

"No. I don't think he meant to be secretive. It had just become force of habit. This is one secret I don't mind he kept. If I'd known Rosie carried a diamond around her neck, I'd have had kittens."

We lived off the tiny profits from the restaurant, eroding quickly now that the Christmas rush was over, and spent days slowly recovering the long-neglected rooms of the manor. Major work would have to wait until funds became available; until then, much could be achieved with elbow grease and a stiff brush. Stifled and feeling claustrophobic, on the few milder days I opened the front and back doors, and the casements in the bedrooms, and pulled stale air from the house. It helped ease the nagging nausea that tiredness brought. At some point I would no longer be able to hide my pregnancy from my parents, and then the real pressure would start.

With the car chugging over more or less reliably, I took the opportunity to slip into Stamford with Rosie and Theo. The jade beads swung to my waist as I knocked at the door of the single-storey building brightened with yellow sprays of winter forsythia, and heard a familiar voice from within.

"Emma, my dear!" Mrs Seaton welcomed me at the threshold of her new home. I returned her hug, much to Theo's bemusement.

"Joan, it's so good to see you again. I love your home, and what a lovely view!" I accompanied her to the big window as Joan sat down in a chair overlooking the silvered waters of the river.

"I'm as happy as a lark," she said, smiling at the children. "So this must be Theo – he likes my jade necklace, I see – and you must be Rose," she said, clapping her wrinkled hands in delight. "Thank you for coming to visit me, my dears. Oh, what pretty flowers; are they for me?" Finger in her mouth, Rosie nodded and held out the bunch of first snowdrops we had picked freshly that morning. "Lovely! I do miss the snowdrops under the hedges; are they still there?"

"They are," I said, sitting opposite and letting Theo down to explore the room. "I've been meaning to visit to see how you are and to let you know how we are settling in to our new home."

"Are you?" she said, her face becoming wistful. "I'm so glad. It was the right move at the right time, and I can't tell you how pleased I am that you took on the old place. I do like it here, though; I see my friends – not that there are many of us left, you understand – I can pop into town, and I can have as much heat as I could possibly want." She laughed and then sobered. "I do hope you and the children are warm enough; the winters can be quite frightful."

"Perfectly, thank you."

She looked at the door for the umpteenth time, a small frown crossing her face.

"Joan, is there a problem?"

"Are you alone, Emma, my dear? Only I thought that perhaps Matthew..."

"He's away at the moment," I said, without meeting her eyes.

"Away? Oh, that must be so difficult for you. You must miss him."

I nodded an acknowledgment rather than risk answering, and we moved to safer territory, exchanging news and chatting as the children watched swans drift past on the Welland's anxious water.

As her limited energy began to wane, and the years sapped the brightness in her eyes, I rose to bid her goodbye. "I meant to write to thank you for leaving the silver dish," I said, as I kissed her age-soft cheek, "and the portrait," I added.

The sparkle returned. "Ah, you found them, did you? I'm sure the dish would have fetched a pretty penny or two, but I didn't need the money and I told Roger I thought it long-since vanished."

"And the portrait?" I asked.

"Now, who would want a tatty old thing like that – except perhaps a historian and the man to whom it belongs?" And to my astonishment, she winked.

We parted with promises to keep in touch, although both aware of the limitations time and years placed upon her. It didn't seem to matter. She knew she would soon slip into the next world, but was content, having done what she could to protect the continuity of the manor, whose guardian she had become.

"Now it's your turn – and Matthew's," she said, with a certainty that seems to come with insight and great old age. "A D'Eresby and a Lynes: it is how it's meant to be."

As I closed the door behind me, musing on her final words, I turned and nearly bumped into a man sporting a silk cravat and an impatient air, standing on the doorstep and filling the space. "Watch where you're going!" he barked, extending an arm between Theo and me and inserting a key in the lock. He made to push past Rosie. She didn't move. He glared down at her. The three of us stood our ground.

"Can I help you?" I said with an edge, restraining Theo as he leaned towards the besuited arm looking for something to chew. I gave him the beads instead. The man looked me up and down, seemingly assessing my bank balance, and then his gaze fell on the long string of big, green stones Theo gummed. His eyes widened, then narrowed.

"Where did you get those?" he snapped, looking at the door as if he could see through it, and then back at me.

"They were a gift," I said, looking him straight in the eye. "Why? Are you an antiques dealer?"

"Don't be ridiculous! Do I look like an antique dealer?" he snorted, as if I cared one way or another.

"Not particularly, Mr Seaton," I replied evenly, "it's just that your reputation goes before you." And holding out my hand to Rosie, I stepped past him and into the afternoon sunshine.

Just when we thought winter over, and snowdrops clustered around the apple trees, the end of January brought late snow on northerly winds.

"Brass monkey weather," my sister puffed, hauling off her

boots in the porch and leaving clumps of snow melting in the heat of the Gurney. "Archie and the twins are sussing out the slopes for the toboggans; think Rosie'll want to join them?"

"I expect so; she's been itching to get out in the snow."

"Why don't you take her, then? You never used to miss a chance of a bit of snow."

I rubbed a hand over my eyes and yawned. "Don't feel like it. Or perhaps it's because it's not like Maine snow. I don't know."

Beth unzipped her purple fleece and hung it on the back of a chair. "You OK? You look a bit peaky."

"Could do with some warmer weather; this cold's getting to me."

She gave me an odd little look, and shrugged. "You should be used to it by now. Hey ho, let's tell Rosie her cousins are waiting for her, and then we can discuss Theo's birthday without interruption."

Rosie was by herself at one end of the great hall, busily constructing a complex marble run. Measuring a piece of knitting against a wriggling Theo, Pat looked up as we came in. "Beth! How lovely to see you, sweetie. You couldn't do me a favour and hold Theo, could you? Henry tried, but he just wouldn't keep still."

Henry grunted a laugh. "And Theo wasn't much better."

Pat flapped a hand. "You know what I mean. All alone today?"

Beth knelt by Theo, gave him a quick kiss, and then held him firmly around his middle. "The kids are outside testing the toboggan run."

"Rosie, would you like to go and find your cousins?" I asked, going over to her. "My goodness, that's a wonderful construction! It looks like the Spaghetti Junction, and I bet it works better, too."

"It's not finished yet, Mummy. Look," and she pointed to an incomplete curve. "I want to finish it first."

Henry joined us, bending towards her with his hands on his knees to admire her work. "That's quite a feat of engineering, Rosie; your father would be so proud of you." At the mention of Matthew, her face straightened, her mouth taking on a hard edge. She turned her back on him and walked away, abandoning the run.

"Rose!" I said, more shocked than cross, but Henry, recovering, held up his hand.

"Leave her, Emma; it doesn't matter." But it did. I could feel it as clearly as if he had used words to describe the rejection he felt. Chewing my lip, I watched her leave the great hall in a blister of antagonism and resentment.

Rosie was quiet at bedtime. She brushed her teeth and waited until I had fought Theo's hands to brush his. I climbed into bed next to her, where she lay on her side with her fingers in her mouth, gazing at Matthew's portrait propped next to the tryptic and pebble on the little chest of drawers by the bed. The single candle in the chipped enamel chamberstick illuminated his face, the dancing flame bringing it alive.

"Shall we say our prayers, poppet?" She didn't answer, and I put my hand on her shoulder. "Rosie?" She shook her head. "OK. I'll say them for all of us."

When I finished and had kissed each of my children as Matthew and I had always done, I gave Theo his Bear, and he wriggled happily, bringing the toy to his face.

"Where's Ottery?" I hunted around and finally located it secreted under the pillow. "Here, sweetheart," and I tucked the otter into Rosie's arms.

She viewed it with scorn. "I. Don't. Want. It!" Rosie snatched Ottery from her chest and threw it across the room where it hit the wall with a soft thump, and fell to the floor. She faced me with glistening eyes full of anger and grief. "I want my daddy! I want my da-ddy!"

"Oh, Rosie." I wrapped my arms around my daughter and held her close, feeling her body heave in uncontrollable sobs, and letting her cry her misery out.

"I really rather thought Pat and Henry would be here for their grandson's first birthday," Mum said with that slightly prurient tone she adopted when something displeased her. Beth rolled her eyes behind our mother and I poured tea from Nanna's silver teapot, on loan for the day.

"They will be; they took my car and must have been delayed. More cake, Dad?"

Dad passed his tea plate – one of the half-dozen spares from their Wedgwood wedding service. "Henry's sorted out the licence, has he?"

"No, Pat's driving." And I hoped nobody stopped her and asked to see *her* driving licence.

"Well, she's certainly done you proud here, Em. Marvellous cake."

"Actually, Dad, hard though it may be to believe, I made Theo's cake."

He inspected the slice in front of him as if it were the result of transubstantiation. It may as well have been, because it was a miracle it had turned out as well as it did. "My, my, Emma, wonders will never cease."

"Rose, darling, won't you try a little of Theo's cake?"

"No, thank you, Granny. Mummy, please may I get down from the table?" I nodded my consent, and she hopped off her chair and went to play with her marble run. I gathered the teapot and cake to take them through to the kitchen. "I'll put some more water in the pot. Back in a mo." A murmured conversation followed me from the room. When I returned, Mum dabbed her mouth with her napkin, looking earnest.

"Emma, Rosie hasn't eaten a thing."

I put the fresh pot of tea down. "She's fine, Mum. You know what children are like."

"Yes, I do, darling, and I really think she ought to see a doctor. It's so important she has the right nutrition at this age, and I know you're doing the best you can in the circumstances. Now I come to think of it, I can't remember ever seeing her eat at all."

Over on the other side of the room, Rosie had stopped humming. Seemingly oblivious to her grandmother's concerns, she jumped to her feet and trotted from the room. A moment later a distant clatter came from the direction of the kitchen. Mum was halfway out of her chair.

"Stay there. I'll go," I said.

In the kitchen, Rosie was standing on the stool in front of the mirror, carefully applying raspberry jam and buttercream around her mouth, taken, I suspected, from the remains of Theo's slice. "What are you doing?" I whispered.

She jumped down and waved sticky fingers. "I'm eating cake."

I opened my mouth, decided I couldn't add anything to the conversation, and closed it again and hugged her instead. "Good idea."

"Everything all right?" Beth came into the kitchen bearing plates, and I spun around as if caught drinking milk from the carton.

"Fine. Everything's fine. Rosie, er, thought she would have some cake after all."

Rosie ran her tongue over her lips. "Yummy," she said.

"Little monkey." Beth ruffled Rosie's hair. "You're as bad as my three. Better tell Mum, Em, so she'll stop fretting." I didn't need to; Rosie had skipped from the kitchen back into the great hall. I admired her quick thinking and artless guile, but for the umpteenth time wished she could be herself and not have to project this image of normality imposed by society. But then I suppose we all do that to an extent, don't we? Pretend to be something we're not.

I picked out the hum of a car engine and recognized it as my own. "That'll be Pat and Henry back," I said, and went to greet them.

"Did you get what you wanted?" I asked.

Henry opened the rear door and leant in to retrieve a sturdy box from the back seat. "We did... and we didn't." Several plastic bags slumped in the footwell.

"Can I give you a hand?" He handed me a bulging carrier bag smelling of new leather. The edge of a buckle, showing at the top, rattled as I took it from him. I peeked in. "A collar, Henry?"

He straightened and, to my surprise, his fading tan deepened. "Ah, well, you see, we... that is, I, thought we would take a little scenic detour through Edith Weston on the way back, and we passed a sign..." The box he carried snuffled and squeaked. I inched back the lid. A small, black nose pushed it open and a hopeful pink tongue licked my fingers. I raised a single eyebrow.

He cleared his throat. "Yes, well, they were looking for good homes..."

"And you thought we might be able to provide one?"

"Well, it's Theo's birthday, and Rosie would like a... I know, I know, I should have asked you first. I hope you don't think I've been irresponsible."

In answer, I stood on the points of my toes and kissed my stepson's cheek. "The children will love having a puppy. *Rosie* will love a puppy."

* * *

"*Awe*some!" Rosie's new word escaped from her lips with a reverential sigh. Kneeling by the box in the snow, Henry lifted out the golden puppy of indeterminate parentage.

"Would you like to hold her, Rosie?" He placed it in her arms, long legs and paws too big for its body, sprawling at angles. Lost for words, she could only nuzzle the puppy's floppy ears as it nibbled her hair.

"He's always wanted a dog," Pat said, shivering in the brisk, damp wind from the north. "He couldn't have one when he was growing up."

"Matthew regretted not allowing him to have animals – the children, also – but it wouldn't have been sensible. If we'd had to move fast it would have meant abandoning them, and a dog was out of the question. As it is, we had to leave Ollie. Thank goodness he was at his winter livery at the time." I remembered our escape from the burning house; a dog would surely have given us away.

"Anyways," Pat said, "Henry wanted to do something for Rosie. He's so aware she misses her papa and he feels responsible for not being there in those early years. I know it might not be sensible, sweetie, and it's another mouth to feed, but Henry will help Rosie train the puppy, and he wants to bridge the gap between them. He wants her to trust him."

"It looks like it's working." Henry was showing Rosie how to hold the puppy to stop it from squirming, and she was doing her best to avoid the remnants of the buttercream being licked from her face, and laughing at the same time. "Thank you, Pat. If it helps them both, I'm all for it."

"I wonder what Theo will make of it all?" Pat asked.

"I'm not sure if I want to find out," I said, envisaging small fingers, pulled ears and sharp teeth. "Better make sure we keep him fed."

23

Break, Blow, Burn

Days lengthened, bringing early signs of spring in primroses crowding under bare-branched hedges and around cracked headstones in the graveyard, and burgeoning warmth drew me outside to follow the face of the sun. Bundled against the easterly wind and keeping a weather eye on Rosie, I sheltered beneath the orchard wall with the journal, rereading Nathaniel Richardson's entries and imagining the play of events taking place a few miles from where I sat now, separated only by time.

Tired of running, Rosie climbed onto my lap. Cuddled together, I read her extracts from the journal mentioning her father and grandfather, until the point when William Lynes turned on his family and brought about its fate. I closed the diary.

"Don't stop, Mummy," she pleaded.

"It's getting late. Look, the sun's setting and my toes are cold."

"Just a teensy bit more. Pl-ease?" The sky was beginning to glow to the west; gold became brass, bronzed, then polished copper, flooding the sky. The blackbird began its evening song and peace lay on the land. "Just a little more, then," I said into her wavy hair, lit by the dying sun.

"Mummy, you missed a bit."

"I don't think I..."

"Yes, you did – there," and she pointed at the entry. Canting her head she read carefully, sounding out the words: "It says, '... *Upon said day the Heavens burned as with a mortal fire...*'"

"You can read that?"

"It looks like Daddy's writing."

"Yes, it does, doesn't it? But this is the sad bit about Daddy's Uncle William."

"Daddy told me."

"Oh, did he? Well, in that case, '... *Upon said day the Heavens burned as with a mortal fire as William came forth with a company of divers men and made war upon this house and did cut from him by grievous means the young master's life.*'" As I read, the bloom to the west intensified until it infused everything with an eerie orange glow. Rosie pointed. "The sky's on fire, Mummy."

Just like it was then. Some things never change. Never. Change.

I stood suddenly, dislodging Rosie. "'The Heavens burned...' Daddy said he didn't remember seeing many torches that night, but Nathaniel said the sky was alight." I grabbed her hand. "Rosie, quick, before the light goes."

"Where are we going?"

"There's no time to explain. Quick!" From the orchard through the walled garden past the barns and into the outer courtyard. From there, using memory to find our way across the darkening flags and under the gatehouse towards the residual sun, then along our track where the land rose to crown the surrounding land. Panting, I slowly rotated, searching the gentle valleys.

"Mummy, what are you looking for?"

In the dusk, I found it. "There, look – that's where New Hall used to be; that's where Daddy was born." Extending my arms, I made a compass of my body. "That's west – where the sun set;

so that's east," I wiggled my right hand, "and so that must be north." I faced the dark sky, with nothing but the first sparkle of a lonely planet to the north-west. "It wasn't a late sunset, and it couldn't have been the torches carried by the men, so what made the light to the north of New Hall?"

"'Thaniel said it was *mortal fire*."

"Yes, he did, and it certainly wasn't street lighting. Perhaps there was a fire somewhere – big enough to be seen from the manor." I frowned, visualizing a map of Rutland. "Uppingham's to the south, Stamford's due east, so Oakham's to the north." I stared at the distant lights of the town. "Maybe there was a fire in Oakham at the time? Well," I breathed, "there's only one way to find out; would you like to come on a mystery hunt, Rosie?"

I'd quickly established that the local archive in Oakham didn't have what I needed and had been directed to the Record Office at Wigston Magna, where I'd arranged to meet the archivist. My friend Greg had moved on, apparently, which was a shame because I could have done with some friendly forces. I eked out the petrol, keeping one eye on the gauge and another on my rear mirrors, half-expecting to see a pursuing car behind us.

"Where's the myst'ry?" Trotting next to me, Rosie eyed the Victorian red-brick building with suspicion. "It doesn't look like a myst'ry."

"I'm hoping we'll find the answer in here," I said, leading the way into a foyer so festooned with leaflets hardly an inch of wall was spared. "We're going to meet the archivist. Do you know what an archivist does?" I picked up the pen sitting on the reception desk.

"Yes, you told me. Mummy, that's not your name," Rosie whispered as I signed in.

"It is today," I murmured, keeping my back to the CCTV camera on the wall.

"Hello," a musical voice said behind us. "Are you waiting to see me?"

"I am," I said, turning around to find an apple-round figure, swathed in a glorious rainbow of colours. "Oh! Hello again! I didn't realize you worked here."

The momentary confusion on the woman's face gave way to a radiant smile. "I know you!" she sang. "Stamford Museum, just before it closed. You were looking for a name. I can't remember which." She waited for me to supply it, but on this occasion I neglected to help.

Mesmerized by the colours in the hand-knitted jumper, Rosie stared in the way parents wish their children wouldn't. "Mummy, she sounds funny."

"Rosie, that's not very polite."

The woman knelt on one knee. "Rosie, is it, love? My name's Judy – Judy Falconer – and I come from Wales. Where do you come from?"

Rosie was just about to tell her, when I intervened. "I'm so sorry. Rosie hasn't heard a Welsh accent before."

"Not to worry, love. I have two little girls and I never know which is going to say something outrageous next. So, you've come to look at the records with your mam, have you, now, Rosie?"

"Mummy's coming to find a myst'ry."

Judy laughed. "Ah, there are plenty of those in here. And are you going to be a historian, like your mammy?"

Rosie gave a firm shake of her head. "I'm going to have lots of puppies and be a sci'ntist like my daddy. I'm going to study... paletology." She held out her dinosaur rucksack as evidence.

"My, palaeontology, is it? That is a big word for a little girl. Do you know what it means?"

Rosie fixed unblinking blue searchlights on Judy's kind hazel eyes. "Yes."

"Oh, right then, well, that's good." She pushed herself to her feet. "We'd better get on. What they teach them nowadays at school, hey, love?"

Sitting on a stack of files, Rosie began to fidget. "What *are* we looking for?"

"Anything that mentions a great fire in Oakham, sweetheart. I've found the one in Loughborough – destroyed over two hundred homes, apparently – but that was in 1666 and in the wrong area." Rosie's eyes began to glaze. "I'll just go through these –" I prodded a pile of papers, and indicated the screen in front of me, " – and then we'll go home."

"Promise?"

"Promise." Frankly, I hadn't found anything to get excited about, so I could hardly blame my daughter for being bored. I hunted around the room and spotted a discarded science periodical. "See if there's anything in here," I suggested, noting her brightening expression. She took the magazine and slid off the chair and went to lie on her stomach out of the way in a corner with it open in front of her. I returned to the database, scouring entries for the summer of 1643 – not that there were many for the Oakham area, nor any references to a fire large enough to be seen from Martinsthorpe.

"This is hopeless." I threw my pen on the table and sat back to stretch stiff shoulders.

"No luck, then?" Judy squeezed between tables and peered shortsightedly at the screen.

I raised a wry smile. "That's exactly what you asked me all those years ago in Stamford."

"And did you then?"

"Did I what? Oh, did I find what I was looking for? Yes," I said, remembering. "I found all that I was looking for and more – much, much more."

"Well then, that was a bit of luck."

"I don't believe in luck," I mused almost to myself.

"That's what my husband says. Tell you what, he's a historian, a bit later than your period – Restoration's his thing – but he knows a lot about the Civil War in this area; studied it at uni, see. He's taking me out for a bit of lunch; I'll ask him then. No point in having them otherwise, is there?" She laughed, but I'd missed the point somewhere.

"Having what?"

"A husband." She sobered. "Oo, sorry, I thought you were married." She nodded towards my rings.

"I am. He's away."

She must have sensed there was more to it than that because her eyebrows took on a sympathetic curve and her voice softened. "Well, let's see what my Tom has to say for himself. You'll join us, won't you? I bet Rosie's famished. You can take the magazine, if you want to, love. Lots of pretty pictures, aren't there?"

"He's beaten us to it," Judy said, spotting a figure sitting in the café window with his back to us, reading a newspaper. Spring sunlight reflected off his scalp as he turned a page. She rapped on the window and waved cheerfully as he turned. "Brought some guests," she mouthed, pointing at the two of us. He stood as we approached the table, folding the paper. "Sorry I'm a bit late, love," she wheezed slightly in the warm air of the café, kissing him, "but this lady's in need of your help and Rosie, here, needs some lunch."

Already smiling, he turned to look at us, but the welcome evaporated as he took in my face, his calm blue fluctuating wildly before settling to a curious teal. "Hello," he said. "It's been a long time."

I frowned. "I'm sorry, I don't think..."

Judy flicked him with her coat. "Don't be daft, Thomas, she won't know you."

Thomas. Tom. Falconer.

"Tom?" I said, hesitant.

He grinned, the years instantly dissolving as I recognized the youth behind the receding hairline and broadening girth. Nothing could occlude the light, and he embraced me like the friends we had once been.

"You know each other?" Judy asked.

"We were at uni together," Tom explained, pulling out chairs for us. "We were on the same course with that supervising tutor I told you about."

Judy rolled her eyes. "Oh, *him*."

"You haven't changed, unlike some of us." He patted his stomach. "I'd recognize you anywhere."

"Nor have you in the way that matters," I responded with a grin. "It's good to see you. What have you been up to all these years?"

"Apart from marrying my lovely wife and fathering the two best girls a man could wish for?"

Judy coloured. "Get over, you daft ha'porth."

He gave her a swift kiss on the cheek and winked. "I teach in a school," he went on. "History to all of the senior school. Thank the Lord for school holidays, hey? I'm afraid Cambridge hols spoilt me so I had to find a job with decent breaks. I earn them, though. Never did understand how our tutors at uni could complain about the workload. Just thought they wanted more time to research. Would suit you though, Emma – you liked research, didn't you? How about you? What have you been up to for the last fifteen years?"

"Teaching," I said, stifling the urge to laugh. "At Cambridge and then in the States. This is my daughter, Rosie."

"Hello, Rosie, it's good to meet you. I like your bag. What's your favourite dinosaur?"

I helped Rosie with her rucksack and she climbed on her chair and studied the pictures.

"This one."

"Ah, the, er, the…"

"An-ky-lo-saurus. It had a thumpy tail like a morning star to go bash, bash, bash…" she illustrated with a clenched fist, "… and a teeeeeny brain. Daddy says it was a armoured cow."

"Wow! I like the sound of that. Do you like learning about dinosaurs?" She nodded vigorously. "What school do you go to?"

I could see her compiling an answer that would avoid lying. "MummyandDaddy school," she said in a rush.

"Oh, right, well," he said, trying not to smile. "That's a very good school indeed. So, you've been living in the States, have you?" he said, turning back to me. "What have you been up to there – apart from teaching?"

"This and that. Tea, please, and a strawberry milkshake," I said to the lad taking our orders, "and Rosie and I'll share a BLT, thanks." I waited for Judy and Tom to decide on their order and then ambushed him with a question before he could ask me to enlighten him about the last decade and a half of my life. "Tom, Judy thought you might be able to help me with a question on the Civil War." I removed Rosie's bag from the table to make way for knives and forks.

"I thought that would be more your line than mine; you're the one with a PhD on the subject."

"Yes, but this is regarding local history and I've been out of the area for a bit."

"Go on."

"Have you ever heard of a big fire occurring in Oakham, or nearby, in July 1643? A fire big enough to be seen from miles away?" Rosie had unzipped her bag and was engrossed in the scientific article, swinging her legs back and forth under her chair.

"I take it you've been through the archives?" Judy gave him a *What do you take us for?* look and he returned it with a guilty smirk. "Well, in that case..." He scratched his neck, thinking, then gave a slow shake of his head. "I can't think of any instances, or none that've been recorded."

"Are you sure?"

"Positive. I teach the kids local history as part of their coursework. Why, what are you researching?"

"I felt sure..." I raised my hands and let them fall in defeat on the table. "There's a reference to the Heavens burning, and I thought it must have been a fire."

"Not one I'm aware of." With his fingers and thumbs, Tom drew a rectangle in the air. "Breaking news: First recorded sighting of a UFO in England's smallest county." He shrugged. "Rutland has to be famous for something."

Judy nudged him. "Not helpful, love."

"It might as well have been a UFO for all I know," I said, a touch gloomy. "Still, at least I can rule out a fire. It doesn't matter; it's probably not relevant."

Tom gave a short laugh. "Now, that's a first. I never thought I'd hear you say you give up when you've scented a kill."

"Thomas!" Judy prodded him again.

"Well, it's true. You should have seen Emma when she thought she was on to something – scary. Do you remember that assignment we were given? Way beyond most undergrads, but you wouldn't give up until you'd completed it. I swear Dr Hilliard gave it to us just to see us squirm, the sadist. Now there's someone who would know the answer. Can't say I ever warmed to him. Took years before I stopped having nightmares about those supervisions. Heard he died, though – in a car crash, apparently. In the States." His wife put a cautioning hand on his arm and indicated the pair of wide, bright eyes absorbing every detail from beside me.

"Sorry, yes." When I didn't answer immediately, concentrating on dividing the sandwich into quarters and sliding a segment onto Rosie's plate, he cleared his throat. "I forgot, you were close to him at one time, weren't you? Sorry," he said again. I didn't miss the frown and slight shake of Judy's head. He must have told her something of my history.

"I'm sure he would have known," I said, evenly, "but whether he would have shared the information is another matter. He wasn't an easy man to deal with."

"He gave you a hard time, didn't he?" Tom said, all humour gone.

I grimaced. "You could say that. You saved my life."

"That's a bit of an exaggeration."

I looked at him square on. "No, I don't think so. Without you things might have turned out quite differently."

His eyes drifted to my neck where my cross hung and he smiled. "I'm glad there was something I could help you with."

Rosie and I were quiet on the way back home along the A47, each with our own thoughts. As we turned onto the Brooke road, she piped up from the back. "Mummy, what's a YouEffO?"

"It's short for Unidentified Flying Object. Mostly, people refer to UFOs in connection with alien spaceships or strange lights, but it can be anything seen in the sky that science can't explain."

"Like Daddy?"

I smiled. "Daddy isn't an alien, Rosie, nor can he fly."

"But science can't explain him, Mummy – he said so."

"Yes, but that's only because he hasn't found the answer yet, not that there *isn't* an answer. When we can't explain something, we say it's preternatural." I pulled into the entrance to a field where vivid green spikes of wheat punctured the earth, and let a white van pass on the narrow road, watching it warily, waiting to see the telltale flicker of studied non-interest in the driver's eyes. He drove past without a second look, disappearing in a plume of diesel fumes around the corner, and I released the breath I didn't know I'd been holding.

"He can fly," Rosie persisted, making her hand into a plane and flying it across my rear-view vision as we drew out and regained the centre of the road.

"What did you do with your sandwich?"

"I hid it in here." She took the folded magazine from her bag and retrieved the dog-eared quarter with a bite taken from the corner and held it up for me to see in the mirror.

"Well done, darling. I know it's not easy. Judy and Tom are kind, aren't they?"

"I like Judy's clothes and Tom is funny. Why did he save your life?"

I debated the wisdom of telling her anything to do with Guy and decided to stick to the bare essentials. "I had a difficult time at university for a while – before I met Daddy – and Tom helped me through it."

"Why?"

"He told me about Jesus."

She was thoughtful for a moment; then, "I like Jesus. And I like my magazine. Judy gave it to me." She flapped it. "It says Heavenly Light." She looked up. "Jesus is a heavenly light, isn't he, Mummy?"

"He is indeed our light. What are you looking at?"

Her sunset head bent over the article spread on her knees, and with her finger under the bold headline and a look of deep concentration, she read, "A-roar-bore-a-lis."

"A-whaty?" I slowed the car right down and took the near-hidden turning to our track between high hedges scattered with buds swollen with spring and ready to burst with the least encouragement of a warm day. The last daffodils withered on the banks, and over the noisy engine, a robin scolded.

"This," and she held the magazine high enough so that I could see the glossy photo bumping and wavering in my rear-view mirror. "Look, see, Mummy, the sky's on fire."

I brought the car to a sudden standstill, and swivelled in my seat. "Rosie, let me see that." I snatched the magazine from her outstretched hand. Ruby flames danced across the night sky beneath the heading: *Aurora Borealis – Heavenly Light*. I read the first paragraph, skipped the technical bit, scanned the rest. The article blurred, swam unsteadily. I remembered to breathe, and shook my head, refocusing. I looked at my daughter, searching for words. "Oh. My. Giddy. Aunt! Rosie, you're a genius!" Unstrapping myself, I launched between the front seats in an ungainly sprawl and hugged her, child seat and all. "You've done it, Rosie. You've solved the mystery of the mortal fire. You clever, clever girl. You're phenomenal!" She beamed up at me, bemused. "Let's get home and tell Pat and Henry what you've discovered."

"And Theo," she reminded me.

"And definitely Theo," I said.

"Aurora?" Henry angled the article to the dying light of day. "It certainly fits the description Nathaniel Richardson gives in the journal, even if there's scant enough information."

"I founded it," Rosie announced with a degree of pride and a smattering of a challenge. "Mummy says I'm phe-nom'nal."

"You found it, did you, Rosie? Well done!" Henry smiled down at her, while fending off Puppy's attempts to bite his heels.

"Puppy, down! Sweetheart, please will you take Puppy outside and run off some of her energy?" Needing little encouragement, the pair dashed off. When I faced Henry again, he had resumed scanning the article. He looked up. "The only thing is that it's unusual to see aurora in mid-summer and this far south."

"But it is possible, isn't it? I remember seeing it once when in Cornwall, and in East Anglia it's traditionally known as Dancing Maidens or Dancing Girls, so it does occur at this latitude." I tapped the entry in the journal. "And it was seen in the northern sky – Nathaniel thought it was the light from the torches carried by William's rabble as they approached from the north, but Matthew said he couldn't remember seeing many torches at all."

"It's not beyond the realms of possibility, certainly, although a red hue is more rare. Hmm – 1643." He shook his head. "I'm pretty certain the Maunder Minimum began sometime around then; I'll need to check."

"Why? What's that?"

"A period in the mid-seventeenth century noted for its lack of sunspots."

"So…?"

"So it relates to solar activity, or lack of it. Solar storms on the surface of the sun discharge vast amounts of energy that give rise to aurora. Sunspots are indicators of that activity, so no sunspots…"

"… no aurora," I concluded, my initial elation fading fast.

"They still occurred, but it's more doubtful in the mid-geomagnetic latitudes where we are now. But I'll check; you never know. Strange, of all people, Dad might have been able to tell us. He lived through the period, after all." He ran his hand over the scratchy growth of his new beard. "Why is it so important, anyway?"

"Intuition, Henry; cause and effect. You know I don't believe in coincidences."

"As a crusty scientist, I'm afraid I need a little more than intuition to come to any sort of conclusion."

"In normal circumstances I would agree, and I'd bite off the head of any student of mine that failed to come up with a viable source to verify a claim. However…"

"This is hardly a normal circumstance. So, is it by the pricking of your thumbs? Or merely clutching at straws?"

I grinned. "Possibly both, but the fact that it happened on the same night that Matthew was attacked might be relevant nonetheless. And I keep getting these words going around and around my head like a song I can't shift: 'Batter my heart, three-person'd God…' Did he? Did God 'break, blow, burn' to make Matthew new? And if so, how? Why?"

"You know, for years I helped him search for answers to a question the context of which I didn't fully understand. I can't help feeling that we might have made better progress had he told me the full story."

"Henry…"

"I know, I know, but it's like knowing only half my father, and now he isn't here for me to tell him how much I regret these last four years, and to get to know him better – and my little sister." He angled his elbows, resting his hands on his thighs, his head bent. He grunted, slapped his palms down on his knees, and rose to his feet with a sigh. "No point in regretting the past, as Dad would say; it's time to be getting on with the future. Do you think Beth would let me use her computer?"

***

"Flying angel!" I sang, balancing Theo on the socked soles of my feet and motoring him around above my head as I lay on my back. He waved his arms and I felt his rumbly laugh deep in his squidgy tummy. "One, two, threeeeee..." Bending my knees I launched him into the air and caught him in my arms on the way down, wrapping him tightly to me. His cheeks pink, he squealed for more.

"Mummy!" Rosie thumped in, depositing clods of mud.

"Boots, sweetheart." She ran from the great hall and returned seconds later, one foot trailing a sock and the other bare altogether. "Mummy, Grandpa and me dug and dug and we dug..." she counted on her fingers, "... two hundred square..." She looked down at her toes, "... feet. Phe-nom-e-nal!" she exclaimed.

"Two hundred square feet? Golly, that sounds a lot."

"It was," Dad huffed, sweat darkening the collar of his shirt. "Couldn't have done it without Rosie's help, though; she did all the maths for me and wielded that spade like a sapper. Real trooper, this girl." Did I imagine that, or did my father just wink at me? He ruffled her hair. "Did you know tha..." He broke off as my head jerked around at the distant sound of a car engine. "Em, are you all right?"

I listened, focused, until the grinding second gear confirmed it to be Henry returning from Stamford in my car. My pulse returned to its regular beat. "Sorry, Dad, you were saying?"

He appraised me from beneath bushy, sandy brows, now flecked with grey. "It doesn't matter. Were you expecting someone?"

"Oh, only Henry and Pat," I said lightly.

"Well?" I asked Henry no sooner than they crossed the threshold, Puppy yelping and bouncing around our feet. I supplied Pat with a hot drink and she went to join my father by the fire to thaw her bones.

"Well," Henry began, leaning against the stone sink and nursing his own mug, "I couldn't find any reference to aurora being noted in the July of 1643 – none, and I would have expected something, especially given the rarity of the colour. However," he added, "the Maunder Minimum didn't begin until 1645 and, despite the lack of sunspots, aurora continued to be observed during that period, so…"

"It's possible."

"Not likely, but yes," he relented, "it is possible." The puppy snuffled around the floor, looking for remnants of Theo's lunch. I picked her up, stroking her soft ears as I looked from the kitchen window, and tried to imagine the scene that summer night. "If we accept that it was an aurora Nathaniel recorded," I said slowly, "what significance might it have had on what happened to Matthew – scientifically speaking, that is?"

"Emma, there is nothing to connect the two events…"

"Except they occurred at the same time."

"Nothing," he repeated. "You are clutching at those straws again. Dad and I spent decades working on molecular changes, DNA, blood typing – the works – and no doubt he spent the previous three hundred years trying to figure it out. The fact is, nothing short of a miracle can explain what happened to him."

"But that's just it, Henry – Matthew is miraculous. Whatever caused him to be the way he is, he is a miracle. That's why they were after him." I sensed, rather than saw, the shift in colours behind me. I spun around. Dad stood in the doorway, empty mug in hand.

"Dad, we were just saying…"

"That Matthew is a miracle, yes, I heard. Why is your husband miraculous, Emma? And *who* were after him?"

My brain froze. Despite five years of evasive fabrication, outright lying came hard.

"We only meant that... I mean, Matthew is..."

"A genius when it comes to medical research," Henry interposed. "That's why he's been headhunted, Hugh. It's a miracle, given the genes he's inherited."

"I see." He did, but not what we wanted him to think. He walked to the sink and washed his mug without further comment, leaving it upside down on the stone draining board to dry. Henry and I swapped glances. Dad dried his hands and turned around.

"Emma, I've been fiddling with the solar cell that powers your mobile. It should be more efficient now."

"Right, Dad. Thanks."

"I expect you will want to get on with your research – whatever that is. I'll show you how to use it and then be on my way. Your mother will be wondering where I am. Come along."

I followed him into the great hall and, sitting on the windowsill in the strengthening sun, he showed me the component he had fitted to the back of the mobile. "Give it a go," he said. "Call Matthew."

"I... don't have his number."

"You don't have your husband's mobile number? Really? Does Henry?"

"No, I don't think so. The signal's not very good where Matthew is."

"And where exactly is that?"

"I can't say."

"Can't or won't, Emma?" He waited, but I had nothing I could say to him that would appease his appetite for information. "All right, then, I'll be blunt. Your mother thinks you must have had some difficulties between you. Is that so?"

I shook my head.

"Have you left him, Emma?"

"No, Dad!"

"Then where is he?"

"I've told you, I don't know. He's on a government project..."

"Don't lie to me."

Taken aback by his directness, I stuttered, "I-I'm not!"

"You all are – you, Henry, Pat. What are you all doing here? Why are you hiding? Why is it that every time you hear a floorboard creak, you jump? Why does my granddaughter never seem to eat anything and my grandson not feel the cold? And your arm – Beth swears that scald should have put you in A&E, and she's seen enough kitchen accidents to know."

I looked desperately at him. "I can't tell you."

"Can't or won't?" he repeated. With an effort he straightened stiff knees and stood looking down on me. "I understand if Henry wants to protect his son – I would do the same – but I won't accept my own daughter lying to me, Em; not after everything we've been through these last years."

He waited, but I merely looked at my hands, twisting the edge of my sweater into knots. "So be it. There is nothing you could say that would shock me. Nothing I couldn't handle." He found his car keys in his jacket pocket. "I'm sorry you don't feel you can trust me. Please pay my respects to Pat and Henry."

I listened until I could hear the car's engine no longer. Leaning back against the stone, the sun's captured warmth couldn't dissolve the chill Dad had left. What he didn't know couldn't hurt him – the maxim Matthew had lived by all his life, and that had backfired with dire consequences when Henry discovered the truth. But, tell me, at what point do you tell someone and entrap them with the same lie that binds you? Dad would then feel obligated to protect Mum from the secret and yet another wall – invisible but as solid as stone – would be erected in their relationship. And where would it end – with Beth, Rob, and their children? Ripples would spread from Matthew's epicentre until they reached the shore of unwelcome ears, and we would find ourselves in flight once more – scattered, disparate, lost.

I picked up the mobile, wanting at least to hear Dad's voice, and switched it on. It blinked into life, a sliver of power in its charging battery. I held the solar cell to the light, remembering Matthew raising his face to the sun – recharging, taking on its strength, growing stronger. The mobile fell with a clatter to the floor.

"Henry!" I bellowed, sprinting from the great hall, colliding with him as he ran to find me, alarm spreading across his face.

"What's the matter?"

"Henry, it's the sun!"

Pat appeared behind him. "What's wrong with the sun?"

But I was at the great south windows, pointing, incoherent words tumbling. "The sun." I stabbed in its direction. Henry frowned. I flapped my hands, garbled out, "Sunspots. You said that sunspots are solar storms – they send out waves of energy."

"Yes, but..."

"Energy, Henry. Aurora indicates solar activity. That night vast amounts of solar energy were released into the atmosphere, creating aurora." I hunted around me, and spotting Rosie's magazine, grabbed it. "Don't you see?" I said, shaking it in his bewildered face. "The huge coronal mass ejections of March 1989 created enough geomagnetic disturbance to black out the entire state of Quebec. Matthew had a steel blade thrust into his heart during the aurora. He... earthed... the energy like a lightning conductor. It has to be that." Face flushing, I waited, panting, as Henry's expression went from disbelief to incredulity, colours pulsing like a cuttlefish.

"Delivering a massive shock to his heart? It should have killed him."

"Yes," I squeaked.

"But it didn't."

"No. Instead he persisted, Henry. We don't know how, but perhaps we might now know why."

"That's a major leap to make."

"Then call it, oh, I don't know – a leap of faith. Matthew once said to me that he was neither likely nor possible, yet here he is – like bees."

"Bees?"

"By the laws of known physics, until recently we didn't think they should be able to fly. It was a mystery until we understood the mechanics of it. But the sum of our knowledge is limited by our experience, understanding and observations, and Matthew has broken the rules. He shouldn't be alive, but he is. He should have died, but he didn't. The question is, how?" Clasping my hands behind my head, I focused blind eyes on the heavily beamed and plastered ceiling, willing myself to see past the obvious, back in time, back to the moment the steel blade pierced his heart. "Henry, you're a cardiologist. If someone's had a heart transplant, can't the new heart be restarted with an electric shock – a bit like jump-starting a car?"

"Putting it crudely, yes."

"Then couldn't the blade, in delivering a death blow, also have been the conduit for restarting his heart?"

"I suppose – theoretically."

"Then what, theoretically, kept it beating?"

Henry looked first at Pat and then at me. "Well," he said, massaging his thumb and gathering his thoughts, "the heart is the only organ that doesn't rely on the brain to keep it beating. It needs an electrical signal to regulate its function, but all it requires to beat is a steady flow of blood. As long as the heart pumps blood, it will receive the high energy molecule ATP, or adenosine triphosphate, which we metabolize from the food we eat, to keep it beating – like a car engine."

"So why do our hearts stop?" I said.

"We run out of fuel. All right, that's too simplistic, but ruling out other factors, such as disease or injury to the heart itself, there is no scientific reason for it not to continue working, as long as it gets what it needs."

"So food provides the source of energy?" Pat asked. "But Matthew doesn't eat and Rosie hardly touches a thing. Where do they get their heart food from?" We looked at each other and then at the light streaming through the dusty windows.

"From the sun?" I asked. "How is that even possible?" I thought of all the times I'd caught him, face to the sun; of the times when he looked after me for days on end until he almost faded, his energy sapped, his vitality waning, his skin greying. I remembered the first time we kissed – the distinct electricity, tingling – like touching a nine-volt battery to your tongue. Then there were the lights in his eyes – not a reflection of the sun, but its *energy*. Didn't he know? Hadn't he realized? "I wish we could tell him." I watched the motes of dust caught in a vortex of air and knew how they felt. What good would this knowledge be to us now? Without him it became... pointless.

"Emma," Henry said gently, "I know you're desperate for answers, but it doesn't explain Dad's strength or speed, or our own ability to heal. None of us received the same injury, yet we all have similar traits."

"Genes, Henry."

"Granted genes play their part, and your own response to that transfusion already proves there's a genetic link between you and Dad. Pinpointing the gene responsible, however, is another matter."

"That's exactly what Matthew was working on when we had to leave. But the data was destroyed when Harry sabotaged E.V.E. to stop anyone getting the information."

"All that work." Pat sank onto a chair. "All those years of research. It doesn't bear thinking about. It must have broken his heart, knowing it was all gone."

"Perhaps," Henry acknowledged, squinting at the sun. Finally, he sucked his teeth and turned to us, rubbed his hands together and smiled. "It's a lovely day. I think I'll take a walk."

24

E.V.E.

Beth bent over, resting her hands on her knees. "I really should have given up food for Lent, rather than chocolate; it's a bit of a trudge out here, isn't it? I'm all puffed out." She straightened, poking the pile of fleshy weeds with her toe. "Golly, Em, I never expected to see you *gardening*. Should you be doing that in your condition?"

Leaning on my hoe, I took a welcome break. "It's quite therapeutic, really. I like being outdoors listening to the birds, seeing things growing. I can see why Dad likes it. The children, too." Over in the orchard, Rosie was enthusiastically pushing Theo in his baby swing, the sound of their laughter amplified by the walls.

"You sure Theo's human?" my sister said. "Archie was a little monster at that age – always crying. I'm surprised we survived."

I remembered all too well. "Archie couldn't help it. Theo's teeth don't bother him that much." Wanting to avoid scrutiny, I didn't want to get into a debate about the relative merits of our children – or otherwise. "I didn't expect to see you today; what's up? Did Dad send you on a recce mission?"

She rumbled a laugh, sounding rather like him. "Not a chance. He's still sulking. Anyway, he can do his own dirty work. You still haven't told me why he has the hump."

I gave an evasive shrug. "You know what he's like. So, what are you here for?"

She took a used envelope from her pocket, on which she had scrawled in thick, black pen something illegible. "I had a call from a foreign-sounding chap asking to speak to you. I denied all knowledge, of course, but he insisted I took his name and number, so I don't think he believed me. He said you would know what it's about." She handed me the tatty envelope. "I wasn't sure about his surname. Dobanovitch, or something."

"Thanks," I said.

"You could have warned me you'd given out my number."

"Sorry, I forgot to say. It's OK. I know who it is."

"You'll need a phone, then, won't you?" She rummaged in her back pocket and found hers. She noted my hesitation. "It can't be traced to you, if that's what you're worried about. Or is it the pasta sauce? It stains terribly. Here," she gave it a quick wipe, "good as new. Go on, call him." I waited for her to take the hint and go. "Oh, all right then, be mysterious. I'll go and talk to the kids. They don't keep any secrets from their aunt."

I grinned. "Thanks, you're a gem. I won't be a mo." I waited until she was out of earshot, then tapped in the numbers. "Hello? You left a message."

"I am glad you called," Levi's European tones sighed down the phone. "I have news for you. That matter we spoke about – it is resolved in a most… satisfactory way."

"Fantastic!" I said, without thinking. "Thank you. How…?"

"I will make arrangements," he interrupted as if he thought we might be overheard, "and contact you again shortly. Good day." The phone went dead.

"All OK?" Beth called from the swings.

"Yes, I think so, thanks." I handed the phone back to her.

"You're looking a bit chipper. Good news?"

"Uh-huh. What are you doing for Easter? Going to Mum and Dad's?"

She looked at me sideways. "Just tell me if you don't want to say, Em. Yeah, probably. What about you?"

"I think we'll stay here and keep Pat and Henry company."

"I'm sure they'll be welcome, too. I can ask Mum."

"No, thanks."

"They must miss Matthew, too, don't they? Still, I bet Easter Bunny's on his way. What do you say, Rosie? Do you think Mummy would like a chocolate egg?"

"Mummy can have mine."

"Mummy probably will, so you'll have to hide it. When we were little, she found the big egg I had been hiding carefully in my knicker drawer and pigged the lot of it."

"And your aunt Beth has never let me forget it," I laughed.

There was one thing I had concluded since my last – disastrous – conversation with Dad, and it was that I couldn't wait for him to come to me. He had succumbed to a chesty cold shortly after our row, and it had taken him weeks to shake it. It had brought home to me just how fragile life could be, and how our time together was on a slow-burning wick that would one day run out.

Taking advantage of the fog hugging the rooftops and passages of my home town, and muffled against the curious eyes of the surveillance cameras, I parked some distance away and walked to my parents' house, and let myself in through the rear door.

The drawing room radiated heat. Unaccustomed, I peeled off layers of clothing under my parents' watchful eyes. "Thanks for letting me come over." I dropped my scarf on the saggy sofa and sat next to it, pulling my hair from my shirt and straightening the unironed collar. "How are you, Dad?"

He pulled the rug he wore around his shoulders, and tucked the ends into his sweater. He cleared his throat, but before he could answer, Mum spoke. "He's not been at all well. He's had two lots of antibiotics and I don't want him stressed, Emma. I don't know what you two have fallen out about, but I've had quite enough of this nonsense."

"That makes three of us, Mum. I haven't come to have an argument."

"Then why are you here?" Dad finally asked, his voice husky and raw.

"I've come for three reasons. The first is to apologize for all the worry I've caused you, and to thank you for everything you have done for me and for the children. It can't have been easy for you, thinking I was in some sort of difficulty, yet not knowing why, or how to help."

Dad maintained a controlled expression, displaying neither acceptance of my heartfelt apology, nor disbelief. I had never really thought about it, but he must have been good at his job. "And the second thing I wish to explain..." *Here goes*, I thought, *this will either work or it won't*. "Dad, you were right, I am in trouble, and so is Matthew."

Mum clapped her hands. "There! I said so, didn't I, Hugh?"

He didn't answer her, but merely said, "Go on."

"Matthew hasn't been seconded by the government, he's been taken by them, and is being held against his will."

"The government? Why?"

"Not the government, exactly, but by a research agency, we think. We don't know which one. He has done nothing wrong – either illegal or immoral – but he... carries... information they want."

"Then why doesn't he just give it to them, darling, so he can come home?"

"It isn't that easy, Mum. The thing is, Matthew believes we are in danger. That's why we left the States. That's why we're here."

"And why would this agency pose a threat to you and the children, Emma?" my father asked quietly.

"Because what affects him, to some extent also affects us." I willed him to make the connection without me having to spell it out.

His eyes slid towards my mother, who was too intent on looking in my direction to notice, and back to me. He quirked a brow. "And Henry and Pat – are they similarly affected?"

"Just Henry."

"I see." And at last, I think he did.

"I don't," Mum said. "If Matthew is innocent, surely he would give them the information they want, and then this agency would let him go? And how are you involved? Have you been working on some project with him?"

"Not a project as such, Mum, but it does involve research. And development."

"R and D – that can be a messy business – top secret, too, I expect. Not something you can discuss, hey, Em? A bit under the radar?"

I thanked him silently. "Yes, something like that, Dad. It's very complicated." It wasn't the whole truth, but there was little point in denying the differences he had witnessed for himself.

I hoped he wouldn't push for further details, and to my relief, he didn't.

"So, what was the third thing you wanted to say?" he asked.

"Oh, that. Well, um – I'm pregnant."

"How did it go?" Henry asked as I plonked my bag on the kitchen table next to a pile of typed papers he had been reading, and made straight for the kettle.

"Much better than expected, thanks."

He watched me pump water at the sink for a moment, then, "So why do I get the impression something's on your mind?"

Water splashed over my hands and left the slate seal-grey and slick. "Is it that obvious?" I sucked in my cheeks, then released the pressure with a pop. "I told my parents the bare bones of the truth – that we're basically on the run from an agency which is holding Matthew because they are interested in his differences. I didn't say what they were, or why we are also different, and nor did Dad ask. He understood the implications and left it at that."

"That's ideal, surely?"

I turned on him. "Is it, Henry? What they now know is a fragment of the picture. To all intents and purposes, I'm still lying to them…"

"Withholding the truth, perhaps, but not lying."

"Aren't I? Henry, remember how you felt when Matthew told you that what you had been led to believe was merely the skin of something much deeper – how betrayed you felt?"

"Yes, but he's my father."

"And Dad's mine – and my mother is as much in the dark. I suppose what I'm saying is that despite my best intentions, I can't tell them the whole truth, can I? Enough to be getting on with, perhaps, but not enough to make them party to the entire lie."

Henry crossed the kitchen, took the half-filled kettle from me, put it on the draining board, and turned me to face him. "What I didn't appreciate until very recently is why Dad didn't tell me the truth. Yes, the time was never right, yes, he wanted to protect me – but it was more than that: he wanted us to live a life free of the liability of the truth. I didn't recognize how precious those years were. I had the luxury of ignorance. We all talk about how we must know everything – the right to the freedom of information – and to a certain extent I agree completely. But with that knowledge comes responsibility, and I'm not certain how many people are ready to shoulder it. I wasn't, was I?"

"You're talking about the control of information."

"Yes, I suppose I am."

"And who has the right to choose what we know and what we don't?"

"Precisely. Freedom of information is an illusion, Emma."

I recalled an earlier conversation with Matthew along the same lines and said a touch sourly, "What we don't know won't hurt us?"

"Something like that, I expect. What I am trying to say is that perhaps your parents are better off not knowing the whole truth, and then they won't have to make any difficult choices should it come to it."

I shook my head. "Yes, that's how I always justified not telling them, but they've noticed some of our differences and I wonder whether it's better they know the whole truth rather than just a fraction of it. Knowledge is power..."

"Whose knowledge? Whose power?" Henry asked.

"Are you saying that you would rather not have known about Matthew?"

"I'm saying that I wasted four years begrudging my father's attempts to protect me, and sometimes... sometimes I wonder whether having all the facts places a burden on me that I don't always feel able to bear. He carried that knowledge for me – as a father, he made that decision and took that responsibility." His mouth had formed a taut line I recognized instantly as Matthew's telltale sign of internal confusion. What was he hiding? The lead weight in my stomach had nothing to do with the vestiges of morning sickness.

"Where is all this coming from, Henry? What are you not telling me?"

"I've debated long and hard over what I'm about to tell you, but I reckon after all you've been through, you might as well know."

I didn't like the sound of that. I gave a cautious, "Go on."

"I think I might have an idea of what Dad was working on. E.V.E. contained software that primarily dealt with decoding and analysing genetic material and looking at mutative responses when exposed to certain stimuli. I didn't realize it then, of course, but he was searching for answers to his own condition."

"He wanted to understand it so that he could reverse the process," I muttered.

"But he also used his research to further work into genetic disorders, and thereby find a cure for them. But that is by the by. You are probably aware of the latest research into the aging process at a cellular level?" I shook my head. "Well, all cells have a DNA blueprint which means aging isn't inevitable. Basically, a body could keep functioning without aging or weakening."

I straightened my top over my gentle bulge. "What – ever?"

"In theory, yes. We are now fairly certain that Dad's exposure to vast levels of electromagnetic pulse induced a change in him. We also assume that there is a genetic link between what happened and the subsequent changes to which we have been subject – I and my family, through birth; you, as a direct result of a transfusion of his blood. It should have killed you, but it didn't. He knew that or he would never have risked the procedure." Henry had started pacing around the table, throwing glances in my direction as he outlined his theory. Now he came to a halt in front of me. "Emma, there's another reason why it was imperative you and the children escaped capture." He paused and seemed to be building up to something I wasn't sure I was going to like. "I think... I believe my father discovered that you hold the answer to the genetic variation."

"Me?"

"You share a common ancestor, don't you?"

"Yes, through his grandmother and my namesake – Emma D'Eresby. But there have been generations of D'Eresbys since then and none of them have had the abilities or... or long life that Matthew has."

"Of which you are aware."

I jerked my head in acknowledgment. "Granted."

"Didn't your grandfather mention something about lights being too bright and the television being too loud shortly before he died?"

"Yes, but..."

"And he died of a heart attack, having had no previous history of coronary events?"

"People do all the time, Henry."

"And when there is an unexplained death, in most cases – including your grandfather's – an autopsy is carried out. These," he said, flourishing the handful of typed sheets from the table, "are the notes made relating to your grandfather's post-mortem."

"Where did you get them?"

"He was referred for an autopsy because the cause of his death was unknown."

"He had a massive heart attack."

"No, he didn't. His symptoms mimicked acute coronary failure, but the pathologist could find no sign of heart disease or anything that could explain the sudden and catastrophic heart failure from which he supposedly died."

"So... what did he die of?"

"The pathologist's report states that he probably died as a result of asymptomatic acute heart failure brought on by cause unknown and leaving no trace. In other words, he didn't know. But do you know what I found most interesting?" I shook my head, but he was already continuing, his eyes so bright that I could almost imagine they were Matthew's. He held up the notes. "In these is a toxicology report, and do you know what he had to drink shortly before he died?" I shook my head again, frowning. "Coffee. Large amounts of strong coffee."

"But he didn't usually drink coffee. He only drank it that day at his friend's wake because he thought it churlish to ask for tea. Dad said he hated the stuff – couldn't stand the smell or... or the... taste..." I trailed off.

"Like someone else we know."

The clues are there if you know where to look.

"Emma, what are the chances of that happening to two people? Medical science has progressed so much recently that it is now able to identify causes of disease that just a decade ago were unrecognizable. Think how far it has come."

"And people would have either not recognized the differences or would have hidden them so they might conform to social norms and not appear different."

"Yes."

"He was always muddy."

"What?"

"My grandfather. In my memory he was always shades of brown – khaki, mostly. I thought it was because he was in the Army."

"And what do you think now?"

I looked up at the ceiling above my head, where a missed cobweb, decorated in dust, waved a lazy salute in the rising heat from the stove, and ran back through shelves in my memory until I had my grandfather pinned in my mind's eye. "Now?" I said, squinting as I thought out loud. "Now I think he was trying to hide something."

Henry raised the sheaf of paper and let it fall to the table.

"My father developed his special capabilities because of the coronal ejection, but he already carried the markers in his genetic sequence – just as you and I do – but in him, the aurora switched them on. That's why we have some of his traits, but not all. Your children's seem magnified because they have inherited the gene from both of you." His mouth lifted. "It's the D'Eresby gene, and you are the key, Emma – *you* are the key."

Long ago, a lifetime away, my grandpa had laid a wasted hand on the handwritten transcripts in front of him. "The journal, Pipkin," he had said. "The journal holds the key." And he had laughed as if at some private joke, words which meant little then, but came rattling in on my memory now. He had been so close to the truth, yet had not seen what lay before him in his granddaughter: through my D'Eresby heritage, I was the key.

Rags of Time

Love, all alike, no season knows nor clime,
Nor hours, days, months, which are the rags of time
John Donne

Easter was late. The pears were in full bloom, the first apple
blossom blushed pink and white in the orchard, and the last long-
necked daffodils drooped in the lengthening grass. Goosegrass
sent sticky-leaved envoys from under the hedges, and magpies,
emboldened by lust, cracked twigs from greening branches for
their nests. Theo and I picked cowslips and wisps of ivy, while
Rosie sourced stones and moss. Then, taking Mrs Seaton's
rusty tray, together we went to the church and made an Easter
garden under Christ's benign eye, and left it on the altar as our
offering. At the foot of her grandparents' tomb, Rosie ranged
jam jars of cowslips, scarlet stems of dogwood, fluffy buds of
pussy willow, and she kissed her father's broken image. There we
sat for a while under the family window, as close to Matthew as
we could, colours descending the columns as the sun climbed,
and casting across the floor. Holding my children close, I prayed
for Matthew, wherever he might be, and thanked God for our
children, for our family, for bringing us home. Because that is
what this place felt like and only the darkness squeezing my

heart was a constant reminder of Matthew's absence.

"I think," I spoke into Rosie's ear, "that Easter Bunny might have paid the orchard a visit."

"Yay!" she squealed and, wriggling from my arms, jumped to her feet.

Pat was adding the finishing touches to their elaborate deception. "Bunny tail!" Rosie whooped, spotting the wisp of cotton wool snagged on a branch. "Easter Bunny's been! Ooo, loo-k – there's his ears…" and, diminutive willow basket in hand and Puppy at her heels, she raced off towards the glossy laurel where a pair of oversized rabbit ears twitched at the wall head.

"They're rather effective at a distance," I observed to Pat.

"Do you think she's guessed? She's such a quick little thing."

"Possibly, but she's enjoying believing it, nonetheless. Don't we all? That's the art of deception."

Pat laughed. "It's what we do best, sweetie."

Henry appeared, tucking the cardboard ears under his coat. "I think we deserve a slice of simnel cake and a cup of tea for that sterling effort."

I laughed. "I think you do. I'll come and help with the veg when the children have finished hunting for eggs. And that's a pretty good Canadian accent, if I might so observe."

"Why, thank you, ma'am," he drawled, with a shallow bow. "I've been working on it."

Bleeding Heart: what a strange name for a beautiful plant. Its delicate candy-pink hoods throbbed with bees in the warm shelter of the wall where I sat. Picking delicate weeds from the crevices between joints where the mortar had crumbled, I watched the children scour the nooks for tiny, shiny Easter eggs, which Rosie carefully collected. Before long, Theo grew tired of wobbly walking and flumped into the grass with Bear in one hand and his basket of trains in the other. He looked like a stripy ground beetle in his colourful dungarees, while his sister flitted backwards and forwards, dropping eggs into his basket. Early insects hummed among the apple blossom against a bluebell sky, petals releasing a fragrance delicate as air. And a memory – translucent as glass – wound itself into my being. I had been here before. Not today, not last month, but years ago, when about Rosie's age and before life imposed the condition of knowledge on my nascent mind. We must have been visiting the manor, and Nanna and Grandpa rested where I now sat, and Beth and I had danced in the long grass under the apple trees, catching petals. It had been a perfect moment of happiness, captured in memory, encapsulated in glass. I felt my eyes burn, and a tear escaped, and then another, and I found myself laughing and clapping as Rosie chased Puppy, at this new-found happiness, this sense of utmost peace, my garden of innocence.

Growing tired of the game, Puppy's ears pricked up and she dashed off under the arch of hazy wisteria and towards the courtyard, leaving Rosie to settle by her brother. I joined them, crouching in the grass. Theo had chocolate smeared around his mouth and an expression of puzzled disgust as he chewed a piece of foil. "I'll have that," I said, hooking the gluey mess from his mouth. "Look, Theo, put an egg *in* the truck." I showed him. In the distance, Puppy started barking.

"Mummy, did parasolophus like choc'late eggs if they were herb-e-vors and chocolate is made from beans?"

"That's it, darling, *in* the truck – good boy, well done." Puppy was now producing a high-pitched yip. Pat must have started preparing lunch. "Um, I doubt it, Rosie. What do you think?"

"Well, if parasolophus did ate choc'late, and velociraptor ate parasolophus, would that mean velociraptors ate chocolate, too?"

"Uh, well..."

"And if velociraptor ate them, then doesn't that make them oni... omi..."

"Omnivores?"

"Yes, omivores. Them."

"The egg is *in* your mouth, Theo, that's right. Omnivore? No, not really, in the same way a cat is a carnivore even though it consumes mice, which eat seeds, among other things." I craned my neck towards the gate. "What is Puppy barking about?"

"I think velociraptor likes parasolophus and choc'late." She crammed an egg in the plastic dinosaur's mouth. "Gobble, gobble, gobble."

Puppy's barking had risen to a crescendo and, for the first time, I felt the hairs on my arms prickle. "Wait here," I said, rising. The barking suddenly ceased. Ripples of tension crossed the surface of my skin. "Rosie," I said in an undertone, "take Theo and go and hide in the bothy. Go. Now!"

She scrabbled to her feet, taking Theo by the hand. He dropped his train and whimpered. "Come on, Theo." She began to pull him, but he objected, opening his mouth to wail, and she hoisted him under his arms. I hunted around for a branch, spade, rock – anything I could use to protect us from whatever was beyond the wall. Rosie had made it to the gardener's bothy with her protesting brother, when Puppy bounded back through the gate, followed by Henry's tall figure. "Wait, Rosie, it's OK." I raised my voice. "Henry, you gave me an awful fright!"

He stopped in the shade of the arch. Why didn't he come into the garden? He seemed surrounded by an opaque pall of uncertainty I couldn't read, and something tugged at my consciousness: a warning? "Stay there and be ready to run," I warned the children. I grabbed the garden fork leaning against the trunk of a tree and with a cautious step, advanced. "Henry...?"

He moved, stepping free of the shadows and into the sun, his hair exploding into radiant fire. A pulse of energy, vibrant, alive, shot between us and I gasped as the bolt hit me in the chest.

Matthew? Rooted, I could only stand and stare until he moved again, breaking the spell. I dropped the fork into the soft soil, my legs carrying me forward of their own volition, and I called out, not hesitant now, but urgent, "Matthew? Is that you?"

From behind me, small feet struck the ground, and Rosie passed me, reaching him in a flurry of limbs and colliding into his open arms. Even had she not already done so, the fire sweeping through my bones and burning my blood confirmed it. He knelt in the damp grass with his eyes closed, holding Rosie to him, her hands wound in his coat, securing him, while Puppy bounced around them, too excited to bark. He opened his eyes and sought me, and his voice cracked as he spoke my name. "Emma…"

But I couldn't move, I couldn't believe it was him.

"Da, da, da," a small, excited voice called, ending in a squeal. Matthew looked beyond me to where Theo tottered through the grass towards us.

"Theo! You're walking!" With Rosie's arms still wrapped around his neck, Matthew crossed the patch of ground and swung him into the air with his free arm, hugging them both, kissing each child, his face alive. Laughing, he pivoted on one foot, searching, and saw me watching. His smile became almost cautious, and his voice softened as he tilted his head in query: "Emma?" Stumbling a little on the tussocks, I joined them, lying my head against his chest, my own arms joining his around our children. "My Emma, my love," he said into my hair. "I said I would always come back to you."

I searched his beard-roughened face, his skin grey, his eyes dark, and all I could find to say was, "I… I thought you were Henry."

Rosie reached out and touched his eyes, his jaw. "It is my daddy." And Theo copied her, patting Matthew's mouth with his chocolatey hand. Their father laughed again, but it caught in his throat and his eyes glistened. He pulled us closer into his orbit. I felt him absorbing my energy, the bond growing stronger, melding, unbroken, until I was certain I could pull away from him enough to see his face without breaking the cords. Uncorked questions piled so fast they tumbled from my mouth.

"How did you get here? What happened? Did you escape?"

His face dimmed. "Later, my love." He let go, putting Theo carefully on his feet and sliding Rosie to the ground. "And who's this?" he asked, going down on one knee and folding the puppy's ears. "She came to greet me in the courtyard and insisted I follow her."

"Puppy," Rosie responded. "She's my puppy and Theo's. Henry found her."

His smile dissolved as he looked at me. "He's here? Henry is here?" He stood, his expression one of longing.

"And Pat," I said. "They've been here since Christmas. They're probably in the great hall or the kitchen."

Matthew bent to kiss me. "I must see him," he said.

Rosie dragged at my hand, anxiety crowding her face as Matthew left us and made for the house. "*Mum-my!*"

"I know, darling, but Daddy won't leave us again." I picked up Theo and together we followed the path Matthew's swift steps had made through the grass.

From the open door to the great hall, I heard Pat's sudden exclamation, and we arrived to see Henry slowly stand, the newspaper he had been reading falling forgotten to the floor. For a moment, the two men contemplated each other, then Matthew took several strides towards him as Henry's face crumbled, and embraced him. "My son," he said, as Henry's shoulders shook.

"Come on," I said to Rosie, quietly. "Puppy wants some lunch. Let's leave Daddy and Henry to talk."

"You look so tired." I touched the lines around his eyes; they were deeper than before – etched with weariness. He captured my hand and held it to his cheek, breathing in my scent, anchoring himself in reality. Light from his family's memorial window struck lines of blue and red across his ashen skin.

"It took me some time to get here. I couldn't risk a direct route – not until I could be certain I wouldn't lead them to you."

"What happened? Who took you? You escaped?"

"No, not exactly. I…" He removed his hand from mine and his mouth clamped shut; it was as if words had become stuck and he struggled to release them. I took a deep breath and willed myself to patience. He uncurled his fists, forcing them to relax. "I don't know who held me; they remained faceless, nameless – part of their bag of tricks, I suppose. They bound me, placed a hood over my head, and took me to a facility somewhere in the north – Alaska, I think – it was difficult to tell. I must have been underground – the temperature remained constant and the only lighting was artificial. And the air was stale – recycled – and I felt trapped and disorientated. It reminded me of a Cold War bunker, and perhaps it was lined in lead, something like that, because I couldn't feel you, sense you. And they left me there, in a windowless room, with a camera trained on me day and night – or I assume so, since I couldn't measure time. They took my wedding ring, Emma, and my watch – Ellen's watch – and all forms of identity. Even my signet ring that I'd worn every day of my life since my father gave it to me. They stripped me of anything that might remind me of who I was, of my home, my family."

I repossessed his hand and held it firmly. "You're here now."

"Yes." He exhaled slowly as if he didn't quite believe it,

looking at the distempered walls of the church rising above us. "I don't know how long it was before they started the interrogation. By then I suppose they thought me sufficiently depersonalized. I was taken to another room and left there alone without chair or table, and then they switched off the light. Then the questions started: Who are you? Where do you come from? On and on and nothing but the floor to tell me which way up I faced, to let me know I was still alive – just this… toneless voice coming at me out of the darkness. But they couldn't take you; they couldn't erase the memory of my family, and I clung to that hope – that you had managed to get away, to find your way here – home – where you might be safe, feel rooted."

"We do," I said. "We love it here. The only thing missing was you."

"I'm glad," he smiled, a tired smile worn thin. "I knew your family would help you if need be, and then there was the nutmeg…"

At that I smiled. "You taught Rosie a different version of the rhyme. I think she rather wanted the diamond herself."

"I'll make it up to her."

"She has everything she really wants, Matthew, and it isn't a diamond. Go on, tell me what happened."

"I hadn't spent a lifetime avoiding detection to be so easily tricked by psychological interrogation."

"So?"

"So they hauled me off to some laboratory or other… I didn't make it easy for them; I've lived in fear of such things for so long that I wasn't going to give up easily. But there's only so much I can do – I have physical limits to my strength, and they found them." Without thinking his hand went to his eyes.

"They tortured you," I stated, covering my mouth as my gut contracted, making me want to throw up.

"Well, what they did certainly wouldn't have been allowed under the Geneva Convention. But then they didn't see me as human – not even an animal – I was more of a machine to be explored and tested. I grew weaker. I had no recollection from my youth of what it is like to feel such weakness – I was like an engine running out of steam." With a quizzical expression, he held his hands in front of him, flexing his long fingers, seeing the muscles contract in his arms, as if looking at them for the first time. And for the first time I noticed small puncture wounds, faint but there, discolouring the surface of his skin.

"They hurt you."

He rested his hand on mine, lacing our fingers. "They didn't see it that way." We sat like that for a time, the yew tapping out the minutes on the memorial window, the sun now striking at an angle through the glass.

"They didn't find what they were looking for. They let me go."

"Just like that?"

"No – there were... conditions."

"I don't understand. Why let you go, when you could reveal what they did to you? Why not just... just kill you? Surely they wouldn't set you free, knowing you could break the conditions they laid on you?"

"Who said the conditions were theirs?"

"What could you possibly...?"

"Emma, there are things I know that they never wish revealed. I've had lifetimes to accumulate secrets. They don't know how, of course, just that I had acquired information which they wouldn't want to become public knowledge. Let's just say that should I disappear, certain details would be released. During my... sojourn with them, I was eventually able to persuade them that, while I lived and my family remained untouched, the information is secure."

"So, will they come looking for us? Are we safe?"

He exhaled, a deep, slow breath, and then looked down at me. "For now."

It was late and the house slept. Matthew adjusted his position so the length of him stretched from my head to my feet, my bare toes curling into his. Raised on one elbow, he lowered his lips and kissed my exposed shoulder in a gesture of such intimacy it made my heart sing. Resting his arm around my waist, he let his fingers gently caress my swelling stomach.

"I cannot begin to describe how I have missed you all," he said. "I'm so sorry for what I've put you through."

"You let them take you when you could have escaped." I had replayed that moment over and over until it invaded my sleep and haunted me there, too. I hadn't meant the accusation to creep into my voice, but it was there nonetheless, the legacy of months of grief and uncertainty, like a mother scolding the child she's just rescued from the path of a car.

"I couldn't risk them capturing you or the children. What is my life compared with yours?"

Theo was tucked up in Archie's old cot in the bedroom next to ours, but it had taken days for Rosie to accept the separation. Neither of us had the heart to insist she went to the room she had chosen to share with her brother until she felt secure enough to let her father out of her sight. We had left her sitting reading cross-legged by the fire, where she had propped his portrait against a chair leg. The flames reflected off the painting, making his eyes come alive in the light. This was the first time we had been alone since his return.

"Henry and I think we know what happened to you that night William attacked – or partly, at least." Bending my head back to look at him, I caught the frown that crossed his face.

"Go on," he said.

"The lights Nathaniel describe as being torches – they weren't. It was aurora, and when William stabbed you, by whatever fluke or miracle, the geomagnetic energy passed down the blade and earthed in you. What we haven't fathomed is why that should have resulted in your extended life."

"Aurora?" Matthew's hand ceased stroking my stomach. He lay back on the pillow and contemplated the richly patterned plasterwork of the peeling ceiling. In the quiet minutes that followed, in which nothing else stirred except the fine hair of his arm that twitched under my breath, he turned his eyes in on himself, interrogating. "Do you remember," he said slowly, "that when they captured me, they used Tasers – repeatedly?"

I shuddered and nodded.

"The shocks didn't subdue me as they'd hoped; they energized me. It was agony, but I fed off them."

"But... but you fell to the ground. I saw you!"

"Because that's what they expected me to do. I had to give them what they wanted so they wouldn't come after you. But it also gave me insight into my own condition, something I could work on through all those dark hours alone."

I wriggled over to face him. "You absorbed the energy, just like you do when you look at the sun?"

"Yes, although I hadn't realized it until then, in the same way you don't think about breathing. I've always thought that the source of my long life is in my blood."

"There has to be a genetic component."

"There is, but there's more to it than that, and you've just supplied the final link in the chain." He sat up, his face becoming animated. "The clue is my heart. You've noted how regularly it beats – it neither falters nor quickens but remains the same?"

"Yes – always."

"And that my temperature never fluctuates and I feel neither extremes of temperature."

"Of course."

"I can run as fast as a sprinter, for longer, and I'm as strong as the strongest man."

I nodded vigorously. "Your skin tingles and you heal instantly... and... and you have tiny lights in your eyes sometimes, like flames, like the sun."

They were burning now as he leant towards me, barely restrained excitement energizing the air around him. "Well, what if the energy kick-started a process in my heart – like a reciprocating engine – a self-repairing organ? A self-perpetuating, biological machine using the sun, rather than food, as its source of energy?"

"Henry and I thought that the sun might be a source of energy, but he didn't know how that would manifest itself in practice. Could it do that?"

He leapt out of bed, grabbing his clothes folded next to mine on the chair and started dressing. "Why not? Electrical currents send messages to cells to regenerate – salamanders do it if they lose a limb, lizards can regrow a tail, even the human liver and our skin can repair themselves – but in me it is enhanced as everything else is: instantaneous cyclical regeneration and repair." His sweater had left his hair awry, his eyes so bright I could hardly look at them. "I am not superhuman, Emma. I'm just operating at an optimum level of human capacity." His voice dropped as if addressing himself and he pulled at his lip, thinking, a sock forgotten in his hand. "Perhaps I might finally have an answer, but I need access to a laboratory, and will have to recreate the data we had on E.V.E..."

"But it was destroyed!"

"Hmm? Oh, yes, the hardware was destroyed and the information stored on it, but the data itself is very much..."

"Alive and kicking?"

He blinked once. "Ah. So you know."

Wrapping my arms around my knees, I grinned. "Henry worked it out. He's not your son for nothing. When were you going to tell me?"

"When I had conclusive evidence that you were the common factor. I was on the verge of it when we had to flee. Your discovery about the aurora, though, has clarified matters somewhat. I know what I need to do to move the research on. I must speak to Henry." The second sock went on and he reached for his shoes.

"At this time of night?"

A sheepish grin replaced the look of utter determination. He let the shoe drop with a thud to the floor. "I suppose I've waited this long, it could wait until morning."

"I think Pat would appreciate not being disturbed as much as Henry will want to work with you again. Tell me, Matthew, now that you know, will you try to find a way of changing back?"

He came and sat on the edge of the bed, avoiding my eyes. "I… don't think that will be necessary. Tell me," he said, "could you still love me if I changed?"

I was about to ask him what he meant, but a tiny fluttering in my womb caught me off guard and his face lit as he felt it. He laid his hand over my stomach, his expression softening.

"What better way to start afresh than this new life, here?" Removing the covers, he touched his lips to my stomach, then tucked the duvet around me again to exclude the chill night air.

"Matthew, if it's a girl, can we call her Eleanor, after Nanna?"

He considered for a moment. "Perfect choice. We don't have to worry about confusing the issue with Ellie any more. And if he's a boy?"

"I'd like to call him Nathaniel, after the man who led me to you."

* * *

Those first few days were like the echo of a dream. We stayed close, frequently touching, seeking reassurance, confirming our identity and our solidity as a family – slipping back into each other's skin. We toured the house and grounds, seeing it with fresh eyes and new hope, while Rosie and Puppy darted around us and Theo watched from Matthew's arms, rumbling his throaty laugh.

We had walked to the crest of the shallow hill, from which he surveyed the redundant fields of the manor leading to those his family had once held, and the remains of his former home. Lark song pierced the blue of the sky and the spring breeze had lost its edge, bringing with it warmth and the promise of summer.

"It's a long time since I farmed this land."

"Is that what you want to do?"

He let Theo down to trot after his sister, and crouched, digging his fingers into the soil. "The farm has been long-neglected, but the earth is good and has a fine tilth. We could do worse than make a living from it. What do you want to do, Emma? Sell up and move on – we can go anywhere – or stay here?"

"Is that what you need to do, Matthew?"

He lifted the soil and inhaled, then let the seeds of earth run through his fingers. He stood and brushed his hands free of the last grains, looking around him. "I have spent so many years running away. Perhaps it's time I stopped."

"And so have I – one way or another. I think this is the first time I've ever felt truly at peace – inside and out. I'm content here, Matthew. I'm happy to put down roots and call this home."

"It's where we came from, after all," he smiled. "If tested, our isotopes would show us to be local folk. Where better to bring up our children?"

"What about Henry and the rest of the family?"

"I've been discussing with Pat and Henry the idea of converting one of the barns into a home for them. We've even spotted a good place where he could have an observatory free from light pollution. As for the others, they will be welcome, of course, but perhaps I need to let them go and find their own way, make their own lives. They can always visit, or we can go to them. When we are certain it's safe, I'll contact them."

We returned to the walled garden and he stood, hands on hips, surveying the rear wing and church roof to his left and, swivelling on his heel to his right, the barns with their light stone glowing in the spring sun.

"There's everything we need here to get the farm up and running again."

"You are joking, aren't you?" I said. "With what – exactly?"

"True, there is much work to be done," he said, looking around us at the dilapidated structures, "but we'll take it one step at a time. Meanwhile," he grinned, a little of my Matthew resurfacing, "the diamond should get us started. Until then we have much to be getting on with. I can see how much you've already achieved. I never wanted you to be in a situation of need, Emma; I didn't expect George Redgrave to betray us."

"After centuries of building up your businesses – all your lands, stocks and shares – you've lost everything."

"Everything?" He looked puzzled. "Emma, my love, I have all that I ever wanted – I have you and my children; I have my liberty and my faith. What more is there?"

As much as I applauded his sentiment – and shared it – there were certain practicalities to address. "Well, the roof needs mending, for a start. The diamond won't do all this, will it?"

He cocked an eyebrow. "It'll certainly get us on the right track. I'm grateful for Levi's help. I never thought I would need to call on him."

"It makes a change, you know."

"What does?"

"You being in receipt of someone else's help; since I've known you, it's always been the other way around. I expect he was happy to be able to repay some of the kindness you showed him."

Matthew looked rather abashed. "Levi is a worthy man. Anyway," he went on, giving my tummy a playful pat, "since we are going to need a little extra in the forthcoming months and years, it's a good thing I set something aside. Come with me." And pulling me to my feet from the hump of masonry that served as a resting place, he tugged the spade from the potato patch and led me to the church wall and the yew tree that stood close by. Between the tree and where the memorial window to his family rose in the golden stone above us, he thrust the spade into the matted grass.

"What are you doing?" I exclaimed, both laughing and slightly exasperated. "Can't it wait?"

"I learned long ago not to place all my eggs in one basket." He continued to dig, fighting roots, until we heard a hollow thud. "There are some things," he said, leaning into the hollowed-out ground, taking hold, and heaving, "that cannot be left to chance. One is the status of your soul. The other –" he braced his legs and pulled, loosening clumps of soil that slipped from the lid of a large, rectangular object – "is the security of your family." Brushing soil from the surface, he revealed an iron-bound box with distinctive wooden panels of seventeenth-century motifs. He ran his hand over it, his expression gentle. "My mother's marriage chest." From his pocket he took the old toothed key that had been in the case, and worked the lock. After a few attempts it gave way, and he undid the hasp. Leaning the lid against the tree, he parted layers of protective cloth. "This," he said, "will see us through." Inside the trunk, musty with age, oiled cloths disguised uneven-shaped objects. He parted one. A gilded edge winked. "My father wanted me to take them to keep safe. I couldn't carry everything, so in time-honoured tradition I buried the rest here until such time as I needed them. It's pre-Commonwealth – some of it from the fifteenth century and my great-grandfather's time – so will fetch quite a bit."

"'Divers goodes'?" I asked.

"Indeed." He looked around us. "I've come home," he said, "in more ways than one." He closed the lid of the trunk, and secured the rusty hasp, grunting as the rough edge skinned his hand. He inspected the grazed knuckle.

"Matthew – you're bleeding!" He held his hand to the light and watched a bead of blood slowly trace its way down his wrist, the scrape only gradually healing, then disappearing. He wiped the blood with his thumb, leaving a smear, seemingly mesmerized.

"I noticed the changes in the days after my capture. The bruises took longer to heal; I felt hunger for the first time in four centuries. And then, when they began to experiment on me, they could find nothing that set me apart from the rest of the human race except, perhaps, for the anomaly in my blood. That's the other reason why they were willing to let me go."

"You... you've changed?"

"Possibly."

I swallowed. Took stock. Drew breath. "It's what you always wanted."

"And what you didn't."

It was true. I bent my head, recalling the anxiety I had always felt at the thought of him no longer walking the Earth, but succumbing to age and disease like the rest of us and returning to the dust from which we are all born. I felt the beginning of tears, and averted my face.

"Emma?"

But these were no tears of regret, but of relief and sheer joy. Death no longer held me in thrall. "It has never been about your strength or your endurability; it's always been about you, Matthew, and what lies in here..." and I touched his temple, "and here..." I laid my fingers against his heart. "I don't believe in fairy-tale endings, just you and me doing the best we can for our family, together."

He took my hand in his, tracing the lines on my palm. "Whatever the future holds, however long our lives might be, we will spend it together." He raised his face to the sun. "I don't know whether the changes will be permanent, but for now, it seems," he said, looking down at me and smiling, "I am merely human, after all."

THE END...
... IS JUST THE BEGINNING.

Author's Notes

Sitting alone on a rise of land overlooking the gentle fields of Rutland stands the remains of the deserted village of Martinsthorpe. Once the site of a medieval manor, the original building was replaced by a grand house in the seventeenth century, imposing itself on the landscape where it could be seen for miles around. It didn't last. Within a hundred years, it too was demolished, leaving all but the stable block to act as a modest farmhouse on which I based Joan Seaton's Old Manor farm. All around the site the rumpled land betrays the extent of the buildings and the village that once surrounded it. To the east is the new expanse of Rutland Water and to the south-west the land rolls away in swathes of wheat and grass to where a long absent manor once stood. This was my New Hall, where the Lynes built their manor only a few miles from their Seaton cousins. It wasn't difficult to imagine. All around this rich landscape lie the remains of the past.

Not all is fiction, however. The manor at Martinsthorpe was held by the de Montfort family, the Fieldings, and the Sextons, and although Matthew's family is entirely fictitious, Emma's is not, and her cousins, the de Eresbys, have roots that stretch into the distant past. Most fiction has a smattering of truth and there is much still buried in the soils of Lincolnshire and Rutland yet to be discovered.

The Secret of the Journal series is about continuity and change, persecution and acceptance. Like most stories, a strand of truth lies woven through it in the fears and hopes of the characters, and the names and places in which they live. History lies embedded in every one of us. We are the legacy of the past and the ancestors of the future. What happened once can happen again and it is our knowledge of the past and our determination to make a better future that can change the outcome for our children.

You can visit the site of the old manor if you take the road from Brooke and find the half-concealed entrance to the hedged track. Then leave your car and walk the modest distance down the green-edged lane. At the end, you'll find a board explaining the site and a single stone building standing alone among the ragged humps and bumps which is all that remains of the manor. And if you're lucky, you might put up lithe-limbed hares that will dart and bounce over the rumpled slopes, leaving you alone to contemplate the past.

COMPETITION!

We have five sets of these brilliant Lion Fiction titles up for grabs!

To enter to win this wonderful prize, simply answer C. F. Dunn's questions about *The Secret of the Journal* series, and fill out the online form at www.lionhudson.com/SecretoftheJournal

Winners will be chosen from correct entries sent in before the end of Friday 2nd December 2016.

I hope you have enjoyed reading *The Secret of the Journal* series as much as I loved writing it. I've come up with a few brain teasers I thought might entertain you.

Other than her teaching post, why in *Mortal Fire*, did Emma want to go to Maine?

What does Matthew lend Emma in *Mortal Fire*?

What is the significance of the nutmeg a) to Matthew and b) to Emma?

As Emma recovers in *Death Be Not Proud*, she hunts down the secrets of Matthew's past. What is the county town of Matthew's birthplace?

Where is Emma's family home?

Emma and Matthew both enjoy Metaphysical poetry. What is Emma's favourite poem?

When Emma and Matthew visit a lake in *Mortal Fire*, Emma has a close encounter with… what?

In *Rope Of Sand*, Maggie plays a central role in the trial. What is that role and who has set her up to play it?

In *Realm Of Darkness*, Emma comes face to face with her past. Who is it?

THE SECRET OF
the Journal

SERIES

MORTAL FIRE
C. F. Dunn

DEATH BE NOT PROUD
C. F. Dunn

ROPE OF SAND
C. F. Dunn
Author of Mortal Fire

REALM OF DARKNESS
C. F. Dunn
Author of Mortal Fire

FEARFUL SYMMETRY
C. F. Dunn
Author of Mortal Fire